Quickening

LAURA CATHERINE BROWN

RANDOM HOUSE

NEW YORK

All rights reserved under International and Pan-American Copyright Conventions. Published in the United States by Random House, Inc., New York, and simultaneously in Canada by Random House of Canada Limited, Toronto.

Grateful acknowledgment is made to the following for permission to reprint previously published material:

Williamson Music and Raybird Music: Lyric excerpts from "Twisted" by Wardell Gray and Annie Ross. Copyright © 1965 (renewed) by Second Floor Music (Administered by R&H Music) and Raybird Music. All rights reserved. Reprinted by permission of Williamson Music and Raybird Music.

Hal Leonard Corporation: Excerpt from "You Can't Hurry Love" by Edward Holland, Lamont Dozier and Brian Holland. Copyright © 1965, 1966 (Renewed 1993, 1994) by Jobete Music Co., Inc. All rights controlled and administered by EMI Blackwood Music, Inc., on behalf of Stone Agate Music (A division of Jobete Music Co., Inc.). All rights reserved. International copyright secured. Used by permission.

RANDOM HOUSE and colophon are registered trademarks of Random House, Inc.

Library of Congress Cataloging-in-Publication Data
Brown, Laura Catherine.
Quickening / by Laura Catherine Brown.
p. cm.
ISBN 0-375-50373-0 (hc)
1. Women college students—Fiction. 2. Young women—Fiction. I. Title.

PS3552.R6929 Q5 2000
813'.6—dc21   00-028094

Random House website address: www.atrandom.com
Printed in the United States of America on acid-free paper
2 4 6 8 9 7 5 3
First Edition
Book design by JAM design

for Corinne, for Jake, for June, for Tony

Every created thing, if it is to be capable of life,
owes its existence to some life destroyed.

—*Otto Rank*

ACKNOWLEDGMENTS

I WOULD like to thank and acknowledge Dani Shapiro, Alice Elman, Karen McKinnon, Amanda Robb, Susie Rutherford, Ellen Schutz, and all the other insightful, considerate readers in Dani's workshop. I would also like to thank Douglas Glover at the Skidmore Summer Writers Institute for his support and encouragement in the early stages of the book, as well as Lydia Mann, who read and made suggestions through numerous versions.

For the immeasurable gift of time and quiet, I am grateful to the Hambidge Center, the Ragdale Foundation, and the Norcroft Writing Retreat. For her constancy and for helping me to believe, I extend my heartfelt thanks to Elisabeth Santiago.

For his enormous generosity of spirit, I would like to thank Joseph Hindy. Finally, I would like to acknowledge my debt of gratitude to BJ Robbins and Susanna Porter, without whom this book would not exist.

CONTENTS

QUICKENING

IMPULSE

HE MORNING I was leaving for college, Mom fainted. She had been playing solitaire at the kitchen table and had stood up too fast.

I was washing the car with Dad, who'd gone inside for matches, then came back out and said, "She's down."

I dropped the hose. Water pooled in the crevices where weeds grew, ran down the driveway and out into the street. "Did you call Dr. Wykoff?" I followed Dad into the kitchen.

"Now, how'm I going to do that, Mandy?"

Of course. The phone had been cut off. We hadn't paid the bill.

The cards were scattered over the table. Mom lay on the kitchen floor, her pilly pink robe half buttoned and wrinkled around her fleshy splayed legs, slippers still on her feet. Her blue eyes bulged and blinked. "It took you long enough," she said as we bent over to help.

She twisted my forearms in a vise grip while Dad, wheezing, cigarette hanging from between his clenched lips, hoisted her up from behind. "Be careful, for God's sake," she said. "You know how easily I bruise."

"Can you make it to the car?" he asked. "We'll drive you to Ransomville General."

"I'm not going to the hospital looking like this! It's just a mee-grain. The dizziness will pass. Help me to bed."

"They're called *mi*graines, Mom." I took one side and Dad took the other.

"Would you listen to smarty-pants!" Mom was short but wide, and solid, still a dead weight after her faint. Her robe smelled of trapped sweat.

"Are you sure you don't want to go to the hospital?" I asked.

"Didn't I just say no? Don't treat me like I'm stupid, Miranda. I had the brains for college, too, you know . . ."

I should have guessed it was about college.

The three of us stumbled through the kitchen door, down the little hall, into the bedroom. The bed springs squeaked and squealed as Mom settled in. "Oh dear," she muttered. "I won't be able to drive with you to your college."

"Gee, what a surprise. But I'm still going." All through high school, I had worked toward college. I had been in the honor society, had gotten a partial scholarship, a federal grant, a student loan, and a work-study grant. This moment of leaving had been the point whenever I thought, What's the point?

"And you can't stop me." I walked out as Dad was turning on the electric space heater and the humidifier, pulling the curtains shut.

"Did I say anything? What's the matter with her!" Mom shouted. "Bring me my pills, Miranda Jane!"

She hadn't left the county in years. It was predictable. Why did it upset me? I didn't even want her to go. My heart banged out of control against my rib cage, in panic and hope that Mom would just disappear, even if it meant her dying. I took the flat plastic box out of the refrigerator and brought it to her. It was separated into compartments designating times of the day and days of the week, the measure of Mom's life.

For her migraines, she took Fiorinal or Naprosyn, depending on the nature of her pain. For the lupus, she took Prednisone twice a day. For her postpartum depression, she had been on Elavil for eighteen years. Halcion to fall asleep. Dexamethasone for her asthma. Premarin since the hysterectomy. And Xanax for the panic attacks.

When I was little, we did drills where she pretended some health crisis and I rushed to the refrigerator to give her a pill. "No!" she would scream. "I'm a dead woman. You've just given me the wrong medication!"

I had since resolved never to take pills, not even aspirin.

"Do me a favor. Tell your father to shave before he goes. He looks like a bum." Her round face was as pale as her worn pillowcase.

I handed her a Naprosyn and a small glass of water.

"Be a daughter to me, please." She pointed to the chair by her bedside table. The humidifier blew steam on the wallpaper, which bubbled and buckled in the damp corner. The room stank of camphor, menthol, and bad breath. I wanted a cigarette. How had Dad slipped out of the room so quick? "I have to finish washing the car," I said.

"Your father said he would finish."

"No, really, I . . ." I edged toward the door.

"Frank!" Mom bellowed. "Tell Miranda you'll finish the car."

I heard the back door slam.

"He said he would finish," she insisted.

I sat down. Her bedside table smelled charred and musty. She had bought it years ago at a fire sale. Cluttered on its surface were a bell, a box of tissues, an ashtray, a thermometer, Vaseline, and a battery-powered blood pressure machine. The place of honor was held by a framed picture of Mom's mother, sitting on the porch, squinting and mean. Dad had taken it. Every night before she went to sleep, Mom kissed this picture. Or so she claimed.

"You're all packed," she said. "You've got your clothes."

How long was she going to keep me here? "Yes. I've got my clothes."

We had gone over them last week, and all the dresses Mom had sewn for herself years ago were mine now, for college. All the little replicas of those dresses, also sewn by her but worn by me until I was twelve or so, were packed in cardboard boxes and piled in the basement. In my bag was the floral-patterned skirt with the ruffle at the bottom and buttons running all the way up. I managed to button it only by holding my breath. It had a blouse with bell sleeves that matched. There was a green dress with a princess collar that choked and a too-tight skirt with a houndstooth-check pattern.

Mom and I just weren't shaped the same. I was taller, rounder, bigger. Mom called me chunky. She had said, "We can let out the waist in that one."

But she hadn't sewn in ages, and I didn't want to be the reason for her starting again. I wasn't going to wear her dresses anyway. I had jeans, T-shirts, normal things. "It's okay, Mom. I like it this way." I had minced after her in a skirt so tight that I couldn't take a normal step.

"I'm sure that sewing machine is somewhere around here." She had opened closets, peeked along shelves, pulled open dresser drawers, wandered out to the kitchen, a wake of hanging doors behind her. But she didn't think of the basement, and I was careful not to suggest it.

"Yes," I repeated. "I've got my clothes." I folded my hands in my lap. My fingertips were raw, chapped, my nails bitten to the quick. Big hands. Ugly hands.

"I remember you as a little girl, picking daisies out in the backyard in your sunsuit. You made a daisy chain for me. You were such a precious thing. Now you're going to college!" Mom inhaled sharply, exhaling a sob.

"Don't cry, Mom. Please." Her sobs always forced me open. I fought it. No. I didn't remember any daisy chains. No, I wasn't going to cry. But the tears welled up and I bent my head to wipe them away, imagining a child in a sundress picking daisies for a healthy, vibrant mother who laughed a musical laugh. It was only a fantasy.

I was surprised she had declined Dad's offer to drive her to the hospital, her second home. She seemed happier in a hospital bed, attached to intravenous devices, her face flushed and cheerful against a clean white pillow. "I got 'em stumped," she would say.

She had actually been written up in a textbook called *Autoimmune Disease: Symptoms and Pathology*. Her case appeared in a section on the difficulty of diagnoses and the flare-up remission pattern of symptoms. Her name wasn't mentioned. She was the thirty-seven-year-old female patient of Bernard Wykoff, M.D. It was back in 1975, ten years ago, and she still kept the book under her bed.

"You can bring me my jewelry box," she said.

I got up, sniffing down my tears, and walked around the bed to the dresser. There were weeping willows trailing sun-dappled leaves by a brook on the ceramic lid of Mom's jewelry box. She thought she was giving me a treat by going through her jewelry, but I was too old. I felt another sob coming. "I don't have time for this, Mom."

"Just open it. Pull out the top bit. *Ow!* This pain is like trolls throwing stones in my head. I should be used to it, God knows. The only meegrain-free period in my life was when I was pregnant with you." She was stroking her stomach, rustling the housedress she wore beneath her robe.

I pulled out the top container of the jewelry box, where she kept her earrings, and squashed inside was a roll of bills.

"That's for you," Mom said from her bed. "For college. For the niceties."

The bills were greasy, soft from handling.

"I've been saving it, and you're going to need some cash. And . . ." She shut her eyes. "Don't tell your father."

The scent of calamine lotion wafted from her skin as I leaned in to kiss her forehead, but she tilted her face back, her mouth pink with the Pepto-Bismol she took to counteract the nausea from the painkillers, and our lips mashed moistly, hers soft and open and mine clenched shut.

"YOU HAVE A future, and your future lies outside this armpit of a village." Dad made a right onto Main Street and we rode past Rolf's candy store, past Polly's Surplus Clothing and an abandoned storefront that used to be a restaurant. He beeped the horn as we rode by the Griffin. Then he made a U-turn. "Just a quick one so you can say good-bye to Mac."

Dad was a fixture at the Griffin. His name was painted on the barstool in the corner near the door. An old-time old men's bar song crooned on the jukebox, something about being fenced in. Though it was the middle of the afternoon, all the regulars were there.

He ordered me a beer and himself a double vodka. "She's off to college now, so this world won't be the same," he told the bartender.

Mac, the bartender, said, "I remember when she was just a little kid with her nose in a book sitting over there by the jukebox."

I loved the Griffin. When Mom was in the hospital or when she was working, it was my after-school place and I stayed until Dad was ready to go home. He had business deals going, always lots of irons in the fire. I did my homework, and Mac gave me bags of peanuts. He let me play the pinball machine as much as I wanted because he had a set of slugs that made it go. But that was when I was a kid.

Now I was a college girl at the bar with the adults. Mac hadn't asked me for I.D., which I accepted as a compliment. The Griffin was a warm, happy place filled with men grinning at Dad. "Long live God and the Boyles, eh, Mandy?" Dad held up his glass and we toasted each other.

The pinball machine had been replaced by electronic blackjack. The jukebox played CDs. But baskets of peanuts still sat on the bar and peanut shells were strewn over the floor. The surface of the wooden bar was cut up and carved with initials and markings and all along it were coasters with drinks on them.

I unsnapped the round copper-colored snap of my purse to check on the money Mom had given me. The purse had been a gift from her last Christmas. I had pretended to be grateful, but it was ugly and old ladyish and I had seen it in the window of Polly's Surplus a week before I received it as a gift. Fifteen twenty-dollar bills was probably the most cash it had ever held, and it made me dizzy seeing those bills rolled up and rubber-banded and thinking what I could get with them.

I could buy jeans so stiff with newness that they'd need breaking in. I could buy lots of books, scented shampoo, a matching bra-and-panty set. And I could buy Dad a drink. I slipped a twenty on the bar. Mac took it and laid down change.

Dad was slurping his drink through his teeth. He always said it tasted better that way. "Tell me again what you're taking, Mandy."

I had my courses memorized—electives and requirements, fifteen credits in all. I was taking the maximum load. "Medieval Literature, Basic Geological Science, Art History, Rhetoric and Logic, and Intro to Philosophy."

"Ah yes. Philosophy." Dad picked up his glass and placed it with a sharp rap on the bar, sloshing vodka. "How do we know what this is?"

"Easy," I said. "It's a glass of vodka."

"But are you really seeing this object in front of me, or are you looking, in your mind, at a concept of the object?" He kept a couple shelves of books in the basement and read them over and over, because he said no new book had been written that could beat out these old ones: Plato, Aristotle, Descartes, Kant, Schopenhauer, Nietzsche, Russell.

Some of the men looked up from their drinks.

"Okay, look," he said. "It's rounded. It's glass or some material we believe to be glass. It contains a liquid substance we bet is vodka." He dipped his finger in and licked it.

"Is the philosopher at it again?" groaned the guy next to him.

Dad was showing off. "You'll have to spend time on Plato. You can't live and not spend time on Plato. He was the guy who knew."

"Knew what?" There were posters for beer on the walls—girls in bikinis wrapping themselves around giant beer bottles. They were faded, curled up at the edges and dusty. A sign over the bar said WHAT DRINKING PROBLEM? I DRINK. I GET DRUNK. I FALL DOWN. NO PROBLEM. It seemed like a philosophy in itself.

"Plato knew how to know." Dad's eyes were twinkling as he tapped his bald skull. "All learning is recollecting what we once knew, Mandy girl. You see, we forget."

A guy with a big thick beard and a baseball cap shouted, "I got a joke! Why is Nancy Reagan like a tampon?"

"Ignoramus!" yelled Dad. "Can't you see we're discussing meaningful things?" A shower of peanuts came from the other end of the bar.

"They're both stuck up cunts!" said the bearded man.

"Jesus, that's disgusting," said Mac.

I thought it might be a cool joke to tell at college.

Dad finished his drink. "How about one more for the road?"

"No, Dad. We have to go."

He started to sing. "I'm a man with many friends, Jim Beam, Johnny Walker, and Old Grand-Dad . . ." Someone threw a wadded-up napkin at him, but he kept singing as he pocketed the change from my twenty and walked outside. I let it go. Two hundred and eighty dollars was more than enough for me, and it felt good to let him have some of the money without disobeying Mom.

The sun was a bright surprise. We got back in the car and continued down Main Street, past the movie theater where *The Breakfast Club* had just opened, past the Miss Ransomville Diner and the Army-Navy store, where we turned right onto the labyrinth of back roads. The leaves fluttered, green and gold, rippling on a breeze. Freedom was in the air, in the sigh of the tires against the road, in the rush of wind that blew the sharp clear scent of autumn and new beginnings across the open windows.

We came out on Route 18, where the Ransom County prison stood not far from the hospital like a square hunk of gray and the barbed wire along its perimeter snagged the deep blue background of sky. Then we entered the ramp onto the thruway and there was no turning back.

THE CAMPUS WAS huge. There were enormous concrete slabs for buildings, towers for dorms, and tunnels that ran everywhere underneath because of the cold, windy winters. I gripped the metal handle on one side of my black trunk and Dad held the other. It wasn't too heavy to carry when we shared the weight of it.

In the center of the campus was a fountain where students hung out, playing Frisbee, wading, sunbathing. Water splashed refracting light, glittering like diamonds and tinkling like a song. This will be familiar soon, I told myself.

I wanted to leap into the water and shout to the Frisbee-playing students, Throw it here, throw it here, I'm in the game! But what if everyone gave me a blank look? Inside, I felt the fear expanding. I didn't know how to throw a Frisbee. I wasn't popular. My best friend, Tracy, left high school when I was fifteen and I never replaced her. I was suddenly cold, though the air was warm. I shrank inside my body. My hands, usually hot and sweaty even in the winter, froze. My fingers were brittle as carrot sticks. I stopped, dropped my side of the trunk.

"I think I'm scared, Dad."

"Remember, Mandy," he said. "You're a Boyle. You got nothing to worry about. C'mon, what do you say?"

Together we proclaimed it, "Long live God and the Boyles!" When he laughed, I forced out a laugh too, not wanting him to know how I really felt.

We carried the black trunk to the elevator in State Quad tower, where other kids were waiting with their parents. When I smiled at them, they smiled back, and the lobby smelled of fresh paint, promising newness.

The other fathers wore practical sneakers with thick soles and khaki trousers or jeans. They weren't fat and didn't wear work pants, shiny with age and pulling at the seams like Dad's. Ashamed of us both, I stared at my boots. They were black leather boots with pointed toes and a silver buckle at the ankle, very new wave. I bought them last year with money I had earned from my job at Lack's department store and I wore them every day. They were soft, broken in, and I loved them.

Dad was wearing his good shoes, black wing tips, scuffed, worn down on the outer edges because he leaned on his ankles. They pinched, I knew. He had worn them a few months ago for a job interview at a real estate agency. Afterward, he lay back on his cot in the basement. "The dogs are tired, Mandy girl," he said. I massaged his feet while Mom stood at the top of the steps, the closest she ever got to the basement. "What are you two doing down there?" We never answered when she screamed like that.

As he dragged my trunk into the elevator, Dad's face was covered in an oily sheen. He was so much fatter than the other fathers that there wasn't room in the elevator for anything else, just me, Dad, and the trunk. I waited until the doors shut before I took his hand, as large and leathery as a baseball glove. From each pore, a single dark hair grew. Next to his hand, mine was small, and my bitten nails invisible.

He squeezed my fingers. "What did I tell you?" he said. I squeezed back. His familiar, capable hands had built a dollhouse and bird feeders, had fixed things; they sanded, whittled, carved, and drew.

Last week he had taken me to the Snack Shack and bought me an ice cream sundae with everything on it. "Look, Mandy girl, look at that!" He pointed out a sparrow sitting in a milk crate sheltered from the sun, a cozy spot, and I didn't know how I was going to see things like that on my own without Dad around to point them out. He had turned his worn-out pale face, sagging unshaven chin, to me. "You're a smart cookie, and don't let anyone tell you different." He stated it with such certainty, he stopped my fear. Then, too, I had put my hand in his, and mine was that much smaller and smoother and more beautiful. His palm sent comfort from him to me.

When the elevator doors opened on the fourteenth floor, I guiltily withdrew my hand and I was grateful to find the hallway deserted as we dragged the trunk past candy machines, a lounge, and the guys' showers and toilets to room 144.

My college-issued key slid easily into the lock. On one side of the room hung a poster that said STONED AGIN, straight out of the 1960s. A crystal dangled in the window above an aloe plant on the window-sill, casting rainbow-colored reflections on the wall. Scarves hung off the doorknob of one of the closets and a woven throw rug lay over the speckled institutional floor. An Indian-print gauze bedspread seemed to float gently above one of the beds.

I sat on the bare mattress on the empty side of the room. The metal bed frame squeaked when I bounced. "How about a glass of water or something?"

Dad jingled the change in his pockets. "I've got to get going, Mandy girl."

"Wait, I'll walk to the car with you."

"You have to get yourself settled in." His enormous sway of flesh, his pungent smell of sweat mingling with tobacco, and his lime-scented aftershave were so familiar, I couldn't grasp them to savor in his absence. His sweater was rough against my cheek. His broad back, with the shoulders slightly hunched, one held higher than the other, shifted sideways through the door. The room echoed without him.

I started to cry, painful stinging jabs. But I was afraid my new roommate would walk in and catch me. I went to the window and cracked it open. Outside, sun reflected off the concrete. Fourteen floors below, brightly clad people streamed across the courtyard in every direction. I couldn't tell which one was Dad. They were like ants with purpose and design, each part necessary to the whole, and I was one of them now.

I plugged in the alarm clock Mom had given me for my birthday. I opened the trunk. Dad had brought it into the yard early on in summer. We had soaped it up and hosed it down. I didn't ask him where he got it. Inside were the blouses, skirts, and dresses Mom had pushed on me.

It wasn't until I had befriended Tracy that I realized it was unacceptable to dress the same as Mom, who claimed she sewed very well, though buttonholes were a problem. Sewing made her feel useful, but half the time skirts didn't hang right and pants were a disaster. "I sew all my own clothes and my daughter's clothes too," she declared to supermarket checkout clerks, women at the beauty shop, church members, neighbors, customers at Lack's, passersby on Main Street, anyone and everyone. It was humiliating.

I had said finally, "No, I don't want to wear a dress sewn by you. I want jeans."

"No? What do you mean no? Who do you think you are?" She had slammed the door to her bedroom so hard that the whole house shook and she cried for hours. Her lupus flared up, inflaming her organs, and she was hospitalized for two weeks. Even after she had returned home and the sewing machine was relegated to the basement, it hung between us how she had almost died.

Beneath her clothes were my real ones: jeans, T-shirts, flannel shirt, sweatshirt. There was also a teddy bear Dad gave me last year for Christmas, a little fuzzy dark brown guy with jointed arms and legs.

I put my jeans in a drawer, T-shirts in another drawer, then socks and underwear. I needed new ones, nice underwear, not these worn-out, clearance pairs thrown into a huge box and pawed through by thousands of hands, irregulars that never quite fit.

I held a pair up to the light. One leg hole was wider than the other, and I remembered high school gym class. "Nice undies," snickered Linda, the popular cheerleader in her perfect matching bra-and-panty set. "Oh, look at that. I want a pair. Where'd you get those?" Giggle, giggle, giggle all around the locker room. No more. Those days were over. I threw them in the trash can.

I placed my spiral notebooks on my desk, sat down in my chair, and caressed the smooth blank pages. From the corridor came voices, laughter, the bumping of furniture and luggage. I started to whistle, like Dad might have done if he were me at his first day of college. I had achieved my dream and landed in my own future. A desk. A dresser. A closet. A bed. All mine.

WIDE-HIPPED, IN A paisley-patterned wraparound skirt, she shook her dark, frizzy hair off her face, stretched her full lips across her teeth in a smile, and held out her hand. "You must be my new room-mate. Like, total pleasure. I'm Barb." Her hand was soft, round. She wore a ring with a stone that looked like an eyeball and she laughed loud and easy. "You wanna go to dinner?"

I was looking pretty okay in my red sweater, jeans, and boots. I followed her down to my first college dinner. My student I.D. stuck to my sweaty palm as we waited with the crowd outside the noise and clatter of the cafeteria. I stepped through the turnstile and grabbed a tray exactly as Barb did. I panicked for a moment as I slid my tray along the counter, remembering how unreal lunch hour had become after Tracy left school and I had no one to eat with. I floated outside myself and watched as if I were dreaming.

For a moment I was back at Ransomville High, in the cafeteria, the large woman who dished out macaroni, her arms huge flaps of shaking skin, shouting, "Move it along, move it along," the voices around me shifting in and out of earshot. *She's a free-luncher, and her dad's always at the bar. Her mom's mental.*

No. This was my new life. Clean slate.

Barb nudged me. "Take a lot of french fries so I don't look like a pig, because I'm going to take a lot of them."

"Deal," I said.

That night I jolted awake to the sound of Barb's snoring, along with an eerie mechanical clicking. In the morning she told me the clicking was caused by the retainer she wore at night so her teeth wouldn't go crooked again after four years of braces. I had an over-bite and a gap between my two front teeth, and I had always wanted braces.

Barb was the me I would have wanted to be. She brought not only a stereo, but a refrigerator, a hot plate, and an electric toothbrush with an extra brush attachment she let me use. She also brought black curtains, a mobile with twirling shapes, an ounce of pot, a black light, and a lava lamp, as if we were back in the hippie days. I couldn't get over it. She had everything.

"The piece of resistance," she said as she drew her bong out of a box filled with newspaper and laid it on my black trunk. I nodded. It was meaningful.

Every new thing I learned about Barb added to her coolness. She had a bumper sticker on her car that said I ONLY BRAKE FOR HALLU-CINATIONS. And at her bedside she kept a little statue, a gift from her boyfriend back in Mineola. The statue was a guy with a lumpy mottled face sitting at a desk, book open in front of him with HOME-WORK GIVES ME PIMPLES inscribed on the base. "What was he thinking?" Barb thrust her little statue in my face. "You see why I need a new boyfriend."

"I need a boyfriend. Period." I wondered if Barb was a virgin. Back in high school, Tracy and I had made a pact. We each pricked our index fingers with a needle, mingled our blood, and I pledged, "I do solemnly swear that I'm a virgin and will fill in Tracy with all the gory details when I lose it."

Tracy said, "Me too."

Tracy's mother had always told us to remain virgins for as long as we could. "You don't want to give it away for free now," she would say as she plucked her eyebrows before work. "You really don't, because, let's face it—your virginity is all you have." I believed her, wishing she were my mother, wishing I were Tracy.

Her mother kept stacks of bodice-buster novels in her bedroom, and Tracy and I read aloud to each other: *Love's Tender Fury, Forbidden Sin, Savage Desires.* Listen to this: "The steamy fires of white hot passion licked at her insides and instead of saying no, as she had intended, Desiré moaned. The virile stranger bent down to kiss each pink flower of a nipple as her breasts spilled out of her tight blouse like ripe fruit." Reading those books made me feel weak and wet inside. Even now, when I thought of Tracy experiencing all that and keeping it secret, I felt almost helpless with anger. Tracy was a liar. She got pregnant and left school to marry the father of her baby. She lived somewhere in Texas now.

Barb said, "We've *got* to find you a boyfriend."

"I can find my own, don't worry about me." But if I couldn't, I trusted Barb to help me out. She kept track of the parties and she knew people already—not only the ones she instantly made friends with, but older kids, sophomores and juniors who had graduated from her high school, people who were grown-up and already living off campus.

"Off campus is where the action is," Barb said. "This dorm stuff is strictly temporary."

"Yeah," I said knowingly, not wanting to admit that I loved living in State Quad tower with the other freshmen.

Constant noise and music filled the place twenty-four hours a day, competing stereos, Barb's included. We played cards with the girls across the hall, and Barb passed the bong around while music blasted on the turntable: Talking Heads, Tears for Fears, the Pogues, the Cure, the Clash, and the Specials. Everyone around me was my friend, especially Barb, who lent me the joy of belonging. We laughed until it hurt.

One night I confessed my virginity to Barb, who said, "Hey, girls, Mandy here's still a virgin!" And they exploded into laughter so contagious that even I thought it was hilarious. "This is a mission and it calls for a smoke." Barb passed the bong to me. I took a hit and handed it to the next girl, who declared, "I smoke to the fucking mission." I was one with them, breathing the same smoke, free of my past, free of myself. This was life, and in the midst of it I was finally alive.

The Ox had smiled at me the weekend before at the Rathskeller on campus and asked me, "How does the world look from the bottom of a beer glass, can you tell me that?" Without waiting for an answer, he had walked away. Everyone knew who he was. He got around. Barb and the girls across the hall thought he was gross, because he was always adjusting his pants at the crotch.

But when he approached me again, his pale hair freshly clipped in a mohawk haircut, when he leaned in so close as I stood by the bar at the Rathskeller that his arm touched mine, and when he said, "I know you, right?" I realized he wasn't gross at all. He was cool, a punk rocker.

"Sort of," I said.

He seemed sophisticated. His arms when he reached for a drink were thick, meaty. I had to look up to talk to him, and then I couldn't stop staring at the blunt crop of hair down the center of his otherwise smooth skull. When he laughed, his teeth were enormous. We drank shots of melon balls. He paid for every single one of them. Then we went to his room, arm in arm. He had a single bed, like mine, like everyone's. But he also had a pillowcase with a picture of Snoopy lying on top of his doghouse, staring at the sky. Snoopy's presence made the Ox seem friendlier, somehow. A guy with a pillowcase like that was a good guy. I fell in love with his pillowcase.

He pushed his mouth against mine like a fist and thrust his thick tongue in. He pulled my shirt up. "I want to see you naked."

"Wait a second." I pulled off my T-shirt and my jeans and lingered over my brand-new red lacy underwear, three for five dollars. "Do you like my underwear?"

"What? Yeah, cool. Let's get them off." We lay naked on his single bed. What a tingling wonder of skin against skin, so much skin. He got on top of me, put it in, and bang bang bang. It hurt, like when I was first learning how to insert tampons. He didn't even feel me up. I had no chance to whisper in a trembling voice like the heroine in *Savage Desires,* "Please be careful. I've never done this before."

Instead, I muttered, "I'm a virgin."

"Yeah, right." He panted in my ear quick, as though he were laughing. His gut flapped against mine. He didn't growl, "You're so beautiful." I didn't shiver with desire. It was over fast and he fell asleep right after. But I couldn't sleep from trying to reconcile this snoring guy with my fantasy. My underwear had meant nothing to him. *Cool,* he had said, *let's get them off.* I might as well have worn my saggy clearance-rack ones.

He was supposed to tenderly hold my fragile, naked body, no longer pure. I was supposed to weep with shame and delight. But the Ox farted in his sleep and I turned away to shut my eyes and imagine it as it should have been. *My bosom heaved as the fibers of my being strained helplessly. My traitorous body moved to his firm manly rhythm, despite my virginal pleas like the cooing of a helpless dove.*

I must have slept, because I awoke when an alarm went off. The Ox moaned, "Shit, I got a game of Ultimate today."

I wiped my mouth on his sheet when his back was turned as he slipped on his boxers, then his ripped jeans. His mohawk was mashed over to one side. I didn't know what I was supposed to do. Now that we had sex, were we going out? How did it work? I got dressed quickly and quietly, so tense that I couldn't even feel my hangover. We kissed good-bye, a sticky, stale, embarrassing kiss.

"See you around," he said, and went off whistling down to the cafeteria.

I went in the opposite direction, although I didn't know where I was. Did "See you around" mean he wanted to see me again? Was it understood that I meet him at the happy hour tonight? Had he even smiled at me? I couldn't recall.

But a warm aliveness burned inside when I remembered him saying, "I want to see you naked," the shiver of my T-shirt as I slipped it off, the miraculous friction of his skin on mine.

I got lost walking back to my room because of the symmetry of the place. All the quads looked alike. But the birds twittered and sang, morning dawned clear. I was in college and I wasn't a virgin anymore. Hallelujah. I found my way home and shook Barb awake. She rolled over, "Whaaaat?"

"Barb? You're looking at a ravaged virgin!"

"Yow!" We went downstairs to the seventh floor, where the dealers lived, bought some pot, and had ourselves a party right then, at nine-thirty in the morning. It was the first time I missed any classes, but this was much more important.

"Who's the lucky guy?" she asked, water bubbling and bowl glowing as she inhaled her bong hit.

"Oh, you don't know him. But he's pretty special all right." I couldn't tell her it was the Ox. It was embarrassing to want to see him again, and I didn't want to risk Barb's disgust. In my mind, I rearranged the good-bye. *"I never met anyone like you,"* he said. *"You're so sweet. I can't live without seeing you again. Please say you'll accept me as your lover." "I'll let you know,"* I replied, *still trembling with the afterglow of our lovemaking.* If no one else wanted him, it improved my chances. Me and him could get something going secretly, and by the time we were together and I was free to admit my love, I would've turned Barb and the others around to the idea that the Ox wasn't actually gross.

"You scored, that's the important thing." Barb passed me the bong. "What kind of birth control do you use?"

I didn't know if I was hearing her correctly over the water bubbling and the sound of sucking smoke. "Um, you know." I started to cough. I hadn't even thought about birth control. I wanted to stay in the colorful, floating world of having scored.

Barb patted my arm. "You should go to the clinic, it's easy."

"Is that like a gynecologist?"

"What planet did you grow up on? Yeah, it's a gynecologist."

"I don't know, Barb. I went to one once and it sucked." I remembered it like yesterday.

Mom had tricked me when I was fifteen. She acted like it was her doctor's appointment and I was just coming along as usual, to sit with a magazine in the waiting room. But when we got there, she had said, "No. This appointment is for you."

Dr. Porter, a gray-haired man with a set mouth and thin, dry lips he moistened by flicking his tongue over them had loomed over me with a gleaming metal clamp while I lay on the examining table, the paper crinkling under my back, legs spread, feet up in the cold stirrups.

Mom clutched my hand. "It's her first time, Dr. Porter. She hasn't menstruated yet, and it just isn't normal when you look at how developed she is." Even though I pulled my hand free, turned away, and focused on the door handle, her shadow nodded at me on the wall.

Dr. Porter, breath whistling faintly through his nostrils, shoved his clamp up me and screwed it open as though he were building a tunnel, hoisting up the tunnel walls. He and Mom and anyone except me could see up into my dark, secret place. He poked a wooden stick in me to take a "sample" and the gushy, moist sound sloshed around the white-walled room. I scrunched up my face so tight, it hurt. The pain was easier to focus on than Dr. Porter's prodding plastic-coated fingers twisting up inside me. The paper on the examining table was damp when he had finished.

"I'd like to speak to Miranda alone." He folded the stirrups back into the table.

I hunched inside the paper gown, thighs clenched together.

"What? She needs me here." Mom patted my head as if I were a dog. I ducked, and she knocked me on the skull with her knuckles. I refused to look at her. But Dr. Porter stared, level and neutral, until Mom turned and left the room. In the end, she would always listen to a doctor. I perched on the table, our roles reversed, for I was in the doctor's office and Mom in the waiting room.

"You can get dressed if you like." Dr. Porter ducked behind a curtain. There was the sound of running water as I slipped on my dress, with a button missing at the chest, slipped on the sweater over it, underwear, knee socks, sneakers.

"Everything seems normal," he said. "We'll get the results of the Pap smear in a couple of days, but I wanted to talk to you about menstruation." The word drifted out at the end of his statement as weightless as straw.

"I already have it." I stared at my sneakers where I had knotted my broken laces and frayed bits poked out, unraveling. I blurted everything. "I've had it for two years already. I don't want her to know. She spies on me."

His gray eyes were watchful as a cat's.

"Is there anything I can do to stop it?" I asked.

He chuckled like it was a joke. "You can't stop it. You have to accept it as part of growing up. And you'll have to tell your mother. She's worried sick."

"She's sick whether she's worried or not."

"Which means she needs your understanding all the more. You know, that's part of growing up, too."

I watched helplessly as he opened the office door and beckoned. "Your daughter has something to tell you."

"What has she been saying about me?" She turned on me. "I know what you're up to. I'm no fool. Dr. Porter, I do my best and I don't get help from anyone, not her father certainly . . ."

"I got the curse." I interrupted, and set my teeth on my thumbnail, my hardest nail, which I could nibble for hours before it finally softened and split off.

"You what?"

"I think your daughter needs her privacy and feels she doesn't get enough of it," said Dr. Porter. I was surprised he understood some things after all, even though he pronounced it *priff-ah-see.*

As we drove home, one of Mom's hands clenched the steering wheel and the other gripped me, twisting my skin at the wrist. "You're a woman now, like me. You won't want to climb trees or run around like you do, because you might dislodge something. Your likes and dislikes will change, which could be a good thing. I don't envy you the first experience of mittelschmerz, and you can't take baths during your monthlies because infection can come up through the bathwater. Hopefully, the meegrains won't afflict you . . ."

"I've had it for two years, Mom. I'm still the same." I stared out the car window, imagining an enormous sharp and gleaming knife snapping out like a jackknife from the side of our car, slicing through everything in its path: trees, telephone poles, houses, people.

But Mom lurched, hit the brakes, pushed the gas, lurched again, released my wrist, and started to cry. First, her shoulders shook, then her entire body trembled as if she were having a fit. "Oh, Jesus, God, help me," she said. "I can't see." She pushed in the hazard lights, blink blink blink, as we cruised fifteen miles an hour in the slow lane.

She finally pulled off onto the shoulder, put the car in park. "What did you say to him about me!" Her face was splotched and red. "How dare you talk to him about me!"

I shook my head.

"Just twist the knife!" She collapsed over the steering wheel. "Why? Why do you hide yourself away? Why didn't you tell me! Why do I bother? I give and I give and I give! What do I get? Lies! Deception! Slander!" She started to gasp, and I looked around for her purse, hoping she had remembered her inhaler.

"You're so cold! So secretive!" Her awful gasping breath whirled through the car. I had to calm her down.

"No, Mom, please. I only want my own life."

"Your life!" She choked. If she died it would be my fault. Both my secret and my reasons for keeping it dissolved, feeble and useless in the river of her tears, her need, her sickness. "I love my daughter, damnit! I almost died to give you life! I wish I had died! I wish I was dead. That's what you want, isn't it?"

"I'm sorry." I started to cry, too—small, ugly, mean tears. The yellow floral dress I was wearing, Mom had sewn for me out of love. The wallpaper she had chosen for my bedroom, the bedspreads with the ruffles she had sewn on by hand, were all expressions of her love, unappreciated by me. "I'm sorry," I repeated. We were both crying, the same, not separate anymore. We merged into one large puddle of tears, and if I hated her, I hated myself.

BARB CAME WITH me to the clinic and sat in the waiting room studying her textbook. I didn't even ask her to come; she just did, a true friend. My knees shook as I walked into the doctor's office. There were pictures of women and birth control methods: pills, coils, and diaphragms that looked like small Frisbees. The doctor was a woman, and she showed me pictures and explained my options.

"I don't want pills," I said. "I never take pills."

When I lay back with my feet in the stirrups, the doctor held a mirror up so I could see my cervix, the tiny dark hole that Dr. Porter and Mom had peered at three years ago. It looked so vulnerable and brought on such a collapsing sense of sadness that I had to look away. In my rearranged memory, I stood up to Mom. *"Get out of here. I need to talk to the doctor alone,"* I demanded. *"But, but, but . . ."* Mom pleaded. And when she stopped the car on the side of the highway, I took over. Though I had never driven before, it came naturally and easily to me. *"I'll do the driving from now on,"* I said.

"I would strongly recommend the pill," said the doctor, "because it's been my experience that young women have trouble with the logistics of a diaphragm, and I would most certainly oppose an IUD."

I relented, because Barb was on the pill and she wasn't at all like Mom. When we emerged from the clinic together, I was armed with a packet of birth control pills, each one tucked in its own indentation, arranged in a tidy circle. I was ready for the Ox. Mystery Man, Barb called him.

Weeks passed. I didn't see him anywhere. I went back to the Rathskeller, but he wasn't there. I went for long walks around campus searching for the room where I had woken up that morning, but I couldn't find it. I looked for his face in every face I saw. We had been naked together. He couldn't just disappear after that. I was worried about him. What if a terrible tragedy had occurred and I, the star-crossed lover, was the only one not to know? I kept my feelings hidden, secret. I was ashamed of my longing.

I didn't go out on weeknights like Barb, though I helped her dye some bedsheets black and hang them up on our walls so our room was the black hole and better for partying. We put our beds kitty-corner but we separated them with my black trunk and arranged the heads at opposite ends. Barb said, "If the heads are together, people will think we're lesbians." She knew things like that. Unlike me, she had already declared her major, and she would have known how to deal with the Ox if I had had the nerve to ask for help.

I had no idea what to major in. But I didn't have to declare it until next year and I figured it would become clear by then. I worked part-time in the library, an enormous building, four floors of solid knowledge. I punched in and wheeled the metal trolley between shelves, returning books. Naturally, the Ox never entered the library.

Intro to Philosophy was my favorite class. If a chair wasn't a chair but only my idea of a chair, what was reality? True knowledge was when you knew the way so well, you could tell someone else how to get there. False knowledge was when you could get there but you couldn't say how.

Dad called. "Well, Mandy girl, we paid the bill. The phone's back in service."

"Dad, maybe I'll major in philosophy."

"Philosophy is a noble thing," he said, as I knew he would.

Mom got on the line. "Nobility doesn't pay bills or put food on the table," she said. "There are rats. I hear them in the walls. The driveway needs repaving, and we might have termites. As usual, your father doesn't care."

I didn't reply.

"I know you don't want to hear it. You're living good up there in your college. But you better make sure you major in something that has a job at the end of it. They've just started a management training program for college graduates at Lack's department store."

"Wow, really," I said. "A fate worse than death" is what I didn't say.

•   •   •

DAD KEPT A dog-eared sign on the dash that said TAXI and he made a few dollars a day meeting the buses at the Ransomville station. Thanksgiving weekend, when I stepped off the bus, he was leaning against the driver's side of the car with a camera on the roof. "I'll be damned, Mandy, you're such a college girl. I almost didn't recognize you."

I shook my hair off my face. It was my best feature, long and red. I hadn't cut it since third grade, when I caught lice and Mom shaved my head rather than give me separate towels and such. But I had outgrown the shame and so had my hair. Shaking it now released the aroma of sweet herbs from Barb's scented shampoo.

"Wait a second. I want to get a picture of you, just like that." Dad brought the camera to his face. "Now, tilt your head, like you did before."

I tilted my head toward the sky which was a perfect shade of blue with a few small wisps of white blowing across. Dad was making something of a scene as cars cruised up Main Street, but I didn't care. Ransomville no longer had a hold on me.

"Okay. Gotcha. Perfect." He scratched his gut, which ballooned out between his suspenders. He couldn't wear a belt because there was nowhere to put it. If he belted his pants above his gut, they looked ridiculous. If he belted them below, they slid down.

"Where'd you get the camera?" I picked up my bag and tossed it in the back.

"I won it in a card game with Slim, down at the Griffin. I put in a fresh battery and it's good as new. This will make us rich, Mandy girl." He held the camera up like a trophy.

"Oh yeah? How?"

"Think of it. So much that happens in this town, where do you find out? The *Ransom County Herald,* right? I'll start there, sell a few photographs to them, and before you know it . . ." The sun flashed like a strobe across the windshield. Dad turned onto Piler Road, our road. We were almost home and I felt it inside my body, in my pounding heart, the blood-speeding fear of encountering Mom.

I looked across at Dad, his first two fingers squeezing the life out of a cigarette and the rest of them on the steering wheel, knuckles large as tree roots.

He glanced back at me. "What do you say we waste a little gas before we go home, Mandy. How about it?"

"Great idea." I sat back, relieved, and watched the peeling gray paint and sagging porch of our house go by. A collection of junk cluttered the front yard. Dad called them "found objects" and he was going to fix them, maybe paint them or use them to build something else. There were old bicycle tires and rusted bed frames, pieces of cars and bits of utensils, broken lamps and a metal cabinet with the doors missing. "Hey, Dad, you can take a picture of your found objects."

"Are you making fun of an old man?" He laughed, then pointed to the side of the road. "There were some late blooms of asters over there last month. They appeared like a miracle. If I had this back then, I could've got a picture." Dad patted the camera lying on the seat between us. "You'll see, Mandy. I'm working on connecting up with Lack's, get in there, do baby pictures and such. You know those specials they have? And I'll go around to schools, too. Remember your school pictures?"

I remembered my face smiling out at me like a stranger year after year, different shots, all marked PROOF. We never bought the set of pictures, but the proofs were free.

" 'Course, I'll need a darkroom. But I got some guys already interested in this, as a business proposition."

How many get-rich schemes had he been through? Last fall, pumpkins were going to be the next big thing. "People don't fully appreciate the versatility of pumpkins, Mandy," Dad had claimed. "They can be used in absolutely everything, not just for carving up on Halloween. They're uniquely American, you know. Only America has pumpkin pie."

We ate so many pumpkin dishes after the failure of his sales that I never wanted to see another pumpkin. I had never questioned how he knew the facts he always quoted. Only now, riding with him on my first weekend back from college, did I wonder. I picked up the camera and stared at the knobs and numbers.

"That's a thirty-five millimeter," he said. "Single lens reflex."

"Sounds like a gun," I answered, pleased with myself when he laughed.

We passed a meadow where sheep grazed, pulling up tufts of brown grass and chewing. They weren't fluffy and white but matted and gray, like Ransomville itself. I aimed the camera at them, but when I pressed the button, nothing happened. "Hey, Dad, how come it's . . ."

"You have to turn it on, Mandy. There's a switch right here, you see it?" Dad almost swerved off the road.

"I got it. You should drive."

"Maybe there's some opportunities for a traveling photographer at that college of yours. I'm sure they could use one, right?"

"I don't know, Dad."

"You don't know. How is it that you don't know?"

I turned the camera on him. His teeth were gray. His face was unshaven, his skin like charcoal where his beard was growing in. Flecks of tobacco were stuck to his lips.

In Albany, when we ventured off campus, there were certain sections of the city filled with folks Barb called townies, whose jeans were brown with dirt, whose teeth were bad, and who grunted in monosyllables. They were inferior to the clean-cut university students, who called each other "dude" and used words like *crucial* and *heinous*. It dawned on me as I pushed the button down and got a picture that in the context of Barb and college, Dad might be a townie.

"Let me ask you, Mandy. What is the nature of this knowing you talk about so cavalierly?"

"What do you mean the 'nature of knowing'?" I put the camera down. Dad was smarter than anyone. He was no townie.

"How do we know anything? How do we even know we exist? How do we know we're riding in this car?"

"Wait a second, Dad. I remember this. It's Descartes, right? I think, therefore I am."

"Aha! *The Meditations!* Yes! But how do we know this entity of 'I' even exists?" He turned right. We had driven in a large circle and were heading home again.

"You're trying to confuse me, Dad." My heart began to pound as he pulled into the driveway.

"She's been looking forward to your coming home. Don't let her tell you otherwise." Dad walked ahead while I dragged my feet. We hadn't finished our discussion.

"She's here, Gert, safe and sound," he called.

Mom was at the kitchen table, the cards laid out before her. She knew lots of solitaire games: klondike, king's clock, patience. On the counter behind her, the TV was going with the sound off and shadowed images flickered in black and white. Her cheeks were flushed and she was smiling with a sparkle and flash in her slightly crossed blue eyes as I stepped in after Dad.

Sometimes when Mom smiled, I could glimpse the beautiful young girl she had been and I recalled a photograph of her, as a teenager with curly red hair, standing in the field behind our house, a mischievous tilt to her upturned lips as though she were daring the camera. "Well, look at you," she said. "My girl back from college."

When she stood to hug me she seemed smaller, as if she had shrunk while I was gone. I wanted only a quick embrace, but when I tried to pull away, her nails scrabbled across my back and she wouldn't let go. Her breath was loud and fast, like sobs. But she wasn't crying. She kissed me full on the lips, stepped back, licked her finger, and rubbed her spit around my mouth.

I recoiled. She noticed.

"You had a smudge on your face, and it made you look like a pig."

Dad started whistling. I recognized the tune, "Sweets for My Sweet." He opened the door to the basement, and I heard him whistling all the way down the steps to his safe place, where Mom would never go.

She would send her voice down there after him, though, screaming from the top of the stairs. "I married a failure!"

Once, when I was studying for my SATs, sitting in the same seat where Mom sat now, I had seen Dad leave the house and I knew Mom was yelling into an emptiness. "He's not down there, Mom," I told her. She had turned on me. "You're just like him, aren't you? Mocking me! Mocking me!"

Nothing was ever simple. I understood that Dad wanted me to hang out with Mom. He would have invited me downstairs otherwise. I sat across from her before she could touch me again. My bag was still by the door, purse on top of it. I took out my cigarettes and lit one. Mom plucked a hair from her head and flossed her teeth with it, staring at her cards.

"Red nine on the black ten there," I said.

She slapped the card down. The dress she wore came from Polly's Surplus, a black-and-white polka-dot number. Her hair was newly colored red, almost the same shade as mine. She had pulled it back in a braided bun. Mom had good days and bad. Today was a good one.

"You look great, Mom. How've you been?" I brightened my voice, forcing a tension around my eyebrows, a stiffness in my cheeks, and a slight clench in my jaw to make my expression just pleasant and attentive enough to remain inconspicuous.

"Oh, you know me. No matter how my symptoms flare up, I'm an independent person. When I have to, I'll get in that car and go. But the ulcer's been bothering me. The Pepcid isn't helping . . ." And she was off on a monologue.

In the safety and confines of our house, Mom made sense. But anywhere outside, her actions were exaggerated and what she talked about was inappropriate. She didn't know how to wind down and let someone else speak. She went on about her irritable bowel syndrome, about how her thighs chafed on hot days, about her food allergies, about microbes in beef and pollen in the air. If she caught someone polite in her web, she moved to the humiliating subject of me and how I was toilet-trained late.

". . . and my liver was swollen last month, so I didn't even have a neck. You know how everything swells when the liver . . ."

Somewhere in my memory were simpler times, when I loved Mom purely and she loved me back, when I lay with her in the bed she used to share with Dad and she stroked my arms, one at a time, with her fingernails, while afternoon soap operas ran through their TV schedule.

She snapped a card. "Ace, I'll take it. Thank you very much." Twilight laid its sameness on the kitchen table and here we were as if I'd never left, as if I hadn't encountered a limitless world continually unfolding, as if I hadn't lost my virginity, as if I were still the same dumb girl.

"Darn it. I lost again." She shuffled the cards now, slow and clumsy. "How about a game of gin rummy?"

"Sure, why not?" Faintly, music drifted up from the basement and I imagined floating out of my skin and down the steps to hang out with Dad while he worked. He was always building something, and I would sit on the wooden stool until I saw a way that I could help, hand him a screw or a nail, hold something in place while he applied glue.

The real part of me was down there with him. The part of me with Mom was just a shell, and Mom didn't even know it.

"So, tell me about college." She examined the cards in her hand as though she were speaking to them, not me.

Her voice summoned me back into my skin. "I love it. In Art History we finished the section on ancient Egypt. And in Philosophy I'm reading Descartes. I just had a quiz in Geological Science. Did you know the earth's surface is made up of plates and when they move that's how land mass is formed? Like mountain ranges and . . ."

She snorted. "Even if I could go to college, I couldn't go to college, not with my health. Dr. Wykoff says to me, 'You're in remission, Gert, and if we're lucky the remission could last for years.' But he still wants bloods every quarter. I told him, 'I'm in pain. How could it be remission if I'm in pain?' "

Why did Mom bother to ask when she wasn't interested? I heard pounding from the basement. Dad was probably working on the puppet theater he had started building before I left.

"I got that timer." She pointed to a device on the counter. "I set it and it goes off. The problem is I don't know which pill I'm supposed to take when it beeps. The thing ought to beep with a different pitch for each pill, but no one's invented a timer yet to take care of all my meds."

I gave up trying to interest her in continental drift or anything else beyond her. I picked a lousy, no-good two of clubs and discarded it. "How do you like being back at work?"

"I guess I'm doing all right since I'm on the schedule again come Monday. Some of the new girls are so careless—no pride in their work. I don't know how many times I have to demonstrate proper gift wrapping." Mom picked a card. She discarded the three of hearts. "They could use someone in the stockroom this weekend, and I told them you might be available, except on Friday morning, when you have to take me to the doctor."

She couldn't make me work at Lack's. "I have a job at college now, Mom. I work in the library." I loved the carefully ordered system in which the books were shelved and their smooth, shiny feel as they slid easily back into place, one by one, as I wheeled the trolley through the stacks. It was so different from the disorder of Lack's, the huge cartons of entangled hangers and sharp-pronged antitheft devices that had to be clamped on every item of clothing. The women were always arguing over who got to take lunch when and whose turn it was to stand guard at the fitting room. It was Mom's world, not mine. "I'm only here until Sunday, and I thought I could do some studying."

"Friday, after you drive me to Dr. Wykoff's, we'll go to Loretta's so you can get a style. Your hair's all stringy. You need a manicure, too. Look at those hands. Disgraceful."

I pulled at a hangnail with my teeth until it peeled away, leaving the thinnest filament of blood and pain. It gave me the courage to refuse. "Loretta does everyone's hair exactly the same. I don't want that."

"Don't get high-and-mighty on me, Miss Snip. Gin." She laid her cards down. A solid flush of clubs from six to queen.

I got up and went to the window. Outside, there existed a vast world where people discussed theories of art and knowledge and love. What was Barb doing right now in Mineola? The name slipped off the tongue like a smooth, sweet toffee, *Min-e-ola*. Ransomville sounded like a jail.

Winter birds squawked outside around the bird feeder Dad had built. It was an absurd thing, a big clown face beneath a thatch of orange hair with wide eyes and a giant tongue hanging down. He had built a few of them. "They'll sell like hotcakes, Mandy," he had said. But he sold only one, to an out-of-towner who chuckled over it.

Behind the bird feeder, the garden was dead. Chicken wire sagged and drooped. Behind that stood two small crosses, each one commemorating a miscarriage that was supposed to have been a little brother.

Mom had wanted me to be a boy, too. Eric should have been my name.

I remembered the hope, the excitement, when Mom pulled me on her lap and kissed me, stroking my earlobes and neck and arms and legs until I got goose pimples all over my body. She sang, "You're going to have a little brother!"

But there was no little brother, just Mom waking up with blood all over the sheets and the car breaking down on the way to the hospital so Mom almost died from hemorrhaging. She still blamed Dad, saying he should have taken better care of the car.

"The Lord took the child," they told me. We all went to church then, as a family. I was probably around eight years old, dressed the same as Mom. Dad carved a cross out of slabs of wood he took from the scrap heap outside the lumber yard. He carved in notches and fittings so the cross looked seamless. It was made of pine. I helped sand the corners and varnish the cross. I also helped push it into the earth behind the garden to commemorate the lost little brother. Mom would stand at the sink, just as I stood now, and stare at the cross from this window with her arms in soapy water, tears rolling down her cheeks.

I would peek at her through the crack behind the door. I was in awe and I cried too, silently, for poor Mom. Until one day she whirled around. "Who's there?"

She honed right in on my hiding place. She discovered me. "It was you that did it, the way you came out! You almost killed me, and now I lost my baby! How dare you spy on me, you sneaky, nosy thing!"

Later she would search me out, to cry with me and hug me. "I'm sorry. I didn't mean it. You're my little baby doll, and Mommy loves you. Let's play dress-up and I'll be the little girl and you'll be the mommy." Then she would give me a stuffed animal. She got the irregular ones free from Lack's, and there was a pile of them in my bedroom.

The second time Mom was going to have a baby, hope sprang up again. Mom and Dad did a fox-trot in the living room, and I prayed three times a day for a little brother to replace the baby who died because of me. But after seven months, Mom had a stillbirth. Dad measured out wood for another cross. Mom took me with her to a special healing prayer session with the pastor at the Church of Assemblies. He said, "Look into the face of the Heavenly Father and be grateful for His eternal love. And we know that in all things God works for the good of those who love Him, who have been called according to His purpose."

Mom laced her fingers together, shut her eyes, and murmured. I sat next to her in the pew, quietly biting my nails, begging God to grant me a baby brother.

When Mom got pregnant the third time, it turned out to be a fibroid tumor the size of a grapefruit that had somehow self-fertilized and actually grown teeth and hair. There was no cross for it in the garden. They were finished with hope. When I was fifteen, Mom had a hysterectomy. She hadn't been back to church since. If only my little brother could have existed. He might have made everything different.

I heard the grunt in Mom's throat and the flap and whir as she shuffled the cards. "Brooding causes meegrains, Miranda. Believe me, I know."

The long, sharp-edged leaves of the spider plant on the windowsill drooped down to touch the faucets. Spider plants would live forever with the smallest bit of care and thrived especially if they were neglected just a little. "Plant looks good, Mom."

"Grows like a cancer." She gathered up the cards. "How about rummy five hundred?"

"That would be fine." I sat, determined to keep the peace.

THE SMELL OF gravy wafted in from the kitchen, where Dad was cooking Thanksgiving dinner, while Mom sat in her usual spot on the living room sofa. The pillow was permanently molded with the shape of her butt and her afghan blanket dotted with cigarette burns. I sat next to her. The TV was going, but neither of us watched.

I was polishing Mom's nails. First I removed leftover red-orange chips and bits from each nail. Then Mom soaked her fingers in a little dish containing a softening liquid. Her fingers were passive under my tending, soft and moist as rubber.

"Do you see how the half-moons above my cuticles are yellow, Miranda? Anemia. I'm better at diagnosis than Dr. Wykoff. He'd be proud of me."

No need to answer. I filed away snags, cracks, and hangnails. I pushed her cuticles down with a small stick that had a blunted end.

"I want that color," she said in the high, soft lisping voice she used when she pretended to be a child. She chose a bright red from her cookie tin full of nail polishes.

"Are you sure?" I asked. Though her joints were gnarled and her fingers crooked, Mom behaved as if her hands were beautiful, calling attention to them with bright red nail polish.

"Of course I'm sure. Don't treat me like an idiot."

I massaged her fingers, and she lay her head back on the sofa and shut her eyes. I painted her nails carefully. It was like staying in the lines of a picture in a coloring book, but because they were contoured it was more of a challenge. I held her hand down, immovable, concentrating. When I finished one hand, I took a deep breath before I started the other. It wasn't a bad way to pass the time.

She gave a nod when I was done and I lit a cigarette for her, placing it between her lips before I gathered up the nail file, remover, polish, and various paraphernalia into the tin. "You can go get the jewelry box." She smoked carefully in order not to smudge her drying nails. She clicked through TV channels just as carefully with the remote control. She seemed content, and it came to me that she didn't expect any better for herself.

I went to her bedroom and fetched the jewelry box, placing it on the coffee table in front of her. We couldn't look through it until her nails were completely dry. She sat and smoked. There was a football game on TV, an incomprehensible smash of bodies advancing up the playing field. Endless replays in slow motion and the annoying bark of a sports announcer made it easy to ignore.

"Wish my soaps were on," said Mom.

Dad came to the doorway, face flushed and smiling, sipping from the coffee mug he drank vodka from. "Can I get anyone a drink?"

"Miranda will get me one." Mom patted my arm.

"Don't mess them up." I put on my reprimanding tone, gratified when Mom laughed and fanned her fingers.

Dad winked and followed me into the kitchen, where a turkey loaf was heating in the oven and gravy from a packet simmered on the stove. He cooked dinner most nights, if dinner was cooked at all. Spaghetti or macaroni, meat loaf, sometimes roast chicken. Potatoes were boiling in the big pot, which meant he was making real mashed potatoes, my favorite Thanksgiving food.

I poured Mom a scotch. "Can I help, Dad?"

"She's happy as a clam." He topped up his vodka. "You're being very good to her. You ought to treat yourself to a small drink, too."

But I wanted to save my mind for studying later. I took the drink to Mom and sat beside her with my art history textbook on my lap. I could read until her nails dried. The kouros boy, with his left foot forward, unlike the Egyptian statues who looked as if they could stand in the same pose until the end of time, was tense with a vitality that seemed to promise movement.

"This belonged to my grandmother." Mom pulled me away from my book. She picked up the jewelry box and put it in her lap, stroking the lid. I watched her nails, those shiny red drops, clacking softly against it.

"They're dry, honest!" She lifted the lid. There was no money hidden there this time. I was disappointed and wanted to return to reading about ancient Greece. It was unfortunate that there had ever been money in that jewelry box, because now it meant a future of disappointments.

Carefully, gingerly, Mom pulled out the newspaper clippings of herself in a long gown with a garland of flowers around her neck: Gertrude, Trudi Peck, queen of the regatta two years running, when her figure was petite, not dumpy, before her dimple had become a wrinkle, before she had gained weight across her shoulders and chest and her body shaped itself like a barrel.

"I was twice proposed to, but I thought I could do better." She shook her head. She had been greedy and now she suffered for it.

Touching each item as though it were precious, she handed me a pair of silver clip-on earrings. "Maybe you can polish those while you're home."

"Maybe," I murmured. The jewelry pieces clinked enticingly. Looking through her jewelry box had always been a treat. It showed me a mom I felt I had known a long time ago and put me in touch with something deep, bottomless, and sad.

She handed me a locket with a twist of her youthful strawberry-blond hair inside. "You see how much lighter and softer my hair was than yours."

She held a cameo brooch to her cheek. "If only you had known my mother. She was too good for this earth. She warned me about your father."

When I held the brooch, I tried to feel a sense of the past and of my mother, like me, sitting with her own mother. My grandmother had died on Thanksgiving Day shortly after Mom and Dad got married. Every Thanksgiving, we went through the jewelry box.

"I was fooled by your father, all right. Not that there weren't nice days. I give credit where it's due. We walked in the summer when he came to court me. My own dear mother was ill, and caring for her was such hard work. Frank was a comfort then." Mom shut her eyes to finger a jade bracelet.

I leaned back and waited.

"Yes, he picked wildflowers and told me what they were." She passed me the bracelet and stared into the middle distance while I imagined her, the regatta queen, with Dad, a handsome bear of a man. Hand in hand they walked, heads together, in their private happiness. Mom used to smile all the time; so she said. It was hard to believe, since her mouth was now like a rubber band drawn taut.

"But I remember it was summer, my allergies were acting up, and the heat became unbearable. You know me, I never perspire, but I was terribly uncomfortable. And the insects followed us." She picked up a ring and scowled at it before she dropped it in my lap. It was a simple gold-colored band made from a metal alloy with a pattern scratched on the outside. I prepared myself for the same old story.

Her voice tightened like a screw. "Your father tried to foist that drugstore ring on me. He thought I didn't care about such trifles. Dense, dense man. As if a wedding ring is a trifle."

The same rings were still on sale at the Rexall drugstore, tucked in folds of cloth in a mechanical display that revolved like a Ferris wheel under a glass case. AS GOOD AS GOLD said the sign. What difference did it make if they loved each other? Whenever I went into the drugstore, I pressed the button to make the display revolve, and the rings flashed as they moved under the light. I thought if anyone ever gave me this ring, I would treasure it.

". . . so I said to him, 'I will not wear that piece of junk.' " Mom twisted the real eighteen-carat-gold band around her finger. It had been her mother's wedding ring. She turned to me as if I had the answer. "For God's sake, am I not worth a nice ring?"

My chest tightened. Why did it have to be like this? Was the hundred and sixty dollars left from the money she had given me enough to buy her a nice ring so that she would get over it already? I reached past her and let the ring fall back into the jewelry box. We had to go through this every year. She couldn't just throw it away.

She sighed, as she had sighed last year and the year before. "This jewelry is all I have. It belonged to my grandmother. Then to my mother. Now it belongs to me. Next, it goes to you." She ran a string of pearls around her fingers, and I felt as if I were one of the pearls on the strand, a continuous circle like the necklace, passing from mother to daughter.

But the catch was broken. "Why don't you let Dad fix this so you can wear them?"

"That man is not touching my jewelry." Mom snapped shut like a locket. She snatched the necklace back and closed the box, spreading her gnarled fingers with their perfect red nails out over the weeping willows as if the pearls inside would transport her to the better, finer life that she deserved. A life without Dad in it, or me.

I reached under the sofa to pull out their one and only wedding picture. Mom kept it under there, because she didn't want Dad to have it in the basement. In the photograph she was posed elegantly in a chair, hands folded in her lap. Her wedding gown, which her mother had worn before her, flowed into a pool of white on the floor. Dad stood behind in his only suit, wing-tip shoes on his feet. He was a broad, brawny man, big, not fat. His hair stuck out in tufts around his ears, and he smiled, open and proud, not looking at the camera but down at Mom, who gazed triumphantly out, wavy red hair framing her face, blue eyes hard as marbles. Her lips curved charmingly in a smile. She had hooked the traveling salesman.

She glanced at the picture. "Mama never liked him. She said, 'Trudi, that man is a junkyard dog.' I thought I knew better than my mother. But I was a fool, Miranda, and there's nothing worse than a fool."

I understood how supreme unhappiness resulted from impulsive acts of rebellion. Mom twisted her lips, her lower lip overlapping the upper one in an expression between contempt and a pout. "The biggest mistake I ever made in my life," she said.

But I thought that if anyone had made a mistake, it was Dad.

"Dinner's served!" he shouted from the kitchen. He had set the table, even putting out the cloth place mats Mom had sewed years ago. She sat at the head, with Dad and me on either side of her. Dad's camera was at the fourth place, like an extra guest.

I pretended to ignore Mom when she picked up her empty plate and sniffed it. But I cringed inside, as though her weird habits were mine no matter how hard I tried to separate myself.

"Oh. I almost forgot." Dad grabbed the camera. "A family at their Thanksgiving meal, how's that for Americana?"

"Must you?" Mom started.

"Just move closer to Mandy. No. Better idea. Why don't you let Mandy stand behind you. Put your faces together."

"This is nonsense," said Mom as I got up and stood behind her, put my face near but not touching hers. She circled her arm back around me, grabbing the excess flesh at my waist. "You've gained weight. You're even chunkier."

"Quit it, Mom. I'm not chunky or corpulent, I'm voluptuous." I successfully combined an SAT word with the term Barb used to describe herself. Barb and I wore the same size, which made me voluptuous, too.

"What are you, a walking dictionary?" Mom snapped.

"Our girl's a thinker and she's got a good vocabulary," said Dad. "Come on, I want to see a smile."

Mom moved her hand to my butt and gave me a soft smack. "You're getting a wide end there."

"Dad, take the picture."

"The flash isn't going. Oh wait, it's . . ."

"It's because of the way you eat, Miranda. You've always eaten like you were starving," said Mom. "I'm a nibbler, myself. Always have been."

"Dad, you should be in the picture." I was going to start screaming in a minute and ruin the meal, the guarded normality and carefully constructed truce.

"We don't need him," said Mom.

The camera flashed.

"Okay, one more," said Dad. "I'll set it on the timer so I can get in this one."

Mom dug her nails into my flesh. "Mom. Stop." I tore myself away.

"You're very touchy today," she said.

Dad bent over the camera, his lips moving like they always did when he concentrated. He looked up quick, meeting my eyes. I saw a pleading there. "I got the timer set, so . . ." He peeked through the viewfinder one last time before he pushed a chair over in his rush to maneuver around the table and crouch with his face between Mom's and mine.

The camera flashed again. The picture was taken. I rushed to my chair and sat down so hard my butt hurt.

The silence was interrupted only by the humming of the refrigerator, a familiar comforting sound. Dad cleared his throat and put a few slices of the turkey loaf on Mom's plate. "Gravy, Gert?"

"You can take half of this back. I can't possibly eat it all."

Dad put two slices back.

"I'll take them." I reached for the platter.

"Good food, good meat, good God, let's eat." Dad laughed and I laughed, too, loud and nervous.

"Better than that college food, eh, Mandy?" he said.

"You bet." I concentrated on the mashed potatoes, a mountain. They were better than at college, where the mash wasn't made from real spuds. But otherwise I loved the college food. There was such an abundance, I could eat for twenty-four hours straight if I wanted and there would still be stuff left over. Here at home, we rarely ate as well as this.

I took a large bite and the mountain became a volcano dripping lava butter. I imagined Barb and her family doing the same. Everywhere, families were eating well, just like us. It was reassuring.

"My God, you eat like a savage." Mom turned to Dad. "She eats like a savage."

I bent close to my plate. She was no one to me, her and her jewelry, sick and stupid. "So, Dad," I said. "Do you know anything about the art of ancient Greece? I have a quiz on Tuesday."

"The Greeks created the apex of civilization," said Dad.

Mom chewed heedlessly, crunching, sucking, and swallowing. I tried to ignore the sickening noise of it, but I felt her watching me, and reluctantly, I looked at her. She leaned over the table to scrutinize. "You're puffy in the face, Miranda. Maybe you're ovulating?" She put her glasses on and her eyes magnified, blinking huge and frightening.

She was trying to make Dad leave the table, because he always did when she brought up menstruation. I looked at him, begging him to put an end, somehow, to Mom's torture of conversation. But his eyes were downcast, his breath puffing through his nose as he chewed.

"In my time, Miranda, when we couldn't afford a belt and pad, we tore up old sheets and we laundered them when we were through. You don't know how good you have it."

Old sheets. She exaggerated everything. I pictured churning soapy water in the washing machine down at the Laundromat, going pink then red, sloshing monthly blood. The mashed potatoes stuck in my throat.

"Rodge down at the Griffin told me a funny joke the other night."

"Yeah, Dad?"

Mom's knife and fork clanked against her plate. And I was going to burst with love for Dad.

"Okay. What do you get when you cross a penis . . ."

"Oh, Frank!" said Mom.

". . . with a potato?"

I shrugged even as I heard Mom's breath growing more emphatic.

"A dictator!" Dad's eyes twinkled. His chin went double, then triple. I laughed till my gut hurt.

"It's a knee-slapper, isn't it, that one?" Dad shouted above Mom's gasping.

"Can't breathe!" She inhaled an unearthly scream. Her asthma had been triggered by hyperventilation. I jumped up and draped her arm around my shoulders. Dad took her other side and with his free hand held the inhaler to her mouth. Together, clumsily, staggering sideways through the kitchen door, through the living room, we got to the bedroom.

Mom fell back on the bed clutching her inhaler, wheezing and

accusing. "The two of you are in cahoots. You're trying to kill me."
Her breath had slowed already. I switched on the humidifier and Dad
pulled the shade down so the bedroom lay in dusk, soothed by the
hum of a steady stream of mist.

We didn't look at each other. I knew better than to talk. What
was there to say? The meal was over. There was no normality.
Mom won, as always. Dad stomped down to the basement without
whistling.

Instead of following, I ran outside without my coat. I ran past the
garden and the wooden crosses behind it, past the tree with the tire
swing, through the poplars bordering the field, and up the slope as a
late afternoon wind blew down from the fields where the hill crested.
Twilight was descending. The air was clear and fragrant. A yellow
leaf spiraled to the ground in front of me. I kept running until I
couldn't breathe. The field was muddy, and dampness oozed through
the hole in the toe of my boot until my sock was drenched and my
right foot frozen. Let it freeze. My heart pounded through the quiet
and each beat thudded out: Alive. Alive. Alive.

I ACCOMPANIED DAD to the Griffin on Saturday evening. He
ordered me a beer and himself a double vodka. But I was more adult
this time around, and sitting next to Dad at the bar was no longer
such a treat. The Griffin wasn't half as cool as the Rathskeller.

Mac said, "You enjoying your Thanksgiving weekend?"

"We're having loads of fun, aren't we, Mandy?"

"Loads." I laughed. It was a lot more comfortable here with Dad
than at home with Mom. She hadn't left her bed since Thanksgiving
dinner, except to go to the doctor. She clanked her broken bell when
she wanted something, and I was counting the hours until I could get
on a bus back to school.

The light was dim. The bar was crowded with more than just the
regulars. People were standing around, folks gathering to console
themselves after the holiday. Here and there, even a few women were
drinking. On the jukebox, Peggy Lee was singing about fever.

An explosive and familiar laugh erupted from a few seats away. I
got up, pretending to head toward the ladies' room but really to see

where the laugh came from. I walked slowly across the warped linoleum floor, turned, and there she was, her hair streaked blond and frizzy from a perm. Her fluffy white jacket hung open. She still had big boobs, skinny legs. One of the village drunks tried to drape his arm around her, shouting, " 'Got the fever!' " But she dodged him, laughing.

"Tracy?" I said. "Tracy Knapp?"

There was a pause before her well-known, once-beloved freckled face broke into a smile, unbalanced because of the mole above the right crest of her upper lip and her beguilingly crooked front teeth. "Holy shit! Mandy Boyle!" Her hair tickled my cheek as she hugged me. She still wore tea-rose perfume. "I'm Tracy Schmidt now. I'm married. Remember? Wow, you are looking *good*! I don't know if I would've recognized you!"

I swelled with the compliment. She had never given them lightly. "What are you doing back in Ransomville? Are you here by yourself? How's your baby?" There were so many questions.

We walked over to a table near the jukebox. "Where are you going?" shouted the drunk guy. I felt the stares of the men and marveled at Tracy's nerve. The women who went to the Griffin weren't young and sexy like her. Dad watched us from the philosopher's chair. I felt it. He had never liked Tracy. I knew it already. I didn't want to see it on his face.

Back in high school, I had always wished so hard to become Tracy. Between classes, the boys flocked around when we walked down the hall. It was her they were after. I found a way to leave my own body, and my soul would fly into Tracy's skin so the crackle of excitement from the attention of the boys was mine, the heat and grasp of their hands pulling my hair, touching my arms, the hot breath of their laughter were all mine, and it was wonderful to be Tracy, to live in Tracy's skin while the empty, useless deflated balloon of my own dragged behind.

But she was a liar and she had broken our blood pledge.

"My baby's not a baby anymore," she said. "He's a toddler."

The last time I saw her, she had just come out of Ransomville General with her newborn and she was staying with her in-laws, disapproving church folks, who hated both the sinner and the sin. Tracy's mother had stopped in, too, on her way to work. She tended bar at Jake's Topless on Route 81 and she wore a frilly dress that showed her panties underneath and shoved her boobs together, displaying a cleavage framed with lace.

Steve was already in the army then, stationed in Texas, waiting for Tracy and Junior to join him.

Tracy sat in a rocking chair, rumbling rhythmically over the wooden floor, back and forth. She held the baby out to me, a screaming wrinkled little old man squinting out tears, his mouth a pink cavern of outrage. My hands shook as I held him. His head was a fuzzy delicate stone, heavy in my palm.

"You have to be careful with the head," Tracy's mother told me.

His crying quieted, a miracle.

"Go on," said Tracy. "Pull the blanket down."

I gently drew the blanket off his body. She leaned over and untaped his diaper. But he had stopped crying. He didn't need changing. She said, "Can you believe that shit?"

"What?" A fleshy tummy, his belly button, his reddened penis, his legs kicking away like a big frog, so chubby they looked as if they bent in three places.

"They circumcised him. They took him away and circumcised him without asking."

"But he's cute," I offered lamely. I didn't know what she was talking about.

"Yeah, it's a cute little weenie, huh?" Tracy taped the diaper back up. I covered him in the blanket, and he stared at nothing with his bright glazed eyes, his mouth moving soundlessly.

Now two long years had gone by and Tracy was sitting across from me in Dad's bar, of all places. "So what's new with you, then?" She leaned on her elbow as she used to when Steve would visit and stand behind her, massaging her shoulders while she made a face across the table at me, wrinkling her nose, rolling her eyes, like, Can you believe this loser? That was before she got pregnant and married him.

"I'm in college now." I shrugged as if I were used to saying that and being there. "Just came back for Thanksgiving weekend."

"Steve's still in Texas, but I've been at the in-laws' for a week and

I'm like to go nuts. I had to get out. But hell, this place is beat. A bunch of old drunks."

Dad was arm wrestling some shorter guy. He wasn't an old drunk, and I resented Tracy for making such a blanket statement. "I really like college, you know. I'm taking a lot of great classes and meeting so many smart people. My roommate Barb's the best," I said. Tracy had never graduated high school.

If I thought I was going to offend her, I was wrong. "You know where we should go?" She grabbed me. "The Tumble Inn. Now, that's a fun place."

I had never been there. The heat of excitement and adventure that Tracy always managed to stir up tingled through my body. We had first met when she was hitchhiking in a shiny purple bikini with a men's denim work shirt over her shoulders, tails fluttering behind her in the wind, blond hair blowing back. Mom and I were on our way to worship at the Church of Assemblies and Mom pulled over.

It was after the second miscarriage, when Mom was heavily into witnessing, a sort of bargain with the Lord. "Shame on you. Have you never heard the name Jesus? He'd square you away. He forgives. I think you ought to come to church with us."

"Hey, like, no thanks, I'm only going as far as the lake." Tracy sat in the backseat of the station wagon, perfectly at ease with all that bare skin showing. She had even reached up and touched Mom's shoulder, oblivious when Mom, who didn't like being touched by strangers, winced.

"Excuuuuse me for being previous." The old drunk guy pulled up a chair, placing it backward at the table and sitting with the back forward, his arms draped over it. "But you two girls shouldn't keep to yourselves."

Tracy stood. "We were just leaving, weren't we, Mandy?"

"Yeah, I guess so. Um, look, I'll meet you outside. I should say good-bye to my father."

"Jeez, your dad's here?" She marched over to him. I cringed.

"Mr. Boyle, how the heck are ya? Remember me?"

"Eminently memorable, you are," said Dad. "Where were we, Mac? I was talking about the economy, wasn't I?"

"Personally, Frank, I'm never sure what you're talking about. If you say it was the economy, I'll go along with that."

"I'm off to the Tumble Inn, Dad." I kissed him on the cheek when he didn't turn to look.

"My daughter's deserting me," he told Mac.

"Yeah, well the Tumble Inn's more fun for the young people," Mac said.

" 'Bye, Dad." I stood at the door until he finally waved to me without turning his head. Then I walked out.

Tracy was waiting by a little blue hatchback. "You like my wheels?"

"Awesome." I was pleased by how natural the college word sounded.

The Tumble Inn was several miles away, a small shingled building with a lot of cars out front. It was much louder than the Griffin. The Clash blared on the jukebox, "Should I Stay or Should I Go?" The floor was covered with sawdust, not peanut shells. A deer's head hung on the wall at the far end of the bar—a twelve-pointer, with a baseball cap hanging off one of the antlers.

Tracy snagged two seats at the bar when a couple of guys got up to play pool in the back room. She took off her fluffy white coat and laid it over her stool so she could sit on it. She ordered a Seven-and-Seven and I ordered a beer. "The in-laws are going to be pissed off at me, but fuck 'em, right?"

"I'll drink to that." I took a big gulp. A draft cost fifty cents here, cheaper than at college.

Tracy wore a sweatshirt that she had cut the collar off into a V neck so her freckled cleavage showed, a lot like her mother. There was glitter on her eyelids. Thankfully, I had paid attention to my clothes before I went out with Dad. I was in my tightest jeans and a dark blue leotard with a lacy white thing over it that I had borrowed from Barb. She had lots of lacy things. I tossed my red hair so it shimmered in the light. It was so long I could sit on it if I looked up at the ceiling.

Tracy blew smoke up into the general haze that had settled over the bar. "You look great, Mandy. I'm not kidding. What are they feeding you in college?"

"You know, sex, drugs, rock 'n' roll." I used an offhand tone and took what I hoped was a nonchalant drag off my cigarette, but I felt uncommonly proud, as if I had finally caught up to her. "How's married life?"

"Sucks a wet one, but that's the breaks." She twisted her gold band past the first knuckle of her ring finger and let it slip off into her Seven-and-Seven, where it fizzed and sank.

"Hey, Tracy, if Steve had bought you one of those rings they sell at the Rexall, would you have been mad at him?"

"You mean for my wedding? Those cheap, stupid fake rings? I wish he had, because I never would've married him."

"Oh." I remembered Steve, clean-shaven, in an army haircut and a rented tuxedo, watching from the front of the church as Tracy glided up the aisle in a long white gown with a stretch stomach because she was seven months pregnant. She got married at the Church of Assemblies, claiming she had found grace and accepted Jesus into her life. Mom and Dad didn't go to the wedding.

Afterward, there was a party at Jake's Topless. Tracy got three hundred dollars during the dollar dance alone. When she threw her bouquet, I didn't even try to catch it. I was fifteen. Getting married seemed impossibly glamorous, far-off, and I envied her leaving Ransomville in a white blaze of glory.

The Tumble Inn was crowded, noisy. A guy with long curly hair, almost long enough for a ponytail, banged his empty beer glass on the bar and the barmaid took the glass and filled it, no questions asked. I was impressed. His eyes were bright and wild looking, roaming the room. The antlers on the expressionless deer head hanging on the wall behind him cast spiked shadows across the ceiling.

AC/DC started up on the jukebox. "*You. Shook me aaaaaaall night long!*"

Tracy shouted, "Remember how you used to bring me cereal in bed?"

"Don't remind me." I finished my beer and looked for the barmaid. Did I have the nerve to bang my glass on the bar? Across the room, the dim yellow light struck the guy's face from the side, accentuating his angles, giving him a wolfish look. He was staring right at me. I turned back to Tracy and laughed as if she had just told a joke. "I remember very well."

I went to her house on Fridays after school and stayed overnight. She lived near a farmer who had some chickens in a coop behind his house, and we would sit, hidden, watching the chickens do it, feathers flying. She showed me how to spray perfume at a lit match and watch the flame plume.

When I slept beside her in her double bed, she would nudge me awake, whining, "I'm so thirsty," and I would get up still muddled with sleep, go downstairs to her kitchen, and bring her back a glass of water. I didn't mind. I would have done anything. She was my friend. She would send me down to the kitchen for orange juice, tea, and cereal, which I poured into a bowl with milk and carried upstairs. Breakfast in bed for Queen Tracy. Lucky Charms was her favorite.

"Uh, Mandy, I need more milk than this," she once said.

I took the bowl back downstairs carefully, as cereal and milk sloshed side to side. I poured more milk in and carried it back up just as carefully, though I left a trail of spilled milk behind me, which I had to go back and clean. Tracy laughed. "Why didn't you just bring the milk up here?" But I hadn't thought of that.

When she started gaining weight, rumors flew around school. She's got a bun in the oven, they said. She's knocked up, preggers. Are you? I asked, because you're getting pretty big around there, you know. She was outraged. You, my friend, you're asking me that? The fact is, I went to the doctor and he said it was malnutrition. That's why my stomach swelled up. I need to eat more and get more vita-mins, especially vitamin A.

I apologized. Carrots are good for vitamin A, I said. I knew because Mom told me. The next time I heard them talking in class, I spoke up, all nervous because I didn't normally take a stand. *She has malnutrition, okay? That's nothing to laugh at. So you can just stop all this gossip.* Then everyone laughed at me.

They had the last laugh, too.

"The drink's on me," said Tracy as the barmaid put a full beer on my coaster.

We raised our glasses. Let bygones be bygones. We had made our separate choices, and I was okay with mine. I had taken only a sip before another full glass appeared in front of me. "This one's on that guy over there," said the barmaid.

Tracy looked around. "Mandy, you sneaky thing, what've you got going?"

When I turned, the guy near the deer's head who had banged his empty glass on the bar blew a kiss. My heart jumped. This wasn't college; it was Ransomville—and nothing like this ever happened here, not to me. I blew him a kiss back, because I had nothing to lose.

I pretended not to notice or care as he sauntered over. Tracy's torn sweatshirt slipped down on one side, revealing a freckled shoulder. We had freckles in common, Tracy and I. But this guy didn't notice Tracy's offer of a shoulder because he was staring intently at me, his eyes flickering like sunlight on a deep green pond, deep enough to drown in. "I got an idea of what the future holds in store," he said.

I was a particular person in this town. I lay low, didn't make waves. But in college with Barb, where there were parties and my personality wasn't predetermined by my parents, I could be who I wanted. All of a sudden, I didn't know how to act. I should never have blown a kiss back at him. He ought to go after Tracy—that was the logical order of things.

"Uh, excuse me." Tracy nudged him, unlit cigarette hanging off her lip. "You got a match?"

The guy ignored her and said to me, "You counting the floorboards or what?"

I knew I had to look up, but I was paralyzed. Matted sawdust lay in clumps around wooden boards streaked with mud. There was a pair of big brown boots, molded to this particular pair of feet, standing on an island of sawdust.

A large, callused hand pushed itself in front of my downturned face. "Name's Booner."

I took his hand, cold and dry. Was mine clammy? Oh, I hoped not. But what did it matter? I'd be gone tomorrow.

He squeezed my fingers. "And you are?"

"That's Mandy," said Tracy. "She's shy. I'm Tracy. I'm her chaperon, because Mandy's a virgin, you know."

My nerve flooded back, filled me with myself again. "Tracy, stop. I am not . . . we were just . . ." But I couldn't formulate a sentence with Booner's gaze, like a beam of golden light, aimed on me and me alone.

"Excuse me, but if you bought Mandy her drink, who bought me mine?" Tracy lifted her glass.

Booner's friends were hooting and hollering by the deer's head. He signaled and two guys came over, introduced themselves. Lumpy, a short, wiry guy, like five-foot-nothing, with a raspy voice, and Hot Shot, a big guy with a beer gut and a walrus mustache, damp at the ends from drinking. "Which one of you bought her drink?" Booner demanded.

"Girls buy me drinks. I don't buy drinks for them," said Hot Shot.

Lumpy said, "Yeah, it was me. That's okay. Enjoy."

"Mystery solved," said Booner.

Linda Ronstadt was singing on the jukebox, and Tracy sang along, ". . . *when we kiss* . . ." She timed it just right and lit a match as she sang, *"FIRE."*

Booner jumped. "Fucking pyromaniac!"

I laughed so hard I felt beer coming back up my nose. I'd only had three. I wasn't even drunk.

Hot Shot went off to play the jukebox. Lumpy said, "I got my seat over there at the bar and I don't want to give it up."

Booner grabbed my arm. "I need to have a word with my friends. Don't go away. I'm coming back. Will you be here when I get back?"

"I'm not going anywhere."

He walked over to Hot Shot at the jukebox. His jeans tightened around his butt cheeks, wrinkling, then straightening. Left cheek, then right cheek, left right left. He turned and caught me watching. I tried to look away, but our eyes were magnetized.

Tracy leaned heavily against me, forcing me to look at her. "When did you get so wild and crazy? You sure've changed." She slurred her words and slurped her drink. I slipped off my stool. I needed to feel floor beneath my feet. The barmaid tapped the wet wedding ring on the bar. "Don't let her leave without this."

I slid it on my finger, but it wouldn't go past my knuckle. Tracy had dainty hands. Mine were big. I could hold my beer glass in my flat palm as if it were a tray. Yet Booner had chosen me. Maybe he liked big hands.

He was standing near Hot Shot and the jukebox, watching me watch him as he downed his beer in one long macho gulp, mouthing a Stones song. *"I'm in tatters . . . shattered . . ."* Suddenly he opened his fingers and dropped his empty beer glass. Crash. It shattered.

"Pitter patter." I held my glass up, because it was empty already and anyone could play the game. I stared at Booner and I was dancing with him, though we were far apart. My body was fluid and I was liquid inside it. I could go anywhere and everywhere, drip and spread beneath doors and into corners, wrap myself around the base of the barstool, slink up his boots. When the word *shattered* came around again, I let my glass fall. Crash, splinter, echoes of fracturing glass when Tracy and Booner's friends dropped theirs, too. In unison.

"All right, you guys just bought yourself a goddamn ticket outta here!" The barmaid came out from behind the bar, a big woman. She pushed me and Tracy, then went for Booner and his friends. "Out. Get out. All of you."

The five of us rolled out into the crisp, cold night. A refreshing sting of wind hit my face. We stood around in the parking lot smiling, shrugging, not knowing what to say. Then Booner lit a joint and passed it to me. I took a hit and passed it to Tracy while Booner lit another and passed it the other way. With joints coming and going, I hadn't exhaled my first hit before the next one arrived.

Tracy started singing, " *'Don't bogart that joint, my friend, pass it over to me.' "*

This was much more like college than Ransomville. Barb once told me that when you got high, you would reach a plateau no matter how much you smoked. I disagreed and thought I might get so high that I'd never descend but would dissolve into the atmosphere. "Do you think we can keep getting higher and higher and higher, or is there a place where it levels off?" I floated up into my own question.

"What the hell are you talking about?" asked Hot Shot.

"This girl has changed since she went away to college." Tracy put her arm around me, the precious scent of roses again. I leaned into her soft white coat.

"Soft as a cloud." I pulled her ring off my finger. "With this ring, I thee wed." I took her hand and inserted her finger into the ring. I loved her.

"I want a piece of that cloud you're on," Booner whispered.

I was no longer arm in arm with Tracy then. Booner's hand touched mine, our fingers intertwined, and his pulse thumped through the tips of his fingers into my hand and up my arm. The stars gleamed like diamond studs. The air was a soft gasp. He nodded toward the woods off the road and together we slipped away, wordlessly, hand in hand.

"Where are they going?" asked Lumpy.

The answer got lost in a wind that blew up through the few leaves left in the trees and they rattled like a million possibilities. I slipped my hand from Booner's because there were too many trees and I couldn't hold it and walk and keep my balance all at the same time. I followed the cracking twigs and the sound of his boots through the trees to a stream that I could only hear as the water gurgled and splashed. Branches creaked. The wind blew.

I stumbled and Booner held me. Then we kissed, a long, wet journey of a kiss. Our tongues touched. We leaned against a tree and slid awkwardly to the ground, clinging to each other until we were kneeling and the knees of my jeans were wet and cold and then I was on my back on a bed of damp leaves. Booner lay over me while the smell of leaves and musty bark and clear cold air drifted around us.

"I never met a Mandy before." His whisper sounded loud, as though it were surrounding me. I wanted to say that I had never met a Booner, either, but he slid his hand up under my lacy blouse to cup my breast. Between his hand and my skin was the stretchy layer of my leotard. Why had I worn it? If we were at college, we'd have a bed in a dorm room, his or mine, and would fall naturally into skin on skin, like with the Ox, only better. Real.

But we were outside in the woods, by a stream, and I was wearing a full bodysuit. I couldn't hear Tracy or Lumpy or anyone. I pushed Booner's hand away.

He lifted himself off me. "You're shy."

And so I was, as soon as he said it. I was overcome with shyness. I thought I might implode or do the opposite, fly off into the air like a popped helium balloon. He touched my face, the calluses on his hand scratching lightly. "I didn't know shy girls went to bars."

My tongue was too big for my mouth, my lips too heavy to move.

But if I kept perfectly still, the transformation would complete itself, turning me into the shy, delicate, beautiful princess I had always wanted to be. He sat up, shook his head. "Wow. And you're in college?"

I cleared my throat. "Yeah. I'm a freshman at Albany State. I graduated from Ransomville High last June." I was shivering and my voice was so unprincesslike that he'd never want to talk to me again.

"I barely graduated from Ransomville myself, six years ago. I work in the city with my buddies back there, and we came upstate to hang out. Our boss has his country house over on Ratchet Road."

"Oh." The city was New York City. In Ransomville, all other cities were called by their names. He drew me close, and I laid my head on his shoulder. It seemed so natural, though I had never laid my head on any man's shoulder before. He cupped my chin in his large hand, fingers stroking my throat. I felt like a cat and shut my eyes. We kissed again, liquid. My lips were getting chapped.

"I wish I could take you home with me," he said. And I became as special and lovable as my teddy bear from Dad. Only better. I was a princess.

All the swooning I had wanted to feel with the Ox, I felt inside now with Booner. The Ox was a jerk and his pillowcase was stupid. Booner was a man.

"Guess we'll head back." He held me steady, and I only wished he had been the one. With him, I might have whispered, *Please be careful; I've never done this before.* And he would have growled, *You're so beautiful.* Hand in hand, we reached the road, where Tracy, Lumpy, and Hot Shot were in a van, smoking joints.

"I want to see my Junior!" shouted Tracy. "C'mon, Mandy, we have to go! Poor little Junior's all alone with the horrible in-laws."

Booner got a pen and wrote my school phone number on the palm of his hand. "I'll never wash this hand again," he said. "I shit you not."

THE WEATHER TURNED cold the first week of December. Barb filled her bong with snow instead of water and the girls across the hall came over after dinner. We played cards: poker, hearts, spit, concentration. But unlike my card games with Mom, we never played double solitaire.

I was good at concentration, because Dad and I had played it. I felt the doubles in my mind before I found them. "Map out the terrain, Mandy. Remember what card is where," Dad would say. "The cards don't lie and neither does visual memory." Mom hated concentration, because the medication scattered her mind. But the endless rummy-five-hundred games with her served me well on the nights in the dorm when we played for pennies.

In my friends' eyes, I was sort of like Barb now, with a boyfriend from home. I didn't have a statue or any physical evidence, just a warm memory of a Saturday night at the Tumble Inn. "He's not exactly my boyfriend, but he *is* from home," I told Barb and sighed, remembering Booner's kiss and how he had stared so intently at me. He had chosen me over Tracy, and even if he never called, I had that to relive.

"If you think he's your boyfriend, he's your boyfriend," said Barb. "You have to chant for what you want. *'Call me, call me, call me.'* Do that for five minutes a day, and he *will* call. Guaranteed."

"Guaranteed by who?" I imagined me, Barb, and Booner sitting in our room under the black light, passing Barb's bong. When Barb put on an old Joni Mitchell tape, draped a transparent scarf over her shoulder, and lip-synched to her favorite song with her roll-on deodorant as a fake microphone, *"My analyst told me that I was right out of my head. He said I'd need treatment, but I'm not that easily led . . ."* I laughed till it hurt and I wished Booner were here at college, too, laughing with me.

In Art History we moved on to the St. Sernin Cathedral in France, with its vaulted nave flanked by aisles that continued around the arms of the transept and the apse. I sat in the dark with the other students while the teacher clicked slides and pointed out properties and innovations. *Romanesque* meant Roman-looking. "The mysterious semi-gloom of this interior was not a calculated effect," said the teacher, "but rather represents the art of the possible."

"Art of the possible," I wrote in my notebook.

"Call me, call me, call me," I chanted between classes. Wherever I went, my imaginary Booner walked alongside. "I never met a Mandy before," he said over and over, a replay of that night, as he sat next to me in the cafeteria among the sea of voices and faces and bright plates of food. I led him through the quad, and he was impressed by the concrete. I showed him the fountain where the water had been turned off for winter.

In Medieval Literature class, we translated *The Canterbury Tales* from Middle English. The knight was my favorite character, because he was both noble and humble, and didn't wear his medals on his chest. A guy in the class carted in a suit of armor to show how immersed in the medieval world he was. He spoke in code with another classmate, playing an endless game of Dungeons & Dragons. The Wife of Bath reminded me of Tracy.

Since I worked at the library, I had a few privileges and I borrowed an illuminated manuscript that I kept on my desk in my room while I translated. It was open to a page with a picture of a maiden in the woods and a unicorn resting its head in her lap. It was like the fairy tales Dad used to read aloud to me.

When the phone rang, I answered like Barb did: "State Quad brick house. We lay anything."

"Hey," a hoarse voice said. "Is Mandy there?"

Every pore in my body seemed to open. It was Booner. He had a slight lisp that I didn't remember. "Just a second," I said, and held the phone receiver in my lap. "Mandy!" I called. I waited. I didn't want him anymore. It was more fun to imagine him than to have this odd, high-pitched lispy voice on the phone.

I posed maidenlike as a unicorn laid its head in my lap and Booner in a suit of armor, chivalrous, in awe of my beauty, knelt before me, reciting in a deep, urgent voice, "Whan that April with his showres soote the droughte of March hath perced to the roote . . ."

"Hello?" I said into the phone.

"Hey, you know who this is?" His voice was valiant then, considerate and, like a kiss, insistent.

"Yeah, sure. It's Booner. How are you?"

"So you're not surprised. You knew I'd call?"

"No, I . . ." I said, with a rush before I lost my nerve or changed my mind. "I *hoped* you would call but I didn't know."

"Well, I'm going through changes," he said.

I didn't know what to say. In front of me was part two of "The Clerk's Tale."

> *But though this mayde tendre were of age,*
> *Yet in the brest of hire virginitee*
> *Ther was enclosed rype and sad corage;*

"Hot Shot says you put a spell on me, because I can't, um . . ."

"A spell?" I had summoned him by chanting. Now I wanted to send him back. I remembered Hot Shot, the fat guy with the walrus mustache. Yuck.

"You know, you turned me down. Girls don't say no to me, but you did."

"Why? Are you irresistible?"

"That's about right." He laughed. "No. I guess I just meet the wrong kind of girl."

Silence.

"I cut myself last week at work. Had to go to the emergency room."

"Oh my God, are you okay?"

"Twelve stitches. My finger's still bandaged. But I'm okay, baby." His voice sent a deep tremor through the phone line. "It was your fault, you know."

"My fault?"

"Shit, yeah. At work. You were on my mind. I wasn't paying attention. Eugene told me, he's my boss, he said, 'You better call this girl before you kill yourself.' "

I remembered how his butt looked in his jeans as he walked toward the jukebox. I slipped my hand under my sweatshirt. I wasn't wearing a bra, and my hand became his hand. I heard him breathing on the other end, blowing in my ear like he had the night by the stream. My nipples hardened against my fingers. *"No," I would moan as my body screamed, "Yes!"* I tucked the phone receiver between my chin and shoulder so both hands could caress my soft, virginal breasts. *"So beautiful," he would growl.*

The door flew open. I yanked my shirt down. "Man, what a day." Barb threw herself on the bed. "Shaky at best."

I put my finger to my lips, signaling Barb to please shut up. I was trembling. "Your boss was the one with the summer house on Ratchet Road?" I said into the phone.

"Yeah, how'd you know?"

"You told me."

"You mean you actually listened?"

"You mean I wasn't supposed to?" This was easy, fun! I was poised on the edge of myself, not wanting to miss a thing.

His words tumbled out. "Look, you can tell me to go to hell or leave you alone or whatever, but I wouldn't mind seeing you again."

"Is it him?" Barb mouthed, with exaggerated gestures. I nodded. She gave me the rounded thumb and finger okay sign.

"Why would I tell you to go to hell?" I asked.

"You know, you're in college and shit . . ."

"Yeah but you have a job and a boss. What do you do again?" Had there been something I hadn't listened to?

"Infrastructure. I make good money, too. Girls care about that, right?"

I thought of Dad and how he never made any money. "I don't care about that," I said. "But I'd like to see you again."

An electronic voice said, "Please deposit five cents for the next two minutes."

"Oh shit, I gotta go," said Booner. "I'll call you again, right, Mandy?"

"Yeah, that'd be great." I listened to the click on his end before I hung up.

"It worked, Barb! It worked! Call me, call me, call me." I jumped up, knocking my books off my desk, and she jumped up too. We jumped around the room, screaming, "*Call me Call me Call me!*"

Then Barb said, "Now you need a college boyfriend to play against the one from home."

My heart sank when I remembered the Ox. "No I don't," I said.

FINALS WEEK CAME around, and Barb freaked out because she had missed too many classes. She crammed madly, zip zip on amphetamines. I hadn't missed a single class, not since I lost my virginity, but the stress was contagious.

Dad called me from the Griffin's phone. Glasses clinked behind him. "They're called finals, Mandy, because you're going to do fine on them. You're a Boyle. And when you come home for Christmas, we'll get that bathroom painted, you and me. I'm stripping the walls already. So study up and make us proud."

I studied. I took a test. I studied. I took the next test. I studied. I took the next test. Three o'clock on a clear sunny afternoon, with snow piled up around the dorms, blinding in the light, puddles melting at the curb, I finished my last final. The semester was over. I had made it through. Hallelujah, all right.

Barb and I began our celebration at the Washington Tavern, because happy hour started earliest there. We ordered a pitcher of beer and passed it back and forth. I drank from the rim. Barb drank from the spout. "We're not proud!" we said, finished the pitcher, and moved on to the next bar.

"I pledge that next semester I'm not going to skip a single class," said Barb. We drank to that.

"It'll be next year by the time we see each other again." I was missing her already. What would I do without her? Take long walks on cold mornings. Paint the bathroom with Dad. Celebrate Christmas. Play double solitaire or rummy five hundred with Mom. Work in the stockroom at Lack's. Maybe I'd see Booner. But he hadn't called a second time.

"Here's to next year," said Barb, and we drank to that.

We drank to meeting in the city over Christmas break.

The kamikaze shots went down later at a bar called the Living Room, where they had a kamikaze special every Thursday night. "Here's the pilot coming in on attack. Down the hatcheroo!" Barb and I drank it up, toasting with shot glasses. "Kamikaze crash!" Clank.

It grew dark outside as the night ran on in a swirl of faces, laughter, and music. Colors and flavors blended and melted. We aimed quarters into shot glasses to add spice and competition. I blew smoke rings like halos floating above the bar. When I saw the Ox walk in, yanking at the crotch of his sweatpants, I said, "Barb, s'time to leave."

"Time to live!" she screamed. But a wide space yawned open and we stayed inside it, going nowhere.

The Ox had dyed his mohawk red. His presence was an insult to me. I had surrendered myself, and it meant nothing to him. I wanted to hurl my shame like acid in his eyes and snatch my virginity back. "That guy, Ox, is truly fucking ugly," I shouted. He heard his name and craned his thick neck.

"*Fugly!*" cried Barb. "Sgusting!"

I remembered how I had searched for him. He didn't even recognize me. To him I was nobody, and I had thought that was love. I hated him. Raw heat flew up inside my body, rage and hatred. "Gross!" I aimed my empty shot glass. The Ox ducked, but the shot glass never even left my hand. What a coward and a loser. Then I felt sorry for him, and for myself.

"I really do want to leave," I told Barb.

"Make like a tree and leave!"

"Like horseshit and hit the trail."

The ground spun under my feet as we staggered out. I didn't want the night to end, but I was too drunk to carry on. "Barb, now what are we gonna do?"

"Candy machines!" shouted Barb. Oh yeah, there were the dorms. And there were the candy machines, a few feet from our room, watching our hunger like sentinels. Sometimes you hit the jackpot and candy came out and you got your money back in the change slot, too. When that happened, you knew the universe was on your side.

"How much change you got?"

"Changes and changes, unbelievable changes." We fumbled, coins clinked into machines, and candy bars slid down. M&M's, licorice, Almond Joy bars, packets of cheese crackers with peanut butter, Milky Ways.

Barb unbuttoned her shirt. "Hot damn, I feel stifled." When she drank too much, Barb stayed articulate, but she took off her clothes and became Lady Godiva.

"Hey, Barb, check it out, our door's open!"

"Holy shit! Our door's ajar!"

"I don't see a jar."

"You don't see that pot to piss in?"

"Pot? We have pot? Cool!" We approached carefully, two cartoon soldiers on sneak attack in a two-dimensional world. Barb pushed me in front of her. "Follow me. I'm right behind you!"

"Shh!"

The desk lamp was on. Sandra, the resident adviser, sat under the light at my desk. She was facing the door, very solemn. I sobered up for an instant. We were in trouble. What had we done? Then the room tilted. I was drunk again. Just deny everything, I thought. Maybe if I smoked a couple bong hits I would fall asleep instead of getting sick.

"Sandra, how'd you get in here?" asked Barb.

"I have keys," said Sandra.

Ew. She was such a tight-ass, always ironed everything she wore. On her door were smiley-face stickers. And on the walls of her room hung posters of kittens with big droopy eyes. She was a junior, majoring in statistics. She wore stockings with her sandals, flip-flops in the shower, and kept her bathroom stuff in a little case with her name written on it, all flowery.

I never knew she had keys. She probably snuck into everyone's room every chance she got. She probably took cigarettes out of my pack. And I had blamed Barb.

"Mandy," she said in such a tight, constricted voice that a chill entered my heart. It was me who was in trouble. "Please sit down."

I sat. The room sloshed.

"It's your father." Sandra's eyes focused on mine. "He's passed away."

I couldn't look at both her eyes simultaneously. Her right eye was my center point. One-eyed monster. "You mean my mother."

"No." Sandra stared at a soggy piece of paper in her hand. "It was your mother who told me. She's at her friend's, at Loretta's, and she wants you to call her."

"You mean my mother," I repeated dully.

"I have the number here." Sandra flapped the piece of paper.

The room tilted. Walls shifted, my bed shook, and I couldn't hold back, couldn't stop. I heaved up all the beer, tequila, vodka, all the happy hours, into the trash can.

C E S S A T I O N

T HE TV HAD been moved to make room for the Christmas tree, a tall, fat trunk spreading out its boughs with the sweet scent of pine. Dad must have meant to surprise me. The lights were strung on. When I plugged them in, colors winked up and down around the tree, echoing in the front window, where wind whistled through the loose glass and forced its way past the heavy plastic that was stapled over it.

The ornaments lay in boxes at the foot of the tree like gifts. Dad had carved most of them from wood. Birds, angels, trains, fish, all sorts of things. I had sanded, painted, and glued on glitter. We always decorated the tree together. Dad strung the lights. I hung the ornaments. Mom didn't get involved.

Dad would say, "Oh no, Mandy, you've got two reds together. That won't do."

"Well, the lights look crooked up there, Dad. And that one's not clipped on too steady."

"It's the tree that's crooked, Mandy. Nature isn't perfect, but we do the best we can." We would lay the tinsel on together, one silvery strand at a time, until the tree shimmered and glowed.

Take it down, or finish decorating? What would he have wanted? Dad's BarcaLounger didn't go back all the way, because it had been moved closer to the wall to accommodate the tree. I sat and watched my breath fog up the air in the cold room. Each second dragged by for an hour and led to the same dead end.

I wrapped myself in his blanket and held his chipped coffee mug, cold and smooth, against my cheek, numb against numb. The ashtray filled with his squashed cigarette butts stood near his chair. I couldn't empty it now, though it stank. I remembered how he would give me his lit cigarettes to put out, a treat when I was a kid. Now I lit one of my own and threw the spent match among his.

"He left nothing but debt, Miranda. Didn't even buy life insurance." Mom shuffled in and sat at her usual place on the sofa, the contents of her robe pocket clinking together: lighter, cigarettes, eyeglasses, thermometer. "Is it too much to ask that a husband buy life insurance so his wife can have a little extra to bury him with?" She reached into her pocket, pulled out her thermometer, and gave it a shake before sticking it in her mouth.

Any room she entered became crowded immediately. I lifted myself off the chair and walked down the hall to the bedroom where Dad kept his clothes, though he hadn't slept there in years. I drew deeply on my cigarette, started to cough, and laid it in the ashtray on Mom's nightstand.

The top dresser drawer stuck when I pulled it open. There were pairs of socks rolled in balls. Mom's and Dad's underwear all mixed together, so much more intimate than their owners. Dad's were bigger, worn-out and dingy. The waistband on one pair was so stretched, he had pinned it with a safety pin. I threw it back and pushed the drawer shut.

In the closet, a navy pullover sweater with leather patches on the elbows, Dad's favorite, drooped off the hanger like it knew it would never be worn by him again. I slipped it on, and the bittersweet smell of perspiration and tobacco, of wool soaked through with rain then dried over a gas oven, surrounded me. It hung like a dress, heavy in the shoulders, the elbow patches almost at my wrists. It was like wearing Dad's skin. Did he feel this small and lost inside his large, rambling body? If only I had thought to ask.

"Miranda!" Mom called. "It's time for my tablet. Could you bring my medication?"

"Just a minute." I rolled up the sweater sleeves. I dragged myself to the kitchen, fetched the plastic box from the refrigerator, and put it down on the sofa next to Mom.

"What are you doing? Are you wearing his clothes? What's the matter with you?"

"What?" I pulled the sweater sleeves down over my hands until they were like mitts.

"Are you *trying* to hurt me, or does it just come naturally? For God's sake, Miranda. Don't rummage and ransack, I'm not ready."

"I wasn't ransacking."

"I'm all alone here! I'm all alone!" Mom's eyes bulged out of her head. She pounded the pillbox. The lid sprang open, pills bounced out, and she reached frantically around the sofa cushions with her flailing starfish fingers.

I holed up inside the sweater, inside myself, skulked like a prisoner behind my eye sockets. The air closed in around me. He had left me alone with her.

"Why do you do this? Don't give me that ugly sneer! Your face should freeze like that. Get out of my sight!"

I was losing my grip. I hadn't seen the outburst coming. Burning beneath my skull, I crept to my bedroom.

"You bring it on yourself!" she screamed at my back.

My room smelled musty. I shut the door, wondering how I could possibly spend another second in the same house as her. I felt weak with hatred. There was nothing to do but get into bed.

Hugging my teddy bear, I curled up beneath the frilly flowered bedspread that Mom had spent months sewing ruffles on. I couldn't tell her I didn't want a flowered bedspread. Not after watching her struggle with it, muttering under her breath as she pushed the foot pedal and the sewing machine stamped out its stitching beat. Thread tangled. The machine stopped. "For God's sake, can nothing ever go right?"

She ripped out thread, tossed the bedspread on the floor, knocked over a kitchen chair, broke a glass, and went to bed.

I had cleaned up after her as quietly as I could, knowing it was my fault that she suffered so. A few days later, she was back at the bed-spread with the same grim determination. It took about a year to sew. But Mom said it took ten years off her life. And I had never even wanted it.

Half my wall was papered with a floral pattern Mom had chosen at Lack's, to match the bedspread. Dad and I put it up. "Come on, Mandy, it's not so bad, is it?" he said. "Your mother means well. And it's cheerful. You gotta admit that it's cheerful." I did it for him, not her. The rest of the wall was speckled white, because we had run out of wallpaper.

There were twin beds in my room, one for me and one for my friends. But I never had a friend stay over. When I hung out with Tracy, I slept over at her house. The empty bed held stuffed animals, accusing me of friendlessness.

Sometimes Dad slept in it when he came home late from the Griffin. He scattered the animals off and fell asleep on top of the bed-spread. I popped awake when his snoring filled the room and found my way back to sleep by timing my breath with his. The rhythm gave me a blissful sense of someone breathing for me, blowing air into my lungs and drawing it out again. In the morning, he was always up before I was and he always put the stuffed animals carefully back on the bed.

But now I would never hear him snore again. A chill circled the room, shifting everything slightly. The sculpted wooden key from the honor society that hung from the closet doorknob tapped against the hollow wood of the shut door.

"There's the key to your future," Dad had said. "It doesn't matter if you don't know what you want to be yet. You're not even a quarter of the way through the snake. It'll come to you. *A* for astronaut. *B* for baker. *C* for clothing designer, and on through the alphabet. Anything you want."

"*Z* for zoologist?"

"*V* for vindow viper."

Mom would say, "Sure, Frank, teach her how to live in a bubble like you when she can't even sleep through the night without wetting her bed. Miranda, listen to me. Learn something practical so you can earn a decent living. No man is going to take care of you, even if you manage to stop slouching and learn to leave off picking your face. Maybe you can work at the gift shop like I do. Learn sales, retail."

Dad would turn and wink. "*A* for anything you want, Mandy girl."

A jab, like a hard muscled finger, poked me in my chest, mean and vindictive. *D* for dead. The stuffed animals on the other bed stared blankly. I felt a lurch in my gut and began to cry. A whisper came from just outside my bedroom door. "Miranda? Please, it's Mom." I realized I had been waiting, and I got up to let her in.

"Mommy's sorry! I know how you feel, losing your father. My smart, pretty little girl! I don't want to hurt you!" She fell into me with a sob. Her wet face dampened the skin on my neck. Beneath her robe, her rounded shoulders heaved and trembled uncontrollably. I became strong and solid, my arms around this helpless crying woman, my mother. "Please let me sleep here with you," she whimpered. It was as if she had sucked the tears and feelings right out of me, leaving me hollow as a doll, my huge, inert body propped up against her heaving, feverish one. I helped her onto the bed, pushing the stuffed animals off. I felt sick with an unbearable sense of no, never, not again. I swallowed it down and pulled the blankets up around her.

Mom fell asleep instantly, moaning slightly as she breathed. I got back into my own bed and turned the light off. The faint tinny sound of TV voices drifted in from the living room, weighing me down. The wind rushed through the trees so loudly that I thought I heard Dad calling out because he was lost. The eyes of a stuffed white owl gleamed from the floor by the bed where Mom slept. They sent an eerie accusing glow, blaming me for everything.

As I fell into a twilight sleep, I remembered hands on my nightgown, tucking me in, a statuette of Jesus on the cross that I kept under my pillow to protect me and prevent nightmares, a hot and cold sensation of love and fear.

I jerked awake to the metallic grind of Mom's jaws echoing through the room. For a moment I thought I was in college and Barb had played a trick on me, shifting furniture around while I slept. Then I saw the shape of the dresser, a heavy black against dark gray, filling a square space against the wall. The triptych mirror on the vanity table reflected unfathomable shapes.

I lay cold, rigid as a plank of wood, remembering as clearly as if it were happening now, though it was years ago that Mom had leaned over my bed, brushing my face with the tassels of her nightgown, whispering, "He's down there again, passed out." So Dad was in the basement. So what? His sleeping there was already habitual.

Mom's breath had rumbled in her throat like a purring tiger. "You're growing up, Miranda. I know you're in pain just as I'm in pain."

I had turned on my side and slid my hand beneath the pillow to clutch the small plastic figure of Jesus, had run my fingers over the bump of his beard, the sharp angle of his toes, the flat, hard edge of the cross.

"You're developing, you're filling out. Your breasts like these . . ." She hissed gently over the s in breasts as the hush of her nightgown slipped off the shadow of her body.

How could she have known about my pain? I had first noticed it one afternoon in study hall, a steady, throbbing, unfamiliar pain that I had eventually tracked to my nipples. The pain grew into hard nuggets, then boobs. Mom spied on me, barged into my bedroom, peeked around doorways, and talked on the phone with Loretta about my being "stacked" and "developed." But she couldn't get inside me; she couldn't have known. I had hidden myself away. I had refused to let her fit me for dresses anymore. I wore large T-shirts. I never said a word about the pain. She was guessing.

"I'll let you feel them. It's a gift." Mom had touched my face. The shadows were fuzzy, my bed spun in the air, and I was falling.

"Give me your hand, sweetheart." She had squeezed my fingers together and guided my fingertips across her goose-pimpled skin. "When you get your first monthly, you'll do the same for me. We'll share everything." She had guided my fingers over her nipples, her every breath a trembling sigh. Her nipples were firm and pressed into my touch, but my fingers were limp. My hand was not mine.

She had whispered, "I wanted to share everything with my mother, but she denied me. She never told me about growing up. She never let me see her. All I wanted was to know."

She had brought my hand into the crease under her breast, where it lay against her skin, and up into the valley between her breasts. She had cupped my palm around one breast and then the other.

"What do you think?" she had asked thickly.

I had twisted my mouth into a silent *ugh* so intense it hurt. My palm was damp, and I had waited for her to leave so I could shake out my cramped fingers.

The bed rose when she stood, and the smooth slipperiness of Mom sliding her nightgown back on had been the real gift. I had lain in bed numb, paralyzed as the light changed from black to deep gray to light gray to daylight.

Was I remembering something real, or was it a dream? I thrashed, twisting my sheets and blankets, while Mom ground her teeth in a deep slumber. I wanted to believe it was a dream. Mom had slept with me sometimes to stop me from peeing my bed, and I couldn't have told her back then that my sleeping habits were no business of hers. I wanted to state it now, to wake her up and scream at her. But I was answering a memory I couldn't be sure of. It hadn't worked anyway. At eighteen, I still occasionally wet my bed.

I wrapped my blanket close around me and tiptoed out to the living room. I turned off the TV. Silence. The house creaked. I downed the sticky dregs of scotch from the glass Mom had left sitting on the coffee table. Then I lay on the sofa, unable to shut my eyes, dreaming a nightmare I couldn't wake up from.

Mom was the baby and I was the mommy. Her huge, heavy skull pushed against my chest, her tongue on my skin, licking. Her damp kisses pressing over my body left me so weak I thought she had passed all her diseases on to me. I was sick and would never get well. She sucked and grunted, whimpered and whined, worse than an animal, horrifying. *Mommy!* she cried. *You're the mommy now and I'm the baby. I'm hungry, I'm scared, help me, Mommy!*

I AWOKE TO leaking blood, the sofa cushion stained red-brown with it, my period, a week early. I turned the cushion over. I had control of exactly nothing. When I walked out to the kitchen, Mom was already awake, ironing a black dress on a towel she had set up at the table. "I didn't sleep a wink last night," she said.

Loretta came over, lips pursed tight around a cigarette, wheeling a suitcase filled with rollers and dyes, dryers, scissors, clippers. The sign that hung outside her house, five houses down the hill from ours, said LORETTA'S BEAUTY SHOPPE.

"The shop comes to us," said Mom. "Miranda, I'm going to need all the help I can get today."

I ignored her. I refused to iron the black dress she had chosen for me to wear. So we were back to dressing alike. Well, it was only for today.

Loretta shoved Dad's crossword puzzle books to the back of the kitchen counter so she could set up her heating curlers. "God took your Dad away while he was in the ambulance, halfway to the hospital," she said. "I'm the one that found him, collapsed by the front door."

I didn't offer her a cup of coffee when I poured myself one. I didn't even want to acknowledge her presence. Mom sat with a mirror in her lap while Loretta stood over her, pulling her hair back in a bun, combing over the thinning patches where Mom's scalp showed through. She curled tendrils in front of Mom's ears with spit and her index fingers. "We'll do you next," she said.

She wasn't putting her spitty hands on me. As if it mattered how my hair looked. I went to the other room and unstrung the lights from the Christmas tree, rolling them carefully and placing them in boxes while Mom got her hair done for the service. I carried the lights and ornaments to the basement, but I couldn't get past the door where the dark cavern of stairway waited like a void to suck me in. I shut the door, placed the ornaments and lights just outside it, and wondered what to do next, how to get ready for Dad's funeral.

A CHILL DRIZZLE sliced through an icy mist, then froze over the trees, the houses, the wires, and the road, encasing the world in glass, a glittering fairyland. Icicles hung from the porch roof in frozen drips. When I ran my fingers across a bush, it tinkled like wind chimes. Dad would've loved it.

I skidded down the path he had been shoveling. Mom was already waiting, her hair looking frozen in place. She fogged up the air with her breath in the passenger seat of the cold car. She only cared about arriving on time. As if they wouldn't wait for us.

The car doors clanged shut unnaturally loud. The engine choked and sputtered as I fishtailed off the icy driveway. Mom pressed her imaginary brake pedal at every curve I took until we reached the Church of Assemblies, which I hadn't been to for almost four years. It hadn't changed. Still the same plain wooden prefab building, no arches or flying buttresses, no stained glass, nothing to study for Art History. Only the cemetery behind it made it look like a church.

Bells on cassette tape played over the outside speakers, worn-out in places so the sound of the bells dragged. I followed Mom inside. There were wreaths on the beveled front doors, but they weren't for Dad. They were for Christmas. In separate pots along the altar, poinsettias were blooming.

But in front of the altar was the casket, a plain pine box, shut tight. A flower arrangement in a black plastic vase, vivid, alive with exotic blooms, birds-of-paradise, tulips, orchids, gardenias, all oranges, violets, reds and pinks, had been placed near the casket. The guys at the Griffin had pitched in for it. So extravagant and futile, I wanted to kick it over.

Mom sneezed and coughed and wheezed, because she was allergic to the flowers. She fumbled with her tissue and tucked it up her sleeve. I watched her hands twitch, but I couldn't look at her face.

"For whether we live or whether we die, we belong to Christ, who is Lord both of the dead and of the living . . ." The new pastor's fleshy cheeks shone pink as a Santa Claus picture.

The church was overheated. The radiator hissed. In the center of the heat, in the middle of the service, the noon alarm wailed out, late by ten minutes, according to Mom's watch. Gray light filtered in through the venetian blinds, and the walls held the reflected diagonals.

Even though my mothball-stinking coat with the rabbit-fur collar choked me, there was a muffled safety in its heaviness. Mom had given me the coat for my birthday last year. I never wore it. I had never even considered an old-lady coat with a fur collar something to want. But this morning she had tearfully hung it off the hanger on my bedroom door. The sleeves were short, the shoulders and neck too small, but I wasn't going to make any trouble. I was only going to get through Dad's funeral like a windup doll. I stepped into the daughter role that Mom had hung on the door, because it was already there.

The squeal of the organ overlaid with uncertain voices cried out a hymn chosen by Mom, Loretta, the pastor, and the funeral director. They had arranged everything.

Eight guys from the Griffin softball team hefted the casket up on their shoulders and proceeded down the aisle and outside after the pastor. We followed. I pretended to sing along about choirs of angels welcoming Dad into paradise. The cold air was almost refreshing, the church had been so hot. Mom clamped her hand around my arm. "What a time for him to go!"

"Stop it, Mom. We're supposed to be singing."

"I'm the one who should've died!"

God, how I wanted to punch the dark, puffy skin around her eyes! Tear her graying hair from its prim bun and rip the tipped, polished nails right out of her fingers. A thousand diseases, and she just wouldn't die! I snatched my arm free.

If only it had been her, not him. If only I weren't stuck in this life with her panting, whimpering, and complaining. I kicked a small chunk of ice off the path, wanting to scream at the pastor, Your God is so stupid, just look at his mistake!

A huddle of folks clustered around the grave for the committal—guys from the Griffin, women Mom worked with at Lack's, church people who went to every funeral whether they knew the dead person or not. And there was Tracy, with a chubby blond toddler tugging at her hand. He shrieked, and as she bent down to shush him, she saw me and gave a rueful wave as if brushing away all the unexpected griefs and saying, Here we are, still alive. She gave me hope.

All over the cemetery, trees and headstones shone under the frozen glaze. And I felt suddenly as though I were enormous and the world was a marble I rolled around in my huge palm. I held it up to the light and looked inside, trying to see what lay ahead. College sparkled there, the place where I really lived, where I was somebody. Then I looked at Mom, who sniffled and went quiet. I wasn't angry anymore. I had college, and that was more than she had. I put my arm around her.

A pit had been dug for the coffin, breaking the surface of the white snow to reveal brown mud and, deeper, black earth. We couldn't afford a headstone. Instead, a temporary placard of hard plastic, with letters stamped in, had been set up by the grave: FRANK BOYLE. JULY 14, 1935–DECEMBER 22, 1985. It was a guess. Because Dad was an orphan, no one knew the date or year of his birth. He had chosen Bastille Day because it represented the destruction of royal tyranny. That, at least, was his.

The pastor droned on: ". . . Lord God, our Father, we commit Frank Boyle unto thee, in whose hands he already is . . ."

The funeral director came around with a bag of dirt. Mom took a handful, spilling it from between her fingers. When I dipped my hand in, the earth was warm, damp and comforting like the dirt in the garden last spring when Dad and I were planting tomatoes, cucumbers, zucchini, lettuce. It gave off a dense, dark aroma, the smell of faith and strength. If Dad were alive, he would tell me, "You're doing a great job, Mandy girl, behaving just right for a funeral."

Sadness was a weight on my chest. I couldn't breathe. When I closed my eyes, only sound existed, the rustle of coats, the cawing of a crow, sniffs and coughs and the creak of the coffin descending. "Well that's that then," said Mom in a voice flat as wallpaper.

The casket was in the ground when I opened my eyes. Mom and I threw our dirt in. Most of it scattered, blown off by the wind. An icy rain was starting, and each sharp drop pierced the frozen gray until the snow was full of holes. A flock of crows flew a loose V through the clouds, veering off to the right in perfect synchrony. I turned with them, and there, in a leather jacket, slouched uncomfortably against the cold and the rain, hands in his pockets and apart from the crowd, stood Booner.

My teeth began to chatter. I wanted to shout, "Booner!" I was glad for my fur collar, because it was warm and I could hide my face in its softness. When I felt the heat of tears coming, I thought, No, not now, and wiped them away.

"On behalf of the family, we invite you all for hot coffee on such a cold afternoon," said the pastor, as if it were part of the sermon.

I craned my neck to watch Booner standing like a hero against the wind. How had he known? He was squinting, bewildered, uneasy, not the wild, reckless guy I had met at the Tumble Inn.

A firm grip closed around my elbow. "Time to set up," Loretta whispered. I followed her through the side door, down the steps to the church basement.

The room hadn't changed. The mural I helped paint in Sunday school hadn't faded. It took up an entire wall, divided in two by a cross that the painted people passed through to salvation after accepting Jesus as their Savior. The heaven side of the cross was filled with blue sky, angels flying around a yellow sun and smiling people dancing barefoot in a green pasture. On the earth side, bowed down and suffering, the people crouched against rain and jagged lightning, weeping as they struggled over rocks.

My job had been to mix white and black paint to make the gray rocks on the earthly side of the cross, while wishing I could paint the sun.

"Your father was an orphan, dear, but you're not. You have your mother and she has you." Loretta touched my face. The gesture felt like a horsefly landing on my skin, folding its bristly legs beneath its wings. She returned to her task of arranging boxes of sugar-dusted doughnuts next to the big metal coffee urn. Her body beneath her tentlike wool dress moved and shook. "He's with Jesus now. It was a good eulogy. He would've enjoyed it."

I wanted to believe her, but I had stopped counting on Jesus a long time ago. And Dad would've thought the service was pathetic. Loretta didn't know anything. I ripped the plastic wrapping off a stack of Styrofoam coffee cups and I felt better doing something useful, but I was searching for Booner among the people drifting in.

"I'm a widow now." Mom leaned on the pastor's arm. "But at least I have my daughter. We've had our disagreements, mind you, but we survive them. I know I have a strong personality. It's the way I am."

I opened a package of sugar cubes and put several in my mouth. The grains slowly dissolved and my gums tingled with sweetness.

"Pastor Robert Wilson. You can call me Pastor Bob."

"Nice to meet you." Flecks of creamer floated on the surface of my coffee like scum on a pond. I held a sugar cube in my teeth to drink through and I stared to the left of Pastor Bob's shoulder, willing Booner to appear.

Instead, I saw one of Dad's buddies coming toward me. "Your father was a good man, one of the best. Always braggin' about you." He didn't say his name, but I remembered him as the guy with the stupid dirty jokes down at the Griffin. He drank more than Dad ever drank. His waxy skin was pocked like an orange peel. He had a small unshaven patch on his chin where he had missed with his razor. His breath stank of cigarettes and unbrushed teeth. He was less healthy, less intelligent, less worthy, yet still alive.

"Mandy, I'm real sorry. Your father was such a big old friendly bear." Tracy hugged me, a brief elusive hug. Her little freckled kid peeked at me from behind her legs, his pale hair poking out all over his head since Tracy had taken his hat off. His eyelashes were practically white around his red-rimmed, leaky eyes. His nose was awash in snot.

"Steve's mom told me. She saw the obituary. She reads them every day—it's her greatest joy." She touched me then, firmer and more comforting.

"Mrs. Boyle, I'm, like, totally sorry." Tracy went to kiss Mom, but Mom tightened her mouth and turned to Pastor Bob. As if she had the right to snub anyone.

"Someone get the child away from the doughnuts." Loretta barged in with two cups of coffee and gave me a look as she handed one to Mom.

"Oh shit." Tracy's kid stood by the table with a doughnut in each hand, clumsily pushing bits between his soft, mobile lips. White powdered sugar stuck to him everywhere. "Come on, Junior." Tracy took a running leap and tried to pry a doughnut from his hand, but he let out a piercing scream.

"Why aren't you being good, honey? He's usually such a sweetheart." Tracy knelt down, her face flushed beneath her freckles. Her permed hair was dry and scraggly like frayed rope, and she looked exhausted, as if she hadn't slept in days. With a sigh, she picked him up, a screaming, kicking sugarcoated bundle, and headed toward the stairs that led outside.

"Are you leaving?" I asked desperately.

"Look who's here, Miranda." Mom's eyes were gleaming as she presented Dr. Wykoff like a visiting celebrity. When he hugged me, I caught a whiff of antiseptic before he stepped back. His pale skin was mottled under the fluorescent light.

"Your mother tells me you'll be staying home for a semester, until the two of you get back on your feet. I think it's a good idea."

I should have known Mom was hatching a plot. I wished I could scream just like Junior.

"It's a sad thing. I told your father to come see me," said Dr. Wykoff. "He neglected his health."

All I wanted was to follow Tracy up the stairs and out the door. But Mom was watching, and Loretta barked from nearby. "I'm sure Miranda will take the semester off. She and her mother need each other right now."

It was a conspiracy. "They're lucky to have each other," someone murmured. I gnawed on my nails, from one finger to the next, until at last I saw my chance. The women from Lack's had surrounded Mom with babble and commiseration. A woman in a woolly hat, one of the church people, was coming toward me and casually I turned my back. Then I bolted up the steps and shoved the door open. Cold air rushed in, making it hard to shut the door behind me.

I had forgotten my coat. I wore only my short-sleeved black dress and panty hose with loafers. The cold was deep and unrelenting. But it had stopped raining. I heard voices in the parking lot and, clutching myself against the frigid air, I made my way hesitantly down the walkway until I saw them at a sleek black car and stopped short. Tracy was smoking a cigarette while Booner stood beside her with his hands in his jeans pockets and his black leather jacket hanging open. Junior was nowhere around.

So that was it all along—the two of them. I should have known.

Tears were like pinpricks stabbing at my eyelids. I didn't want to cry. I turned back toward the church basement, my dreams of escape hanging heavy in my gut like indigestion. My menstrual blood was probably leaking out all over. I shouldn't have come outside.

"Mandy! Come here! We're over here!" Tracy waved frantically.

"Mandy!" Booner called.

A reprieve. I ran to them.

"I had to get outta there," said Tracy. "They were all giving me the evil eye. Then I ran into him." She jerked her thumb at Booner and laughed. "He was afraid to go in."

Junior was sitting in the driver's seat, pudgy hands on the steering wheel, rocking from side to side. The car's license plates said BOONER, which struck me as cute rather than silly. "Um, how are you, Mandy?" Booner pulled his hands from his pockets. "I mean, under the circumstances and stuff." His eyelashes were long, dark, and perfectly curled. He looked shy.

I jumped and rubbed my arms, blew into my hands. My skin was going numb and I didn't know what to say. "How'd you know about this?"

"Your, um, whatchamacallit." Booner's eyes changed from brown to green to yellow. He had pulled his hair back in a ponytail. "Your roommate. I think I called just after you left."

I shifted from one reality to the other, from the church basement to college to Booner, from Mom to Tracy and Junior. None of us would have been standing here at this particular moment if Dad weren't dead. That was the one true fact. The cold seeped into my bones. "I should probably go back in."

"Wait." Booner opened his arms. "Come here, girl."

"Oh." I glanced at Tracy, unsure.

But she was smoking her cigarette while she watched Junior through the car window, waving at him in the driver's seat, making him giggle.

Booner's jacket creaked like a saddle as he wrapped himself around me. The icy zipper cut into my cheek, but his body was warm and he swayed, easing the unbearable ache just slightly. His shirt was soft. He was big, firm, and gave off heat.

"Mommy!" Junior screamed.

Booner's arms stayed warm and close around me. Whatever happened outside them was no concern of mine.

"Excuse me, you two, but I have to get going."

My legs were cold and my toes had numbed in my loose loafers. Booner released me into the icy air.

Tracy was pulling Junior out of Booner's car. "I'm heading back to Texas in a couple of days, Mandy. Steve's got the housing situation worked out. But I'll call you before I go." Tracy kissed me on the cheek and headed for her little blue hatchback. When Junior let out a howl and rammed himself headfirst into her legs, she laughed and hugged him. "Come on, little monkey."

I envied the world they created with each other, the oneness. I wanted to be part of it. A cold wind blew across the parking lot, scraping my skin raw. "Booner, I have to go back in before I freeze to death."

"Come on." He started walking toward the church. I hadn't anticipated that. I followed him, walking stiffly with my frozen, brittle legs.

The warmth that filled the basement intensified how cold I felt. I huddled, shivering. Booner put his arm around me. "You doing okay?" I couldn't answer. I couldn't reconcile him with the church basement.

Mom was sitting in a folding chair in front of the mural, holding court. "But Dr. Wykoff says I'm the healthiest sick person he knows."

Dr. Wykoff had his coat on. "It's true, Gert. You continually amaze."

Clenched up with the urge to get it over with, I led Booner toward Mom. We towered over her in the folding chair. "Booner, this is my mother. Mom, Booner."

"You must have played softball with Frank." She squinted up at him.

Mom never even went to Dad's softball games. She was so full of it. I was the one watching him play for the Griffin, the bleachers warm under my thighs and the sun hot on my back. Once Dad was talking to another guy in the outfield and as he talked, he spit on the ground, squinted up into the sun, and turned his baseball cap around. I saw by his gestures that he was telling a joke. The other guy laughed and laughed. Dad couldn't really hit or catch or run, but he made people laugh. I was so proud I almost applauded. "No, Mom, he didn't."

"I came because of Mandy." Booner gazed at me, which caused Mom to look, and then Dr. Wykoff, Loretta, all the other women, and Pastor Bob stared at me.

Time stopped. I shrank inside myself, an ugly menstruating windup doll. Why was everyone staring?

"It was Frank's ticker that did him in, and I'm the one with the mitral valve prolapse." Time became fluid again as Mom drew the attention back to herself, taking the burden off me. "I should've been dead years ago."

"He's with Jesus now," Loretta said for the second time in an hour.

Such a good man. Always ready to laugh. The Lord took him. So sorry he's passed. What a shame. People were leaving, and Mom twisted her head this way and that. "You're not going already, are you?" She didn't want to grasp that her moment in the sun was ending, that the attendees of the funeral were taking it away with them, leaving nothing but empty condolences behind. Lips bent, pursed, and stretched around moving teeth.

"I guess you and your old man were pretty close, huh?" Booner held my hand, and I felt the ridge along his index finger where he had cut himself while thinking about me. In the presence of Booner's voice and touch and sheer physical being, I couldn't quite grasp Dad's absence.

"They were as close as a father and daughter could be," said Mom. I hadn't realized she was listening.

"I got to go back to the city. And I'll be there until after New Year's. But I can call you, right?"

"Are you leaving now, too?" I became Mom, not wanting to believe the ritual was ending, because afterward, what was there?

"I got to."

"I'll walk you out." I grabbed my coat and followed him out to the parking lot.

We stood by his car. "I'll call you," he said.

Adrift, lost on a current. "You promise?" I asked feebly.

"Yeah, I promise." He cupped my face in his hands, and when I stared into his eyes, my face became a beautiful oval, held together with love.

CHRISTMAS CAME AND went. I had bought a candle in the shape of Rodin's *Thinker* as a gift for Dad and I didn't know what to do with it.

Mom gave me a makeup mirror with three light settings—daytime, evening, and office. "Wow, thanks, Mom," I forced out, trying to appear as grateful as I could.

"I thought it would be useful to you. I thought you would like it."

"I sure do, Mom. It's great."

She opened my gift of a sweatshirt that said ALBANY STATE and let it fall in her lap with the torn Christmas wrapping. "How nice."

"I thought you could wear it around the house." It had seemed perfect when I bought it, all cotton. I had tried it on, and it felt so soft and warm against my skin, I wanted it for myself.

"Around the house," she repeated. "God knows I don't go anywhere."

She clicked the mirror she had given me to the evening setting and looked at herself. Changed it to office, then daytime, then back to office. "I think I'm an office," she said.

New Year's Eve arrived. At midnight, Mom and I, in the living room facing the TV, she on the sofa and I in Dad's BarcaLounger, shrugged and said, "Nineteen eighty-six, what do you know. Whoopee." We didn't kiss. If Dad had been alive, he and I would have gone outside, lit sparklers, and waved them through the dark sky, spelling out *1986*.

When the phone rang, I dragged myself off the chair to get it. Our phone was back on, courtesy of Loretta.

"Hey, Happy New Year," shouted Booner, far away, unreal.

"Happy New Year to you, too."

"How're you doing?"

"I'm okay," I yelled into the phone.

"Do you have to shout." Mom's questions were like statements.

"I've been working!" Booner yelled over noisemakers and happy screams. "I'm coming upstate soon!"

"Sounds like you're having fun."

"It would be more fun if you were here!"

Was he saying this because he thought I wanted to hear it? "You don't have to lay it on so thick, okay?"

"What?"

"Nothing."

"See you soon!" Music, laughter, and singing interfered, and he hung up, cutting off a din of happiness way beyond my reach.

A condolence card arrived, addressed to me. Mom opened it anyway. It was a large, thick white card with scalloped edges. On the front, beneath a cluster of embossed morning glories, it said, *In Deepest Sympathy.*

Inside, scrawled at the bottom, indented deep into the paper with a ballpoint pen, were the words "Sorry. Love, Barb." I touched the grooves of the letters and imagined her gripping the pen so tight that her knuckles whitened, holding it close to the tip like she did when she took notes. I tried to imagine myself as her, writing *Sorry.*

I dialed her number in Mineola and left a message on the machine.

Pine needles fell off the naked Christmas tree like rain. I dragged it out behind the house and across the field and left it in the snow. I swept up the needles and waited for Mom to notice. She spent a lot of time in bed, summoning me with the broken bell at her bedside, clink clank. I brought her cinnamon toast on a tray, a bowl of fruit cocktail, whatever she wanted. I was on my best behavior, preparation for returning to college so she would have nothing over me.

At Lack's, I worked part-time, stocking shelves and counting inventory. At least I wasn't in sales and didn't have to talk to anyone or look presentable. I wore sweatpants and didn't bother to wash my hair. Who was going to see me? No one who counted. The women who worked in the gift shop accosted me in the stockroom. "How's your mother? How's your mother?"

"She's managing," I said. Each day ground on toward the next, grinding me down. My face was tired after working at Lack's. I felt as though it deflated as soon as I got home. Under my oily skin, pimples were forming, and I wished I could just take my face off, give it a rest, wash it under the tap in the kitchen and air out all the nerves beneath my skin.

I couldn't stand walking into the scraped-out bathroom, seeing those primed walls. Yet I had to. I needed a shower. Two buckets of paint stood side by side under the sink. The scale said I weighed 142, eight pounds more than I thought. There was a tiny TV in the bathroom, perched on an upside-down milk crate, constantly on. We had one in practically every room in the house, as if we were rich, because Dad could fix TVs that other people threw away.

His Soap on a Rope hung from the shower head, grooved and cracked, deep and dry. Unused. It had been a gift from Mom one

Christmas. "Is it a hint?" Dad had been joking, but Mom didn't laugh. "To be honest, yes. You smell, Frank, and I think you ought to wash more often."

"I guess I asked for that one." He didn't speak again for hours. I sat next to him, waiting for him to say something, anything, defend himself. He said nothing.

I took the quickest shower I could, turned the hot water on full until it scalded, steaming up the room. I pulled on my sweatpants and sweater before I was completely dry and, with my hair wrapped in a towel, went to the living room to sit in Dad's chair. I pushed against its padded back until it reclined as far as it would go. The footrest rose as the chair went back and I was almost lying down, but it wasn't relaxing. I was stiff with tension and cold, waiting for January to end, waiting to return to college, to life.

"What?" Mom shuffled past me on the way from her bedroom to the kitchen. Her eyes were glazed over. "Did you say something?"

I shook my head. When I looked in the mirror, I saw my eyes were the same as hers, whether it was daytime, evening, or office. I heard the kitchen chair scrape across the linoleum as she pulled it out to sit down. She switched on the TV and I heard beeping, bells, and canned applause, a game show. "Come on *down* . . ." Beneath the TV noise, cards were slapped against the table. Mom was playing solitaire.

I could imagine her sitting there, exposed and pale in the stark afternoon light, turning cards over as she bit her lower lip. Her glasses were hanging on a string around her neck, the right earpiece attached to the lens with Scotch tape and a paper clip. When her cigarette burned itself out in the ashtray, she would light another one.

At least she was warm in there. We kept the oven going, the door wide open like a mouth exhaling heat and coziness. The rest of the house was so chilly that ice formed inside the windows. It was a bone-gnawing chill that wore me out. But it was easier to deal with the cold than to sit in the same room with Mom.

Dad's sweater draped heavy off my shoulders, itching my neck, my breasts, every inch of my skin. My calves tensed; my legs twitched. I leaned forward in the chair, pushed down the footrest, and stood up.

I walked to the window, where a world of gray outside changed only slightly day by day, lightening, darkening. The muffled snow-packed front yard, the road, and across the road a cluster of birch trees stood perfectly still, the same color as the snow that covered them, softening the sharp ends of their branches. It seemed as if winter would last forever.

I walked to the wall that separated the living room from the kitchen and rested my ear against the cold, bumpy surface. "Okay, we're ready for the Showcase Showdown Round . . ." said the TV announcer.

"Red queen, about darn time," said Mom.

I'm sorry for everything, Mom, I wanted to say. Then I would tell her how I had felt that long-ago night. *It wasn't a gift,* I would say, and she would say, *Forgive me, Miranda. I'm sorry.* When we both finally understood each other, life would open up, and I would, too.

But the only way I could love Mom was to stand in another room with my ear pressed against the wall between us, no talking, no looking.

When the doorbell rang, I jumped up to get it. A man stood on the front steps, in a cap and a pea coat, his cheeks chafed red with cold. "Hello, Miranda." He blew on his pudgy chapped hands. "You remember me? Pastor Robert Wilson, from the Church of Assemblies." He smiled. "You can call me Pastor Bob. I thought I'd stop by, see how you and your mother were getting on." He took his cap off and twisted it around in his hands. He was bald but for a few flattened tufts of gray around his ears.

"We're fine, thank you." I started to shut the door.

"Who is it?" Mom bellowed from the kitchen.

Pastor Bob shouted past me, "Hello, Gertrude! It's Pastor Bob." He twisted that hat like he was wringing it out.

I let him inside. "She's in the kitchen. Follow me."

Mom looked up from her cards, peering around me at Pastor Bob. "Would you like some coffee? Miranda would be happy to put on another pot."

"Why, sure. Now, that's kind of you to offer."

Two more weeks, I thought as I dumped out coffee grounds. Two more weeks. In the dorms heat blasted constantly, so Barb and I walked around in shorts even when it was so cold outside that it hurt to breathe. Two more weeks and maybe Barb would let me live with her over the next vacation and I would never have to see this house again.

"I don't know what I'd do without her." Mom stood up to squeeze my shoulder. She had to reach up to do it. She clung to me.

The sink was stacked with dirty dishes. Crumbs covered the kitchen table, and the counter was cluttered with a variety of casseroles, cookies, and other contributions from church members.

"How *are* you, Gertrude?" Around and around, Pastor Bob twisted his hat, until I wanted to snatch it away and throw it out the window.

"One day older and closer to the Lord, I suppose." Mom lit a cigarette and took a wheezing drag. She actually thought menthols were easier on her throat.

"And Miranda?" said Pastor Bob.

"What?" I put out three coffee mugs, clanking them loudly against the table.

"We're here for you at the Church of Assemblies. Will you remember that, Miranda?" He laid his arm over my shoulders, a weight I couldn't duck.

The previous pastor had tried to get me to start a Bible study group in school when I was fifteen, Wednesdays during lunch hour. You of all people, he said, you, who we in the church have taken under our wing and fed and clothed, you should be more grateful to the Lord. He brought over boxes of food and clothes when Mom went on disability and Dad was unemployed.

Dad said, "Pastor Michaels doesn't *mean* to be a horse's ass, Mandy. But look at this. Are we going to eat this?" He held up two cans of dog food. "No one's that desperate. How much charity do you need in your heart to give away stuff you don't want? It's the hypocrisy that sticks in my craw."

He put the dog food and a few other useless items back in the box and drove it to the church. Word got around that Frank Boyle had returned charity to the church, something no one did. Mom had cried, "Bad enough you put us in poverty, but then you can't accept the charity you've forced them to give you! You're useless!"

"I'll walk hand in hand with Frank in heaven, and it makes me feel better knowing that," Mom was saying, though she had never walked hand in hand with him on earth, not in my lifetime.

"The one thing we can always be sure of is Christ's love." Pastor Bob sat down, setting his hat on the table. The bastard was in Dad's chair. "Blessed are those who mourn, for they shall be comforted."

Mom nodded. "The afterlife is my only comfort, aside from my daughter. We've decided she'll stay here with me and not go back to college until next semester."

"What a fine idea," said Pastor Bob.

We had decided no such thing, but Mom kept on about it, as if the saying made it so. Could she really make me stay?

The coffee machine gurgled, and I watched the thin brown line trickle from the filter to the pot. Dad's crossword puzzle books sat in a stack on the counter, covered in crumbs and dust and jelly smears. I opened the one on top to a page with a gibberish of squares neatly filled with capital letters. Dad had always used a pen, because he never made mistakes. I ran my finger along the letter *M* and was surprised to actually feel indentations from his writing. *M* for Mandy. *Sky's the limit, Mandy girl.* He had winked at me. "Dad would've wanted me to go back to college right away," I said loudly.

Mom put her thermometer in her mouth as if she hadn't heard.

"That's why I'm going back in two weeks." I spoke in my most matter-of-fact voice as I poured out the coffee. Then I put out milk and sugar and sat down in my usual seat, beyond reproach.

Mom squinted at the mercury in her thermometer. "My temperature's fluctuating like crazy."

"I'm here to listen." Pastor Bob stirred five teaspoons of sugar into his coffee.

"I need someone to take care of me," said Mom. "I can feel a relapse coming. My muscles are starting to hurt. And that one wants to go off again as if nothing has changed."

"I have to go back. All my stuff is there."

"You can have that when I'm dead." Mom nodded toward my coffee mug. "It'll probably be sooner than we imagine."

The mug was big, with daisies around the rim, and it could hold almost two cups of coffee. But it wasn't hers to give. I had found it with Dad on one of our excursions to the local dump, where we found lots of good stuff—bottles, plates, cups. Once Dad found a silver ring with a purple stone in it. "People just throw things away," he had said. "And, Mandy girl, that's what makes America great." At school they held their noses. "Ew, cooties, garbage-dump Boyle." Everyone found out everything in Ransomville. Mom had said, "A husband of mine wandering around the dump, picking up garbage."

"I hear tell you were once an active member of our congregation," Pastor Bob was saying to Mom.

"It's my health that went kerflooey and I just couldn't do it anymore," she answered.

Her health hadn't been the reason. It had been the excuse. From where I sat, I could see the corner of the boxes I had left just outside the basement door. I pushed my chair back to make a slow, inconspicuous move.

Mom was starting to cry now. ". . . and I always wanted a large family, you know, where the older children take care of the younger ones."

I stood slowly, sensing the atmosphere in the room change. Mom ticked away at the Formica table, tick tick tick with her nails. Her crying was about to come on full force. Pastor Bob made a funny noise from the back of his nose.

I left my coffee at the table and walked slowly, quietly toward the basement door. I picked up the boxes of lights and Christmas ornaments. The steps creaked. It was dark, and I leaned against the wall as I descended, my arms full of boxes. The last time I had come down here, Dad was alive. I felt a chill terror of deadness, chaos, and the dark, a horror that there had never been and never would be anything to hope for. There was no comfort and nowhere to go. I forced myself down the steps.

When I reached the bottom, I turned on the lamp, laid down the boxes, and switched on the electric heater. There was a bit of gray-blue carpet in the corner with an odd rectangle cut into it, as if to accommodate something jutting from the wall. Dad had found the carpet outside the accounting office on Main Street. It set out the parameters of his living space. It held the cot in the corner where he usually slept, which was bowed down in the middle by the nightly weight of his body. I went over to sit on it, then collapsed on the sheets. They smelled sweet from his sweat.

Tucked under the cot were the wing-tip shoes Dad wore when he took me to college. His work boots stood at attention next to them, as well as his brown fake-leather slippers, flattened at the heels and worn through the soles. Nothing was real but these objects, so familiar and once so full of life but drained of it now. They were shells whose only statement was: He's gone.

At the foot of the cot, tangled together in a sharp heap, was a clutter of lamps, airplanes, and mobiles Dad had built from beer cans. He had planned to sell them at flea markets, but no one bought them. I disentangled a sharp-edged airplane and placed it on top of the heap.

Against the opposite wall, under an old blanket, I recognized a sad triangular shape. When I pulled the blanket off, a two-story doll-house stared back at me, furniture upended, toilet in the kitchen, and bed in the living room. Dad had started building it as a baptism gift. He didn't finish until I was a teenager and too old for dollhouses. Eight years in the building, because he wanted it perfect. But he let me play with it in its half-finished state. He put in two staircases, front and back. He made little windowsills and flower boxes. He built little beds, and I sewed pillows from scraps of material in Mom's sewing bag. I helped him paint it. Now there were cobwebs inside.

In the bookshelves, his books quietly leaned against each other. Nearby, a collection of balls filled a cardboard box: softballs, base-balls, golf balls, Spaldeen balls, tennis balls, kickballs, a deflated basketball. There was a stillness to everything. Covered in dust and hidden by a bird feeder was Mom's old Singer sewing machine, an intrusion among Dad's things.

"Miranda!" Mom sent down a long shadow from the top of the steps. "Where did you go? Are you down there?"

"Yeah, Mom." I wiped my eyes on my sleeve. I opened a black case on top of the bookshelf, and nestled inside was Dad's thirty-five millimeter camera. I held it in my hands, solid, heavy, and full of pos-sibility. I put it around my neck, remembering the photographs he took Thanksgiving weekend and wondered where they were. I looked through the viewfinder, focusing on Dad's worktable.

All his tools were scattered haphazardly, drill, soldering iron, saw, clamp, collapsible ruler, an overturned coffee can with nails and screws spilling out, and much more. It looked as though any second he would return from wherever he was. *Better get started, eh, Mandy girl?* He would laugh. *Sure thing,* I would say.

Even though his tools and his work space looked incomprehensibly messy, he always knew exactly where each item was. Dad could fix pipes, cars, squeaky hinges on doors, and stuck locks—anything. He could twist a piece of wire into a flower, put a hammock up from tree to tree, build whatever he had a mind to. But without him, the tools were pointless. The mess was nothing but a mess.

I WAS WATCHING the shadows from the trees lace the snow, a delicate quivering veil, when a sleek black car disrupted the unchanging universe with the churn of its engine. It seemed aggressive. It drove up into our driveway and parked next to the station wagon.

Booner got out, locked his car door, and walked up the front path.

The house was filthy, embarrassing. I wasn't wearing makeup, my jeans were dirty, and Dad's sweater had become my second skin. Panic knocked around in my skull. Should I hide in the basement, pretend I wasn't home? I quickly opened the door before he could ring the bell, in case it woke Mom.

He stood on the porch squinting, sort of smiling, a full head taller than me. "Hey, good to see you."

He had said he would come and he did. How little it took. Just someone coming for me, not Mom, asking about me, not Mom. And I started to cry, still holding the door against him, cold air streaming into an already cold house filled with nothing but death and sickness. I didn't know whether to step outside so he wouldn't see the mess or to surrender and just allow him in. It was unbearable, this ache from the inside out. I despised it.

He pushed on the door, stepped inside, and enfolded me in his arms, pressing my cheek against the cold slipperiness of his leather jacket. I was crying like Mom had cried the night she insisted on sleeping with me. Did he feel the same disgust I had felt then with Mom in my arms? It was humiliating. I had to stop.

But he stroked my hair and pulled me closer and I couldn't breathe from the cry stuck in my throat. A strange moaning noise came out of my mouth.

"My goodness, Miranda." Mom's toneless voice inserted itself between my sobs. She sniffed deep and guttural up her nose and down her throat, a noise that set my teeth on edge. My tears dried instantly. Anger was a solid rock. I heard the rattling of her robe pockets and knew she was settling into her usual place on the sofa. "I heard the racket and it woke me up from the deepest sleep I've had in, oh, I don't remember when."

Booner hadn't moved, hadn't shifted his arms from around me. Had he even noticed Mom entering the room?

I heard the lighter snap. Mom inhaled deeply off her cigarette. "Who's this?" she asked.

Whatever happened now was out of my control. "This is Booner, Mom. You met him at the funeral."

"Where did the Christmas tree go?"

"Booner, this is my mother."

"How do, Mom."

"I always hated sweeping up pine needles. It aggravates my sinusitis. But I woke up one afternoon from my nap, and there was the tree. Now I wake up from my nap and it's gone. I tell you, I don't know what's going on." She stood up unsteadily. "He left debts from here to Timbuktu. He didn't even have insurance to . . ."

"Mom, don't," I said.

"I embarrass my daughter." She turned, almost flirtatiously, her hair matted around her face. She was exhaling through her nostrils, two smoky trails that poured out of the dragon lady. "Miranda, aren't you going to offer our guest a cup of coffee or something?"

I looked at Booner, big boots, tight-fitting jeans. His eyes looked brown in the shadows of our house. I noticed a black mark indented on the bridge of his nose. He smiled without showing his teeth. "Coffee'd be okay," he said.

"Come on then." Mom took small, unsteady steps toward the kitchen, pausing for a moment to lean against the doorway. Booner followed Mom, and I brought up the rear, chewing my nails, two fingers at a time.

He sat across from Mom, who put her box of pills on the table like an offering. I fumbled with the filter and the coffee. I couldn't let my vigilance slip. I had to protect him from her. I watched him take it in—the kitchen full of dirty dishes and leftover food, the spider plant's leaves, brown and crackling. I saw him notice the open oven door. You should see me in college, I wanted to say. I'm nothing like this.

"Isn't this a pretty color?" Mom held up a bright orange pill.

"I take my coffee black," Booner told me.

"Well, I take milk and sugar." I tried to brighten my voice, to sound normal.

"Dr. Wykoff says to me, 'Gert, you're not going to die and there's only one reason. You're too stubborn.' "

Booner touched my hand. "I thought maybe you'd want to go for a drive or something."

"That would be nice," said Mom. "I need a few things from the market." She pulled her robe tight around her, "but I have to get dressed first. Botheration."

There was a pulsing in my skull, that familiar dreadful feeling. Her or me? I kept my voice low, an apologetic murmur, so as not to upset her and further embarrass us both. "I think Booner was inviting *me* for a drive."

"What?" she asked, quick as a slap. "Miranda, whatever tricks you're up to, they won't work. Not right now."

Booner was quiet. The coffee pot gurgled. "Isn't Pastor Bob coming by?" I asked her. "He seems to care a lot about you."

"Pastor Bob is a great comfort to me. Boner, do you have a relationship with Jesus?"

"His name is Booner, Mom, not Boner."

Booner raised an eyebrow, just one. The only other person I knew who did that was Dad. I poured the coffee and sat down.

"Can you fix cars?" Mom asked.

"I know a thing or two about cars," said Booner. "Good coffee." He raised his mug at me.

"The heater in the station wagon isn't working," said Mom, "and it makes a clanking noise under the hood when I turn right."

"The heater works, Mom," I said.

"Clanking noise?" Booner's mouth twitched like he thought it was funny.

"Let's go for that ride then." I didn't care about finishing my coffee. There was too much coffee. All day long until my stomach hurt.

"Wait. Let me give you a list of things to get at the market."

The wait was interminable as I watched Mom clutch her pen and painstakingly write out her list: canned pineapple, canned soup, canned string beans, canned peaches.

At last. I put on my coat and followed Booner out the door. He tossed his keys in the air and caught them. The sound jangled in the cold quiet. I was tongue-tied. Should I apologize for Mom? The task was too enormous. Part of me was still with her in the kitchen. I knew she would be pouring herself some scotch, taking out her cards, maybe setting up a couple of ongoing solitaire games. I had behaved badly. I had left her alone with unanswered needs. But it served her right.

"You sure have a lot of keys," I said.

"Guy like me needs a lot of keys." He unlocked the passenger door first. "I washed the Camaro for you."

"You did a great job." I touched the shiny black hood, flattered at the care he had taken. I glanced at the BOONER license plate. "Nice plates." I slipped into the seat.

"Gotta let 'em know I'm coming." The door shut with a resonant click, like a vault, and Booner turned the key in the ignition, starting it up with a smooth rumble. His car smelled of leather, like his jacket, a rich, deep man smell.

We drove along back roads through a quiet white world of snow. The heat blasted and my fingers and toes swelled with warmth. Dad and I used to drive around in the winter, too, just to warm up. I could almost hear him. "How about wasting some gas, Mandy girl?" We also drove around when the weather was nice, Dad with an open beer between his legs, pointing things out, flowers budding on a bush. "Look, Mandy, it's the burning bush!" "Would you look at this, Mandy. It's a lady's slipper, right at the side of the road. They're endangered, you know, and mustn't be picked."

I realized my cheeks were wet.

"Hey, are you crying?"

"My father . . ." My throat clogged. I couldn't talk.

"I never knew my old man, so maybe I'm lucky that way. Nothing to lose." Booner pushed in the lighter. A moment later it popped out and the rich odor of marijuana filled the front seat like incense. "My old man was my old lady's one-night stand." He passed the joint to me, and I drew deeply on it. Smoke rolled down my throat. I rested my head against the seat, shut my eyes.

"You know what? Maybe he's better off now than when he was alive. Maybe things get better when you die." A slight whoosh took my gut as Booner rounded a bend in the road. My head floated above my shoulders like a balloon fluttering slightly but staying afloat. I only wanted to laugh, to feel a sense of the future, to not be trapped in some gray, muffled gauze and have nothing to do but cry.

"When something bad happens like someone dying or losing your job, the best thing to do is tie a good one on, you know," said Booner. "It takes your mind off things for a couple days, what with getting drunk and then having a hangover."

I didn't answer, but it was the best logic I had ever heard.

"Let me tell you something funny, okay?" He plucked the joint from my hand. "Everyone calls me Booner, but my real name is Todd, Todd Boone. No one's allowed to call me that."

I opened my eyes. Booner stared at the road, calm, assured of his own wisdom. His profile cut a silhouette against the window. "You know what they called me in school?" he said.

"What?"

"Todd the clod."

I laughed. I had been waiting for the funny part. He stretched his hand over my leg and I covered it with both my hands. His were cold. Mine had warmth enough to share. I thought about Mom and decided Booner was right: Dad was probably better off.

White trees wound along the road and suddenly the Tumble Inn was right in front of us and Booner stopped the car. A lightness filled me up. He gazed at me for a long moment until the roots of my hair tingled and my hands went from warm to hot. My face burned, but I didn't look away.

"Those big old eyes of yours." He took my face between his two large, rough hands and kissed my lips, my eyelids, the tip of my nose. My head swam. I slipped into a dream, and in the dream Dad was alive, his death wasn't real, and Booner's kiss was part of the unreal dream.

When he let me go, it was as if my face stayed in his hands and I was faceless. "You want to go in?" He jerked his head toward the bar. I didn't want to go in. I was afraid and I only wanted us two, alone in our world, winding along the roads. I shook my head.

"I'll just run in and get a bottle of something," he said. "We'll drink and drive. Is tequila all right with you?"

I nodded. Tequila was perfect. Booner was perfect. Sitting alone in his car and waiting for him was perfect. When he came back, he turned on the radio and Mick Jagger was singing "Waiting on a Friend." Also perfect. We passed the bottle back and forth. Booner started up the engine and pulled out onto the road.

"Tequila to kill ya, Dad used to say." It was as if I had summoned him and he was here in the car with us, grinning, taking his turn with the bottle.

Booner pulled over at the side of the road where, just ahead, there was an abandoned house with the snow-covered roof caving in and the porch steps and railing broken. We had downed half the bottle easily, but I didn't feel drunk, just relaxed finally, like a long exhale I was still in the middle of.

"I used to live there," said Booner.

"Wow, really," I said, not knowing what to say.

He swigged down tequila. His Adam's apple moved with the loud sound of his gulp. "I lived there for almost a year, until one day I came home from school and my mother had moved out."

"No."

"Shit, yeah." He swigged again. "The school bus dropped me off and no one was here, no furniture, nothing but garbage. She left all her garbage."

"What did you do? Did you call the police?" It was my turn to swig.

"Hell no. What could I do? I waited. All night I waited. I fell asleep on the floor, and in the morning the school bus came and I got on it and went to school."

We were silent. The sun had set, and in the twilight, it seemed that every object was the same shade of gray, nothing lighter or darker than anything else. It was impossible to distinguish shapes. Even the house had receded.

"I was nine fucking years old."

When I turned to him, he hugged me hard, tight, and pulled me toward him over the gearshift. "I don't know why I told you that. I never told anyone." He pushed my hair back, pressing hard against my head, and then he kissed me, a fierce kiss. He bit my lower lip and a surge of heat and pain flooded my mouth. My collarbone tightened around my throat with craving. I felt desperate for him, breathless. The gearshift dug into my rib cage, and there was only the sound of our lips smacking and sucking. His hands moved up my sweater, spreading a trancelike, tickling feeling all over me. "I want you so bad," he whispered.

"I'm here," I said.

He pulled back, and I backed off the gearshift. "I know where we can go." He started the engine again, flashed the headlights. Night had descended and shadows revealed themselves as darker than what they shadowed.

I didn't want to think or make decisions or disrupt the trance or the moment. This was where I wanted to be, this heightened, throbbing sense of aliveness. Nothing existed but holding on to that. "Is it far?" I asked.

"Nope." He smiled, reached over, and laid his hand on my leg, a warm heavy promise. I sipped from the tequila bottle, aware of nothing but his hand and the fire-hot liquid trickling down my throat.

He pulled up in front of a large farmhouse, completely dark. When I opened my door, the cold wind slapped me awake. The stars were out, a light sprinkling like tiny burn holes in a black shroud. I followed Booner up the porch steps, then inside and up another flight of steps. We made a lot of noise stumbling. At least it was warm. "My room's here." We bumped into a doorway, and then Booner pushed me onto a bed that creaked and bounced. He lit a flashlight and I saw there was a dresser with a mirror that reflected the night sky outside and the silhouette of branches wreathed across the window.

I shivered, afraid. What was I doing? Why was I here? Mom's pale, puffy face, moon round and moon white, hovered in the corner of my eye. I had to go home. But when Booner sat down, the bed shifted and slid me closer. I reached for him. We fell back, still in our coats. I kicked my boots off, but Booner was still wearing his. He pulled a heavy pile of blankets up over us. There were no sheets, just itchy blankets, below me and above me.

"We gotta warm you up, girl," he whispered in the hot, airless world of me and him beneath the blankets. He helped me out of my coat, pulled Dad's sweater up over my head, and unhooked my bra. Then he sucked my breasts, nibbled my nipples until they were raw. I held his head against me while he sucked. His hair curled itself around my fingers. My body moved on its own.

I heard his boots drop to the floor, a hollow sound, but I couldn't recall his pulling them off. I heard his belt buckle clank and the sound of our breathing ricocheted through the room. Then we were naked, skin against skin. His chest was firm, matted with hair, and as itchy as the blanket. He moved his hand between my legs.

His body was heavy and solid, and beneath him, embracing him with my legs, I felt soft and pure and small, almost nonexistent. He pushed himself inside me, pinned my head back against the pillow with his hands, his lips against mine.

A jolt like electricity, and I came in waves, helpless to the feeling. I moaned beneath his kiss. He moved like he knew exactly how I felt. If a bomb dropped or the house caught on fire or the earth opened to swallow me up, I would be helpless. I started to cry. "I never felt this way before . . ." Booner strained and swelled, and in a spasm of loud panting, he came. Then it was over and we collapsed into each other. The room spun. He whispered, "Baby," and hugged me hard. I couldn't catch my breath, but I didn't want to breathe. Or think. Or feel too much.

A pale glare through the window woke me. Booner was snoring with his mouth open, drooling. My mouth felt like the inside of a wool sock. Sickness sloshed just below my throat. I shook Booner awake. "I have to go home." He was up in an instant. We dressed quietly. I didn't look at the house except to notice the bareness of the room we had fallen asleep in.

It was cold and the sky was gray, the clouds looking ready to dump a foot of snow. Booner blasted the heat as we drove down Main Street, past the Griffin, the Army-Navy store, all the familiar places, different in the light of 7 A.M., with me raw between the legs. Every shift in my position aggravated the soreness.

Booner cleared his throat. "This isn't a one-night stand for me, you know."

I didn't know what to say. I wanted never to leave his car.

"Unless it's a one-night stand to you. But if it is, I'm a real poor judge of character." He sounded wistful.

I put my arm around him, this boy whose mother had abandoned him. "It means everything to me," I said. He turned up Piler Road. "You can let me off here."

He ignored me and kept driving uphill.

"Okay. You can let me off at the end of the driveway here."

But he ignored me and pulled all the way up, parked next to the station wagon, and turned the engine off. "I think it would be rude if you didn't invite me in for coffee." He took my hand and kissed my knuckles.

"Oh, I don't think that's a good idea."

"Come on." He got out of the car and opened the passenger door for me. I stepped out slowly, reluctantly. Hand in hand, we walked around to the back. Mom was awake, vacuuming the kitchen floor in her pilly pink robe and slippers. The TV blared on the kitchen counter. Another show was on in the living room.

"Good morning, Mrs. Boyle," Booner shouted over the din. "I brought your daughter back safe and sound."

"Pain." Mom vacuumed around Booner's big, scuffed boots. "When I'm in pain I have to move. I cleaned the stove top. I defrosted the refrigerator at three A.M. I'm up at all hours, all by myself. But I'm not lonely. You know why? Because this"—she jabbed her finger at the TV—"keeps me company."

On the kitchen counter was a cake. Booner, ignoring Mom, said, "Check it out, Mandy. Cake. You think I can have a piece?"

I was hot, uncomfortable maneuvering around the open oven door. "Uh, sure. Yeah."

"I never used to think about angels. Now I can't turn on the TV without hearing something about 'em." Mom turned the vacuum cleaner off.

"I'm sorry, Mom." I took hold of her arm, but she pushed me away, pretending to wrap the electrical cord around the vacuum cleaner handle.

"Don't you dare," she muttered.

"Where do you keep your plates?" Booner opened the wrong cabinet door.

"Oh, right over here." I was reaching toward the adjacent cabinet when I noticed that the crossword puzzle books had disappeared from the counter. "What did you do with Dad's crossword puzzle books?" I asked.

"I'm through with you." Mom's voice spread itself like poison around the room. "If your father knew about your behavior, you think he'd approve? I know you could care less what I think. But I didn't raise you to be a whore. Where's your self-respect? You think you can just . . ."

"You've got it wrong," Booner interrupted. "Whatever happened was my fault. She's a good girl."

"I'm putting my foot down. Miranda, you're not staying here with me. I won't let you. And I don't care where you go, just as long as you get out of my house."

Booner said, "You're being unfair."

I was sore between my legs, itchy, stinky, and despised, but he was standing up for me. The two of them were arguing over something they both thought of as me. They didn't realize I didn't exist.

"You don't know anything. I almost died giving birth to that one, and is anyone grateful? No. I get a lifetime of grief. She was hairy as a monkey when she came out of me. I said, 'What's this? This isn't a baby!' "

I felt a surge of heat and fire and life. Why hadn't she died? "Shut up! Just shut up! You're the evil one!" I screamed. "You have to go, Booner. Get out of here." I tried pushing him toward the door, but he was as rooted as a tree. My shoulders hurt and I became aware of myself standing, pushing against this immovable guy while Mom sat far away, separate. I wasn't just a part of her in a boundless space. She couldn't control or absorb me like an amoeba. I didn't have to fight. I had already won. I could go back to college.

"You got me dead wrong, Mom." Booner stared her down. "And you got your daughter wrong, too."

"Miranda's always been selfish, ever since she was a child, always pushing me away." Mom's voice was thinner, weaker, reciting a familiar speech. "She thinks of one person and one person only. Herself. I loved my mother. On my birthday I sent her a card, because it was more her day than mine and it was harder for her . . ." She sat, her voice trailing off. "I'm in pain." Her pale blue eyes gazed dully ahead. "I'd like to get some sleep. Is it too much to ask for sleep?" Her face sagged into her neck, her neck sagged into her shoulders, and she seemed to sink into her chair, full of nothing but defeat.

HIATUS

I COULDN'T REMEMBER why I had registered for Psych 101. Probably because Barb was a psychology major. What a stupid reason. I sat in back of the lecture hall, my notebook open on the foldout desktop.

Other students in colorful clothes with books and bags and buttons talked and laughed. They were loud, exaggerating their gestures as they shifted in their seats. Where did they draw their energy from? Why was I myself and not one of them, so lucky, so alive?

Miles away, down at the lectern, a teacher's assistant droned on about behaviorism. His mouth moved like a puppet's. My fingers curled around my pen, but I didn't know what to take down. Out of all the words that poured from teachers' mouths, what were the important ones? How had I known last semester? Somewhere in my room was a textbook I would have to read.

Intro to Psych meant that this was Monday, Wednesday, or Friday, my last class of the day, and the pressure was off until tomorrow. I had been back for two weeks. When I walked across the windy campus after class, my bag was heavy with Dad's camera inside and I was careful not to bump it into anything. I carried it everywhere. I had even bought film and carefully loaded it, winding it around the spool, though I hadn't taken any pictures yet. I didn't want to.

When I finally returned to my dorm room, all I wanted was the reassurance of the click in the lock when I turned the key.

But I felt a light touch on my shoulder. "How are you, Mandy?" It was Sandra, the R.A. What did she want, with her eyes all misty? She was cloying, like too much perfume. I forced out a smile. "I'm fine, Sandra, thanks. And you?"

She squeezed my shoulder. "Good to hear it," she said, smiling away, pressing her teeth into her lower lip until it turned white with the effort of that smile. "I thought maybe you'd want to stop by after dinner for the Wednesday support group."

"Oh, I don't know." My room was waiting for me. She had asked me last week, too. How many times would I have to refuse before she stopped asking? She had hugged me two weeks ago, the day I returned. "It's good to see you back. Anytime you want to talk, Sandra's here." Her kindness took on a wheedling tone that reminded me of Mom.

"I'm sorry, Sandra. I really have to go." I shut the door behind me and I was home in my warm, dusky room, filled with the comforting smell of slightly soiled clothes. I turned on my desk lamp. I took the camera out of my bag, clicked the lens cap off, and wiped the lens with my bedsheet. Looking through the viewfinder, I saw the world in a frame, which shifted when I did.

I framed my nightgown, then a T-shirt and jeans twisted up in my sheets. My pillow was crammed in the corner between the mattress and the wall. My blanket lay on the floor. My dresser drawers were pulled open, with clothes hanging out all over the place. The black sheets sagged off the walls. They needed a new round with the staple gun. But I didn't have the energy, and they had been Barb's idea in the first place. Let them fall.

I moved the camera frame to the window, where Barb's dust-coated crystal hung, glowing in the light, darkness behind it. Below the crystal, the leaves of her aloe plant drooped over the clay pot, drained, wrung out, and tinged with gray, too close to the radiator.

The plant's death wasn't my responsibility; it was Barb's. I placed the camera carefully in my top desk drawer, along with the detachable flash, the light meter, and the extra lens. Then I sat back in my desk chair and waited for Barb to come home.

Shrillness ripped the silence, jarring, jangling. I picked up the phone. "Hello."

"Hey, girl." His voice was as gentle as the collapsing sound of his sigh when he shot himself up me, making me ache for him and the magic of his hard man's body, the warm close safety of his arms around me.

"Booner."

"Yup, that's me. How you doin'?"

"I'm okay, I guess. I just got back from class and . . ."

"Let me ask you something. Why are you there if I'm here?"

"What?" I wrapped myself in the long phone cord, turning, turning, turning, then reversing, unwrapping, unturning. Booner exhaled deeply, a distortion of breath like a hiss through the phone. "Well," I said into the silent pause. "It's good to hear your voice."

"Wish I could see you," he said. A trickle of sweat tingled a trail from my armpit to my waist, shuddering along my skin. I remembered Booner's body, his chest matted with hair, his eyes watching from the bed after I shook him awake in that bare upstairs room. A longing I didn't know what to do with scattered my focus. I was supposed to say something. What was it?

"Please deposit five cents for the next two minutes," said a recording.

"Shit. I gotta get a phone if I'm going to make a habit of calling. This is a pain in the ass." Coins clanked angrily.

"I'll call you back," I said. "Just give me the number."

"Yeah, I thought of that, but there's no fucking number on this phone."

I sat on my bed and pulled Dad's shoes out from underneath. One of the shoes gave off the sweet smell of herb from the bag of pot I stored there. Last semester I had only visited the dealers on the seventh floor if someone else was going. This semester, they already knew my name. I didn't spend money on anything else.

"Fucking cold out here and pouring rain and some pig stuck a wad of gum in the fucking phone . . ."

Behind him I heard traffic, horns honking and a car alarm. He seemed far away, lost in an unknown world. "Are you mad at me?" I asked.

"Hell no. Why would I be mad? It's just that . . ."

Heat rattled up through the radiator, dry and relentless. I remembered the puff of hair along his shoulders, an aura in the light. There was no one else I knew so well. He was it. "Just that what?"

His voice burst. "How do I know what you're doing up there in college when I can't keep my eye on you?"

"Come visit me," I said, and it was like a door blew open and cool blue air unfurled around me.

"How about you coming to visit me?"

"Please deposit five cents for the next two minutes."

"But I put in fifty fucking cents before! I should get more goddamn minutes than that!"

The recorded voice didn't answer.

"All I want is . . . look, I'm not a lot of good with words, and I'm out of change."

"But . . ."

"You take care of yourself. I'll call you in a couple of days, all right?"

What about my going to visit? His voice was like a rope thrown at me from far away, and if he hung up, I had nothing to hold on to. If only he were here with me. But that was impossible.

"All right?" he repeated.

"Yeah, all right." Click. Dial tone. I wanted to scream, to rip the phone out of the wall, to tear my bed apart. My heart was pounding too fast. My hands shook as I crumbled pot into the bowl of Barb's bong. I had to calm down. Long inhale. Hold it in. Exhale slow. I lit one of Barb's incense sticks. I took another hit. My heart slowed down, beating out: All right; all right; all right. Smoke rose off the incense, a fragrant filigree. I took another long, leisurely hit of pot. I deserved it. All right. Incense smoke curled around the room and seemed to solidify, suspended in the moment, trapped in the thick, heated air. Lace in a paperweight. All. Right.

●   ●   ●

IN WOMEN'S STUDIES class, we pushed the desks against the wall and moved our chairs into a big circle. "This is a more ovular, less hierarchical way of holding a discussion," said the professor.

We passed around torn-out pages from fashion magazines. Bring in five pages. A simple enough assignment, but I had forgotten.

"As women, we're bombarded by false images and we're expected to believe we ought to look like this," said the professor. "No one looks like this."

We passed around a centerfold from a porn magazine. A blond model posed on luscious satin pillows, her lips like glazed sweets, parted slightly. Her gauzy pink robe opened carelessly to reveal the candied mounds of her breasts. Her long legs in thigh-high stockings were also slightly parted.

"The pubic hair is conveniently shaved off," said the professor, pacing behind the circle of chairs. Girls murmured in agreement.

The page was thick and glossy. If I could step out of my own body and into hers and arrange myself on pillows while everyone passed me around, I would know I was beautiful. To not have hair or pimples or bad breath would be the best.

I remembered sitting in the bathtub when I was so little that the tub seemed large. Mom took a giant step into the water, and I shivered to glimpse her hairy center with a small pink tongue flapping. I was supposed to share the water with that thing, surrounded by those jiggling thighs, and I was horrified.

Her scar ran like a puckered ribbon from her thatch of hair, up her sagging belly, and ended at the deep indentation of her belly button. "This is your fault." She ran her finger along the ribbon, and the water level rose as she sunk her body in. I began to cry.

"What society does"—the voice of the girl next to me carried as though she spoke from a megaphone—"is make us girls feel really bad about ourselves, right?"

"When women are objectified, they internalize the self as object. They fetishize themselves," said the professor.

There was no reason to panic. I was in college now, raising my consciousness. I was safe inside a circle of women.

The professor asked, "How many of us hate our bodies?"

When everyone in the room raised their hands, I put mine up, too.

But I had liked myself until I grew boobs and hair and got my period, until I understood I was becoming Mom.

Now I realized I did hate my body. I hated it.

I stood up, wobbled slightly, and slipped through the circle.

"Where are you going?" asked the professor.

"I'm sorry. I don't feel well." My backpack lay on a desk outside the circle. I swooped it up and ran from the room, ran across the campus center, bitter wind in my face, streaming windswept tears. I didn't stop until I reached my dorm. Thankfully, I had the elevator to myself. Up fourteen floors, down the hall, into my room. Safety.

My breath was loud and bounced off the walls, but my sheets, as I lay on the bed and pulled them up over me, were a soft loose skin. I put a towel on my face and breathed inside my cocoon, my tent. Mom used to say, "Come inside my tent, little sweetie, and play with me." So I crawled in and lay against her warm, soft naked body, playing with her breasts while she stroked my back, my arms, my tummy until my body dampened and I itched all over.

Sick. She made me sick. I had thought it meant she loved me. I had liked it. I was sick. My eyes ached. My throat caved in around my tongue. Where was Dad? Why didn't he help me? I choked. I sobbed. I couldn't stop.

I HAD ALWAYS looked forward to dinner, the messy, good-natured jostling, the clatter of trays and cutlery, the dull metal coffee urns, and the feel of the cool, smooth table under my arms. The smells that emanated up the stairs, mostly meat and oil and bread, were enough to make my mouth water. In the land of plenty, dinner was the high point of my day.

But since I had been back, each dinner had offered its own disappointment. After 5 P.M., a line formed and the cafeteria was crowded until at least seven. The usual shouts of "Get in back, asshole!" came from up and down the line as a group of skinheads shoved to the front. Last semester, I had shouted too, just to be a part of things, though I didn't care who cut in line, because there was plenty to go around.

This semester, I saw that those who cut in got the best while the rest of us suckers waited on line and everyone could shout until their throats were raw. How hopelessly unfair the world was. It was pathetic to shout. What was the point? It was bewildering. I felt the prickling, painful sensation of tears coming on.

"Hey, Mandy! Thanks for holding a spot!" Barb burst into my private circle, spiraling cold air, frizzy hair tangled around her cheeks, her mouth thick with lipstick.

"No problem." Tears vanished, and I hugged Barb, safe in the mist of her patchouli.

"How was your day? How've you been coping?" Her eyes were dark as a warm night.

I tried to think back on my day, wanting to invest it with normality, to spare Barb from worrying. "You know, classes." But there was nothing to say about any of my classes. "Every time I see Sandra, she invites me to her support group." I snorted laughter, waiting for Barb to laugh, too.

"It might be a good idea. Are you thinking about it?"

She, who last semester said that only fairies and fat girls joined Sandra's support group? I couldn't believe what I was hearing. "Hell no," I said.

"Get in back, asshole!" someone shouted from the end of the line. We had reached the turnstile when up loped Tiff, a guy with a long, horsy face, who ran his fingers through the brown waves of his hair like a girl would. "Yo," he said, kissing Barb full on the lips. I showed my I.D. and walked through.

I liked to pretend Tiff didn't exist, but he had been following Barb around like a dog since we'd gotten back to school. He chewed loudly, bolting down his dinner. When he finished, he pushed his tray away and drummed the heels of his hands on the table, shaking the soda in my glass. I wasn't even halfway done.

"I hear it, I play it," he said. He was a drummer in a band.

"I have a mother of a quiz tomorrow," said Barb, "and if I don't study, I'm dead meat. My grades were so bad last semester, the 'rents gave me an ultimatum. They're gonna yank me if things don't look up."

"Wow, really." I had gotten all A's. Even Mom couldn't argue with that.

"The theory is whatever state you're in when you study, that's the state you gotta be in when you take the test," said Tiff. "For example, if you're tripping when you study, you better be tripping when you take the test."

Tiff was full of stupid theories that Barb seemed to give more worth than they deserved.

"Seriously?" she said.

"Serious as a heart attack," said Tiff.

I saw Barb's face turn white. "That's so insensitive, Tiff. Don't you know that's how Mandy's father died?"

"Oh please, Barb. It's okay." I lit a cigarette and threw the match into my half-eaten lasagna.

"Hey, I'm sorry, man. It's gotta be a bummer," said Tiff. He and Barb gazed at each other, excluding me, even as they were talking about me, about Dad. I was the source of my own exclusion. Then I was going to cry, but for all the wrong reasons.

Barb nudged me. "Got an extra cigarette?"

I handed her the pack.

"Can I get one of them, too?" Tiff licked his lips before he wrapped them around the cigarette.

Last semester, Barb and I had always lingered in the smoking corner, talking and smoking and watching the people come and go. But when Tiff stood up with his tray, Barb stood, too. And I saw no point in lingering.

I SKIPPED MY Intro to Modern Literature class. I would be okay as long as I got the reading assignment done. *Jude the Obscure* lay on my desk and I opened it, trying to read. But the letters seemed nonsensical. They jumped around, blurring words until my brain hurt, a white light of pain. Was I developing migraines?

The edge of the shade flapped back and forth from the wind blowing in through the sliver of space where the window was cracked. But even the wind didn't cut through the heat rising thickly from the radiator beneath. At my job in the library, I placed books back on shelves only so someone could remove them again. It struck me as absurd, my entire artificially created life.

Barb hadn't come home last night. Her bed was made, the gauzy spread tucked under her pillow. Her desk was clean, pens and pencils in their jar. Her lamp had been dusted. Her clothes hung in the closet.

When did she become neat? I used to make my bed every morning. I didn't see the point anymore, since I was only going to sleep in it the next night, which meant making it again the next morning. If I could do it once and be done with it, I would. But the unendingness of the task was exhausting just to think about. I couldn't recall ever feeling different than this. Yet I knew I had been tidier than Barb. She had stolen my habits, and I wanted them back.

I opened the drawer and pulled out Dad's camera. My camera now. I hung it around my neck, checked the battery. Everything okay there. I went to my bed, kneeled down, and pulled Dad's shoes out, then arranged them near Barb's rug and held them in the camera's view. No. That was no good. It was a boring arrangement.

Laughter from the girls across the hall floated to my door before the sharp knock. Rap rap rap. I leaped up. Saved! I flung open the door so quick that they jumped back, startled. "Oh, Mandy, hi. Is Barb here?"

"No. I don't know where she is."

"We were going over to the campus center. There's a midday concert series in the student lounge. We thought you and Barb might want to go, too."

"Wow." One of the girls leaned on the door. "Where did those big old shoes come from?"

Dad's shoes were set up pigeon-toed in the middle of the room. My camera hung heavy around my neck. Nothing was sacred. They were crowding the doorway, and I wanted to hide. I slowly closed the door on them, pushing against the weight of the leaning girl. "I've got a lot of work to do."

"All right, see ya!" Off they went down the hall to the elevator, taking their laughter with them. Wait! I wanted to say. But I felt empty. They hadn't even tried to talk me into going.

I kneeled down by Dad's shoes. Inside the left one was the bag of pot. Inside the right, with the smell of oil, shoe polish, and foot stink, the obituary from the *Ransom County Herald* was tucked away. As small as the surgeon general's warning on a cigarette box, it said: "*Frank Boyle of Ransomville died December 22, 1985, at home. He was 50. He is survived by his wife, Gertrude Peck Boyle, and one daughter, Miranda Jane Boyle. Services will be at noon, Monday, December 23, at the Church of Assemblies, Ransomville. Burial will be in the Pine Hill Rest Center, Ransomville.*"

No job, no community memberships. He didn't have those kinds of distinctions. His talents were unique, but the obituary said nothing of the things he built—nothing about his garden, his philosopher's chair at the Griffin. None of that was in the paper. His dying was the only official evidence that he had lived.

I waited for the awful hollow thud inside my chest, the ache that came whenever I remembered Dad. I had grown used to it. I expected it. I wanted it. But nothing happened. He didn't exist in college. He hadn't even spent an hour here. I was losing him again; even the pain was disappearing.

I sat on the floor and pulled his shoes in my lap. I had his shoes.

What a relief to hear a key turn in the lock. Barb bopped in. "Hiya!"

"Barb." Tears trailed heat down my cheeks.

"Aw, poor you." She sat on the floor next to me. "Want to talk?"

"I'm trying, you know, to get by, but I feel so different inside." I searched for the words to comprehend and then communicate, but there was nothing. "I can't pay attention to things and I don't know what's going on and it all just seems so stupid . . ."

"Depression." Barb, the psychology major, nodded. She intertwined her fingers in the folds of her Indian-print skirt as she reduced the enormous, wordless, bottomless well of my feelings into one simple ordinary word that couldn't possibly contain them.

"I'm studying this right now. I'll talk to my professor about you." Barb took care of the rats in the psych lab for her work-study grant. She touched one of Dad's shoes, and I shoved her hand away.

"Hey, it's okay." Barb's voice took on a kindergarten teacher tone. It was as if she were talking to a stubborn retarded child. "They're nice shoes. They were your father's, right?"

Ashamed of how much I wanted to talk about them, I ran my fingers along their shiny surface, feeling where the indents had become part of the leather. "He used to wear them to church, back when we went to church. And he would draw little eyes on the base of his index finger and lips along his thumb and move his mouth just like the pastor's mouth." I laughed, remembering how I had laughed back then, how Dad and I had walked home three miles hand in hand while Mom drove.

"He sounds like quite a guy," Barb said quietly.

"He was. He used to mow the lawn when I was a kid and he would leave heart-shaped areas unmowed for me, because he . . ." *loved me,* I was going to say. But I remembered I had asked him to stop. I had been embarrassed, like Mom. "Can't you just mow the lawn, Frank?" she had said.

Barb gazed straight ahead. Was she even listening?

"Oh never mind." I reached behind to my bed, where I had left the camera, and I laid it in my lap with the shoes. The camera was heavy, clunky, and unchanging, a certainty.

When Barb turned toward me, her eyes were uneasy, as if a storm were rolling in. "Where'd you get that camera?"

"It was Dad's. Thirty-five-millimeter single lens reflex." I understood she was worried, and I resolved to behave more normally. "Anyway." I pulled the bag of pot out of the left shoe. "How about a puff?"

"I won't say no. A friend with weed is a friend indeed." When she grabbed the bong off the trunk, her I.D. fell to the floor. "Hey! I was looking all over for this." She kissed it and held it up toward heaven, as if to say, This is me. Here I am, and isn't it great?

I had been as secure as that last semester.

"Wait." I framed her, holding her I.D., in the viewfinder. "I have to get a picture of you just like that."

I focused in, but I was too close and couldn't get her whole face with the I.D., too. I backed up, stood on my bed, then took a step onto my desk.

"Mandy, do you have to make such a production? It's just a picture."

"Hold it up," I ordered. She lifted her I.D. card. Here I am. I am me. Click. I took a picture and wound the film for the next shot.

"You know what?" she cried. "I have the best idea ever! You should sign up for a photography class. Really! It might help."

I took a picture of her enthusiasm.

• • •

I AWOKE TO the sun peeking in below the window shade. It was after 11 A.M. I had forgotten to set the alarm. What class did I miss? Astronomy? Modern Literature? Psych 101? No. I missed Thesis Composition, where I was already lost. Suddenly, I felt like everything was slipping out of control.

Then the phone rang and I could tell by the pitch of the ring, the slant of sun, and the spinning dust motes in the shaft of light on my blanket that it would be Booner. I was glad I had missed my class. "Hello," I said in my sexiest, huskiest voice.

"You sound as bad as I feel." Mom's flat tone held a demand.

"I'm fine." I dragged myself out of bed. We hadn't talked since I left home. It had seemed better that way. Now her voice was like a punishment.

"I called to say you forgot your sweatshirt. You know, the one that says 'Albany State.' "

"It's yours, Mom. I gave it to you for Christmas." Through a haze of disappointment, a sharp knifelike anger at Mom penetrated almost pleasurably. I hated her doubly for not being Booner.

"Oh."

Silence. I went to my desk and sat down, glancing at the mess of notebooks, papers, and textbooks I had been ignoring for days, or was it weeks?

"I was just getting ready to go to a class." My voice sounded like a recording of a lie.

Mom coughed harshly into the phone. "I'm just getting ready to receive Christ. Pastor Bob has welcomed me back to the church with open arms."

Pastor Bob didn't visit out of the kindness of his heart. No. He was looking for souls to steal. "That's great, Mom." I forced enthusiasm into my voice. What did it matter? It was a relief she wasn't going to hound me about coming home. Yet I envied her the open-armed welcome she had received. It was as if we were competing and she was getting more love from the world than I was, which meant there was less to go around. I held my breath, phone suctioned to my ear.

"I can't remember why I stopped worshipping. I truly believe that Jesus loves everyone, especially those who stray."

I remembered perfectly well why she had stopped worshipping. It was after the hysterectomy. "Because you wanted more kids and you couldn't have any," I said. "They told you to teach Sunday school, and you didn't want to do that."

"I physically feel Christ's forgiveness." Her voice got louder without becoming more lively. "It's as if I'm a lamb held in his arms."

"Mm-hmm." I leafed through one of the notebooks on my desk, page after random page of notes in my own handwriting. *Stereotype vs. archetype* was underlined. *Stereotype: Society's image. Archetype: Image in the collective unconscious.* I had written these notes during Women's Studies class, but I felt as though I were trespassing in a stranger's book.

"Dr. Wykoff's all for it, says it can't hurt. And since, you know, I can't get to church, Pastor Bob comes to me," said Mom.

"Why can't you get to church?" I asked, as I had been expected to ask. Then I stopped listening. She was going to repeat herself anyway. *Images of women: social stereotypes reinforced by archetypes.* I hadn't gone back to Women's Studies.

". . . but I took some Motrin. We know Naprosyn is out of the question, because aggravating my ulcer's the last thing I need. Not that I blame Dr. Wykoff for it, but . . ."

Five stereotypical roles existed for women in literature: 1) castrating bitch—I didn't want to be that; 2) whore with heart of gold—that appealed somewhat; 3) virginal innocent—that was the one I wanted; 4) temptress—hardly; 5) nurturing Mother. I pondered that one. What a stupid bunch of notes.

". . . I said, 'Dr. Wykoff, how many spontaneous fractures have you seen in your life? Not many, I'd bet.' "

"Spontaneous fracture?" I shut the notebook. I believed none of it.

"What do you think I've been talking about? If it wasn't for the dizziness, I wouldn't have bumped my foot against the table. But it's okay. I'm here with my leg elevated, and Pastor Bob's due soon. I need Christ's love to bridge the gap between me and God. I'm taking the steps."

"I thought if you took them once, that was it."

"You must be very happy to be back in college," she accused.

"Mom, I *have* to be in college. I need an education. Dad always said . . ."

"The problem with you is you think you can do everything on your own without God's help. But all you have to do is ask. He's here. The first step to Christ is to admit your spiritual need. I think we both should do that."

"Why exactly did you call, Mom?" I felt a dizzying sense of girls in dorm rooms tied to their mothers through phone lines. When I was born, I had come out choking on the umbilical and the doctor had to disentangle me. We had both almost died, Mom and I, the story of our lives.

"Loretta's been an angel to me. I told her the other day, Jesus has already forgiven me and I know that because he gave me an angel," said Mom.

I stood and turned, twisting myself in the cord.

"Your bedroom's still your bedroom, anytime you want to come back." She was smoking a cigarette. I could hear it: inhale, exhale.

It seemed that I hadn't left, or maybe she had come with me. It didn't matter whether I was bringing her cinnamon toast on a tray or taking notes in class.

"I never imagined I would end up alone," she said.

"Maybe you should've thought of that before you . . ." I stopped. Before she what? The minute I tried to put words around it, whatever it was evaporated into a shadow whose details I couldn't see. They were always out of reach, dark and taunting.

"What's that?" asked Mom. "Oh, there's the timer. I have to walk to the kitchen, and with this foot, it takes half an hour. If I was a horse they'd shoot me."

"But, Mom . . ."

"Good-bye, Miranda." She was gone.

I slammed the phone down. It rang again almost immediately. So she was sorry she hung up? "Yes, what is it now?" I answered.

"Hello," said a crisp, clear voice. "I would like to speak to Miranda Boyle."

"Speaking."

"I'm calling from the office of the work-study grants regarding your job at the library. Apparently, you haven't been keeping with your work schedule."

"What? I only missed a couple of times. I'm sorry. I'll go in right now."

"That isn't the point. A schedule was set up to accommodate you, and if you've made a commitment to work, you have an obligation to . . ."

"Yeah, look. I'm expecting a call, so I can't stay on the phone." I hung up.

When it rang again, I was gripped with panic, my crazy pounding heart beating up into my throat. But maybe it was Booner! I wanted Booner! I picked it up furiously. *"Hello!"* I screamed.

"I'd like to remind you that a work-study grant is a privilege and can be revoked. There's no point in being rude. I'm only doing my job."

"I'm sorry," I said. I let the phone receiver dangle with that voice jabbering away out of it. I left the room and walked down the hall to the girls' showers, where the air was hot, dense, and humid. I sat in a bathroom stall, surrounded by graffiti. To the left, someone had written: *Better a bottle in front of me than a frontal lobotomy.* A crude drawing of a penis had been scratched into the stall door at eye level. *My pussy needs dick,* it said. Someone had written beneath: *Oh, that's intelligent.* It felt stable here amidst the dialogue. The hook on the stall door cast a crooked shadow, like a visual echo, and I wished I had thought to bring my camera.

Never mind. I listened to the voices drifting in and out among the stalls. Classes didn't matter. My job at the library didn't matter. Mom didn't matter. Water poured from faucets, splashed in showers, and flushed down toilets. Nothing mattered.

"TIFF AND I are going for a drink. You want to come?"

I noticed Tiff's face fall. The loser wanted Barb to himself.

"All right," I said, more to annoy Tiff than because I felt like drinking.

A labyrinth of tunnels ran underneath the concrete buildings of the campus, connecting the four symmetrically arranged dormitory towers to the campus center and the school buildings. We took the tunnels, since it was so cold, walking three abreast, Barb and I with Tiff between us, saying nothing. His sneakers squeaked.

Pipes lined the roof. Posters announcing rallies and parties and clubs to join hung at intervals on bulletin boards. Tiff put his arm around Barb. I wanted the warmth and caring of an arm around me—Booner's arm, pulling me close. But he didn't have a phone and hadn't called in over a week. Okay, the arm of someone who looked like Booner. Anyone. I craved it.

Tiff and Barb seemed to know exactly where they were going. How did they know if I didn't? Life was passing me by and I wasn't paying attention. "Blink and you miss it," Dad used to say. I remembered my first day of college, how I had pulled my hand out from Dad's because he was fat and sweaty and I was ashamed. I had squandered his hand, wasted our time together. I had taken it so much for granted. If I had known, I would never have let his hand go. "Dad never saw these tunnels," I said without thinking.

"My father never saw these tunnels either, you know." Barb extracted herself from Tiff to put her arm around me. So there, Tiff.

"My father never *will* see these tunnels," Tiff declared, as if it were a competition.

"I really think . . . You know, don't take this wrong," Barb whispered, "but you might be helped by, uh, talking to someone."

"I'm not a mental patient, Barb." It was annoying how she brought that up. And in front of Tiff, too. Not that he cared, walking alongside in his big, stupid green sneakers, waiting for Barb to finish with me. "If you just treat me like I'm normal, then we can all be normal."

She gave me a fake punch, a jab in the arm. "You mean like, Hey, how the hell are ya?"

I felt another surge of annoyance. It was futile. There was no such thing as normal anymore. But I forced a smile out. "Yeah, something like that."

We climbed the stairs to the Rathskeller. It was crowded. The jukebox played "Mack the Knife" and a table full of kids shrieked along.

"What do you want?" said Barb. "I'm buying."

I shrugged. "A beer, I guess."

But she ordered a gin and tonic, and so did Tiff. I felt like a country bumpkin with my beer. Silly third wheel, invited out of pity. Anger, that burning ember in my gut, rose to my throat until I was drenched in sweat along my neck, my forehead, behind my ears. *You just wait until your father dies,* I screamed inside as they cast love-bird eyes at each other. *You'll see how it is then, with your goddamn gin and tonic.*

We stood, three in a huddle with our drinks. Tiff and Barb had somehow situated themselves so no one else could push by them, but I was standing in an informal path, shifting here and there as people moved around me. I hated crowds. I took a huge gulp of my beer. Tiff tapped his foot to the music.

"My mother's been calling," I yelled over the din to Barb. I finished my beer because it slid down like water.

"How is she?" Barb yelled.

"She's taking the steps to Christ!"

"What?"

The first step was to admit your spiritual need. The second was to repent. The third was to believe that Jesus Christ died for your sins, and the fourth, to receive him into your heart. Mom was going to drag me into this. I would have to formulate a plan. I said to Barb, clear and loud, "My mother's getting born again. Again!" I wanted her to laugh so I could laugh, too.

The song ended. "It's very common for people to turn to religion after a serious loss." Barb's tone implied that we were going to have an in-depth discussion about it. I wanted to avoid serious conversations.

Tiff said in his usual superior tone, "Religion is the opiate of the masses."

What a jerk. I went to the bar and ordered another beer. Cool, bubbling elixir. Nothing mattered anymore, I had to remember that. Not Barb. Not Tiff. Not Dad, not Mom, not college, not Christ. Nothing. I reached into my back pocket for my cigarettes. Barb and Tiff each bummed one off me, and I thought about quitting just so they would have to buy their own.

Someone pushed me, another annoyance. But then that someone stopped. "Hey, you're in my Modern Lit class, right? Professor Bailey? Tuesdays and Thursdays?"

"I am?"

"You haven't shown up in a while." He was cute, short. Nothing like Booner, but he had a nice loud laugh, a big ha-ha-ha that boomed out, like Santa Claus's. If he had noticed I hadn't been to class lately, maybe I wasn't invisible. He held out his hand. "Jack," he said.

I held out mine. "Mandy."

"You need another beer?" Jack pointed to my empty glass.

"Sure."

In heaven there ain't no beer, that's why I drink it here, Dad used to sing. How nice life became when someone who knew me suddenly emerged from the crowds.

Tiff and Barb sipped their drinks and smoked my cigarettes. They were my friends and I loved them. Why had I been so angry at them for ordering gin and tonics? Let them drink what they wanted.

"Man, that class makes me ill. All that reading. A drag, isn't it?" Jack looked pained, and I wanted to comfort him.

"There's crib notes, I guess." Last semester I had scorned them. Fake learning.

"You don't have to tell me." He laughed. "I need an English elective before I can graduate, otherwise I wouldn't even be in that class."

"You're a senior?"

"Sort of. This is my fourth year, but I think I'm on the six-year plan. See how it goes, you know?"

I nodded. Whatever he said, he said with a beautiful smile.

"You have nice hair, you know that?" He flipped a long loose piece behind my shoulder. I remembered Booner saying the same thing. Maybe it was true.

"My best feature." We smiled at each other.

Culture Club were singing "I'll Tumble 4 Ya." A small space cleared and people were dancing. Jack asked if I wanted to dance.

"Sure." What a wonderful feeling to sway on a wooden floor in the arms of a guy from my class, feeling his breath in my ear blowing warmth and excitement. When the song ended, he kept his arms around me.

When he asked if I wanted a shot of something, I said, "Sure, why not?" We went to the bar and he bought shots of vodka and Boggs, dark red like cough medicine.

Barb said, "It's late. We're leaving. Are you ready to go?"

Behind her, Tiff's face folded into a frown.

"No, you go on," I said. "I'll catch you later."

Later, when Jack's wet lips sucked around mine and my tongue was in his mouth and his hard-on pressed against me through our clothes and he asked if I wanted to smoke a joint, I said yes.

I was scared I might get lost walking back alone through the tunnels. Arm in arm with Jack, I didn't have to think about it. We existed in a suspended place with only the two of us. Instead of going toward the tunnels, we went outside to the vast student lot where his car was parked.

"A friend with weed is a friend indeed." I laughed as if Barb's wit were my own.

He boomed out his lusty ha-ha-ha. This was magic, like it had been with Booner, and wasn't it great that I didn't need him? Maybe I would have lots of guys. I'm afraid you'll have to wait in line, I would tell them. Make an appointment. I'm a busy woman.

Jack lived off campus. "Just got this really nice rug," he said. "You gotta see it." It was touching, a man buying a rug. He hurtled down streets, and I didn't even wear my seat belt. I didn't care. If I died, I'd walk hand in hand with Dad up in heaven. Oh, that was silly. That was something Mom would say.

"You look good sitting there," he said, suffusing the front seat of the car with love.

I caught a glimpse of a rainbow decal on the downstairs window as we staggered past. There may have been a rug, but the place was dark and I didn't see it, or feel it underfoot. When he showed me to his bedroom, I felt woozy and overcome. "I love you," I whispered. I said it so softly, he probably didn't hear.

"I love you," I said again when we were naked and he put it in me. And I was going to burst with love for this guy, lurching helplessly on top of me, panting in a voice that wasn't Booner's. My love was so large it would leak out and spread around until there was nothing left of me. But Jack could hold it all together. Jack would contain it.

I awoke with a throbbing head, a green ceiling way above me. Jack's beautiful clear blue eyes were wide open on the pillow next to me. He said, "I better get you home." He was cool. He was better than Tiff. He had a car and he lived off campus. We had driven here.

I liked his hand clamped around the gearshift, adorned with a silver ring carved with symbols.

"Jack," I said, preparing to say it a lot.

He turned to me. I hoped my hair wasn't too much of a tangled mess. His name was Jack. I didn't want to let him go. "Jack is such a great name," I said. "Jack and the Beanstalk. Jack and Jill. Captain Jack."

"Look, you're a cute kid, but you shouldn't get any ideas. I mean, we can have a good time, but I'm not looking for a girlfriend or anything."

His words put me in danger of crying. I pressed my fists against my eyes. No. Push it down. Then I remembered the rug he had never shown me. I opened the window and freezing air whooshed in over us. The rug had been the point, and it had probably been a lie. Last semester, Barb told me that if you really want to put a guy down, insult his anatomy.

"Don't take it personally," he said. "I just don't want to get serious about anyone right now. I got a lot going on in my life."

"Why would you think," I said, wiping my eyes, "that I want to be your girlfriend?" What I wanted to experience again was that moment of joy when I had been nobody and then became somebody when he had said, Hey you're in my class, aren't you? But it was gone. "What about your rug?"

"My rug?" He pulled up in the campus-center parking lot.

"You were going to show me your rug. Don't you remember? Your brain must be as small as your dick." I slammed the car door. My heart slammed inside my skull. If we had ever had a chance, I had just blown it. I walked across the cold, desolate podium to the gray courtyard. Bits of snow were scooped in the corners, whittled away by wind and rain. Towers loomed up ahead and the university looked more like a prison than a promise of freedom.

I TOOK TO staying in bed all day. I hadn't been back to Women's Studies. I couldn't go back to Modern Literature. I was afraid to go back to Thesis Composition, and it was useless to return to Psych 101.

I waited for Barb to come home for dinner. Hunger finally drove me downstairs without her. I gritted my teeth, waited in line. I almost took my tray to the table where we always ate and where a few of the girls in the hall were eating, but I changed my mind. I sat alone. I had done it in high school, I could do it again. It was easier this way, no phoniness.

I went up to the salad bar, but there were only a few shreds of lettuce left. A long black hair floated on top of the dressing. So what, salad didn't matter. I didn't want salad. I returned to my tray and tried to eat my meatloaf.

But the guy next to me scraped his fork against his front teeth with every bite. It set my nerves on edge so bad I wanted to stick his fork in his eye. The gravy on my meatloaf congealed as I stared at it. The mashed potatoes were made from freeze-dried flakes, very salty and fake. I needed Barb. Why hadn't she come home? Like the gleam on the butter knife came the cold fear of realization. She was avoiding me.

I couldn't sit anymore. I got up, left my tray and uneaten food at the table, took the elevator back to the fourteenth floor, and I didn't relax until I was safe in the room. I crawled into bed. I needed to sleep, just sleep until I felt up to living this life.

Barb came home eventually. I didn't know what time it was. "Hey, Mandy! Did you already eat?"

"No," I moaned. "I don't feel well." My head was heavy, like a boulder on my pillow. My throat was swollen. Was she avoiding me or not? She was trying to throw me offtrack.

"Do you want me to bring something back for you?"

"I don't know." I lay there in a twilight, floating between wakefulness and sleep. When Barb burst in again, it seemed no time at all had passed.

"Sorry I took so long. I got a sandwich for you." She put the goods on my desk.

I got up slowly. Spread out like a feast over my notebooks were a tuna-fish sandwich in a plastic bag, an apple, and eight cookies, oiling the napkin she had wrapped them in. "Wow, you're such a good friend." Gnawing pangs of hunger rumbled in my stomach. I started with the apple, eating slow. I got hungrier as I chewed. I was starving. I ate a cookie. Then the sandwich. Then the rest of the cookies. The swelling in my head eased. Maybe I wasn't sick after all. "I feel so much better, Barb. Thank you."

Just to be on the safe side, I spent the next day in bed. At night when Barb came home and asked, "Are you going down to dinner?" I thought of the crowd clamoring around the bright hot lights and I couldn't face it, couldn't handle balancing plates of food on my tray, pushing and shoving, squeezing myself into one of the long tables. I felt my head swell. My throat clogged. My nose stuffed up. "Would it be the biggest pain in the butt for you to bring me up a sandwich again?"

Barb obliged. Again, I ate everything, and felt almost healthy when I had finished. How could I keep this going for the rest of the semester? I had pinpointed the source of my trouble: the cafeteria, the noise, the wait, the huge quantities slopped onto plates.

But the next night Barb didn't come home. I forced myself out of bed and downstairs, like a robot. There were no trays when I finally got through the turnstile. I waited for the guy to bring a pile of clean ones, still damp, from the kitchen. The fork I pulled from the container had crooked prongs. The woman dishing the rice scraped the sides of the pan with her huge metal spoon, so I got all the hardened, burnt grains that had been stuck there.

I ate what I could, put on my friendly face and imagined removing it later, hanging it off a hook and letting it droop.

"Well, if I get a C on this test, I'm still okay for my B in the class, at worst a B-minus."

"I do my best studying in the middle of parties. I don't know why, but . . ."

"I'm hoping for the transfer to come through . . ."

"Where's Barb?" someone asked, a voice aimed at me.

"What?" Sure, everyone wanted Barb. She was so vivid and alive, with her bright brown eyes and hair, her loose skirts and her patchouli perfume. She glowed. She pulsated. Compared to her, I was a gray half-living shadow. "I don't know where Barb is. Probably at Tiff's. What does it matter, and how the hell am I supposed to know anyway?"

I saw a group of girls, all alike, looking at me. "You don't have to yell, Mandy," one of them said. "She was just asking."

"Yeah, right." My face puffed up like a hot air balloon, swelling, red, until someone could have burst it with a pin. Oh God. I was ruining everything! I couldn't even talk anymore. I needed Barb. She had kept me as part of the group by the sheer power of her friendliness and life. Why was she turning away from me now? Why?

Because I was obnoxious to be around. I had to stop. Tomorrow I would approach the day with a whole new attitude. I would take a shower, go to classes, straighten things out with my job at the library. Stay on top of it.

I WOKE, SHOWERED, and went out to enroll in a photography class. They were held in the art building, where I had never been before. I stepped into a spacious lobby enclosed in glass, with a gallery on the ground floor. I spoke to someone, showed her my camera, but she said, "It's too late in the semester to sign up. I'd definitely recommend that you take a class next semester. It seems you have a strong enough interest." She was trying to be kind and patted my shoulder, but the impatience came through in her voice and I kept hearing the words *it's too late.*

How long had I been back? I tried to figure it out, counting the days on my fingers, but I couldn't concentrate. A month? It seemed too late for everything. The days passed like a background hum, one following another. How many classes was I taking, anyway? I had missed so many, they seemed like situations occurring in a dream. In the disintegrating world, I didn't know anymore what was real. I was exploding into a panic. I had to get a grip.

My bed was real. Cigarettes were real. Dad's shoes were real. The camera was real, but it was too late. Mom was too real. I didn't know if Booner was real or not. I pulled the covers up over my head and felt a comforting inertia roll through my body.

Barb came in. I heard her put a tape in the stereo. Talking Heads started singing "Take Me to the River."

She snapped the shade up and light flooded the room. She was real, the way she stood there like a goddess with light haloed behind her. I wanted her to stay just like that, forever. But she was always moving. I jumped out of bed, snatched the camera from my desk drawer, and caught Barb just as she was turning toward me, her face somehow small and frightened in her mass of hair.

"Take a photography class, Mandy," she said. "You gotta do something. You're getting weird."

"Weird? Is that one of your *psychological* phrases?"

"Don't be mean to me. I've had a hard day." She sat on her bed, which she rarely slept in anymore since she was so often at Tiff's.

I sat in my bed, the sheets still warm from my body, and cradled the camera in my lap. "You don't know what a hard day is, Barb. You have everything you want."

She heaved a sigh, stared at her feet. "I don't want you to take this the wrong way, but—"

Warning. Warning. I didn't want to hear this. I tried to interrupt. "It's too late in the semester to take a photography class."

But Barb was full speed ahead. "Every time I come in, you're lying in bed. It isn't healthy. You never go anywhere. Look at all the dirty plates and crumbs. You haven't changed your sheets since you've been back. It's disgusting. The room smells. I can't live like this."

"You don't like being my roommate, is that what you're trying to say?" I wanted to swing the camera into her skull, to get through to her, to make her know, to make her feel, unforgettably, how empty the world was.

"You're like a piece of furniture, Mandy. Last semester you never missed a class. You used to go out and laugh, party. I think you need help. You should see an adviser or something. You're always here, like a lump. Don't you see what I'm trying to say?"

"I'm a lump," I said lumpishly, a lump of wax melting into my mattress, part of the general filth in the room.

"It's not that. But you seem so fixated on your father's things. You know—the shoes, the camera. And it's been two months. Eventually you have to move on."

I remembered that Barb's parents were divorced and she hadn't seen her father in four years. Still, he was alive. "You want me to move," I said.

"*No!* I'm just saying you should talk to someone who can help you." She gathered up some clothes, stuffed them in her backpack. She was going to abandon me, move on from the lump. *No. Please don't.*

"I'm talking to you now. Aren't you someone? Aren't we talking?"

"I got you the name of a professional." She held out a business card. Dr. Somebody, Psychologist, Ph.D. I barely looked. It was probably her professor. She was probably after an A.

On the stereo, Talking Heads sang about water, about love and trouble.

"I'm not one of the rats in your lab."

She zipped her backpack shut. "I'm trying to help."

"Don't bother." I stared at my knees as she left the room and I was still staring at my knees when she returned a few seconds later. The door opening created a wind that rippled the pages of the notebook on the floor. "I can't help you, Mandy. I don't want to leave you like this, but I just can't help you."

If she didn't want to leave me like this, she didn't have to, did she? "I'm fine," I said, and waved her away.

"THEY'RE ALL SO supportive. Pastor Bob says I have exactly the right skills for the church store," Mom told me over the phone. "You would be proud of me, the way I've been getting around. I said that my little Miranda was as faithful a worshipper as myself."

"That's great, Mom," I said mechanically. She was so full of it.

"Do they have a Christian group there? Campus Crusaders?"

"Sure, Mom, but I have to go."

"The only problem is the driving. I haven't been able to go any-where without suffering a panic attack."

"Oh, look at the time. I have to get to class, Mom."

"Seven o'clock at night, they have classes?"

"Night classes! I'll call you soon, okay? 'Bye!" I hung up the phone, cutting off the only person who ever called me. It was Booner I wanted to talk to. I smoked a hit of pot and then another. Okay. I sort of stepped sideways out of myself and surveyed the world like that. Maybe I would be all right after all. I smoked another bong hit, then another and another. There's Mandy in college, sitting on her bed. She needs company.

Through the door I heard the voices of the girls across the hall returning from dinner. They were talking about partying and happy hour. I opened the door quick. "Are you all going out?"

"Well, we're just . . ."

"I'll get my coat." They weren't my friends, but they were friendly enough. Too friendly to tell me I couldn't go with them. "Party on!" I said amiably.

Who needed Barb? The know-it-all, I'd show her. Go out like the old days. Beer, the elixir of life. First stop: the Rathskeller; next: O'Heaney's.

"If your home isn't home and your dorm room isn't home, a bar can be your home," I said, nudging one of the girls.

"Whatever you say." She downed a shot of beer. "But what I want to do tonight is score."

"Score!" The rest of the girls held up their glasses, a ring of glasses reflecting the light.

The next stop: Washington Tavern, where we got a table. We drank beer through straws, shot glasses, paper cups, and mugs. But unlike when Barb and I went out, no one drank straight from the pitcher. It didn't matter. There was enough togetherness. Friendship in college came and went, smooth and easy as water. I would get the hang of it. Tonight, these girls were my best friends, smiles around the table, everyone laughing, animated. I was one of them.

Beer slid down, an endless number of pitchers between us. My glass remained perpetually full no matter how much I seemed to drink. Starting tomorrow, I would get back on track. The straight and narrow. Straight as an arrow. "Here's to tomorrow!"

"To-fucking-morrow!" said one of the girls, granting me existence by toasting with me. "I toast, therefore I am!" I said. We bought some shots of something. I didn't know what.

Starting tomorrow: study, read the assignments, write the essays. I would pull all-nighters, like other students did. A pitcher of kamikazes arrived. Then another. Why, I hadn't drunk kamikazes since . . . I had an announcement to make. "My father died, but I have to move on! I know how to have a good time!" I shouted. "He was the man! I don't call him Dad! I call him Dead!" Now, that was funny. A funny thing that was also sad. Funnysad. My eyes welled up. The girls around the table wobbled and glowed.

But I sensed wrongness. This wasn't the place to bring him up. The table was getting crowded. Guys had joined us. Yet I had summoned Dad by cracking a joke, and now he was with me, as if he were actually alive! I wanted to explain this, but some dumb guy sat down and started talking to me. It seemed I couldn't get a word in edgewise.

I decided to talk right over him, because I had conjured up Dad! "You never knew my dad. Like, he was always a big guy, but not fat, not fat at all. Until it happened all of a sudden. He gained a lot of weight. He turned into a fat man! His wedding ring didn't fit him anymore. 'Course, he got it from the Rexall."

Another face replaced the one I was addressing. "My dad's hand was so big, it kind of like swallowed up my hand." I raised my hand and turned it, a holograph without a frame. Eyes rolled away like planets disappearing. Strangers stepped in and out of my range of vision like distant stars through a telescope, and when I didn't want to see them, I put the telescope down and gazed at a space filled with colors and shadows. The back of a head refused to turn and look.

"I will not be ignored!" I was proud of myself for shouting this, and Dad would have been proud of me, too. "Long live God and the Boyles!" I shouted. I was as clean and pure as a freshly healed sore when the scab finally falls off on its own.

MY EYELIDS WERE stuck together. My lips were swollen, and my tongue thick as a drying sponge between coated teeth. The ceiling flattened above me, straight and white. Beneath me, a bed. I was wearing my flannel nightgown. The shade was up and the room painfully bright. I remembered dancing to the Ramones "I Wanna Be Sedated." But the night stopped there. No more. What class had I missed this morning? What day was it? My muscles hurt, and there was a stinging burn between my legs.

Bang bang bang. The door vibrated between knocks. "Hey, come on! Let me in!" A male voice shouted harder, faster. Louder knocking.

Barb's bed was empty. But hadn't I seen her last night? Her face had appeared, one of the stars in the far-off universe. I thought I remembered an argument, something about a horse and Tiff. Or did I dream it?

Bang bang bang on the door.

I stood slowly, as carefully as Mom with a lupus flare-up. Feet heavy. Bones aching. I opened the door a crack. There was a guy, fist up for that one final punch. I squinted at his pale, freckled skin. Gray eyes, wide open. Fresh, showered, clean, smelling of cologne, like he'd been up for hours already. There were creases ironed in his jeans. White teeth. Short hair. Mom's term popped into my head: *well groomed*. He had probably taken the steps to Christ and he was a member of the Campus Crusaders.

"Miranda. Hi. Morning. I need my shoes."

"Your what?" How did he know my real name? No one called me Miranda but Mom. Oh, now I got it. He was from the Church of Assemblies. It was all connecting. He came for Dad's shoes. Mom found out that I had taken them. "Did my mother send you here?"

"I know where they are," he insisted.

Where had he come from? I allowed him in, and he walked straight toward my bed. In my ratty flannel nightgown, worn out in areas where the pale blue flowers were white and threadbare, I was ashamed. I leaned against the door, clutching the knob. Through the pounding in my skull, I dimly remembered screaming with helpless laughter, falling down with it. Arms around me during a slow dance. A silver globe turning, casting metallic shadows that flew and glinted off moving bodies. A funny thing that was also sad.

I watched the guy as he knelt down by my bed, lifted the trailing blanket, and peered beneath. But I couldn't ask his name. He reached under, shoved aside dirty laundry, pushed away the food-encrusted plates from the cafeteria. He withdrew from under the bed a brown leather, loafer-type shoe.

"How did that get there?" My voice shook.

"The other one, the other one," the guy muttered, paused. Then he went over to the stereo. Jammed between a speaker and the window-sill was a matching shoe. He held it up like a trophy. "You threw it back there last night. Don't you remember? There's something else, too." He leaned over the speaker, pulled it toward him, and behind it, on the floor, this clean-cut stranger whose name I didn't know found a pair of green cotton men's underwear. My knees buckled. I stumbled to Barb's bed and lowered myself. I remembered nothing—not his face or his dimples or his gray eyes, not his hands, with neatly clipped nails. My ribs wouldn't move to let me breathe. They were all stuck together. My room was a locked box. I was trapped.

He folded his underwear neatly, pulled out a plastic bag from his backpack, put the underwear inside, and lock-sealed it shut. Like evidence from a crime scene.

I couldn't ask, "Did we do it?" How could we have done it if I didn't remember? It was a trick, a setup. But I was sore between my legs, burning. I folded my arms over my chest and hunched inside myself.

"See ya around." He walked out the door. His aftershave drifted up my nose and I sneezed. I put my face in my hands, but my palms smelled like sweat. My stomach clenched. I needed help. No I didn't.

I crawled back to bed and under the covers, where it was warm and dark and safe. I curled up, my knees near my mouth, my breath hot against them. I tried to recreate the night, figure out where this guy had come into it, but I couldn't get beyond the thudding pain in my head. My eyes hurt in their sockets. I started to shake under the covers, sweating and shivering simultaneously. I had come to this. This was me.

The phone blared. I snatched it up. "Hello?"

"Hey," said Booner. "You sound half-dead."

A weak, grateful warmth rose up inside me. The one person I didn't need to beg forgiveness from. "Yeah, I'm sick with something."

"Check it out, I got a phone installed. No more pay phone."

"Wow."

"I got some things figured out, too. I gotta go upstate for Eugene this week because his summer place got vandalized, but I'll be done with that by Thursday, so I could come to Albany, spend the night, and on Friday we'd drive back to my place in Queens and you'd stay the weekend."

"You have it all figured out."

"I'm a problem solver."

"So how am I getting back to Albany?" I asked. Not that it mattered. I pictured the guy putting his underwear in a plastic bag.

"Oh shoot. I forgot about that," said Booner.

"I could take a bus. I don't know how much it costs . . ."

"I'll give you the money. No problem with that. All you gotta do is say yes. How about it, little girl?"

"You haven't called in a while," I said.

"I had to deal with things here, get the phone and shit. Been working night and day. How about it? Come on, you gotta say yes. You don't know what I had to go through to get Friday off."

"It's a great idea, Booner. Yeah, sure."

"All *right*!" He whooped like he was cheering for the home team. He was cheering for me, which made me a girl who somebody loved. Not a loser, but a good person. Pure. Worthy. Smart. Who I wanted to be.

WHAT DID GIRLS who went away with guys for a weekend bring with them? I packed a pair of black jeans, shampoo, deodorant, birth-control pills. I had no perfume. I threw in Dad's camera, Dad's sweater. I laid a few sticks of incense among my clothes so Booner would think I smelled beautiful. I tried to imagine I was him seeing my things for the first time.

I soaked my white bra in bleach to get the dinge out. I placed my one tight sweater in my bag and threw in a lacy shirt of Barb's. She'd never notice. I added an extra pair of socks. They were all worn-out in the heels. But the lacy red underwear I bought last semester was still in good shape. I put in my nightgown. I pulled it out and tried to find a large T-shirt instead.

But the room! What a pigsty! Candy-bar wrappers trailed from the door to my bed, up my blankets. There were scraps and chocolate crumbs scattered over my pillowcase. I gathered up the torn bits of paper. I pulled the sheets off my bed, collected all the clothes around the floor, and carried everything down to the laundry room. I had only a few days to prepare.

I put a tape in the stereo, Joni Mitchell, and remembered Barb, last semester, singing into her deodorant: "*My analyst told me that I was right out of my head. He said I'd need treatment, but I'm not that easily led . . .*"

I took the dishes into the bathroom to wash them. I gathered up the notebooks and textbooks on the floor and stacked them neatly on my desk. I stapled up the drooping black sheets. I dusted the crystal and threw out the dead aloe plant. I wiped down the speakers, changed the bong water, and borrowed the hall vacuum cleaner.

"SO THIS IS it." Booner's hands hung large and bulky at the end of his arms as he looked around, taking in the room and diminishing it. He was a man with his own apartment. He didn't share a bedroom, a shower, or a cafeteria. My dorm room was childish with its small single beds and student desks.

The tag on Booner's sweatshirt stuck out from under his collar. When he stood and stretched, he knocked my jacket off the hook and didn't seem to notice. His shirt slid up, revealing his stomach, hard and hairy. His jeans hung off his hips. He sat down in my desk chair, making it appear spindly and frail. His eyes lit on Barb's poster that said STONED AGIN.

I hunched inward, paralyzed on my bed, my hands tucked between my knees. What to do next? I should have planned something, but I hadn't been able to imagine past the grand entrance, which was painfully extending beyond my imagination.

He examined the neatly stacked books on my desk. The psychology textbook on top was a big, thick thing. "You got enough books here or what?"

I laughed, bounced a few times on my bed. But that was so stupid. "God," I said. When I looked at him, he was gazing at me. He was too large to take in.

"Come here, girl." He patted his thighs. "You look too cute to sit so far away."

I obeyed and lowered myself gingerly on his lap, afraid to allow my full weight. But he pulled me down, circled his arms around me, and there was no need for words. No need to be nervous. His neck was smooth and hot to nuzzle my face against. His arms held me like I was solid but also light and easy to bear. The knobs of his spine were prominent and strong. He had cut his hair, and it tickled my face.

"I missed you, baby." His lips tasted even better than I remembered. Lips against lips, then his tongue touched my tongue, electrifying and wet. How had I gone so long without his tongue? I pushed against him, pulled his lips into my mouth.

He stroked my back under my sweater and pushed my sweater up, panting with need. I couldn't let his mouth go, not even to whisper that I had missed him, too. He lifted me as he stood and I straddled my legs around him. Awkwardly, we moved to my bed and lay down.

A rattling outside the door gave me time enough to pull my sweater down and sit up, pretend I was coughing. Booner shifted so he was sitting next to me. The two of us were facing the door by the time Barb barged in. "Whoa, sorry. Didn't realize. Just need a notebook . . ."

"It's okay, Barb," I said.

"Got anything to go in that thing?" Booner pointed to the bong.

Barb was staring. Let her look.

"Yeah, I have a little." I reached under my bed for Dad's shoes, guiltily remembering the brown loafers that had recently landed there. But to Booner, I was innocent and he would never find out about that. The fewer people who knew about it, the less likely it was that it had happened at all. "There's not a lot left," I said.

"What's this? Seeds and stems?" But he filled the bong and took a hit.

"This is Booner," I said to Barb. "Booner, Barb."

"Oh." Her voice was full of false friendliness. "You're the guy she met at the bar and you broke all the glasses."

"Word gets around." Booner gave her half a smile as he passed the bong to me. He didn't need Barb. He knew who he was.

"He's staying the night," I said. "Then I'm visiting him for the weekend."

Barb nodded, surprised. Did she think I had no life without her? Well, guess again, Barb! I passed her the bong, and she shook her head. I had never seen her awkward or at a loss for words before. But under Booner's stare, she stuttered, blinked, shrugged. What power he had! And his power became mine, because he was mine.

"Well, um, I gotta get going. I guess I'll see you Monday? We'll go to dinner?" She hugged me, but I stood like a plank, like I did when Mom hugged me.

The door shut. Booner and I were alone again, but Barb's intrusion joined us like an extra incentive. "That was my roommate. I haven't seen her for days."

"Man, what a thing to have to put up with." Booner pulled me back down on the bed, moist lips on my neck, hands under my sweater. "So where were we?" Then my sweater was on the floor somewhere, my bra pushed up around my throat. Booner's zipper was undone, his hard-on peeking through. As he laid his touch all over me, I remembered he didn't wear underwear.

"Mm." His moan stroked like another caress, and it said, Mandy, you are a wonder to behold, not gross, not in need of counseling, not requiring a Ziploc bag.

We were naked without a thought, and I began to tremble as soon as he rolled on top of me. Hard, fast breath, the weight of his body, his skin against my skin. I wrapped my legs around him as he pushed himself inside and I experienced a fragile unfolding. Each thrust was a baton of pleasure, arching up into an almost unbearable thrill. The crystal clinked against the windowpane. The feeling was too strong. I shivered, shut my eyes. My skin tightened around my bones. "Booner," I whispered. Completeness.

"Talk to me, baby, does it feel good?" Booner was still thrusting after spasms of pleasure exploded and ebbed away inside me, like water twirling down a drain. When he moved, the bed shifted, hit the wall with the strength of his push, and he didn't notice. He was where I had been only seconds before. A lift, a swell, a slight sigh, and he gushed warmth inside me, subsided, and collapsed.

His hair smelled of baby shampoo. His skin was moist where it touched mine. The sheet was too small to cover us both and his feet extended over the bottom of the mattress, hitting the desk. I had never seen my dorm room as so supremely inadequate.

We lay in silence for I couldn't tell how long. Then I reached past Booner for my cigarettes.

"Bad habit," he said.

"You smoke pot, so you shouldn't talk."

"At least pot gets you high." His muscled arm lay across the blanket, heavy, reassuring, the hair all growing in one direction. I blew the smoke away from him so he wouldn't think I was disgusting.

His stomach grumbled.

"Are you hungry?" I asked.

"I thought you'd never ask."

"Do you want to go down to the cafeteria? You could say you forgot your I.D."

"Cafeteria? Naw, I don't think so."

"That's good," I said, "because I hate the cafeteria."

We walked through the tunnels and there was something in Booner's slouch, in his stride, each step firm and purposeful, that made him look older than the others around campus, more weathered, more handsome. He squinted when he looked at the posters and the other students. The college guys looked wide-eyed and stupid by comparison. I felt full and deep walking with Booner. I had acquired dimension.

We found a booth at the student center and Booner lounged in his seat, stretching out his legs so people had to detour around them. There was a group at a nearby table, talking like everyone in college talked, blah blah blah, midterms, quizzes, papers, tests. They talked about themselves and their grades like it was life and death.

"Silly little kids." Booner grinned his careful, handsome half-smile. "Hiding from the world, acting like whatever they do and think is important. I don't know if you belong here. You're not a silly little kid, are you?"

"Blah blah blah, if I don't get an A I'll die," I said. We laughed like we were one person accidentally separated into two bodies.

The waitress came over and we ordered the special: cheeseburger deluxe with french fries and a pickle. Booner touched my hand. "Why are you in college anyway?"

I shrugged. Because I was smart. Because I got in. Because otherwise I'd be with Mom in Ransomville. "To get an education, I guess," I said.

"You guess. An education. Those people at that table, are they getting an education?"

"Dear Mom and Dad, I love you. Please send money!" shouted a particularly doofy guy at a nearby table. The rest of them laughed.

"Face it," said Booner. "You're only here because it's like a toy store to hang out in for four years or whatever until you have to face reality."

At another table, two girls argued. "But that is *so* goddamn socialist!" shouted one to the other. "Get it through your head. Liberalism is dead. We're in a free-market economy!"

No, I wasn't like any of them. But Booner sounded like Mom. I couldn't find the right words as I groped stupidly for reasons to be here. "I think I'm in college to learn about life and stuff."

Our burgers arrived, steaming and huge. I didn't want burger juice to drip over my fingers, and I used a new napkin every time I wiped my mouth.

"You learn about life by living it." Booner swallowed his mouthful before he started talking. "What am I saying? College is for rich kids and I wish I could go, but some of us have to work for a living."

"I work at the library."

Booner's eyes, those green-brown, brown-green eyes, swallowed me up. "I wasn't talking about you." He smiled. "You using enough napkins there?"

They lay around the table, balled up and greasy. I hardly ever ate out. It was embarrassing. I would sometimes eat at Miss Ransomville Diner with Dad, but I never ordered a burger. I ate the same thing every time: a grilled cheese sandwich, french fries, and a chocolate shake. But the last time I ate there it had been too weird. I had gone searching for Dad at the Griffin after school. Mac told me he had gone to the diner, and I found him there, in the booth where we always sat, with a couple of men I had never seen before.

"This is my daughter," he had said proudly. But the men paid no attention to me.

"Order anything you want," Dad told me. Then he started talking to the men. "The time is now. I got investors lined up, so I need a decision. I can't wait around any longer."

With a thrill, as I ate my grilled cheese, I realized Dad was conducting business.

"I dunno," said one of the men, gazing dully out at the parking lot. "We gotta check with some others."

"Check all you want. Check for the rest of your lives, and meanwhile it'll get yanked right out from under you." Dad pushed his plate away, and I suddenly thought he was going to do a magic trick. He could find quarters in people's ears. But instead he laid out a business card with just his name and phone number. FRANK BOYLE, ENTREPRENEUR.

I sloshed my chocolate milkshake around my tongue. "Can I order dessert, Dad?"

"The problem with the deal is you, Frank." The other man narrowed his eyes. "Not a single person I checked with has anything good to say about you."

Dad's face paled beneath his stubble, gray and white. "I don't know who you talked to." His voice sort of squeaked. I looked at him and thought he should've shaved. He shouldn't have ordered a hot roast beef sandwich that left strings of meat hanging between his teeth. He shouldn't have lit a cigarette that left specks of tobacco stuck to his bottom lip.

My stomach hardened, round and cold. I had gobbled my food too fast, eaten everything on my plate, and I was ashamed.

"Come on," one man said to the other, and threw a crumpled ten-dollar bill on the table before they slid out of the booth.

"Wait a minute, wait a minute. You invited me to lunch, remember? I'm a working man. I got a wife and child to support."

They looked at him as if he were a beggar on the street. "Sure, Frank, whatever you say." The man threw out another ten and a couple of wrinkled ones.

Dad's face had flushed, no longer white. He kept eating, though he had finished his roast beef. There was still the basket of bread, the cracker packets, and the bread sticks. He took the bread he didn't eat and wrapped it in a napkin. "For your mama." He winked as he handed it to me. I looked away. I understood implicitly that this meal was a secret.

As soon as I got home, I vomited the grilled cheese and french fries, the chocolate shake, and the piece of banana custard pie I had eaten for dessert. Mom held my hair back while I retched over the toilet. "I certainly hope you're not developing esophagus problems like me. No daughter of mine should have to suffer like that. I'm thinking we ought to call the emergency room." I loved her then, for holding my hair off my face, for rubbing my back, for not being secretive, for just being Mom.

The tap of a boot on my shin. "Hey, daydreamer." Booner leaned toward me. The shifting colors in his eyes drew me in. I felt a trembling begin in my belly, and I was afraid I might be sick. Chills ran up and down my body, and I couldn't quite place where I was. I felt slightly dizzy.

The check came, a solid reality. Booner started digging in his pocket, but I beat him to it and pulled out my own ten. My jeans weren't as tight as his.

He reached out, cupped my hand gripping the ten-dollar bill, and pushed it back toward me. "You don't think I'm a cheapskate, do you?" His eyes bored into mine, intense and powerful, until I had to look away. I said, "No, I just thought . . . oh, never mind." I tucked the money back into my pocket and tried to push down my embarrassment.

Afterward, we returned to the dorm. Booner didn't want to go out, didn't want to see Albany. "You're all I came to see," he said. "I don't need to run around."

We lay on my bed watching *The Golden Girls* on Barb's TV. Booner lounged godlike in his nakedness. I wasn't used to that. I had always hidden myself. I knew how to change my clothes without revealing anything to Mom. Fast and clever, I would pull my arms out of my shirt and put my nightgown over my head, then pull the shirt off through the neck of my nightgown. Ta-da!

"This one thinks she has something to hide," Mom had told Loretta.

"You're shy." Booner projected shy charm over me like soft rain. He took my hairbrush off the dresser and brushed my hair, stimulating electric shivers along my scalp from the roots to the ends. "I've been wanting to do this a long time," he said.

I sat like a princess. It had never occurred to me to want something so specific. Something as simple and beautiful as Booner brushing my hair, I couldn't have imagined. It felt so good. I wanted it to go on forever.

WITH THE RADIO going, the journey from Albany went by like a flash in Booner's warm, smooth Camaro, and soon we were in New York City. We passed skyscrapers that glittered back reflections of a cloud-scudded blue a thousand times, separate mirrored squares that filled the car window and beyond. Countless figures paced the streets in fast motion as though mechanically driven. Huge crowds crossed when we stopped at red lights. A quickness surrounded them, surrounded the sheer vertical buildings with store after store after store, dizzying to absorb.

We turned off the busy avenue and onto an iron bridge. Below lay the river, densely gray. The tires wailed as we crossed. The bridge shuddered. The streets were narrower on the other side, the buildings smaller, squat and uninteresting.

Booner pulled into a driveway in front of a two-story redbrick house with an empty terrace on the second floor and a garage directly beneath. It was ordinary, identical to the houses on either side. The curtained windows revealed nothing. They were blank, respectable. In front of each building, a lawn was nothing more than a frozen brown rectangle, with bristly twigged bushes beneath the front windows.

"Is this where you live?" What a disappointment. I had imagined Booner's place as freewheeling and messy, somewhere I could feel at home. But this house was conventional, tidy, stifling as the Church of Assemblies.

"Naw, I just gotta stop in." Booner came around and opened my car door. I felt, as I stepped out, like a princess descending from her coach. He took my hand, and walking up the path with him was pure freedom. There was no decision I had to make. I trusted him, and my body tingled with the memory of his touch.

The air was warm, as if preparing for spring. The wind felt fresh on my face. Puffy white clouds floated across an expanse of blue, the kind of clouds that shaped themselves like horses or fish, the kind Dad and I used to watch as they shifted and wandered across the sky.

"I want to introduce you to Eugene, my boss," said Booner. "Guy's like a father to me." His words floated over and I caught them in my mouth like melting sugar candies.

On Eugene's pinkie finger gleamed a gold ring, monogrammed EE. A thick gold wedding band circled his ring finger. The palm of his hand as he shook mine was as rough and warm as a tree in the sun. "So you're the girl Booner can't quit talking about." His eyes crinkled into friendly slits and drew me in.

He was bigger than Booner and softer, his muscles running to fat. His face was slightly squashed, and though he was already past thirty, he looked like a boy showing off his large white teeth. "What have you been up to, kid?" He hit Booner on the back of the head, like a man might do with a big dog.

"C'mon, Eugene. Stop." Booner ducked, letting out a high-pitched laugh. His face creased into a too-wide smile, showing small sharp teeth with gaps between them. He was such a man compared to the college boys, but in Eugene's presence he became a child. I didn't want him to be a child. I wanted the man and I stood there woodenly, not knowing what to say or do.

Eugene's wife was beautiful and there was a lot of her. "Hello, hello! Come in, sit down. I'm Rose Economopolous. So nice to finally meet you. We've heard so much about you." Her voice caressed as she ushered me into the living room. "I've known Todd for almost as long as I've known Gene, and I've never seen him so happy since he met you." The heavy mauve carpet swallowed up the sound of our footsteps. Throw rugs were scattered over the carpet. Rose's highlighted blond hair shone under the lamp as she sank into the armchair next to me.

I thought no one was allowed to call him Todd. I felt a stab of envy like a cramp that came and went. Rose didn't count. She was fat and wore an apron that she wiped her hands on, a housewife. She was wearing too much eye shadow on her heavy-lidded brown eyes. Yet when she pushed her hair off her face, her lips slipping over her teeth in a smile, she dazzled. I looked away so as not to stare rudely.

The walls were white, with peach-colored trim along the top. Not a crack in the paint; not a flake or a fingerprint marred the perfection. From the ceiling hung a chandelier with crystal balls dangling. They would have made great earrings. Barb would have loved them. Then I remembered how she had walked out on me with her "I don't want to leave you like this" and I decided the chandelier had nothing to do with Barb. Neither did the crystals and neither did I.

A piano, polished and gleaming as Booner's Camaro, took up a corner of the room. Ceramic shepherdesses posed prettily on the coffee table. Double drapes behind the sofa blocked the light. The hush was like at church, a place where I had to watch my behavior.

Eugene and Booner sat on the sofa. Booner slid a round tin from his jacket pocket, twisted it quickly open, pinched a clump of stuff, and shoved it in his mouth. When I saw his cheek bulge I realized it was chewing tobacco and I thought how out of place it was in this living room.

Booner and Eugene were both out of place. They rumbled their man voices, churning up conversation. While Rose, perfectly poised, bestowed her calm and loving gaze first on them, then on me. The armchair slowly swallowed me until I shifted my position, perching higher and closer to the edge. Then it slowly swallowed me again.

"What do you think of that, Mandy? It would be interesting, eh?" Eugene teased from the sofa.

I should've been paying attention. "Sure." I forced a nonchalant smile out as if I knew exactly what was going on, not making too much of it, just enough.

"See," Eugene said to Rose. "She doesn't mind."

What a privilege to perch on the edge of this armchair with these people who loved Booner and would also love me. Rose was positively swimming in her smile. "Is it true you're in college?" she asked.

I nodded, the spotlight on me. "I don't care where you go!" Mom had screamed. "Just get out of my house, you cold, selfish girl!"

"I go to Albany State," I said, loudly.

"I was going to the community college here in the neighborhood before Gene and I got married," Rose said. "Sometimes I think about going back. It was fun."

"Yeah." I tensed my face into what I hoped was a pleasant expression. College had stopped being fun, but there was no point in bringing that up with Rose.

"You don't look so sure," she said.

Eugene said, "All the jobs are in Staten Island now." Booner nodded in agreement, staring at his boots.

"They always talk about work," said Rose. "They can't help themselves. But I like to talk about the important things. How did you two meet?"

I was surprised she didn't know. If Booner was so close to them, didn't he tell them everything? "At a bar." I smiled, remembering Booner's reckless way of banging his empty beer glass on the bar, remembering how he had chosen me over Tracy, the wind in the trees, the rush of the stream and the twigs cracking. "Thanksgiving weekend."

"A bar?" Eugene broke in, eyebrows raised. "You spend a lot of time in bars, then?"

"She's not one of the four F's, Gene," said Booner.

"The four F's?" I was puzzled.

Rose touched my leg. "Hey, do you like cookies? I just made some. C'mon." She stood and turned gracefully despite her size, swaying her hips to avoid hitting the piano. I followed, like a child, through another room with a large-screen TV, a huge sheet of a mirror, and, on the opposite wall, an enormous fish tank, bubbling, bright with aquatic plants and tropical fish.

Pretty little striped fish, yellow and black, flickered, turned, floated. Long sleek blue ones swam in a group from one end of the tank to the other. Swim, turn on a dime, swim. Snails stuck to the side of the glass, globs of immovable mucus. A big orange fish with whiskers basked alone by a fake little tree, at peace in its silent watery world, while the other fish glimmered and swam around it. "Nice fish."

"They're recent. Eugene got them for me. They're supposed to bring peace of mind."

"Does it work?"

"I don't know. I'm too busy right now." Rose laughed.

The kitchen was immaculate. Oatmeal cookies cooled on a cookie sheet. Rose took a spatula out of a drawer. "Do you want some coffee? I can make a pot. It's decaf."

"I don't want to be a bother."

"It's no bother at all." She turned, arms akimbo, and set her soft brown eyes on me. "Booner was right. You *are* a sweetheart."

I felt my face flush and began to scoop cookies onto a plate with the spatula.

"You don't have to do that," said Rose.

"I like to," I said. "My Dad and I used to bake cookies together."

"Your dad cooks?"

"Well he used to. He . . ." I stopped for a moment just before the word. ". . . died." I felt the heat flood my face, pulsing in my skull and radiating outward. But I had said it. Simple. I wasn't going to cry.

"I'm sorry. When did he die?" Rose stared, arrested with the coffee filter still in her hand. I hadn't meant to stop the action.

"A couple months, almost." My hands felt limp. The weight of the spatula became unbearable, and I put it down. This would get easier. I would get used to saying it.

"Oh my goodness, so recently?" She set the filter on the counter. "Booner never said. Mandy, I'm so sorry."

I was slipping into a dark corner, awkward and weak. "It's okay, Rose. I didn't tell you just to make you feel sorry for me."

"I think you need a drink." She poured something dark into a small fluted glass. "Just go on, drink it. I'd drink with you if I didn't have a baby on the way. I'm laying off everything."

I downed it and a sweet, warm feeling spread through my chest. "You're pregnant?"

"It'll be our first." She smiled, wagged her finger at me. "You probably thought I was just fat, didn't you?"

"No. No." I lied. I regretted having thought she was fat, since she was one of the nicest people I had ever met. "Uh, congratulations."

"I didn't tell you just to make you congratulate me." When Rose laughed, I laughed, too, and hiccuped. She put her arm around me, and for that instant, the world was a calm, stable place.

"You'll be a really great mother, I bet."

"Well, I hope so." She picked up the plate of cookies. "Are you ready to go back out there, or do you want to sit for a while?"

"No, I'll come out. Thanks." I floated after her over the mauve carpet. Eugene and Booner were examining something small, rectangular, and black. I wanted to ask Booner, Why didn't you tell them my father died? You came to the funeral. You knew how much it meant to me.

But wondering about it fogged my mind. Through the fog emerged the image of a sharp-toothed Booner laughing a strange high-pitched laugh as Eugene batted him in the back of the head. And I wasn't sure I wanted to know the particular why of anything.

"Cookies!" sang Rose.

"Check it out." Booner held up the small black item. "A beeper!"

"Very impressive," said Rose. She turned and winked at me, bringing me into the circle where Booner was perfectly understandable, lovable.

"I've known this guy since he was a no-good teenager," Eugene said, addressing me. "Has he told you the truth about himself, or has he handed you a pack of lies?"

"I don't know." I took a cookie off the plate and bit into it. Soft, sweet, and chewy. I wanted to eat the whole plate of them.

"This guy would steal guns and then try to sell 'em back to the cousin of the guy he stole 'em from."

"That was a fluke, Gene," Booner stammered. "And a long time ago."

"Leave the poor things alone." Rose offered the plate to Booner.

He took a cookie, his big hands looking out of place against the cut-glass platter. "We gotta get goin'," he said with his mouth full, then swallowed and rattled his keys. "Let's roll, baby."

"Nice to meet you both," I said politely.

"Likewise. I think you're so good for this guy." Rose hugged me. She was large and soft and scented with baby powder.

"Thanks for stopping by," said Eugene. "I'll beep you later, right, Booner?"

Booner cupped the beeper protectively. He slung his other arm around my shoulders, his keys jangling against my coat. I put my arm around his waist, up under his leather jacket, his velour shirt soft against my palm. We walked like that down the path to the end of the driveway.

"They definitely liked you." Booner turned the key in the ignition, draped his arm over the seat, and stared proudly at me. I almost asked about the guns, but there was such a good feeling in the air that I could have chewed it up and swallowed it.

Booner's street was filled with identical brick buildings five stories high, each one connected to the next. What set Booner's apart was the small tree out front, fenced in behind a little square patch of dirt. Across the street, a dog ran back and forth, barking inside a fence surrounding a vacant lot.

"Home sour home." Booner carried my bag. I walked alongside him, past the tree and up three steps to the front door, which was locked. He shook out a key from his enormous key ring and unlocked it.

"Do you ever get sick of carrying so many keys around?"

"Got to carry 'em," he said.

We went through a dusty little vestibule, through another door, up one flight of steps, then another. The bulb was burned out on the third landing, and I held onto the railing, picking up dust in my palm. The stairs creaked.

At the top, Booner unlocked an apartment door. We stepped into a stuffy, airless kitchen ripe with the stench of fermenting garbage. "Wow, Booner. This place is kind of stinky."

"Yeah well, Princess, I don't really live here, I just sleep here. Mostly I'm in my car or at work or at Eugene's." He took his jacket off and laid it on a folding chair at the kitchen table, a card table. I draped my coat over his. The soles of my boots stuck to the dirt-streaked linoleum floor as I followed him to a closet. Sliding doors, off their runners, leaned up against the closet frame. There was a shelf next to these, covered with pennies, nickels, dimes, quarters, and piles of ATM receipts that Booner brushed aside to reveal a white Trimline telephone. "There's the phone," he declared proudly.

The bathroom was off the kitchen, and the door had swollen to become too large for its frame. It was missing the doorknob and I pulled it shut with my fingers through the hole. Small octagonal spaces dotted the floor where tiles had come off. The toilet seat was cracked. When I flushed, water moved around the bowl but nothing drained. I tried again and held the handle down until finally it swirled and flushed.

The living room was dominated by a wall-to-wall orange shag rug that had browned with age but remained garishly bright compared to the dark green sofa. Large, heavy gates covered the two living room windows, blocking the light. Against the wall was a long coffee table with a TV on it. Piled precariously on top of the TV were copies of *Car and Driver* magazine.

Everywhere I looked, I saw where I could be useful and it was a good feeling, a comforting, familiar feeling. Take that garbage downstairs. Light a stick of incense. Scrub that kitchen floor. Glue down a few tiles in the bathroom. I felt a rush of hope and energy. There was room for me here. No pretensions or respectability. It was what it was.

Booner squatted near a brand-new wooden cabinet against the opposite wall. "Got this system a few months back." He pushed on the glass door and it sprang open. "There's the speakers. Small, but great sound. I got a tape deck, turntable, CD player. And down here, the controls. Got the bass, equalizer, the works."

"Wow, really," I said.

He stood up, took my hand, and led me to the doorway off the living room. There was no door. The adjoining room was long and narrow, just wide enough for the double mattress on the floor. The window in the bedroom was also gated. Beneath it, heat wheezed up through an old rusted radiator. Outside the window was a fire escape. There was no carpet, just a linoleum floor patterned with big pale flowers, scratched and worn, like the floor at home in Ransomville.

Directly across the doorway was a dresser with a mirror, browned and spotted. There was our reflection. We caught each other's eye in the mirror. "That's the bed." Booner pointed to the mattress and cupped the back of my head with his palm.

"It's beautiful," I lied. It wasn't beautiful. Nor was it a bed. Just a mattress with a jumble of sheets and a blanket. But what mattered was who slept in it, and I remembered the feel of Booner's body next to mine, the safety and wonder of his skin. His heartbeat wouldn't change even if we slept on the bare floor. I leaned into his hand, imagining how we would wake up together on that mattress.

"If it's just me, you know, there's no point in having a nice place I gotta take care of," Booner said.

I looked up at him. Not at his reflection but at the man. I was eye level with his Adam's apple. I saw his throat, his neck, and then his chin, a prominent chin with a slight cleft. This was a man who saw no point in having a nice place just for himself. The hint of a mustache shadowed his upper lip, and I wanted to lie with him on the mattress right then, his arms tight around me and mine around him, neither of us saying a word, but understanding each other completely.

He turned away. "Come on. I'll show you the good part."

I followed him back through the living room and the kitchen, outside the apartment to the hall and up a small iron staircase. He unlatched the door at the top of the stairs, pushed it open, and we stepped out onto the roof. The air blew in my face, soft and damp. Pink light spread with the dusk over the city. A geometric array of rooftops wedged dark shapes against the pink. Yellow squares of light twinkled from the windows of other buildings like Booner's.

Beyond that, a water tower off in the distance glowed white like something from outer space. The moon was a soft, pale circle. The North Star winked faintly. A bridge glittered in the distance, red lights of the cars moving away, white lights coming in, snaking across.

The rooftop was full of odd protrusions, vents, pipes, and posts that seemed to serve no purpose. There were air bubbles in the tar. At the front, the roof just ended, like the flat end of the world. But between Booner's building and the next one a wall, waist-high, offered protection from falling. I gripped the edge and peered down. Two stories below, laundry hung off a line strung across an air shaft, white baby's shirts going gray. The ground below was a small rectangle.

"You're the first girl who's ever seen this place." Booner cleared his throat and slipped his arms around me, and I understood that he was lonely.

Pigeons rose, flapping off the roof's edge in a flurry of gray wings.

"It's beautiful," I said.

It seemed perfectly natural, when I unpacked my suitcase, to fold my clothes into one of the empty drawers in Booner's dresser and to lay the camera carefully in there, too. The hours we were going to spend together stretched ahead. What if we ran out of things to talk about?

"You like pizza? You want pizza or something?" Booner was rolling a joint. Back at college, it would be getting on toward dinner time and I would be dreading the cafeteria.

"I love pizza."

"Here." He handed me the joint and a lighter. Then he walked to the phone and ordered a pizza. We each took a couple hits, and I began to melt into the sofa. But Booner put his coat on. "Think quick." He tossed my coat at me, laughing when I ducked.

We went downstairs, outside, and around the corner to pick up the pizza. The little tree out front waved its bare, sharp branches in the pale glow of a streetlight. There was a comforting lack of conversation, with Booner carrying the pizza box like a tray. When there was nothing to be said, he said nothing.

There were no dishes in his kitchen, just a huge supply of paper plates, enough to feed the whole city. I opened and shut all three of his empty cabinets. He owned one metal fork, one knife, and one coffee mug.

"I'm not up nights washing dishes." He bit into his pizza, efficiently severing the cheese with his sharp front teeth. He was sitting on the sofa, a paper plate on his knees.

"True." I sat on the rug with the knife and fork, cutting my pizza into bite-size pieces. Booner switched the TV on and the movie Carrie was showing. The girls in the locker room were throwing tampons at Carrie because she hadn't realized she was menstruating. Blood was running down her leg. I had seen the movie several times, and I knew those girls would get theirs. The nagging mother would get hers, too. Knives would fly around the kitchen.

After I finished my first slice of pizza and then a second, my eyelids felt heavy. I couldn't pay attention. I picked up the pizza box, closed the lid, and put it in the refrigerator.

"Hey, come here." Booner lay in the shadows of the sofa. I kneeled on the rug near him, and at last, the point of everything, our mouths mashed together into one wet mouth. He shifted further into the sofa. "There's room for you here. Don't be shy."

He slipped off my shirt, my pants, my bra, my panties. I pulled his shirt up over his head and his pants down off his body and we hugged, naked and close. But the sofa was too narrow and for a breathless moment I thought we might roll off.

"Let's go to bed," he whispered. He kept his arms around me, walking behind me into the bedroom, and we lay on the mattress. He put his knee up between my legs and everywhere he touched he left an afterglow that longed for him. His touch had love in it. His fingers probed between my legs and I opened like a leaf uncurling, caught in a sticky place of desire, a place I didn't ever want to leave.

•　•　•

WHEN THE ALARM went off, it was still dark except for the street-lamp spreading its pale light in through the metal gate, casting an alluring pattern on the ceiling and on the walls, enclosing the room. Booner pulled his clothes on, not having washed or brushed his teeth. But I had to wash up. He waited at the door, tapping his foot, rattling his keys in a friendly, joking kind of way. "Girls always gotta be cleaning themselves."

At the last second, I grabbed the camera. It gave me something to hold on to as I followed Booner down the steps to his car. The city was quiet, streets empty. The camera sat in my lap like a child. I felt protective.

As Booner drove, I stared at my reflection in the passenger-side window, a ghost, barely visible. He stopped at a diner, left the engine running while he ran inside. He came out with two cups of coffee and two bagels with butter. He didn't bring sugar, so I drank the coffee without. I would get used to it. Sugar was for babies. College was for babies, too. I dreaded the bus ride back to Albany, dreaded Barb's false, pushy friendliness, dreaded classes. I shoved it out of my mind.

"What exactly do you do?" I asked.

"It's a specialized aspect of sanitation engineering." Booner spoke as though he were reading from a book, sounding out the words. The neighborhoods changed as we drove, from apartment buildings to warehouses and garages, with garbage littering the curbs. Broken glass winked under streetlights.

"You know those gratings at the curbs where steam rises sometimes?"

"Yeah." I thought I knew what he was talking about. There was one on every street corner.

"Those are drainage basins. I clean them."

"They're not sewers?"

"A lot of people make that mistake, Mandy. But catch basins are for drainage when it rains or snows or something. Sewers are where your shit goes when you flush the toilet. Two totally separate things."

I opened the camera case, checked the battery, and the red light blinked. But Booner poked my leg with his index finger, poked it hard. "So now you know what they're called, right?"

"Drainage basins."

"There you go. Another mistake a lot of people make is they use the catch basins to chuck out their garbage, and that causes blockage and flooding in the streets, which causes potholes, which causes the same idiots who threw their garbage in the first place to sue the city when they bust their ankle or their car tires." Booner bent a finger to emphasize each cause, until his hand was clenched in a fist.

He was more talkative than I had ever seen. I focused the camera on his fist, the large tight knuckles callused and discolored, like a row of hills. No rings, no nothing. They weren't decorative hands. They were working hands, but there was a softness in their touch I felt lucky to know.

Booner pulled up in front of a garage with a small sign out front that said GENERO CORP. He left the car running when he got out, opened a side door with one of his countless keys, and disappeared inside. Seconds later, the metal door clattered up. Booner came back to the car and we drove in.

The space was huge. The smell of diesel fuel, grease, and damp rags hung in the air, thick as fog. Four yellow trucks were parked next to each other. On the bed of each one was an adjustable upright section, with a cable attached to a pulley, which connected to another piece of metal that came out at an angle. A hook, a power shovel, and chains were attached.

"This is high-tech equipment." Booner's voice echoed in contrast to the solid sound of his knocking on the truck. "It's made of the same stuff as battleships. That's the stanchion, the winch, the boom." He was pointing to the upright and a sort of barrel at the foot of it, then the piece of metal that came out at an angle.

"Wait, can I get a picture?"

He leaned against the truck, his hair curled around his face and ears and sticking up around his scalp. But the camera wouldn't work. The red light inside the viewfinder showed a blinking arrow pointing down.

"You know what it boils down to, Mandy?"

"No." I opened up the f-stop on the lens, and magically, the arrow disappeared and the camera worked. I felt a surge of joy that caught me by surprise. It was so unfamiliar, yet I knew it. I had felt it before.

"Stupid people," said Booner. "You can't change human nature, and if people weren't so fucking stupid, I wouldn't have a job cleaning up after them."

For a moment as I focused, converging the broken halves of Booner in the viewfinder with the truck behind him, I caught a sense of the hidden possibilities in all things.

He led me to a corner where a wall had been built around a toilet. On the other side of the wall was a shower head with a plastic curtain running around a metal rod. Very makeshift. "Me and Hot Shot rigged that up one scorcher a few summers back."

"Just rigged it up, huh?" I focused on the sag in the piping that held the plastic curtain, but it wasn't worthy of a picture.

"You gettin' everything?" Booner was laughing as he led me into an office, another makeshift room in the opposite corner, surrounded on three sides with Plexiglas, fishbowl-like. There were two desks, each with a phone. Booner pointed to the smaller desk, a tidy square in the midst of a mess of papers and tools. "There's a ditz who works here, taking calls and estimates and shit. But I could see you there."

I sat in the chair and wheeled around, imagining how it might be to wave at Booner from behind the Plexiglas, to see him all day, to know exactly where he was, what he did, minute by minute, a familiar figure in a world full of unfamiliar activities, guys in trucks unclogging catch basins.

The chair accommodated my butt perfectly and the desk seemed like a small clear space where I could fit myself in, safe, protected, and sure. Everyone would know me and I would know where I belonged, so unlike college, where I was lost and anonymous and hardly anyone knew my name. So unlike Ransomville, where there was no space for me. "When can I start?" I made like I was joking.

But Booner was already heading back toward the trucks. "Here's our vehicle for the day. Get in, baby."

The engine roared and rumbled, jostled my bones, my brain. Booner shifted gears and the truck belched. The dashboard was full of stickers: REAGAN/BUSH '84. ROCK LIVES. SEX VIOLATORS WILL BE PROSTITUTED. GUNS DON'T KILL PEOPLE. PEOPLE KILL PEOPLE. CUSTOMERS WANTED, NO EXPERIENCE NECESSARY. A hairbrush filled with dirt, lint, and hair slid across the dash when we went around a bend. A frog bounced on a string off the rearview mirror. It made the truck appealing, like a big toy that everyone was allowed to play with.

Booner shifted the gears with an unconscious strength and grace that filled me up as I watched. We rolled over a long suspended bridge, the Verrazano-Narrows. The sun rose in the east behind us; the sky flushed pink ahead. "I got three basins to do today." His voice vibrated.

I nodded as if I understood.

The truck broke the early-morning quiet of the neighborhood like an army advancing as he pulled up at a corner. Booner checked his map against a scrap of paper on which he had scribbled something indecipherable. "Yup," he said, mostly to himself, and reversed the truck, the air-lock brakes squealing over the general rumble. I felt sorry for the people who thought they could sleep late on a Saturday. But we were important, here to do a job, regardless of anyone's sleep. Like Mom, roaring through the house with the vacuum cleaner at five o'clock in the morning. "I'm in pain and when I'm in pain, I clean." She would crash into the wall, bang into my bedroom door.

A thrill ran through my body as I got out of the truck. Mom didn't know where I was. She didn't even know where to look.

I focused the camera on Booner as he worked the winch controls. He was shouting, and though I couldn't hear, the effort tightened and strained the muscles of his neck and face. He pointed as he worked, and I took a picture of him pointing and shouting. I understood that he was trying to teach me.

He lowered the boom, attached the hook to the grating on the basin. I stepped back as it rose, hoisting the grating off and shifting it to the side with a screeching metal-against-concrete scraping sound. Then he operated the power shovel, scooping heaps of dripping sludge from the basin, swinging it around to dump it in the truck bed. There was so much noise and movement, I didn't know what to take a picture of next, so I lit a cigarette and watched. It didn't take long. A few shovelfuls and then Booner hooked the grating, dragged it back over the basin.

I climbed into the truck for another jostling, rattling ride to the next basin, where Booner repeated the entire operation. This time, front doors along the block opened up, ejecting children, all bundled in coats, scarves, hats, mittens. Little boys, red-faced, puffing, shoving, as impressed by Booner as I was, gathered around the truck, wrestling each other out of the way.

Booner stopped to remove his jacket and sweater, which he handed to me. The leather jacket was heavy, bulky, and his sweater was damp with perspiration. I held them in the crook of my elbow and took a picture of him working in just a T-shirt, his chiseled biceps bulging like a hero's. This was his world. I was glad I had brought the camera. Otherwise, I would have had nothing to do but stand here. Booner waved the boys away, but as soon as he turned back to shoveling muck and garbage, the kids inched closer.

He gestured to one of them, who scurried over for the money in Booner's outstretched hand. The kid ran across the street to the store on the corner, two friends chasing after him. They came out, fighting over a can of soda, which they presented to Booner like a prize. He gave them a thumbs-up, stopped, and gulped some soda down.

He could've told them to get me a soda, too. If I'd had money in my pocket, I would've bought one for myself, but I hadn't thought to bring any. The cash from my student loan and my last paycheck lay folded in my suitcase at the apartment, along with some of the cash left from Mom's roll of bills.

Once it was gone, it would be gone. Even if Mom had hidden more money away, she wouldn't give it to me now. I needed my job at the library. I was lucky I still had it after all my screwing up. But the thought of going back there, back to classes and all the rest, threw me into a panic.

Booner waved, scattering my worries. All the kids turned to look: Who was this special person, acknowledged by their hero? I looked at them through the camera and a couple of them posed, throwing their arms around each other, all eyes momentarily on me. To see and be seen, all of us together for an instant. Click. I took the picture, feeling myself a necessary part of Booner's world.

A beautiful silence settled. With the truck turned off and the grating returned to the basin, Booner leaned back and finished his soda. The kids clamored around him. "What's that? Are you finished? Can I see the inside? Did you get everything?"

"Gotta get going," said Booner. "One more."

The truck grated and rattled as Booner reversed into the street. The frog bounced around the rearview and the seat vibrated behind my head when I leaned back against it. "I can't believe those kids actually stand around on a cold day, watching."

"Kids love this shit," said Booner. "When I was a kid, I couldn't get enough of watching guys work construction and that kind of stuff."

We were driving to the final basin. "You can help with this one," he said.

I placed my camera carefully under the seat before I got out.

He handed me a pair of gardening gloves and showed me how to hook the grating and work the gears to lift it off. He kept his hands over mine as I shifted, then he backed away to let me shovel. It took brute strength to move the gears, but yanking them didn't work, because the shovel swung wildly. I got that. My shoulders ached. I couldn't do it if I tried to watch myself doing it at the same time. I got that, too.

Neighborhood children gathered to watch here, too. The ache in my shoulder subsided. I had an audience and a sense of what it might be like to inhabit Booner's powerful body. When I waved the kids away, they backed off, just as they had with him. I wrenched the gear, swung the shovel, and heaped sludge in the back. "You're better than a boy, and that's the God's truth, Mandy," Dad used to say.

Forget about working at that desk in the garage. I wanted to go out in the trucks like the guys. If Dad could see me now. If Mom could.

Then Booner was shouting, his face contorted, slicing a horizon with his hands. I couldn't hear what he was saying until he clasped the tops of my hands and swung the shovel back into position. "Good job, ace." He hooked the grating and dragged it back over the basin, his T-shirt drenched, even in the cold February afternoon. Grime streaked his face. He secured the shovel. We were back in the truck, driving off. And I had cleaned a drainage basin. Not a sewer.

"Not bad." Booner gave me a half-smile. "You might just have a future in infrastructure."

We bounced and bumped along. The streets were busy now with traffic, but Booner was fearless and we were in a truck. Cars got out of our way. "Are we going home now?" I asked.

Booner laughed. "You just wait. It's time for phase two." He turned off at an exit and traffic lightened. Only trucks traveled this road. The smell hit first, a wall of stink so strong it leaked into my skin when I held my nose. I couldn't breathe. My eyes watered, my ears clogged. I checked to make sure my window was rolled up. But Booner's was halfway down.

"Your window, Booner! Shut your window!"

Silently, his mouth wide open, Booner reached over to pull a clothespin from the glove compartment. He emitted a helpless squeak of laughter as I snatched it and clamped it on my nose, never mind the pain, the numbness. Booner finally caught his breath, still laughing. "You should smell it in August."

It was the Fresh Kills landfill. Garbage trucks barreled at us from the other direction, massive Dumpsters free of their loads but dripping with filth. We stopped at a booth, where Booner turned the truck off and got out. A stooped, grizzled old man limped from the booth. Money changed hands.

A big, hairy fly drifted and buzzed, trapped in the truck, bumping up against my window. It brushed my lip, though I flapped my hand to shoo it. I jumped. I squirmed. I twitched. The clothespin snapped off my nose and I clamped it back on.

The old man followed Booner back to the truck, waving a scrap of paper, shouting in a voice so gruff that what came out was gibberish. Booner snatched the paper. "I don't need this shit. Just give me the goddamn receipt." He got back in the truck, leaving the man with his arm still upraised, stuck in his futile gesture.

"Why were you so cruel to that poor old guy?" The effort of talking made me feel as if I were underwater.

"Cruel? You gotta be kidding." Booner drove along a winding road cut through the garbage. "He's a fucking corrupt old geezer who's got more money socked away than you or me could even dream of." He shook his head. "You always gotta have an opinion, don't you?"

My nose was a point of pain and I still felt sorry for the old man, but otherwise I had no opinion. All over the dump, roads had been cut through with yellow YIELD signs at the crossings. It was like a little city of garbage within the big city of New York. Booner knew exactly where he was going. "Guess where the Lone Ranger takes his garbage?"

"I don't know." Seagulls flocked overhead, hovering, cawing, and crying. They were gray, not white like pictures of seagulls I had seen by the ocean.

"To the dump, to the dump, to the dump dump dump."

I didn't laugh.

"See that?" Booner hit me on the leg and pointed out a bald man in hip boots, wandering among the garbage with a metal detector. Another guy sorted through a pile, carrying on his back a huge plastic bag of empty cans. A woman and two children scavenged through a mountain of stuff. "Wherever you go, someone's worse off than you," said Booner.

I had gone through garbage at the local dump with Dad. They were fun outings, treasure hunts. Compared to this place, the local dump at Ransomville was a pleasant park. What would Dad have thought of this? I could almost see him, winding up. "There's gold in them there hills, Mandy!" He would have devised some ingenious way of escaping the smell without cutting off all circulation to the nose like this clothespin did. I removed it, feeling the pang of tears. But now was not the time for crying.

I took the camera out from under the seat and framed a hill of garbage with a seagull alighting, its wings spread as it glided in for a landing. Beautiful. Click.

At last, Booner pulled into a cul-de-sac, moved the gears, and tilted the truck bed. Mud, sludge, and garbage slid out onto a hill. We were home free, unloaded and barreling out of there. The angle of the sun slanting across the dashboard indicated late afternoon. Booner's hands were black with grease, dirt embedded in his fingernails. He had smudges on his cheeks, and his greasy hair stuck out all over the place. He looked rugged. I didn't want to know how I looked. I took a picture of him. "What is it with you and that camera?" He shrugged, easygoing, not demanding an answer or even a response.

Back we drove to the garage, where Booner handed me a hose. I rinsed down the truck while he made a call. Then we drove in the Camaro back to the apartment with the little tree out front. I resolved to get a picture of that tree before I left.

"Ready for a shower?" Booner said. "I know I am."

Water splashed and bounced off my naked body. Steam filled the room. We hugged, wet and slippery, as drops ran warm as praise over us. Booner grew hard. With my back pressed against the wall where the tiles ended, gritty with peeling paint, I wrapped my legs around Booner's body and he thrust himself inside me. I was hot and wet inside and out.

We thudded together and my tailbone banged against the wall, faster, faster, faster. I was giddy, flying, floating, a sparrow in a rainstorm with the most appealing helplessness, cushioned by Booner's large hands cupping my butt. Then it was over. I slid down the wall. Booner supported me, and I laid my cheek against the wet, matted hair on his chest. "Aw, man," he said over and over. "Aw, man."

I wanted to keep all the pieces of myself inside one continuous sensation, but when Booner turned from me to grab the soap, I felt as though I were slipping away, separating into a million droplets, sucked down the drain. I clung to him as he rinsed. "Hey, it's all right." He disengaged my arms and stepped out of the shower. I was stuck with myself. I lathered my hair. I soaped off his love, tried to feel a sense of solidity.

The shower curtain stuck to the inside of the bathtub. He needed a new one. The ceiling was a mess. The walls were just peeling away, revealing countless lives and tastes that had lived in this apartment and used this bathroom. It needed the work, the care, the love that Dad had given ours. How he would sweat as he scraped paint off. He and I were going to finish. He had prepped the bare walls before he died. I had done nothing.

I rushed through rinsing and ran into the kitchen, naked and dripping across the sticky linoleum floor. Booner, in just his jeans, top button undone, knelt on one leg, polishing his boots. He looked like he was posing, drops scattered over his bare shoulders, muscles toned and hard. I pretended I was carrying my camera. Click. Great shot, a man polishing his boots. He was completely in charge of himself. That was what I wanted to be.

His eyes flickered appreciation, green-brown-green, making me beautiful. I lifted my arms and moved my hips like I used to in front of my bedroom mirror when Mom wasn't home and couldn't spy.

With Booner, I wanted his gaze always and only on me. I swung my hips, rolled my shoulders. Look at me, look at me.

"You better watch it, girl. You're right in front of the window." He turned back to his boot, running a cloth over the toe.

The kitchen window was the only one without gates. It looked out into the air shaft and the building next door, a few feet away. I danced over, sidled between the stove and the sink. Let them look, whoever they were in those curtained rectangle windows perfectly parallel with the brick wall.

I felt Booner's eyes like heat on my back, siphoning away my usual fears. Pigeons clustered outside on the windowsill, their round eyes circled with yellow. They were cozy. Their feathers puffed out, keeping them warm. They had an iridescent rainbow of oil on their necks. The soft sound of their cooing slipped in through the glass, a friendly hello. "There's all these pigeons out here, Booner."

I hadn't heard him stand up from his crouch, hadn't sensed him just inches behind me, until hands firmly gripped my shoulders. "Didn't you hear? I said get away from the window." He clamped down and turned me firmly around, stepping in front of the window, covering the sight of me with his body.

I resisted, but I might as well have resisted a refrigerator. He guided me away, walked me into the living room, and pushed me down on the sofa. "This is New York City. Full of perverts. It's not like your little fairyland college, okay? Perverts! And I'm the only one allowed to see my girl naked."

My eyes were level with the zipper on his jeans and a mat of hair on his stomach, which bulged slightly over the unbuttoned waistband. I was still damp from the shower, trickling moisture on the cushion, with my flesh out in the open, air pimpling across my skin. A warm inner heat began between my legs and moved up into my chest, creeping over me. I didn't know how to react.

I remembered his sharp teeth at Eugene's. He hadn't told them about Dad. He bought himself a soda, but he didn't buy me one. At the same time, I saw him uncertain and bewildered at Dad's funeral. I remembered that his mother had left him when he was nine years old.

Maybe it was silly to stand naked in front of a window. At college no one cared what I did because I was a nobody. But Booner cared. He had defended me against Mom. He wanted to protect me from perverts. I didn't want him to be angry. I wanted love again, like me and him in the shower. Love existed as a pure place he had shown me how to enter. He wanted to protect me. I smiled.

"You think it's funny?"

"No." But an uncontrollable urge to giggle gave me an ache in my gut and I couldn't look at him glaring down at me. I bit my lip. I smothered my mouth with both hands until I finally got control. "I won't stand naked in front of the window," I said. "I didn't realize."

"Yeah, that's what I thought." He reached down and stroked my cheek with his callused hand. I tilted my head to lay my face in his palm. How freeing that Booner knew with complete certainty what to do and what not to do. I could rely on him.

"Hey." I grabbed his arm. "You should put gates on the kitchen window, too, like all the others." Now, that was funny. An apartment with nothing in it but some beat-up furniture, a used TV, and a stereo, but gates on all the windows.

"This sound system is worth a lot of money." Booner went to the cabinet, riffled through tapes.

"Yeah, right." I laughed within the newly set limits. "That's what I'm saying."

He muttered, almost to himself, "Someone might steal *you*."

In the silence that followed, I carefully tucked a froth of pale acrylic filling back into a rip in the sofa cushion, so touched that I couldn't look at anything else.

IT WAS SATURDAY night and we were going out. Booner moved his beeper from one side of his jeans to the other. "Here? Or here?"

"You're wearing your beeper?"

"Hey, girls love these things. You know what it means? Twenty-four-hour call. I'm indispensable."

"Oh, baby!" I snatched his beeper and laid a kiss on it.

"See what I mean?" He smiled his sideways smile, not revealing his teeth.

I brushed my hair and started to braid it, one simple fat braid.

"No braid," said Booner. "It looks good just loose."

So I left it hanging long and free down my back. I wore my black jeans and a tight blue sweater. Mascara, lipstick. And I followed Booner down to the car. The streetlamps seemed to exhale pools of light at intervals along the sidewalk. There was a thrill in the air, sharp as broken glass.

Booner made a right onto a busy street lined with coffee shops and restaurants and a movie theater. Steinway Street, according to the sign. "This is the main thoroughfare of the neighborhood," he said, as if he were reading a traffic report.

"Thoroughfare?"

"Yeah, that's what they call it."

He switched on the radio and the Fixx were singing "Deeper and Deeper." A car with flames painted on the trunk cruised slowly in front of us. Another sports car trailed behind.

From the opposite direction, a yellow Corvette approached. The license plates said HOT SHOT. Booner honked his horn and the driver waved.

"Remember him?" said Booner. Behind the Corvette, a van rode high on its tires. Booner honked again. "Another one of my buddies." He slid the metal tin from the chest pocket of his jacket, pinched out a clump, and shoved it into the side of his mouth.

"Why do you do that?"

"What? It's just chew. I know it's a bad habit. I'll give it up soon." His cheek bulged.

"Doesn't it cause mouth cancer?"

"Don't those cigarettes of yours cause lung cancer and tit cancer and any other kind of cancer you can think of?"

I laughed. "Not tit cancer. No. I don't think so." But it was permission enough to crack open the window and light a cigarette with a perfect feeling of compatibility.

Booner parked on a dark residential street with a bar on the corner, flashing a light in the shape of a duck. "This is where I hang out," he said. "The Drake."

I got out and stood near him. The Corvette and the van had tailed us here and both parked, too. From the Corvette, a fat guy heaved himself out of the driver's seat. His jacket hung open and he hoisted his pants up by his giant belt buckle as he approached. I recognized the walrus mustache and the beer gut from the night I had met Booner at the Tumble Inn.

"What's up?" he said.

"You know, I worked today and shit. Stopped by Eugene's yesterday and . . ." Booner's voice drifted into the cadence of a monologue.

I finished my cigarette and ground it out under the heel of my boot.

"And who might you be?" Hot Shot asked.

"This is Mandy. She's staying the weekend. I told you she'd be here." Booner muttered to me, "He thought I was full of it."

Hot Shot was a hulking shadow in the dark. "All right, how much did he pay you to come down here?"

"Pay me?" I knew he was joking, but I didn't have a comeback. What would Rose Economopolous say if she were me? I remembered a phrase that Booner used with Eugene. "I'm not one of the four F's, you know, whatever they are," I said.

Hot Shot's tight, oily voice pushed out the words like pieces of something solid: "Find 'em. Feel 'em. Fuck 'em. And forget 'em."

"Don't even listen to him," said Booner with babyish pride.

Booner needed new friends. "Listen to what? I didn't hear anything." I felt strong, way above this guy with his beer gut and his silly car.

"We'll get along just fine. Or we won't," said Hot Shot. "I leave it in your hands."

"He's just jealous." Booner put his arm around me.

We walked three abreast toward the van, which was closer to the light of the bar. It was impossible to ignore the painting of the nearly naked woman on the passenger side. She glowed under sparkling paint, a science-fiction fantasy, all tits and ass and wild hair flying. A scanty Vulcan costume covered up her vital parts, a metallic bikini against a glittering midnight blue background. Her breasts ballooned as large as her head.

"Hey, howyadoin', waddaya think?" A short, wiry guy came around from the driver's side, eye level to the woman's breasts. It would've been a great shot if I'd had the camera. I recognized him from the night at the Tumble Inn, too. He had bought Tracy a drink.

"Lumpy, it ought to be illegal," said Booner.

"Yeah. Obscenity laws," said Hot Shot.

A sharp rapping came from inside the van. Lumpy shrugged and opened the door. "Sorry," he said to a woman, who dismounted from the passenger side like royalty in stilettos and tight jeans, her hand on Lumpy's arm.

"All I ask is a little respect." Her blond hair fluffed out like a halo of light around her face. "You guys are all alike with that stupid picture on the van. You hear me, Lumpy?" She shifted nearer and screamed in his ear, "*Stupid picture!*"

I liked her already, even before she held out her hand. "Since no one's going to introduce us because they're all animals, I'm Donna. I'm the one unlucky enough to be that guy's fiancée." She turned her hand around so the rock of her ring flashed under the flashing bar light.

"Nice ring," I said. "I'm Mandy."

"It's got a flaw. Of course, Dreamboat didn't see it. But we're going back to exchange it next week."

"She's got eyes with a built-in radar." Lumpy laughed as if he were coughing.

"Hey, I told you not to buy anything without me!" Donna moved quickly, in short, fast bursts. "C'mon, let's get a drink. I gotta find out what you see in that guy." She tilted her head toward Booner and steered me toward the Drake's entrance. Behind us, the guys discussed the van.

"The metallic paint's the bitch," said Lumpy. "It takes the longest to dry."

"I bet it does." Hot Shot guffawed and Booner's laugh was a long, low chuckle. I stretched toward him, unwilling to break the invisible thread between us.

"Booner, I'm taking Mandy inside!" Donna screamed.

"Yeah, Mandy, it's okay. I'll be right in."

When I turned, he pursed his lips, blowing a secret kiss that I carried with me into the Drake. Pat Benatar was belting out "Hit Me with Your Best Shot" on the jukebox. And I felt infused with confidence, holding that kiss as I entered the party zone with my new friend, Donna.

"What do you want? I'm buying. You want a White Russian?"

Donna made a beeline for the bar. My sweater, which I had considered tight, fit me like a big sack compared to the low-cut snugness of hers, which hugged her breasts like a layer of skin.

"What's a White Russian?" I shoved my hands into my pockets.

"You like ice cream?" she asked. "Then you'll love White Russians."

Two creamy drinks arrived. We toasted. Vodka, Kahlúa, and milk. She was right. It tasted like ice cream. I wanted to slurp it down in one long swallow and immediately order another, but Donna pulled daintily on her straw and I imitated her.

"So." She spread her fingers out, rock flashing. Her long nails were painted a burgundy color and decorated with a white zigzag of lightning. "I just got them done today. Manicure, pedicure, facial, the works."

"They look great," I said. "I never had a pedicure."

"Never had a pedicure? Honey, you haven't lived!" She snatched my hand, examined my swollen, sore, chapped fingertips and nails hopelessly bitten raw. She winced, just like Mom. "Here, do something useful," Mom would say as she twisted the lid off her nail-polish remover.

"I know they're bad," I said. "I can't stop biting them. My toenails are a lot nicer." I chewed on my straw. The guys came in as I slurped the last cold sweet drop of my White Russian. Booner was telling Lumpy and Hot Shot, "Yeah. Mandy came with me on the job today."

"Ew! What, are you crazy!" Donna covered her mouth in horror. "That is so unbelievable!"

"Hey, she did good. I'm thinking Eugene could take her on," said Booner. "She could work in the office—you know, instead of that ditz who's working there now."

"She might be a ditz, but I like her," said Hot Shot.

"You would, Hot Shot."

Donna held up her empty glass. "Lawrence! I'm empty!"

Lumpy got her another drink. Booner whispered in my ear, "That guy is so pussy-whipped, he can't think for himself anymore."

Pussy-whipped? I tried to picture it.

"You need another drink?"

"Yeah. But, Booner, I want to work on the truck, I don't want to work in the office."

"Whoa," said Hot Shot. "You heard that, Booner?"

"She's a better worker than you are, Hot Shot."

Lumpy said, "You saw Rose? She looks ready to pop her toast any minute!"

"Eugene got her some fish, because with her ankles so swollen, she can't get around much anymore."

"He gets her anything she wants."

"Eugene said he might come down for a drink, too, you know."

"They always talk about work." Donna touched my arm. "I could give you a makeover, you know. I do my sister all the time. And you have natural features. I could do it."

But I was already wearing makeup. I swallowed some of my newly filled drink, cool, milky, and sweet.

"We've been doing up some blow outside." Booner put his face between Donna and me, very close and conspiratorial. "Lumpy said Donna would take care of you, Mandy. Am I right, Donna?"

Donna laughed, a breathy laugh. "I guess that means it's time to powder our noses."

I slipped off my barstool and followed her. I had learned long ago with Tracy that if I didn't get what was going on, I should just keep quiet. We walked into a pink stall. Donna reached into the pale leather seashell of her handbag and took out a folded piece of paper filled with white powder.

Her every gesture contained a certainty of purpose as she scooped a small heap on her long pinkie fingernail and extended it to me. I stared at it.

"Go on. Sniff it up. No, not like that. You gotta hold one side of your nose shut."

I sniffed shooting fire through my right nostril. If Barb could see me now! She always got invited to back rooms at off-campus parties for the real party, where the coke was happening. I wanted to tell Donna about Barb and college and how I came to be here in this bathroom stall. But Donna held out another nailful, and instead of saying anything, I sniffed it up my left nostril. My heart rushed and fluttered. My bowels loosened slightly. A surge of life and energy. I could jog in place, climb the walls, laugh so my laughter bounced off the bathroom tiles.

Donna was sniffing powder now. But no matter where I looked, my eyes were drawn to her tight sweater and her pushed-up chest. She noticed and, without any shame or self consciousness, squeezed one of her own breasts. "I'm wearing a special bra, keeps them up. My sister had a party like a Tupperware party only she had all this sexy lingerie for sale. We had a few drinks and tried everything on. It was a ball. It really was."

"They look great."

"Next time she has one, I'll invite you." Donna, glowing against the pink of the bathroom stall, held another nailful of white powder out to me and I pictured myself trying on sexy underwear with a room full of strangers.

When Mom had bought me my first bra at Lack's, she had stood behind me with a hand on each of my shoulders, practically shouting to the saleswoman, "We think she needs a training bra." But the saleswoman said, "I got news for you. She's too big. Stand up straight. It's hard to fit the young ones, because they don't stand up straight." She had opened drawers, an entire wall of drawers, each holding different brands and sizes of bras. There weren't enough breasts in Ransomville to fill them all. But that was the only time I had ever tried on a bra before I bought it. I couldn't bear the thought of parading around like that in front of anyone, as if Mom would somehow find me and whisper, "I'll let you feel them. It's a gift."

"Go on. We'll finish it up," said Donna.

I shivered, held one nostril shut as I sniffed up the other. Mom couldn't reach me, didn't even know I was missing. I could cut her out of my life like a tumor.

The toilet gleamed and a water lily floated in the bowl. No, it was wet toilet paper. A harsh white taste trickled down the back of my throat. "Wow," I said. "I love this stuff."

"You and me both." Donna held out another nailful for me. Someone banged on the outside door as I sniffed up the powder.

Donna shifted her folded piece of paper to scoop out some more. Her practiced, efficient gestures, the economy of movement, and those nails were so impressive that I wanted to imitate them. With her pale skin and her gray eyes, she was as beautiful and precious as a doll. Her lips were plump, perfect. She flicked her tongue around the paper like a cat's, and licked off all the extra dust. Then she let the paper fall into the toilet.

Light from the fluorescent fixture pinged and zapped across the room. "You gotta get out now, because I gotta pee." Donna laughed and it was infectious. I laughed, too. Our laughter joined together.

"Come to think of it, I could pee, too." I laughed again at the sound of my own voice. Donna was giggling, groping for the button on her pants and shoving me out all simultaneously.

I went into the stall next to hers and felt instantly lonely until her voice wafted over. "Thank God I don't have my period, because my jeans are so tight I would probably get toxic shock syndrome and, lemme tell you, I couldn't deal with that."

I laughed. "Yeah, really." Until the thought jolted me. When is mine due? Just my luck—I'll get it this weekend. I checked the toilet paper. No blood, thank God.

"I'm done!" Donna let her stall door slam.

I flushed and stepped out in a hurry, not wanting to be left behind. Donna was washing her hands in the sink, rubbing her palms together quickly. Her bracelets clinked together. I watched her dry her hands with a paper towel, then take out a makeup case from her purse. She dusted some blush on her cheeks. Her skin was perfect— not a single freckle, not one pimple—unlike mine.

She applied her lipstick, pursing her lips, turning her face to the side in the mirror.

"Here, let me do you." Her face stiffened with concentration as she loomed toward me. I shut my eyes and felt the smooth pressure of her lipstick run over my lips. When she was done, my mouth looked almost like hers, plump, full, and perfectly shaped, only bigger. I pursed my lips like she had done, turned my face to the side. Maybe it would be fun to get a makeover.

A drink waited at my place at the bar. Booner had parked himself where Donna had been, which meant I was sitting next to Booner now.

"Would you jump in my grave that fast?" she said to him.

I felt bad that she had lost her seat, but I liked being near Booner. I gulped down my drink. My tongue felt electric. I couldn't stop moving. This place was entirely different than the Griffin or the Rathskeller or the Tumble Inn. The bar was horseshoe-shaped and large. Glasses hung off ceiling racks, reflecting bluish light. The metallic surface of the bar was cold to lay my elbow on. In the center was a mini dance floor. Donna headed toward the dancers. She wiggled her hips on the outskirts, looking like she wanted to join them.

A Madonna song played on the jukebox. I danced in my seat, shrillness breaking out inside me as I watched the dancers move like mechanical puppets across the floor to "Like a Virgin." Each move made perfect physical sense coordinated with the next one, an uplifted arm followed by a swing of hips. Perfect! I wanted to shout, and wished I brought my camera.

I felt a tap on my shoulder and I twirled back around to Booner, who was holding out both hands, clenched in fists. His fists were strong, loving, beautiful, and I would be able to see them whenever I wanted because of the picture I had from our morning on the job. "Pick a hand, any hand, and you will understand!" He shouted above the music. Faces seemed to flash by as though he and I were going around on a carousel. I pointed to his left hand. He opened his palm. Empty.

"All right," he shouted. "You can take another chance!"

I pointed to Booner's right hand. He turned his fist up, opened his fingers, and in his palm lay a small blue velvet box. "What's that?"

"It's for you. Take it."

The box was light, the velvet smooth as a purr. I lifted the lid very slowly, but my grip was shaky and the box snapped shut. Booner plucked it out of my hands. "I'll open it for you."

His fingers trembled. I was transfixed. It couldn't be a ring like Donna's. Booner and I barely knew each other. The black crescents of dirt embedded in each of his fingernails contrasted with the smooth blue velvet of the box. I tried to drag my eyes away, but I couldn't. The music seemed to pause in a bubble around Booner and me, a bubble that contained his shaking fingers and dirty fingernails. There was nowhere else for me to look.

Inside the velvet case was a delicate gold chain with a tiny diamond pendant shaped like a teardrop. It glimmered in the light just as the song ended, in the gap before another began. The dancers paused on the dance floor, wiped the sweat off their foreheads. "Oh, Booner."

"Oh, Booner," someone imitated in a high-pitched voice. My face burned and I knew the red splotches were rising from my neck to my cheeks. Hot Shot's walrus mustache twitched, leaning into our space. "Oh, Booner." He smooched at Booner, ridiculing.

The Specials came on the jukebox with "Rudi, a Message to You," and I was thankful for the noise of it.

I wanted Booner to shove Hot Shot so hard he'd go flying. But Booner didn't seem to notice. Even worse, Booner was beaming at me, his face collapsed into creases that I had never seen before. He usually gave such a careful half a grin, and, dismal, I understood why. When his face was wide open, he looked like a dork. I wanted to hide until we were alone. Why would he give me this necklace at the Drake so his friends could laugh at him?

Behind him, Lumpy said, "Mandy, you better appreciate that necklace, because it's probably the only thing you'll ever get out of that cheapskate."

"You should talk!" said Donna.

"He's not a cheapskate," I said.

Hot Shot was laughing so hard his gut shook with a life of its own.

"Don't laugh at him," I said.

They laughed harder. "Aw shit," Hot Shot said. "He's got you fooled."

"Put it on." Booner widened his smile, showing the gaps between his small sharp teeth. He looked like a pathetic little kid whose mother had abandoned him, and I didn't want to put the necklace on, not while his friends were still laughing. His stubby-ended fingers, callused and encrusted with dirt, trembled as they touched the thin gold chain. As I helped him untangle the necklace from the crevices of the box, I was horrified that my hands were shaking even worse than his. And what if my neck was too thick for such a delicate chain? All of his friends would see.

His cold fingers at my nape sent shivers like wind across the surface of a pond. He fastened the clasp. I shut my eyes and rested in the darkness of my eyelids like an ostrich. When I opened them, someone had bought me a shot of something, which I guzzled immediately. It burned down my throat into my belly. Southern Comfort. It calmed me. I reached for my cigarettes, which I had tucked in my sock so I wouldn't have to carry a purse.

I felt the chain around my neck, the diamond teardrop in the hollow of my collar bone. I put my arm around Booner, leaned in close, and whispered, "Thank you," in his ear. And thankfully, he stopped smiling. He turned. His lips touched mine. His friends howled and clapped and stamped. Booner didn't acknowledge them. "You bring out the best in me." He spoke into my ear, but his voice entered my heart. If he could ignore his hooting friends, so could I.

I sat a little taller, tilted my chin up, ran the diamond drop along the chain. He put his arm around me, unafraid to show his friends, the world, that he cared. Love was a surging ball of energy bouncing between us.

Joan Jett screamed, *"I love rock 'n' roll, so put another dime in the jukebox, baby!"*

"Let's go." I took his hand and we went to the dance floor, escaping his friends in the tumble of the crowd. Lights flashed on moving bodies, colors swirled, music throbbed, and when I shifted my head, the chain caressed my neck. He loves you, it said.

"Are you really leaving me tomorrow?" Booner slurred, laying his heavy head on my shoulder.

I tightened my arms around him, tiptoed to whisper into his ear, "Only if you want me to."

PALPITATION

BOONER HAD ALREADY left for work by the time I awoke to sun streaming in my face and nothing to do but wait for him to come home. Nowhere to go. No money, no clothes but what I had packed for the weekend. Sunday had come and gone, but I hadn't returned to college. "Stay as long as you want," Booner had said.

I lay naked on the mattress under an electric blanket with the control set to seven on a dial that went to ten. I was gloriously warm. Moisture formed between my breasts, under my arms, and in the crooks of my elbows. Around my neck hung a delicate chain with a diamond teardrop. I poked my toes out and the air was so cold that I yanked my foot back under.

While Booner was at work, the apartment was purely and entirely mine. I could take my time getting out of bed. No one needed or expected me, or even knew where I was. When I finally got up, I boiled water for instant coffee. I lit a cigarette and placed myself firmly in the day. Then I turned on the radio and danced over the orange shag rug to Van Halen's "Jamie's Cryin'." I was reeling, weightless, flying.

I took the garbage out, one bag at a time, four trips up and down the stairs. I found cleanser under the kitchen sink to scrub the linoleum with. The black streaks that had seemed like permanent scratches actually came clean. I scrubbed until the floor gleamed pale yellow like shiny old mustard, faded almost to white in areas. It reminded me of home, scratched up where color had worn off in a path from the front door to the living room, a history of habits.

Next, I attacked the bathtub, with its big clawed feet. I scoured until my arm ached and whole areas of the tub lightened from gray to white as I worked. Miraculous. It had only needed me to reveal its true splendor. Dad and I had worked this way, sanding wood for the puppet theater or the dollhouse or the cross for Mom's lost baby. *Elbow grease, Mandy girl, elbow grease,* he would say. We would get lost in the pleasure of working. As I scrubbed madly, he was with me. He was everywhere around me.

The tub so gleamed and sparkled when I finished that the rest of the bathroom looked doubly shabby by comparison. With a thrust of joy and energy so strong I felt I could sprint around the apartment endlessly, I knew my purpose. I would paint the walls bright white and make of this bathroom a brilliant, sparkling sanctuary of purity and cleanliness. I would do it in honor of Dad.

I grabbed the camera and took a picture of the bathtub, remembering suddenly the pictures Dad had taken over Thanksgiving weekend. Whatever happened to them? I wanted to go home and get them immediately. But of course that was out of the question.

On the kitchen table were three keys and a twenty-dollar bill. The keys were mine. Booner had had them cut for me yesterday. And I had come to expect the twenty-dollar bill, since there had been one on the table the past two mornings when I got up. The worried face of Andrew Jackson refused to look at me directly. So far, there had been forty dollars. I didn't have much cash of my own and I couldn't refuse Booner's money. I would pay him back. I would get a job. I slipped on my sweatshirt and my jeans and shoved the twenty in my pocket.

There were many stores on Steinway Street and I browsed through them. I bought underwear, socks. I bought a paperback, *Madame Bovary,* that we had just been assigned to read in Modern Lit, and I thought if I could become self-educated like Dad, I wouldn't need college at all.

I had a roll of film developed, too. There was a picture of Barb with an angry expression, holding up her I.D. like a weapon. The photograph of the tree in front of Booner's building came out perfectly. Its branches stretched and pointed up toward the sun like a dance movement, inhibited by the small cagelike fence around it. My favorite picture was of Booner's silhouette against the truck window, a shadow against light. The picture of his fist around the gearshift ended up blurry and unfocused. It must have been the movement of the truck.

It was warmer in the Laundromat around the corner, where I carried our dirty clothes, than it was in the apartment. The Laundromat was filled with the comforting smell of fabric softener and the lull of washers going around and around in a rhythmic slosh. I wore a sweater of Booner's and a pair of his jeans, way too big, but I didn't care what I looked like to anyone except him. I just hoped I wouldn't get my period like an unpleasant surprise while I was wearing his pants. Now, that would be humiliating.

I read *Madame Bovary* while the clothes were washing, knowing it was only for myself that I was reading. There wouldn't be a test on it later, or a discussion. I wouldn't have to run into that guy Jack in class. As a bookmark, I used a picture of Booner drinking a soda as he leaned up against the yellow truck. He looked like a child, proud of himself.

When the buzzer sounded, I transferred the clothes from the washer to the dryer, where they flew in circles, slapping up against the glass. I turned back to *Madame Bovary,* but I couldn't concentrate. I kept remembering Dad. At home, he usually did the laundry, piling it up in a basket to take to the Washing Well. He would set it going and then walk over to the Griffin. He would take a break from the Griffin to put the clothes in the dryer. Sometimes he completely forgot about the clothes until after the Laundromat had shut, and I would pick them up the next morning so wrinkled that Mom said they were unwearable. I would run them through again. The waste of money made her crazy, she said.

I shut the book. I went through my pictures again and stopped at the photograph of Barb standing by the window the day she had told me I needed professional help. I remembered that when I took it, I thought she looked beautiful with light shining on her. But it was an unflattering picture. She was washed-out, her mouth holding a strange crooked openness, and she had a double chin. She had no idea where I was right now, and I wanted to tell her, if only I knew what to say.

A bulletin board full of cards and flyers and messages hung on the wall above the table where people were folding their clothes. It reminded me of college, just a little. Popping right out was the headline CAN YOU HANDLE YOUR CAMERA? Under the headline was a list of courses at the New York Photography Center. I took the flyer off the board and folded it up with the clothes when they had finished drying. Then I carried my basket of warm, clean laundry back outside, around the windy corner, up five flights, and home.

Behind everything I did, I was waiting for Booner to come home from work. He stank of sweat and garbage and pushed me away when I tried to kiss him. I wasn't hurt. I understood he was ashamed of his filth and his smell. He pulled off his clothes, left them in a heap on the clean kitchen floor, and headed for the shower. I waited for him to emerge, naked and damp, hard and muscular as a god, droplets clinging to his skin, eyes twinkling, mischievous. I waited for him to kiss me. I loved waiting. I had never felt so free.

"What did you think of the bathtub?" I asked. "Did you notice I cleaned it?"

"Yeah, I never knew it was so bright." He dampened me with his wet, naked hug.

It was easy to leave college behind. There was no one to stop me.

Booner said, "Let's get some pizza or some Kentucky Fried." Eventually, we drove to a diner, where he ordered a burger deluxe with french fries, a pickle, and Coke, no ice. I ordered grilled cheese, french fries, and a chocolate milk shake. I poured ketchup on my plate and dipped my sandwich in at every bite.

When the check arrived, Booner paid and I stared at the oozing residue of oil and ketchup, wondering how I was ever going to repay him. He never mentioned the twenty-dollar bill I found in the mornings on the table and neither did I. I followed him out to the car and slid into the passenger seat, my seat. "What about this job at GeneRo Corp.?" I asked.

"Yeah, I gotta talk to Eugene about that."

"What about if I took a photography class?"

"Yeah, right." He drove fast, his eyes on the road, and he parked with quick precision. I watched his hands on the wheel and waited for their touch.

At night, we lay on the sofa with the TV on, though we didn't watch. Booner kissed the top of my forehead, kissed the tip of my nose, kissed my neck. The ache he brought out in me began in my breasts and moved down with his kisses, right down to my toes.

We moved to the rug, and he flicked his tongue along my belly button, my inner thighs, pushed my legs apart, and, oh, the heaviness of his head there, his eyes bright in the dusk of the room as he glanced up. "You like that." I stopped existing except as desire and I felt the lurch of coming, heard him lap me up, lapping with his tongue, his thick, precious, lovable tongue.

Then it was my turn to do him. He kneeled above me on all fours, looking down at me, crawling over and touching my lips with the tip of his penis. "Kiss it." I was caught between distant thoughts about flunking out of college, about getting my period, and about how I should call Mom because she had no idea where I was and my own moist, helpless pleasure with the memory of coming into Booner's tongue. I surrendered to the pleasure while the tip of Booner's penis smoothed my lips and I opened my mouth to play my tongue over an indented part of the head.

Booner drew my hand over his balls. "Touch there, like that." It made me weak, his knowing so surely what he wanted. I sucked until my jaw cramped and my cheeks ached, until I felt the slight swell as he moved, and I was caught with a sickness in the back of my throat at the sweet-salty taste of his semen. We left our clothes on the sofa and walked into the bedroom, where Booner fell asleep instantly and began to snore. I managed to sleep by timing my breath with his until I didn't even hear it.

THE NEXT DAY, I walked up Steinway Street to a hardware store, where I bought cans of white paint, plaster, spackle, scraper, brushes, and a drop cloth. Dad would've been proud. I also found, in a discount clearance bin, long beaded curtains. I carried it all ten blocks and started to scrape the bathroom walls as soon as I got home. Just a little prep work and then I'd take a couple days to paint it.

Huge chunks of plaster dropped off, only to reveal another layer of paint. Then a chunk three layers thick fell off, which meant I would have to scrape even further down. Cockroaches scurried in and out of the cracks. It was going to take more than just a little prep work before I got to the painting part. I thought of the bathroom at home, unfinished, all prepped and waiting to be painted.

I gulped down tears. But I didn't stop scraping. I could cry all I wanted here. There was space, and no one I had to squelch my tears in front of. My grief was mine like my camera was mine like my limbs were mine. No, it was more mine than anything I owned, and I nursed it like a little life, crying as I worked, sobbing over the wall and the gritty, grindingly endless layers of ugliness.

At about two in the afternoon, I began to feel the now-familiar urgency of preparing for Booner's arrival and I had to call it a day on the prep work. I had completed only a portion of the wall above the bathtub. There it was, like a wound on a homely person. I cleaned the tub again, rinsing off paint chips and plaster.

When Booner came home and headed right for the shower, I waited until he came out. He didn't mention the scraped wall above the bathtub or the cans of paint under the sink. "Hey, Booner, did you notice anything different in there?"

"Looks like you have plans." He gave a guarded smile.

"See what I bought?" I spread the beaded curtains out on the kitchen floor.

"What the hell is that?"

"Curtains. For the bedroom."

"Shit. Some curtains."

"I thought we could screw them in over the bedroom doorway. Don't you think they'll look cool?"

"I don't know." Booner scowled. "Why do girls always gotta do this kinda stuff?" I pictured Dad's power drill and coffee cans filled with screws and wall fasteners cluttering his worktable in the basement. He would approach the mess and find what he needed in a second. *Let's go, Mandy girl,* he would say, *no time like the present.*

"What do you mean?" I asked. "What kind of stuff?"

"You know." Booner kneeled down on one leg and picked up a strand of the round plastic beads as though they were going to sting him.

"C'mon. They're cool." I felt sort of desperate. I hadn't even considered that he might not like them. They were a hippie item that Barb would have loved. "Okay, Booner. You don't have to do anything. I'll put them up. You'll see. You'll love them. Where do you keep your tools, you know, like a drill, screws, and stuff?"

"I got a hammer and some nails." He took a folding chair into the bedroom, and I followed him with the beaded curtains. "The things you make me do," he said as he climbed onto the chair.

But I had told him I would do it and he was holding the hammer wrong, hammering the nails in crooked.

"You know, Booner, you should swing with your whole arm, because . . ."

"I know what I'm doing." He glared, hammer poised. "Don't push it, okay?"

I shut up, hurt. He didn't have to use that tone of voice. Every bang of the hammer made me blink. I covered my ears and the banging was muffled. I released my hands and the banging returned. Covered. Released. I created a *wah-wah-wah* by blocking and releasing my ears. It was fascinating, like a science experiment, though I didn't know what I was trying to prove. Maybe I had been pushing Booner and it was wrong to buy the curtains. Maybe he was mad because it was his money. Maybe he was starting to get bored with me.

Once he got them up, Booner stepped off the chair and stood, arms folded across his chest. "Go on." He tilted his head at the curtains and I was relieved to see his half-smile. I touched my diamond drop and walked through the doorway, then back again. Pink plastic beads rattled, smoothly parting over my body.

Booner stepped through them, too, glanced at himself in the mirror above the dresser, and came back. The beads lingered over his bare chest. Hand in hand we walked through once more, together, entering the bedroom. "I feel like I'm walking into the fucking queen's boodwar," he said.

"Guess what? This *is* the fucking queen's boudoir." I talked to his reflection. On the dresser stood a bottle of Windex and a roll of paper towels that I had brought in earlier, thinking to clean the mirror. I decided to wipe it down now, try to get the brown stains out. But they were under the glass, beneath the reflective surface. The mirror was stained from within.

"You're such a little kid," said Booner, watching.

"I'm more mature than you," I answered, admiring the reflection of the beaded curtains.

"Yeah, right." He came up behind me, circled me in his arms. I tried to wriggle out, because I hadn't finished wiping the mirror. But he tightened his grip and I couldn't move. I felt a twinge of a headache at my temples that I recognized as annoyance, a leave-me-alone feeling that surprised me. Because love was never being left alone—that was the point of love. Booner's hands were clasped together at my stomach and I leaned back into him. He rested his chin on the top of my head and gazed in the mirror, not at me but at himself. In his arms, I was a part of him. He was solid, and even if I leaned back with my full weight, he could hold me easily.

I looked at his half-shut eyes in the mirror before I allowed mine to close. I settled into the slight sway of his body and felt him grow hard. He slid his hands up my shirt, breathing faster. I leaned back into him, more to get on with it than because I was surrendering. We never fell asleep without making love first.

I SLEPT THROUGH Booner's leaving for work and popped awake suddenly. Countless cracks spread a random pattern across the ceiling. They branched out from one huge crack, wavering, shifting, expanding, then contracting. The room tilted. Sour liquid sloshed up my throat. I gulped it down. The ceiling swelled and magnified, and I was going to be sick.

I crawled off the mattress, hit my knee on the floor, and, with my hand clamped over my mouth, stumbled through the living room and around the kitchen corner into the bathroom. I slammed the toilet seat up and retched. The walls spun. I thought I was finished, but as soon as I moved my head, my stomach heaved again, chafing my throat with vomit. I was choking. Snot burned through my nostrils as tears ran down my cheeks. I was all alone.

I wanted Mom to come into the bathroom and pull my hair back like she did when I got sick at home. "No!" I would try to shake my head, but she held me fast. It had made me angry then. I willed her away, but she was ever-present and triumphant, wanting me sick, just like her.

She would sit on the edge of my bed and spoon bouillon into my mouth when I was ill. Maybe I was wrong about her. Maybe she was just trying to take care of me the only way she knew. If she were with me, I would only hate her. But I couldn't stop wanting her. I didn't understand. I started to cry again, then stopped. I was sick of crying.

I heaved myself dry, hollow. I had nothing left. I held the flusher down for a count of ten as water and vomit swirled in sickening circles. Was it the pizza with sausage that I ate last night? The memory of hardened dough, bright red sauce, and cheese coagulating in whitish flaps brought another onslaught of spasms, but nothing came out.

My mouth felt swollen and fuzzy inside. I was shaky. I pushed myself up off the floor, still unsteady. I wiped my nose with toilet paper and looked in the mirror. The girl staring back was pale and bleary-eyed. White crud was stuck to her lips. My lips. I licked them. Sticky gook had gathered in the corners of my eyes. I blinked and picked it out.

I ran hot water, splashing it on my face until it scalded. I turned on the cold tap and cupped my hands, shifting them from one spigot to the other, trying to collect a bearable warmth in my palms. Then I turned off the hot, cupped some cold water, and drank, slurping it up in my puke-lined mouth. I looked a little better after that, almost human, though not as good as I wanted to look even if it was just me and my reflection. Flecks of vomit clung to my hair.

In the shower, I washed it all away. The bathtub was pure white, but paint chips fell off the walls from the velocity of the spray, as if I were washing off a layer of the wall. I felt normal again, not sick in the least, and I wondered. Was I turning into Mom, with strange bouts of disease coming over me? Water sprang off my skin, running hot down my back, my shoulders, my breasts. They were tender. I would get my period soon. Then, with a sickening, heavy logic, I thought: morning sickness.

In the spiraling helplessness of panic, *no* was the solid pole I held on to. Not me. It couldn't be. Don't be ridiculous. If I kept better track of my period, I wouldn't be in this panic. Of course it wasn't morning sickness. It was the pizza. I toweled dry, toweled off my worry.

I pocketed the twenty-dollar bill, reluctant to get used to it, because one day Booner would decide not to leave it and I needed to prepare for that. I found myself plugged into Mom's constant "You can't live on dreams" motif. I wanted to take a class, but I had to get a job. I needed my clothes and my things.

I dialed my dorm room. It rang once. "Start talking." Barb had changed her way of answering the phone.

"Is this State Quad brick house?" I asked.

"Mandy, wow, where the fuck are you? Jesus Christ, it's been a week! I was going to call the cops. Your mother called twice. I told her you were at the library, but, like, it's . . ."

"I'm in an apartment." I said, half-scared, half-proud. "In Queens."

"Queens? What are you doing there?"

"I'll probably stay awhile. I'm, uh, with Booner." I touched the diamond teardrop, ran it along the chain. "I'll get a job and . . ."

"Wait. You're going to stay with that guy? You're mental."

Easy for Barb to say, with her house on Long Island, her boyfriend at home, her boyfriend at school, all her clothes, and all her things. Easy for her to call me crazy. "He loves me," I said. The diamond was cool and moved along the chain with a soothing smoothness. "I wonder if you could send my stuff."

"You can't do this. What about your midterms? Sandra asks about you every day and . . ."

"Does that mean you won't send it?" I interrupted.

I knew she would. Barb was resourceful. She would pack my stuff in boxes, mail it off, and add a story about her crazy roommate to her collection of stories. There was a girl she knew who drank formaldehyde out of a jar in her parents' refrigerator, thinking it was blue, refreshing Gatorade, and who was still living only because she went macrobiotic. There was her drug-dealing paraplegic classmate who drove a van with the brake and gas pedal situated near the steering wheel and who, when drunk, had killed a pedestrian. There was a guy who had fallen into a blazing bonfire at a big party and no one had known he was seriously injured, with third-degree burns, because they'd all been tripping out on mescaline. Now there would be me.

"Is there anything I can do to make you change your mind?"

Who needed college? Freaking out about tests and sleeping with stupid guys and drinking too much—what a waste of time. "I can't think of anything," I said. "But, Barb? When you tell people about me, say I met a great guy and fell in love and I moved on to better things."

"Mandy, life's not like that anymore. C'mon. You took a Women's Studies course. And to tell you the truth, he doesn't seem like such a great guy."

"It's not for you to judge, Barb."

"It's just that first semester, you were a totally different person, you know? The way you're acting, it's not you."

"Maybe the first-semester person is the one who isn't me. Did you say you'll send my stuff?" How could she know who I was if I didn't even know? I gave her Booner's address and phone number and said good-bye quickly. I felt nothing.

I dialed home. Ten rings and no answer. Where was Mom? I called Loretta.

"Your mother is fine. She's getting out of the house, and she's been very involved in the church store."

"It's just that my roommate at college said Mom had called me, but I'm not there. I'm, uh, staying with a friend in New York City. I think I'm going to get a job."

"Give me your phone number. I'll have her call you." Loretta's voice was crisp and businesslike.

"She's fine, you said?"

"She's been praying and healing, and I don't know if *fine* is the word I'd use, but with the help of the good Lord, she'll manage. True concern is shown through gestures. Do you understand what I'm saying?"

"Do you have a pen to write down the phone number?" I didn't even want to try to understand Loretta. I knew her games. I gave Loretta the phone number and hung up feeling empty. But almost immediately a sense of dread, like I hadn't felt in days, filled the emptiness. What if Booner answered when Mom called?

I dialed the number on the flyer I had found at the Laundromat. "I wanted to find out about registering for a class."

"Sure. You can register over the phone. We just need your credit card number."

"But I don't have a credit card." The only person I knew with a credit card was Barb. This was going to be harder than I thought. It seemed that every damn thing was harder than I thought. I needed a job.

"Then you'll have to register in person between the hours of ten and four, but I would recommend you do it as soon as possible. Space is limited."

"How much is the class?"

"Three hundred dollars."

I felt a strange clarity and strength. I had some change left over from Booner's twenties. I still had cash in my suitcase from my last paycheck and my student loan. Technically, I'd be using it for the right thing.

With the camera around my neck and the flyer advertising the class in my back pocket, I walked ten long blocks along Astoria Boulevard, where traffic never stopped. Cars rattled over potholes and trucks rumbled and screeched, shaking the sidewalk, a constant roar, the city's breath. Back home in Ransomville, the ground had been solid under my feet. Except for the wind rushing through the trees and the calling of the birds, it was quiet there and I had walked slow because there was no sense in rushing.

But in the city everyone walked fast, and I did, too. The secret was not to look frantic but to just zoom ahead. I was getting good at it. I sped past warehouses, a couple of delicatessens, a lumberyard, more warehouses and garages, past Nathan's, where guys hung out morning, noon, and night with cigarettes behind their ears. I pretended I didn't hear them whistle at me. I just quickened my pace until I reached the elevated subway.

I walked up the stairs, bought two tokens, and got a complimentary subway map. I was set. I slipped through the turnstile, walked up more steps, and got onto the platform heading downtown, toward Manhattan. It was about ten degrees colder up here. Wind gusted across, and the platform swayed slightly. Only a few people were waiting for the train, and they huddled in the shelter of the stairway. But I felt exhilarated.

The shudder beneath my feet came before the train gleamed around the curve. I studied the map as I rode and checked off the stops as I passed them. Ads lined the train walls above the windows, for computer school, chiropractors, hemorrhoid doctors, and dermatologists. I got off at Twenty-third Street and walked east, camera around my neck. I was in Manhattan, the magical, twinkling world I saw from our roof. This was as real as working on Booner's truck. I felt the wind rushing through my coat and the breathlessness that came over me from walking so briskly.

Booner never took subways. If he had to go anywhere, he drove. This gave me an edge. I had discovered something on my own, completely apart from Booner, and I wanted to stop people in the street to announce my accomplishment. I hadn't felt so free since those first clear days at college, when it seemed that all I had to do was be alive and all the knowledge would come to me because everything was meaningful and for a purpose. Before everything got complicated.

I reached the New York Photography Center and, as if I were dreaming, signed up for the class Black-and-White Camera and Darkroom for Beginners. There was a youngish guy behind a counter who accepted a partial payment in cash, gave me a receipt, and said, "See you Saturday, nine A.M."

"That's in two days," I said, surprised.

"That's right."

For the first time in a week, I was nervous. I had laid down a root. Things were becoming inevitable. I bought a roll of black-and-white film, which added to my nervousness as my money supply dwindled. But when I took a picture of a streetlamp, it calmed me. I needed to focus, to change the aperture opening, and I couldn't do that and be nervous at the same time.

I took a picture of a store window with smiling mannequins whose arms were broken off. I shot a flower display behind heavy plastic at a delicatessen. I stopped and ate a slice of pizza by myself, praying that it wouldn't make me sick, and I waited for the hours to drift by so I would feel an urgency to get home before Booner did, to wait for him to get out of the shower.

I SET THE radio alarm to go off at 7 A.M. on Saturday, to give myself plenty of time. "What's Love Got to Do with It" yanked us out of sleep.

"What the fuck?" Booner muttered.

"I have to get up," I said. "I signed up for a photography class. It meets on Saturdays at nine."

"You did what?"

"And it starts today." I hadn't told him sooner, because I didn't know how to bring the subject up and it hadn't simply presented itself.

"What are you talking about?"

"Well, it's a darkroom class, you know, developing pictures, because I have the camera and I want to learn how to use it and . . ."

"Why did you go and do that without telling me?" Booner stared up at the ceiling. I moved my hand to stroke his chest, his lovely matted hair. He pushed me away. "I don't know you at all, do I?"

"Don't be mad."

But he pouted like a two-year-old and refused to look at me. "I don't even fucking know where this class is."

"It's in Manhattan, on Twenty-third Street. I went there a couple days ago to sign up." I spoke quickly. "I just really want to learn how to develop pictures, and it seemed like a good idea. You know, I've been here over a week and I . . . maybe I should go back to college."

"You *went* there? Holy shit. What the hell else are you doing while I'm at work?" Booner shifted his head back and forth on the pillow. "You're going to leave me. Is that what you're saying?"

"No. I want to stay here as long as you want me to. I . . ." I paused, afraid to say the words, to cheapen the widening sense of gratefulness I felt toward him.

"How the hell did you get to Manhattan without me?"

"I took the subway." I couldn't help feeling a little proud.

"Aw, man, you took the subway? By yourself?" He sat up. "You want to take a class? Take a class. I don't have a problem with that. There's shit I got to do today and I wanted to do it with you. But you have other plans. You want to be riding around on the fucking subways. That's fine. I'm easy."

But his tone of voice didn't sound easy. "What were you going to do?"

"I was going to get something to eat at the diner, wash the car, stop by Hot Shot's, see if he's got weed for sale. Maybe drive down to the park."

Was I ruining our love? I touched the necklace that I never removed, not even when I went to sleep. He wanted to show me his life, and I was denying him that. But . . . "I've got an idea, Booner. Why don't you take the class, too? I have a subway map, it's easy. We could develop pictures together and . . ."

"That's your thing. I don't take subways, and I'm through with school. I learn from life."

"But I was wondering then. If I'm staying here, maybe that job you mentioned, you know at GeneRo, working with you?"

He looked thoughtful. "You mean it?"

I nodded, suddenly breaking out in a sweat under the blanket. "I could pay half the rent, and we could be equal partners and . . ."

"I'll look into it. And while you're off having fun, I'll be washing the car for you. The things you make me do. I never met a girl that wanted to take a class."

"Rose said she wanted to take classes at the community college," I murmured.

"Yeah, Rose. You have all the answers, don't you? I'm not letting you take the subway. I'll drive you there." He put his arms around me, and I cuddled damply in his warmth.

"I love you," I whispered.

He answered by squeezing me so tight it hurt and my back cracked and I couldn't breathe except in short, shallow gasps. He held me like that for so long, I knew it meant he loved me, too.

When we made love, I knew he loved me. When we got dressed

and went down to the car, he opened my door first. Love again. He stopped at a coffee shop, came out with two cups to go, and he remembered sugar for mine. As he drove, I sat in the front seat of his car, camera in my lap, carefully drinking my sweet coffee, filled with the assurance of his love.

I was late, because we hit traffic on the Fifty-ninth Street Bridge. Booner pulled up in front of the building and I kissed him good-bye. He was wearing metallic sunglasses that reflected my face back at me, warped and weird. "When should I pick you up?" he asked.

"You don't have to. I *like* taking the subway."

"You like the subway." He shook his head. "Sick puppy." But I thought I heard a certain pride in his voice, and I held onto that when he peeled out, screeching a U-turn with his black Camaro in the middle of the street. I walked into the building and looked up my classroom on the large sheet posted in the lobby. It was like college, in a good way.

There were ten people in the class plus the teacher, an older guy with a scraggly beard and sharp, inquisitive blue eyes. He wore a gray T-shirt that said FUZZY BY NATURE, and his name was Doug Harrison. "Hey, good goin'. You brought your camera with you. All right."

He was talking to me! He reached for my camera, and I was proud when he held it up, demonstrating f-stops and depths of field to the class. "I'm going to give you assignments and you're going to shoot rolls of film. Then you're going to develop negatives, and by the time you come in next week, we'll head straight for the darkroom."

A small middle-aged woman nudged me. "How did you know to bring your camera in?"

"I don't know. I just brought it."

A guy raised his hand. "I'm wondering, since I need my artistic freedom, why we have to get assignments? Because I'm, like, totally self-motivated and I'd rather do an independent study sort of thing."

"The assignments are given to force you to learn all the techniques I can teach, especially ones you might not go toward independently. Any other questions?" Doug Harrison handed out sheets of paper with recommended readings, shows, and a list of supplies.

"You want to get a tank like this." He held up a cylindrical metal jar with a tight-fitting cover, which he pried off. "This cover is what makes the tank light-tight. It has this opening"—he pulled a small cap off and tilted the cover toward us—"so you can pour in the chemicals without letting in any light. It's called a light trap. You'll need reels that fit right in the tank, like so. And it's essential that you have a thermometer and a timer. We supply the chemicals."

More things to buy. More money to spend that I didn't really have. I definitely needed a job. A murmur had begun among the students.

"People! I'm talking! Okay. The trickiest part of this is loading the film onto the reels, because it must be done in total darkness. Once you do that, you shut the top and the lights can be on for the rest of the process." He talked with authority, but he smiled at the same time, as if to say, C'mon, this is fun. We're having fun!

We trooped after Doug Harrison to a brightly lit room full of sinks. He demonstrated with an unexposed roll of film, snapping it open with a can opener. He cut off the leader and laid the film into the grooves of the spiral reel, rolling it on. He manipulated it with such dexterity, I was impressed. I wanted to try.

When he finished, he placed the reel in the tank. He pushed the cover on and began to explain the chemicals: developer, stop, fixer. First, he poured in developer. He shook the tank with circular movements. "We're agitating here to make sure that every negative gets the same amount of developer." He emptied the tank and poured in the stop.

I took notes, wanting to remember every detail. Others were taking notes, too. But not the independent-study guy. Nor a woman with intricate black and white bracelets tattooed on both wrists. She folded her hands together, tilted her head, and blinked continuously, not taking her eyes off Doug Harrison for one second.

"It's very important to be careful, to pay attention to each and every aspect of the process here, because the negative is the source of the print and you can't make up for a bad negative."

Three hours flew by. The assignment for the week was to take pictures of things in our daily lives. It was starting to rain when the class ended, and I held my camera inside my coat. It began to rain harder as I walked to the subway and I started to run. Drops jabbed the wet pavement, slanting in my face.

The station was four long blocks away and I was drenched, giving off the musty smell of wet wool, by the time I slipped my token in the turnstile. I shivered as I waited for the train, but it didn't matter. I had my camera, an assignment, notes, and a purpose. You can't make up for a bad negative, I thought. Then, unexpectedly, I think, therefore I am.

SUNDAY I AWOKE to the sound of the rain tapping against the window. Hard, fast, sharp little drops spat through the cracks in the ceiling, landing in a tinny rhythm in the pan that Booner had placed at the foot of the mattress. Booner's arm pillowed my head. His other arm was wrapped around me. I was warm; my breath condensed against his skin. He tightened his grip, shook me. "When I wake up and you're here, I think I'm still dreaming."

"You mean a nightmare?" My voice muffled against him.

"No way." He rolled on top, his clammy skin against mine, his body heavy, pinning me down. He was hard and we were sweaty, gummed together. I wanted to get out from under, but he swallowed my mouth in his kiss and a trickle of heat and desire dripped inside me. It felt so good, I was ashamed and shut my eyes to hide the shame.

His hand was large and full of purpose, moving between my legs, and though his breath was stale, webbed with the acrid stench of last night's Chinese food and unbrushed teeth, my own disgust heated my body as much as his hand and the sound of his moan. I was thankful the horrible urge to vomit hadn't come over me. Then I went wet and creamy and felt as though I were dreaming, waves upon waves in a rush through a tunnel, twisting and turning. He began to thrust and I exploded.

"Oh baby, oh baby, oh baby," he chanted as he came. Then he lay inside me and I didn't care if I couldn't breathe. To lie like this beneath him was the heaven I believed in.

But the phone rang. He rolled off me and I panicked. It was probably Mom! Why had I called her? I jumped up, ran through the beaded curtains and across the orange carpet, where I knocked the ashtray over. "Hello!" I panted.

"Yeah, Booner there?"

"Who's this?" I was so relieved I felt dizzy. I stretched the long phone cord over to the forbidden window where the perverts lurked behind their curtains, and I smiled at the pigeons huddled on the windowsill.

"It's Lumpy. This is whatsyername, right, Mandy. How ya doing. Put Booner on, woodja? I gotta ask him about later."

Naked except for my necklace, I looked down the air shaft, tingling inside to imagine eyes on me, framed by the window. And I wasn't really me but a picture of me, watched through the lens of an invisible camera. I felt alive with the tingling, conscious of my own aliveness. Maybe someone was actually watching me!

I walked back toward the shelf and put the phone down just as the beads rattled and Booner emerged from the bedroom. "It's Lumpy," I said.

He picked up the phone. "Yeah, what do you want?"

I grabbed the scraper off the kitchen table. This was a perfect time for working on the bathroom. I stepped naked into the tub and started where I had left off, scraping out from the center. Soon I was sweating. No problems, just opportunities, Dad used to say. There were countless layers of paint to scrape off, but I would do it without crying, scratch away until I reached the structural level. Then the painting would begin.

But this bathroom was much worse than our bathroom at home. Dad would never have stood naked in the tub, working. He was probably ashamed of his body. Once when his robe, which was loosely shut with the skinny tie he used as a belt, had parted to reveal the flesh of his massive gut, rolling over his belly button, I had quickly averted my eyes, ashamed on his behalf, afraid to see any more.

Sweat poured down my body, dripping even between my thighs, like blood might. I looked down at myself, but there was no blood. Just sweat. Chunks of paint stuck to my skin. Why didn't I have my period yet? I scraped harder, scraping away that stupid, scary question. An ache began in my shoulder and moved down my arm. Maybe I was developing tendonitis, like Mom, or bursitis or soft-tissue arthritis.

"Man, every inch of you shakes when you do that." Booner was leaning in the doorway, arms folded across his chest.

I felt ugly then, humiliated. A quivering mass of naked flesh, like the glimpse I had caught of Dad's stomach. "Don't you have anything better to do?"

"Nope. I like what I see."

The blush that swept over me felt like an added heat beneath my sweat. Not wanting to look at Booner, I watched my hand lay the scraper down on the sink.

"Eugene's having some people over. Girlfriends, too. Good thing Lumpy called, because I forgot all about it."

"Oh." This bathroom project was convenient. I was already naked, already standing in the tub. I only had to shut the curtains and turn on the shower. *Fwoosh.* Rinse off.

Booner stepped in naked as I was shampooing, and we made love again, standing under the shower. "Bet no one ever did you like this, huh?"

When I didn't answer, he said, "What, I can't hear you."

"No," I said, embarrassed.

"No what?"

"No one ever did me like this."

"That's right." Booner's need was tireless.

After we got dressed, I watched him hook his keys on his belt loop and I felt privileged to know so intensely and so well the man beneath the clothes.

"You're always looking at me with those bedroom eyes," he said. "Those jeans tight enough or what?"

"C'mon, Booner, stop."

"I'm not allowed to compliment my girlfriend?" He pinched my butt as we walked out the apartment door, and I took the stairs down two at a time so he couldn't do it again.

It was a short trip to Eugene's place. Booner swerved and lurched through traffic with the rain sliding down the windshield. In no time at all, we were walking up the path to the tidy brick house.

Before Booner even rang the bell, Eugene opened the door. "Thought you'd never get here!" A fat cigar hung from between his lips. When he puffed, it sizzled slightly. He handed it to Booner and lit another for himself.

"Aren't you supposed to give these out *after* the baby's born, Gene?" Booner puffed once and coughed. I wanted one too, just to be a part of things, but no cigar was offered.

"I couldn't wait that long. It's weeks away." Eugene ushered us into the living room. There was no one in it. The room was like a museum. There were no ashtrays, no indentations in the sofa pillows, nothing amiss or out of place. The ceramic shepherdesses had gathered no dust.

Booner was still coughing, trying to stifle it. He clapped his hand over his mouth and attempted to talk through his fingers, eyes watering. I felt sorry for him and hit him on the back to help him get the cough out.

"Jesus, she's beatin' up on me!" he squeaked.

"Mandy, I don't know how you do it, but it's good to see you're sticking with this guy." Eugene's approval as he put his arm around me was like warmth on a cold day. I almost leaned into him as if he were Booner. But he wasn't Booner. I got confused. My cheeks burned. I pretended to check my camera case.

"That's a nice lookin' camera. I'm glad you brought it. I told Rose to remind me to get film, but she forgot," Eugene said. "Booner told me you were into taking pictures."

"She brings that camera everywhere, Gene." Booner wiped his eyes.

"The guys are out in the garage. We got beer, snacks, cigars, anything you want." The velvet tickle of the hair on Eugene's arm along the back of my neck unnerved me. "C'mon, Mandy, Rose and the girls are in the family room."

"Family room!" Booner snickered. "So that's what you call it. You're all set, aren't you, Gene?"

"If you're gonna have a family, you need a family room. Right, Mandy?"

I allowed him to lead me away. Why was Booner exiled to the garage? There was no time to wonder. Eugene opened the door to the family room and an outburst of voices and laughter.

The room was full of girls and women all dressed up in sweaters with sequins and stretch pants, or dresses with heels and stockings, talking, laughing, gesturing. The air was filled with perfume. No one else was wearing jeans. No one else had a hole in the toe of her boot. Pink streamers were draped along the ceiling from one wall to the other, twisting prettily. "Rose!" Eugene pushed me in, gentle but firm.

Rose was lounging in a rocking chair in a flowing lavender dress with what looked like an enormous beach ball in her lap beneath her dress. Her legs were crossed at her ankles, fat and soft as water balloons. They were frightening. They looked like they might explode any second.

But she smiled and waved. "Mandy! Nice to see you!" And if I could have been as beautiful as Rose when she smiled, I'd take her ankles anytime. I turned to thank Eugene, remembering my manners, but he was already out the door, sprinting back to the garage, to Booner and the guys.

Rose talked over me. "Tina, that's Booner's girlfriend. You know Booner?"

"Oh, you poor thing!" exclaimed a short woman with hair pulled back in a velvet hairband.

Another girl said, "Booner's got a girlfriend?"

Rose pointed at me as if she were proud. I touched my diamond teardrop. It was something special, sending love through my fingers and giving me strength. Booner should have warned me to dress up. Lucky guy could throw on any old thing. What did it matter if he was hanging out in the garage? Not that I had anything nice to wear. Not that I even liked dressing up, since it meant churches, funerals. I touched the camera.

"Hi, howyadoin', I'm Arlette." A harsh voice belonged to a woman who held out a limp, deeply tanned hand with gleaming red nails so long they curled over. "I knew Todd Boone ages ago, and you're an angel, lemme tell you, because that guy . . ." She stopped. Her eyes, outlined in black, were avid on me. Her hair was a mass of dark brown curls. She wore a red leather jacket with a red leather miniskirt and shook her shoulders as she continued. "Me and him once had a thing, and in those days it was, like, if it wiggled, he jumped on it. Know what I mean?"

"I wouldn't know about that," I said firmly, and opened my camera case. She must have been one of Booner's four F's: find 'em, feel 'em, fuck 'em. And forget you, Arlette.

I checked the battery and the red light blinked. I took the lens cap off and wiped the lens with a tissue. I should have been using a static-free cloth, but I had to get a job before I could buy everything I

needed. I picked a tiny wad of dirt out of the crevice where the battery went in and stared down at Arlette's black spike-heeled boots,
waiting for them to get the hint and walk away. They didn't.

"Don't get me wrong." Those blood talons scratched my arm.
"That was years ago. Water under the bridge as far as I'm concerned."

"Mandy reformed him, Arlette," Rose called out from her rocking
chair. "She's so good for Booner! He's a changed man."

"Ah, she's reformed him. That's sweet." Arlette said "sweet" like
an insult before she walked off toward someone else.

Reformed him? I wanted to find out exactly what Rose meant,
but she was already greeting another woman. Someone held out a
plastic cup full of pink punch and I looked up to thank her, a woman
with a regal nose and long, dark hair streaked with gray. "Are you a
photographer?"

"Well, um, yes and no." I touched the camera. I couldn't take
a picture and hold my punch at the same time, so I sipped it in a
ladylike way. "I'm taking a class."

A little girl of about eight swerved through a group and slipped her
hand into this woman's hand. "Hi," she said, almost defiantly, to
me. Her hair was parted perfectly straight down the middle and hung
in two pigtails.

"Hi yourself." I laughed, wishing I could have been so defiant at
that age, at any age. "What's your name?"

"This is my daughter, Grace." The woman looked down at the girl
just as the girl looked up at the woman, and it was a perfect picture
of identical mirrored profiles.

"Wait, I'd love to get a picture of you just like that." I put my cup
of punch on the floor between my feet. But they were already looking
back at me. "Look at each other," I told them. "The way you just
did."

They turned to each other, framed in my viewfinder. But they
weren't perfect anymore. The girl smirked self-consciously. Her
mother rolled her eyes. Never mind. I took the picture anyway, so I
wouldn't embarrass them.

"Mommy." Grace tugged at her mother's arm. "I want to keep the
list. Can I keep the list when she opens presents?"

"Presents?" I picked up my punch.

"There's fifteen of them now. I just counted." She pointed behind me, where along one wall was a table full of food next to the peaceful fish tank. Below the fish tank, gifts were stacked, wrapped in bright paper with ribbons and cards. Grace's dark, serious eyes hungered after then. I remembered hunger like that and the enticing look of wrapped gifts, the mystery that disguised the inevitable disappointment when they were unwrapped and turned into alarm clocks and purses from Polly's Surplus.

As if a cold rock were sinking to the pit of my gut, I realized it wasn't, as Booner had said, Eugene and Rose having people over. This was a baby shower, and I hadn't brought a gift.

The cigars made sense then, and so did the segregation. Mom would have known. She would have said, *You don't go, eat people's food, and drink their punch without bringing a gift. Nobody likes a freeloader, Miranda*—which would've been a dig at Dad. She always said baby showers were bad luck, too. When she got pregnant the second time, the ladies from the church surprised her with a shower, after which she miscarried. No one gave her one when she was having me.

I needed to get away from this observant little girl, who probably knew full well that I hadn't brought a gift. I finished my punch in a long cold gulp, held up my empty cup, and said, "Guess I need another." I shifted around a fat woman reeking with perfume, slipped through a group of three laughing girls, and reached the food table, covered in a paper tablecloth decorated with teddy bears.

In the center of the spread was a molded plastic punch bowl surrounded by clear plastic cups stacked upside down. I ladled some punch into my cup and small, square pieces of fruit plopped in. I slurped around them. There were platters with cold cuts and rolls laid out, waxy, fake-looking food. I wasn't hungry. What I wanted was a cigarette, but no one else was smoking.

Why didn't Booner tell me this was a baby shower? Why hadn't I known?

The fish flicked by with their oblivious sideways eyes, opening and shutting their mouths, observing the world from behind a safe glass container. Above the fish tank the sheet of mirror, with no spots or warps, reflected the room exactly. I watched the sea of faces in makeup and lipstick. Mouths moved. Eyes blinked and squinted in laughter, bulged with intensity, and then softened. It was like watching the fish, only larger, and with voices.

Okay. I was the operator and my body became the heavy machinery. Push the smile control. Roger. Wilko. Now, move. I pulled and pushed and shoved the controls and operated my stiff, clanking machine of a body through the room. Check the smile apparatus. Roger. How are the arms doing? Hands empty? Ten-four. Okay, we're moving out. Clank, push, rattle, churn, creak, lurch through the room. I was at the controls. Turn the doorknob.

Ah, the living room lay before me, bathed in a hush. I shut the door and breathed in the quiet. Then I stuck out my tongue, scrunched up my eyes, jutted out my jaw, opened my mouth, made a few hideous faces to counteract all that awful smiling. Much better.

I sat in the armchair I had sat in, was it only last week? It seemed like a lifetime ago, when I thought I was staying for the weekend. I had thought Rose was fat. A stabbing pain in my skull screamed for aspirin. The bathroom was up the heavily carpeted stairs. The smooth metal railing was cool on the inside of my palm.

I switched the light on. There were saucers of potpourri and a floral scent floating through the room, sweet as the punch. The light fixtures by the medicine cabinet were little, smiling angels, sending out twin glows. I shut the door and locked it. Matching towels folded in thirds hung off the rack, too clean to wipe my hands on.

The sink was fake marble tinted pick. Seashell soaps lay in a dish shaped like a snow angel. I ran cold water, splashing droplets over the pristine surface. I rinsed my face and felt almost normal. I cupped my hands and drank. The room began to spin. Was the punch spiked? I sat on the toilet with my head down, waiting for the dizziness to pass. Though my temples were pounding, I was calm, having escaped the baby shower. Maybe I could quietly wait here until it was over.

There was a path of mashed carpet from the door to the toilet. I slipped the camera off my neck. Without lifting my head, I opened the cabinet beneath the sink to look for aspirin. There were menstrual pads, spare toilet paper, bathroom cleanser, bubble bath, and a dented cardboard box that said FIRST RESPONSE. It was open and inside was something in a foil wrapper. I pulled it out, checking behind me, though I knew I was alone.

The question that had been hinting at me for days struck me now, head-on and unavoidable. When was my last menstruation? My teeth began to chatter. I didn't keep track of my cycle. I couldn't even remember today's date. I didn't want to know. I shut my eyes and shifted my position on the toilet seat. The foil wrapper crinkled in my lap.

Would Rose notice if it was gone? If she noticed, would she suspect me? If she did, would she mention it to Eugene, who would then mention it to Booner? I could deny it to the death. I read the instructions. *Hold the plastic strip by the thumb grip under your urine stream. Three minutes later, the results will show in the result window.* Simple.

I had nothing to lose. In a fever, I tore open the sealed wrapper.

A sudden knock disrupted me. "Hello? Anyone in there?"

"Just a minute," I shouted cheerily, falsely. I should've known. Even here I couldn't sit in the bathroom in peace. I turned the taps on so I could pee quickly on the test strip and get it over with. But I was too nervous. Nothing came out. Another voice erupted just outside the door. "Yeah, I'm waiting, but someone's in there."

It was useless! I put the test back in the foil with the directions, wound layers of toilet paper around it, and shoved it into my boot. I would pee on it later. I wiped off the sink, wiped off the handles on the cabinet underneath to get rid of the evidence. Then I picked up my camera, took a deep breath, and opened the door.

Arlette and another woman were standing against the wall. It figured. "Sorry I took so long." I shrugged, with a false smile. "I got my period, you know, surprise?"

Arlette gazed at me like she knew I was lying. But the woman said, "Isn't it always the way?"

I couldn't go back to the party yet. I ducked down the hallway, staying near the wall like a spy, and slipped into a little room with the same thick mauve carpet as downstairs. Bright ceramic goldfish adorned the opposite wall. Beneath them stood a crib with a black-and-white mobile dangling above it. A changing cabinet with diapers was set up at the foot of the crib. Everything in the room smelled clean, new, and innocent.

An empty photo album lay on a brand-new white dresser. Each page was designated: first smile; first tooth; first step; first word. It was just waiting for the baby. I flipped through the blank pages, imagining the quirky face of a chubby little pink-cheeked infant smiling and gurgling at me. A familiar fog rolled in, sweeping over the ache for life to be different, for me to be different.

I was a thief and a freeloader. Trespasser, too. The test jabbed at my ankle and I was stuck with my crime, unable to put it back, because I had already torn it open. I sat on the floor, leaned against the wall. Cloth books, stuffed animals, and bright plastic toys cluttered a small shelf. Ruffled curtains hid the window. If only Rose were my mother.

I pulled out my cigarettes and lit one, polluting the baby's room with smoke. There sat my camera, watching with its neutral eye. If you're pregnant, you won't be allowed to smoke, it said. You won't be allowed to drink or get stoned. But if I were Rose, I wouldn't want to.

I flicked an ash on my jeans and rubbed it in, remembering how I had envied Tracy and Junior at the funeral, laughing together in their own private world. If I were pregnant, I could have that. I would love my baby and it would love me back.

What would Dad have said? *A for anything you want, Mandy girl.* I took another drag, needing to breathe in something more substantial than air. How could I be the mother when I wanted to be the baby? I shut my eyes, my cigarette almost gone. "I think I might be pregnant," I whispered aloud in the room, fighting against the inertia of silence. I was tired suddenly, drained, worn-out, and afraid.

I had to go back, sit by Rose, be with her, absorb her. I held tight to the railing as I walked down the carpeted steps to the living room. No, it was more like a dead room encased in its own emptiness. I dropped my cigarette filter into the pot of a fake rubber tree. Then I opened the door and walked into the baby shower.

The first person I saw, standing pertly in navy stretch pants and high heels with her weight on one leg, was Donna. She was tilting her pointy chin up, her face surrounded by a cotton-candy puff of bleached blond hair. Compared to everyone else, she was my best friend. We had shared drugs in a bathroom stall. We were close. I loved her. "Donna. Hi."

She licked her cherub lips deliberately, carefully, as if a motor inside said, It is now time to lick your lips. Everything she did was logical, considered, and certain. She would never steal anyone's pregnancy test. She sipped her drink like a little bird. Her cheeks pulsed, and she waved to me with her pinkie finger.

"It's great to see you! You look great!" I gushed.

"Thanks, Mandy." Donna laughed an airy little laugh and turned back to a woman I didn't know. "So I said, I'm not wearing my sister's hand-me-down wedding dress. I am buying my own dress . . ."

I aimed my camera at her, because she looked so beautiful and absolutely perfect standing there like an angel, not fake like the ones in the bathroom, but a real angel. Click.

"Don't you dare!" she screamed. "I hate having my picture taken!"

But it was too late. I already had it. "Why?"

Arlette put her arm around Rose. "Take one of us!" she shouted. "You don't mind, do you, Rose?"

I didn't want a picture of Arlette, but I had no choice. Fake it. Don't focus. Crop her out and get a picture of Rose in her pregnant glow with her round, warm, flushed, and happy face, center of everything. When Rose talked, the room listened. "I'll never forget the first time I felt the baby move," she said. "Something touched me from inside like a little massage. I told my doctor about it and he said, 'Oh, that's the quickening.' That's what it's called."

Lucky Rose to be so happy, to be named after a beautiful romantic flower, to live in a house she loved, center of this party with streamers and everyone celebrating. Her every gesture said, I'm happy to receive this attention and I deserve it. I'm glad to be giving you the opportunity to bestow your appreciation on me.

I basked in her light, gazed down at her huge, pregnant mound covered in flowing lavender. Her hands lay softly over it. Did we have more in common than she imagined? "When are you due, Rose?"

"Two weeks." She shifted in her rocking chair. "Mandy." She grabbed my hand, and before I could snatch it away, she guided it over her mound. "Don't be afraid."

And I felt a pulse inside her, leaping, pausing, kicking. A strange feeling drew me in, turned my stomach over, shut my throat around my tongue, and tightened my rib cage. "Wow. It moved."

"Not 'it,' " corrected Rose. "She's a girl, and she's some kind of acrobat."

Ooh. Wow. A collective cooing over the acrobat.

Grace and two other little girls with eyes full of wonder put their hands on Rose's belly. When I shifted my position to touch my own stomach, I had to take a step back, and when I did that, I felt the test poking into my leg.

The women sitting on the sofa were passing around strange-looking pictures. I couldn't make out what they were. A woman with curly black hair and a downy mustache handed me one that looked like a black-and-white TV screen with static, nothing but static. Rose said, "Which one is that?"

I turned it toward her. "Oh, that was the first. Look, you can see her there. She looks like a little bean." Rose pointed to a small, dark kidney-bean shape in the corner of the picture.

"Cute." I shrugged. It looked like nothing. But I understood I was holding a sonogram picture and I passed it along when another was passed to me. Was there a kidney bean inside me, surrounded by static?

I handed the picture to the woman next to me, went directly for the punch, and drank a cupful in one long gulp. I ladled in more. "Come on, presents!" A chorus erupted among the women. "Open the presents! Open the presents!" There were so many of them piled up, we would be here all night, and all I wanted to do was hide in the bathroom and take the test already, to know if it was true.

The little girls ran back and forth, carrying gifts over to Rose, piling them up at her feet. How did they know to do that? Did someone tell them, or did everyone know just exactly what their role was and where they stood with each other? Grace sat on a pillow on the floor, pencil poised, tense. Her mother said, "Pay attention. If you want this job, you're going to have to pay attention." Telling someone else, mother to mother, "She never pays attention, but she always wants to do things. I don't know what's the matter with that girl."

At Mom's one and only baby shower, did she sit in the center like

Rose, the cause of the celebration? Was she smiling and happy? What did I do? I couldn't remember. I had been too young to do anything useful, and I'd never been to a baby shower since.

Rose opened her gifts and passed them around, one at a time. Little hats, diapers, rattles, feet pajamas, and everyone squealing about the size. Ooh, so little! How cute! How adorable! Look at that! I took a picture of Rose holding up a pair of miniature baby overalls. I got one of the girl with her pad and pencil, tongue between her teeth as she studiously wrote down who gave what.

I took a picture of the woman in the velvet hairband as she was saying, "Girls are so much easier than boys when they're little. They're such sweethearts." Her lips shaped themselves into a heart as if to prove her point.

Rose smiled at the camera, but I photographed her ankles.

Someone said, "In China, they leave baby girls on mountaintops to let them die. They're eaten by wild animals."

"Get out of town!"

"No joke. Guys outnumber girls something like thirteen to one in China."

I pictured mountains of dead baby girls in pink buntings, with soft pink lips and round, surprised expressions, like stacks of dolls gazing up to heaven.

"Thirteen to one! I wouldn't mind!" Arlette strolled in, sniffing deeply, all voice and nails. "A girl can pick and choose in that situation. Believe me, there's a *man* shortage in America."

I plucked a piece of fruit from my cup and popped it into my mouth. What was Booner doing right now? When could I be with him? What would he think of me if he knew I stole this test? If he even knew I had to take it?

"I'm thinking about getting my tubes tied," a woman said. "I got three. That's enough."

"God forbid something happens to one of the them," said Rose. "Excuse me for saying."

"Don't get your tubes tied, get your man fixed! Right? Am I right?" The mustached woman cackled like a witch and laughter rippled around the room. We were all in the same boat in the end.

"Say cheese," I said, honing in on her just as she turned in the light and the shadow on her face made her look like Hitler.

A girl declared she would have a baby by the age of twenty-five whether she got married or not. "Even if I gotta go to a sperm bank," she said.

The older women clucked and sucked their teeth, aiming their collective disapproval on the girl. I took a picture of her face. She was young, fresh, and determined, willing to speak her mind.

"Hey, Mandy, cop a squat." Donna patted the sofa, shifting over so the others around her also had to move to clear a spot for me. The mustached woman resented it. I saw her roll her eyes and shift as little as possible in a charade of making room. Get over it, lady, you'll never see me again. I would never do this again. I would go back to college, far away from these people. I perched on the edge, thanking everyone for accommodating me, thank you, thanks, and smiling sweetly, hoping to cover up my evil thoughts.

The woman with the hairband asked me, "So, are you and Booner really serious or what?" I didn't know what to say.

"I've known Booner for years because of Lawrence, and when he started going out with Mandy, he turned into a nice guy. I didn't know he was a nice guy. I never used to like him." Donna bathed me in the love of her smile as she turned the rings on her fingers. She even had a gold ring with a little charm on her thumb. She was my best friend, and I leaned my head against her. "Thanks for saying that."

"I meant it," she declared. "I don't just say things, I mean them."

"You walk the talk," I said. It was something they used to say at church, and it meant your word was good. Donna looked puzzled, but the conversation had already slipped away.

"I just love working in Manhattan," someone across the room was saying.

"Me too." said Donna. "I'm a legal secretary. It's so interesting. In meetings, my boss likes me there with him and I take notes and everything. Do you work, Mandy?"

"I don't have a job right now, but Booner was thinking about my working for Eugene, you know, in that little office in the garage."

"You don't want to do that, believe me. Get a job of your own. There's lots of jobs in Manhattan." Donna shook her head, quiet and insistent, gesturing with a careful wave that this was not meant for Rose to hear. But Rose's attention was far away. Someone had made a hat out of the decorative ribbons and placed it on her head like a crown. She was laughing.

"Manhattan's great, because you can shop on your lunch hour and there's so much goin' on. You work for GeneRo . . ." Donna shuddered. "There's nothing. I did it for a little while. There's nothing there."

"Well, I don't know if it's going to happen anyway." I thought of my fantasy, waving at Booner from behind the glass in the makeshift office while the trucks belched and rumbled. I couldn't do that with a baby on the way, getting slowly fatter behind the desk until I filled the entire cramped office.

What were the guys doing right now in the garage? Making ribbons out of measuring tape or bits of tubing and wires? All this smiling hurt my face, but everyone else was smiling, too. Did that mean we were all in pain? My mouth was dry, but the thought of more punch set my teeth on edge. Reality lived in my left boot. I didn't want to know. I took a picture of Rose in her ribbon hat. She wore it well, noble and lovely as a queen.

Donna and the mustached woman lit cigarettes, which opened up permission for me to do the same. I put my camera on the coffee table in front of me, reached into my back pocket, and pulled out my cigarettes, a little squashed, a little bent but smokable, for sure.

Donna, who could smile, talk, smoke, and chew gum at the same time, lit her purple Bic and held the flame in my face without missing a beat. ". . . and my sister got that artificial insemination thing, because something was wrong with her husband's sperm count."

Arlette screamed, "What was he, shooting blanks! Hah, hah, hah!"

"He treats her so well ever since she became a mother," said Donna, not even acknowledging Arlette.

Someone passed me a piece of cake on a paper plate decorated with roses. Chocolate with vanilla icing and little candied hearts. I broke the icing with my fork and took a sweet, moist bite. Between each bite, I took a drag off my cigarette and rolled the smoke around to savor the different textures. It was so delicious, I wanted to keep eating and smoking forever.

"Smile, Mandy. It can't be that bad," Rose called from her rocking chair. I forgot about smiling. How was I supposed to chew and smoke and smile at the same time? I looked around. Others were.

"Smile if you got it last night!" laughed Arlette.

"You're terrible," said Donna. "What I really want is my own little baby, just like you, Rose."

I was sick of babies, everyone talking about babies. I pressed my cigarette out, reached past the mustached woman for the nuts, and shoved a fistful of cashews in my mouth. I chewed so frantically, I bit my tongue and tasted blood as the sting of tears needled at my eyes, and I couldn't sit still for another second.

I stood up then, edged myself out between the sofa and the coffee table. I picked up my camera and the small stack of sonogram pictures lying there, vulnerable to spills. I brought them to Rose. "You might want to put them somewhere safe," I said. She took them, laid them on a box that contained a baby-monitor set, and smiled at me. "Thanks."

Her smile and her thanks forgave me for not bringing a present, for stealing her test, and I wanted to hold that forgiven feeling in place so I could return to it later. A little girl was going around collecting the torn wrapping paper and putting it in a big plastic garbage bag. Others stood as I did, part of a general movement. Rose pressed a pair of tiny pink pajamas against her cheek. She was thanking everyone. "Thank you, it's been so nice. Thank you, thank you." As if everyone else needed forgiveness, too.

I slunk out to the living room and sat in the armchair. The girls' world was behind me, shrieking laughter and good-byes. The guys' world was in front of me, hidden behind the door to the garage. The tinny sound of the radio trickled out and deep-throated men's laughter rumbled beneath it. But here, between worlds, in the big soft chair, was I.

I touched the sharp edge of the pregnancy kit through my jeans and my boot. I would use it as soon as we got home, then I would throw it out the window by the sink. And after that . . . what? I touched the chain around my neck. Love was a long, slow swoon. Love was Booner with his key ring and his curly hair, giving me a look from across the room and eliminating everyone in the world with the power of his hazel eyes. Love was him drawing me in.

As if I had summoned him with my thoughts, the door to the garage swung open and there he was, blessing me with a smile full of warmth and tenderness. "What are you doing sitting in that chair all by yourself? Daydreaming?"

"Nothing, really. Waiting for you."

"Come on." He held out his hand. "It's time to go home."

THE TESTING KIT remained in my boot until the next morning. Booner was at work when I awoke under the blanket with the bed to myself. I felt nauseous again, ran to the bathroom, and threw up. I was getting used to the sickness and its swift, almost immediate passing, like a quick, sharp thunderstorm reminding me that I existed.

I took the kit out of its torn foil wrapper, sat on the toilet, and peed on the plastic strip. Then I laid it on the cardboard tray it came in and put it on the sink to wait for the answer. These people thought of everything, even a cardboard tray so pee wouldn't drip on the sink.

As I waited—one minute, two minutes, three minutes—the result window turned partly purple. I checked the instructions. Purple meant positive. Positive meant pregnant. I shut my eyes. No. I slid my eyelids up and read again through the tiny print. "97 percent accurate in laboratory testing," it said.

A dreadful clang echoed through my skull.

But surely there was a mistake. I paced through the apartment, across the kitchen floor, which had gotten dirty again despite my cleaning, across the shag rug, then the smooth linoleum of the bedroom. I turned and walked back over the rug, then the gritty kitchen floor, feeling one surface then another under my feet, circling around the ominous truth. When the phone rang it was a reprieve. "Hello?"

"I would like to speak to Miranda Boyle, please."

"Mom!" I almost cried. How had she felt when discovering that she was pregnant with me? Was she sick, too? Disgusted? Scared? Happy? I had so many questions that I couldn't ask.

"Miranda, I'd appreciate it if you didn't involve the neighbors in whatever dirty laundry you need to air."

"What?"

"Loretta cares deeply about me. But she's not at your disposal."

Woodenly, I gripped the phone. "I'm sorry."

"Everyone wants something. The people in hell, they want ice cubes."

I waited for a clue as to how to respond, but none came. There was a momentary silence.

"Where are you," Mom asked in the flat hard monotone she had assumed since Dad died.

I spilled the truth. "I've been staying with Booner. Remember Booner?"

"I should've guessed as much. What exactly do you do all day?"

I didn't say: I sleep a lot, like you. I smoke pot, watch TV, do the laundry, and get sick in the morning. By the way I'm pregnant. "I'm taking a photography class, Mom," I finally said. "You know, with Dad's old camera."

"He's been six feet under for three months and I'm still getting bills. Two hundred dollars for a ten-minute ambulance ride. Forty dollars for oxygen. I bet you thought oxygen was free, just sittin' out there in the sky. Nothing is free, Miranda, especially dying."

"I'll be getting a job soon. I'm starting to look for one today." As soon as I said it, I knew I would do it. Otherwise, I'd simply pace around the apartment in a panic for the rest of my life.

"I might have to be hospitalized for this next round of tests. The dizziness is back. But I'm behind the wheel again, praying to Jesus the whole time I'm driving. Obviously, it works. With Him as my co-pilot, I live to tell the tale."

"I was having a hard time in college, Mom. Booner helped me . . ."

"I said to Pastor Bob, 'What do I know? I'm not an educated woman. I'm just the mother.' " I heard the snap of cards on her end. She was playing solitaire. "You're going to force me to say it, Miranda. I'm lonesome for you. I don't know why you don't come home."

If only it were true that she was lonesome specifically for me. I started to cry. "When I get my job, I can help with the bills."

"Dr. Wykoff told me we'd get closer, being that Frank's dead and gone. I told him, 'Not with my daughter.' What does it matter. I'm not long to join your father."

"Don't say that, Mom."

"I speak my mind. It's the way I am. I drove to Lack's yesterday. Everyone says, 'How's your daughter.' I said, 'What daughter. I don't see my daughter. Do you see a daughter . . .' "

"I could come visit if you like," I said weakly.

"Being a widow is no bargain. My only comfort is the love I have in Jesus and the everlasting life He offers."

In the silence that followed, I held the phone tight against my ear and turned to face the shelf where all the change was piled up and wrinkled ATM receipts fluttered.

"You have trouble in college, you come home," said Mom.

"*This* is my home now, Mom." I stretched the phone cord toward the living room, where my camera sat on the coffee table, offering possibility, hope, strength. I thought of the crosses commemorating those babies that had never come to be. Maybe I would have a miscarriage, too. "I can't stay in Ransomville. And you don't really care about me."

"Good grief. Who went to your baptism? Who went to your high school graduation?"

"Not you!"

"Why didn't I go. Can you tell me that."

"You didn't go because you were sick. You're always sick!"

"Why didn't your father go."

What was she getting at? He didn't like organized events. "Why are you trying to turn me against him, Mom?"

"I'm only trying to make a point. He's the one who turned you against me. You followed him around like a puppy."

"That's a lie!" All those times she made me dress like her, lie with her, be her, the times she yanked me into her bedroom for the third degree: What have you been saying about me? I wanted her to pay. "As if you would've come to anything of mine even if you weren't sick. All you ever cared about was yourself! You know what, I'm glad you didn't come to my graduation!"

"I don't need the cruelty, Miranda. The only sin I've committed is the sin of being a concerned mother."

"Is that why you called? What do you want?"

"I put food on the table. You think your father would've done that? I made sure you were properly clothed. I was the one who said you shouldn't go to college in the first place. You conveniently forget. You listen to this fellow you're with and God knows who else, but it's too much to imagine you would listen to me. Your temper has always been a serious problem. But now you're not even thinking straight."

A burning began up along the back of my neck.

"I'll pray for you," she said. "It's all I can do. But I'm very disappointed. I'm truly at a loss."

All about her, as it had always been about her. I pictured the people at the church—oh poor Gert with her poor health and dreadful daughter. I was sitting on the linoleum floor. "I have to go, Mom. Can I call you later?"

"I never go anywhere. You know where I am."

I waited until I heard the dial tone before I let the receiver go. It hung off the shelf, emitting a recorded voice. "Please hang up. There appears to be a receiver off the hook."

I sat, paralyzed, in a heap, staring at a mud stain on the linoleum. My stomach hung over the tightly pulled drawstring of my sweatpants. "I'll never treat you like that. I'll love you, I promise," I told whatever was living inside me. I pushed myself up off the floor. Then I took the scraper into the bathtub to scrape away those layers of other people's lives, each layer someone's idea of what color a bathroom ought to be. I would make it white. I scraped out from the center, but it was sloppy, ugly. I needed to work more efficiently, more orderly.

The smallest wall was the one behind the toilet, so I moved there. On my hands and knees, I scraped from the floor up. I was going to be thorough, finish an entire wall and count down from there. Three to go. This bathroom would shine with perfection.

"You gotta get it right, Mandy girl, that's the point of working on a thing." Dad put his half-finished puppet theater aside in order to start a new one. "It's all wrong, see."

He was at the Griffin for my baptism and my graduation. He was at the Griffin when I was in the church choir and we gave a concert. He was there when I was born. When Mom went into labor, she drove herself to the hospital. That was how her story went. She named me Miranda after a kind, understanding nurse who helped her through the almost deadly birthing of me.

My knees ached, and I rolled a towel to cushion them while I was kneeling, the way Mom did when we prayed together so many years ago. Our prayers had gone unanswered. She never had the second child or the third. Mom and Dad never got along better, which was what I prayed for. After the hysterectomy, Mom said that praying was hogwash. Now she was praying again. What a hypocrite. Dad would have said, "There's no harm in praying, Mandy girl. No sense in it, either." My eyes watered, liquid dripping. I scraped harder, faster. See, Dad, see, I'm doing it like you always told me to. But I would never hear him tell me, *Good job, Mandy*. He would never again say, *Don't listen to your mother. She doesn't mean what she says.*

I stood and threw the scraper behind the toilet, snatched the pregnancy test off the sink, and hurled it out the perpetually open bathroom window, the goddamn window that was painted open. I stamped my foot so hard on the floor pain exploded in my heel. When I jumped in the shower, I turned on the hot water until it burned, then I ran just the cold until I couldn't stop shaking. I was determined to think about nothing, remember nothing, feel nothing.

I was numb as I got dressed. I needed a job, needed to earn money, make a life for myself. But I had run out of cigarettes. When I went around the corner to buy a pack, I also picked up the *Daily News*. In the vestibule, I stopped to open the mailbox and was shocked to find a small yellow card addressed to me. MANDY BOYLE C/O TODD BOONE. There was a package at the post office I would have to claim. I walked ten blocks to pick it up. The package was from Barb, the biggest I had ever received in my life. I carried it home, arms and shoulders aching with the weight, sweating in my coat while an icy wind chafed my face, smacked me out of the numbness.

"Dear Mandy, here's your stuff. I'm sorry for whatever I did or didn't do. Good luck and I hope you keep in touch. Let me know what to do about your trunk. It was too big to send. Love, Barb."

Enclosed with the note was a pair of long, dangling silver and turquoise earrings that I had always admired on her. I held them to my heart for a moment and then put them on. They felt heavy, pulling down my earlobes, pulling me back to the life I had given up. When I shook my head, they clinked lightly as if to say, *We're here.*

I unpacked Mom's dresses and shook them out. I hadn't worn a single one the whole time in college. Beneath the dresses were my textbooks, which accounted for the heaviness of the package. And tucked in the corner were Dad's shoes, scuffed and stretched out as if they had just recently been on his feet. Tucked in the right shoe I found the obituary, ink-smeared and fading.

I placed the shoes on the top shelf in the kitchen closet, pushing them all the way back toward the wall so I was the only one who would know they were there. I felt severed and alone, too small to fill the space stretching enormously and endlessly out before me.

I hung on to the need for money. I couldn't do anything without it. I lit a cigarette and started looking through the classifieds. The "Gal/Guy Friday" section seemed like a decent place to start, with over four columns of ads.

I made a few calls. One after another, the person on the other end told me to send my résumé. But I didn't have one. "Hello, my name is Miranda Boyle and I'm calling about your ad in the *Daily News*." I began to sound like a recording.

Finally, my calling paid off. "We're looking for someone who can really hit the ground running. Can you come in today?"

"Sure. Whenever you say." I felt as though I had already hit the ground. And running sounded good. I could do that.

"Do you know how to get here? We're in Grand Central Station. Where are you coming from?"

"I'm coming from Queens, but it's okay because . . ." I paused to unfold my subway map. "It looks like the number seven train goes right there."

"Okay, Miranda. How about we'll see you in two hours?"

"Great." In a chilled panic, I pawed through Mom's dresses. I chose the least wrinkled one, a scratchy wool number that smelled just faintly of mothballs. I pulled on a pair of tights and slipped on my loafers. They were a little run-down. Even Booner's shoe polish couldn't disguise the worn heels and torn seams. But they would have to do. My boots were out of the question.

I arranged my hair in one long braid. All in all not bad. "Go for it," said the girl in the mirror. In the box from Barb I found the purse with the big snap. I brought my backpack, too, to carry the roll of film I had taken at the baby shower, plus a developing tank and reels. I would do it all.

I threw on my coat, ran downstairs, and rushed along Astoria Boulevard, a city girl with a quick pace. When I reached the subway station, I huddled in the stairway to wait for the train, sheltered from the wind, like the others. It wasn't crowded and I got off at Queens Plaza, where I needed to switch to the train across the platform. In this second one, I saw an ad staring straight at me: A female doctor with a friendly smile, hands outstretched, stethoscope around her neck: Pregnant? We can help. I changed my seat to face an ad for a podiatrist.

Grand Central Station was so large and the ceiling so far away that I couldn't look up without feeling dazed. I was adrift in the whispering currents of other people's air. If I tried to look at individual people, I lost my focus in the blur of faces, the echo of voices and thudding of countless footsteps swirling around me.

The Graybar Building was accessible through Grand Central Station. The lobby floor was polished to a slippery sheen. I slid across it. A security guard sat behind a desk, impassively watching. Not wanting to ask him anything, I studied the directory on the wall and felt victorious when I saw CORPORATE LIAISONS INCORPORATED, SUITE 1406.

I straightened the seam on my dress. The warped, mirrored metal of the elevator walls reflected myself back at me, distorted, blurred. The elevator buttons went from 1 to 12 and then from 14 on up. There was no thirteenth floor. I put the detail away to tell Booner. Since he didn't get to Manhattan much, he didn't know a lot about it. I would become the expert here.

"Thanks for coming in on such short notice." Priscilla Sherman was classy, thin; even her face was narrow. She had pulled back her straight brown hair with a ribbon, but pieces had fallen loose and wisped, flyaway, around her face. Even in her tailored suit, trailing the scent of expensive perfume, she seemed tense and shook my hand quickly with a limp, slightly damp grip.

Leonard Glass was an older man with a trim mustache and a fringe of dark hair outlining the round dome of his bald head. He squeezed my knuckles until one of them cracked. "You're very young. That's one point against you already." He smiled like he was making a joke. "How old are you anyway, sixteen?"

"I'm twenty." So I wasn't exactly twenty yet, I was just a few months away, almost there. "I'm very mature," I told Leonard, making eye contact. I had said those same words on my college interview, along with: *I relish hard work. Accomplishments mean a lot to me, and I will work like a dog to achieve. In five years I see myself with a college diploma and a job with a future.* There was a book Dad kept in the basement about how to interview successfully. I had read it back then, and I remembered it now.

But when I had said those things for my college interview, I had believed them. Now, I felt as though I were reciting empty words, like at church. Leonard went first, then Priscilla, as they led me past a large, shiny wooden desk that filled the reception area. Next to it, a flattened packing crate leaned against the wall.

I followed them into a conference room with an oval table of deep red polished wood in the center of which were flowers arranged in a round vase; gardenias and daisies, daylilies, baby's breath, and birds-of-paradise. *Wow,* I almost said. I sniffed deeply but they didn't seem to have an aroma. Instead, I took in the strong synthetic odor of newness, which was just as appealing.

Priscilla motioned for me to sit. I folded my hands in my lap, careful to hide my bitten nails and raw, chapped fingertips. I imagined sitting here every day, as brand-new as my surroundings.

Framed prints hung off the walls. JUMP AND THE NET WILL APPEAR was written in large, elegant letters beneath a photograph of a hawk wheeling through a cloudless blue sky. WHAT THE MIND CAN CONCEIVE, THE BODY CAN ACHIEVE said a photograph with a picture of a tiny human figure, arms raised in triumph at the top of a huge mountain. DON'T LET WEEDS GROW AMONG YOUR DREAMS it said beneath a picture of a garden. I wanted to believe every single one of those statements. My heart beat quickly with a want I hadn't felt in a long time.

"Coffee?" asked Leonard, slurping his own.

"No, thanks."

"Why do you want this job, Miranda?" When Priscilla smiled, her large teeth and flexible mouth transformed her otherwise thin, wan face into a beautiful welcome. She used my real name, which caught me off guard for just a second before I remembered I had referred to myself that way on the phone. I wanted to say, Please, call me Mandy, but didn't.

"Well, I was in college for a semester and my father passed away and . . ." The words slipped out easily, a bubble in a stream of water, but I was getting offtrack. I took a breath. "And I need the money."

"Rule number one," said Leonard. "Never say you need the money. Cheap is ugly."

"Oh." I shrank into my chair. *Drink coffee,* it had said in Dad's interview book. *Be alert. Answer questions directly. Know about the company where you're interviewing.* I had refused coffee for fear of spilling it. I was more nervous than alert. I had just sidestepped the question, and I knew nothing about Corporate Liaisons Incorporated.

"So your father passed away and you had to leave college." Priscilla raised her eyebrows. A small furrow formed between them.

It was more of a statement than a question, which meant I didn't have to answer. It was too complicated to contradict her anyway. Dad hadn't paid my tuition, and his dying had no effect on the partial scholarship, state grant, federal grant, work-study job, or student loan. An anesthetic heaviness took over my body as I remembered the towers, the class discussions, the guy with his shoes, the noisy cafeteria, the chronically slow moving line of people at the financial-aid office, and the wall of indifferent faces at the counter.

No. I shook the fog away. That life was over. This was my new life. "I live in Queens now, but I used to live upstate." It wasn't going well at all. They were both looking at me as if expecting me to say more. "My mother's been sick, and she still lives upstate," I added.

"So you live in Queens," Leonard said. "When did your father die?"

"Around Christmas."

"You know, that's amazing, because my father died around Christmas while I was at college, too." Priscilla's eyes fastened on me. "He was sick for a year with cancer and it was absolutely the most painful time in my life. Of course, I was a senior, which makes a difference, but I truly believe this is not just a coincidence."

I didn't know how to take that. I fought the urge to start crying.

"Priscilla, you really should've been a social worker." Leonard cleared his throat. "What we do here, what Corporate Liaisons Incorporated does is recruiting. We're a recruiting agency."

"Ah, recruiting."

"So you know what a recruiting agency is?"

"I think so." I thought of the army, the navy, the air force, the marines.

"Shall I, Leonard?" Priscilla flashed her transforming smile. "What we do is this: We find out where there's space open in a firm and then we fill it with someone from our pool of candidates." In the neutral gray of her eyes, I saw a pool of water filled with candidates, swimming like the fish in Rose's fish tank.

"We're different than the other ones out there," said Leonard.

"We're specialists," Priscilla chimed in, leaning forward. "We specialize in the placement of tax professionals. Other agencies out there—not only are they not specialists, they're not even professionals. You've heard what they say about recruiting firms, right? Sleazy, hard-sell, fly-by-night. Well, that's not us. Leonard and I both worked at a firm where we felt compromised and . . ."

"We decided to start our own business." Leonard, too, leaned forward in his seat, fired up with enthusiasm for their new company. "We aim to build long-lasting relationships with our clients. We also have a higher aim, to bring up the reputation of the industry as a whole."

"We find the right place for the right person and the right person for the right place," announced Priscilla. "That's our corporate motto."

"That's great." I was getting fired up too. "And you need a gal Friday like me to help you do it!"

Leonard nodded. "We had someone, but she ducked out at the last minute. She left us in the lurch. We don't want someone like that."

"I'm definitely not like that." My voice was surprisingly strong and sure considering my future had changed so drastically this morning. "I'm dependable, and I work very hard. I've always worked. In college, I had a job in the library. In high school, as soon as I could get my working papers, I worked in—" I searched for the word that

Mom always used to describe the job at Lack's. Never mind I hated working there because she and her spies were everywhere. "—retail!" I grabbed hold of the word almost joyously.

"Doesn't seem like much experience," Leonard said, addressing Priscilla.

She tilted her face, holding her hands together as if in prayer. "What's wrong with your mother? You said she was sick."

"She's got a lot of things wrong with her."

Priscilla looked attentive.

"Well, for example, she's had lupus for years." The urge to bite my nails was becoming irresistible. I sat on my hands.

"That's a very serious disease," said Priscilla. "She must be courageous and strong to live with that for years."

If Mom were here, she would agree. And Priscilla wasn't asking me. But when she had a lupus flare-up—her eyes like little chinks in her swollen, rashy face, lurching painfully, unable to breathe, and crying in a thick shaky voice, "Call the doctor"—Mom was more monstrous than courageous and more frightening than strong.

I was gripping the seat of the chair so hard my fingers cramped.

"You must be very strong yourself, hustling for a job in the city," Priscilla added.

"We can't pay a lot. You see we're a start-up company." Leonard's glasses glinted in the light.

"I understand." I tried to put on a straight and strong expression.

"You know what?" Priscilla looked from Leonard to me and back to Leonard. "I feel good about this. You seem professional. You're bright, and if you're willing to learn, how about we give it a try? Are you open to training?"

"Sure. I'd love it." I imagined Dad's hand on my shoulder. "I have a good feeling, too," I blurted out. "I really like the office here and what you said about long-lasting relationships and bringing up the reputation of the industry." I felt a warmth in my belly, a desperate heat for a good feeling, for a solid, stable sense that wouldn't slowly revolve to reveal an ugly underside.

"A trial period. How about we give it a trial for a month and then we revisit the issue?" Leonard drummed his fingers against the table. I nodded and wondered how pregnant I was and if I'd show in a month. But I couldn't think about that, and I focused on Leonard's hands, which were pale and clean, not a callus, not a stain, so unlike Booner's or Dad's.

"If you play your cards right, Miranda, you can really take advantage. Because we're such a new firm, the future is wide open." Priscilla spread her thin, delicate fingers out against the table, as if to demonstrate the wide-open future as she saw it.

She wore an opal ring on her index finger, and on her giving-the-finger finger, she wore a gold band ringed with diamonds that looked like the kind of wedding ring Mom would have loved to receive from Dad. "I feel very good about this," she repeated.

I touched my necklace to feel the love it gave off. I shook my head slightly and the silver turquoise earrings clinked. I could become like Priscilla. Professional. Eager. Beautiful. Sympathetic to people with lupus.

"You'll start tomorrow, then. Nine o'clock." Leonard cracked my knuckles again when he shook my hand.

I took the elevator with my warped fun-house reflection back down to the lobby with the slippery floors and the impassive guard at the desk. "I have a job!" I told him. He nodded with the barest flicker of a smile, of recognition. But it was enough.

I walked slowly through Grand Central Station to the subway, savoring my sense of achievement while people rushed all around me, past me, by me as though I were a rock in their stream. A pregnant rock. I halted, my stomach twisted in fear. A man in an overcoat bumped me with his briefcase and moved swiftly on without saying "Excuse me." He enabled me to continue walking, focused on his rudeness.

In my backpack were my tank and reels, thermometer, and completed roll of film. I got on a train going downtown, got off three stops later at Twenty-third Street, and walked three blocks to the New York Photography Center.

As soon as I entered the building, the shabbiness was comforting. It was old, but it worked. The stairs were worn in grooves where feet had walked for many years, and my feet, too, were adding to the erosion.

I had my notes. I had the film, all the equipment. I walked into the darkroom, where I wound the film onto the reel in complete darkness, carefully rolling it so that no part of the film touched any other part of the film. It was amazing that so many photographs existed in the world, considering the complexity of the process by which they were created. So many steps to take before the finished picture: capture the image; develop the negatives; and finally, develop the print. Each step required precision and careful attention.

I covered the tank and carried it into a room across the hall where the walls were lined with sinks. I paused, sniffed, and inhaled deeply the salty, stinging chemicals, a comforting, pungent smell that reminded me of Dad, yet I didn't feel like crying. I opened my notebook on a table near the sink. I checked the temperature of the developer, as my notes instructed.

"You're in my Saturday class, right?" A voice growled from the doorway.

I jerked around. I had thought I was alone, but Doug Harrison was standing there. "I didn't mean to startle you." His eyes were blue and vivid. His beard parted in a smile.

"I was just developing these negatives for Saturday." Thankfully, I hadn't poured in the chemicals yet.

"You're taking initiative. That's good. You like doing this?"

"Yeah, I love it, because my father . . ." I stopped. "I just got a job . . ." I stopped again, feeling the heat of a blush rise from my chest to my face. "Things are really . . ." I stopped once more. Why was I stuttering, blurting out everything, saying nothing?

I stared at the floor then, unable to face him. But I noticed his white high-top sneakers spray-painted all different colors. The laces were undone; his jeans were cuffed. And I was wearing a wool dress of Mom's that puffed out strangely above the waist.

This isn't me, I wanted to tell him. But it was me. Unfortunately.

"You got the temperature right on that?" When he reached for the thermometer, his fingers brushed mine and snapped back with a static electric shock. "Supercharge." He smiled, so naturally and spontaneously that it was contagious. I felt myself smiling in return. And I couldn't imagine him practicing in front of the mirror when he thought no one was looking, the way Booner probably did.

"I'll let you get on with it," he said. "But stop by my office afterwards if you like. It's up on six. I love saying that. I never had an office before."

I didn't say that I have an office now, too, and that I never had one before either. Of course, my office wasn't actually mine and I wouldn't really have it until tomorrow, but those were just details.

I poured in the chemicals and agitated the tank to spread them evenly over the negatives. Mom used to complain that I was agitating her, and it pleased me to think of her in the tank I was shaking. The timer buzzed and I poured in the stop, then the fixer. Then I rinsed the negatives.

I unwound them and hung them to dry, a long reel of small rectangles containing miniature pictures. There were a few abstract patterned pictures of the gates on the windows in the apartment and a few of Booner. And many, like peepholes giving onto a drama, of the baby shower. The strange black teeth in the ghoulish crescents of the women's grins laughed at me, making it impossible to ignore that enormous heavy fact I kept trying to forget. You're pregnant, knocked up. You've got a bun in the oven.

Was this how Tracy had felt? She was probably afraid to tell me back then. She hadn't kept it from me out of spite, out of selfishness, as I had thought at the time. What would Booner say? How was I going to even bring it up? I felt the worries circling, but there was nowhere for them to go. I wiped my damp hands on my dress and walked upstairs to the sixth floor, looking for Doug Harrison's office.

All along the corridor walls were glass cases in which student photographs were displayed, like windows onto individual worlds. Pictures of fire escapes, of people laughing, of animals and architecture, close-ups and landscapes, children and old people. HUMANITY AND SOCIETY said a sign above them. Maybe one day I'd have a picture hanging here! An inner jolt of excitement pushed me along the hall.

I passed an open door and there sat the teacher at a long table, surrounded by books piled on the table and the floor. Behind him was a window so dirty that no light filtered through. To the side was an old brown sofa with sawed-off legs. It sat very low.

"There you are!" He called out to me. "How'd it go? You get your negatives developed all right?"

"Yeah, I think so. I left them drying."

"What's your name again?" He waved his hand over to the sofa, but when I sat down, I felt too short, too close to the ground, so I perched on the back of it with my feet on the seat. I felt free enough to do that.

"Mandy Boyle."

"Hmm." He was looking over a computer printout. "I don't see a . . . you're in my Saturday class? Boyle?"

"Yup." There were just hundreds of postcards of black-and-white photographs hanging on the facing wall. Each postcard was a separate vision. There was so much to learn! I hadn't felt this way since my first few weeks of college.

"Miranda," he said. "Not Mandy."

"But everyone calls me Mandy."

"Why? Miranda's a beautiful name. Can't I call you Miranda?"

"Sure, if you want." He sounded like Mom, and I wondered suddenly what time it was. This was the longest I had ever been gone from the apartment, and even though I knew it was stupid, I was afraid it wouldn't be there when I returned.

"So, you're not a full-time student?"

I leaned back against the wall, cautious and hesitant. My face felt hot. Any second he might suddenly say, "I only take full-time students and I'm afraid you can't be in my class." I didn't know if I could handle that. "I just got a job and I'm taking a class, that's all."

He held out a postcard with a picture of what looked like a smooth rounded landscape and I noticed his hands were covered with speckles of white plaster or something similar. Maybe he was redoing his bathroom, too.

I peered at the postcard and realized with a blush that it was flesh folding in a body part I couldn't identify. I turned the card around. *Charis Gallery*, it said. "*Flesh Landscapes, by Doug Harrison.*"

"Wow. That's you."

"If you go to my show, you get an A."

"I guess I'll go then." I handed him back the postcard.

"It's yours to keep," said Doug. "Plenty more where that came from."

I had a flash of sitting next to Dad while he did the crossword puzzles in the morning, of the comforting scratch of his pen while birds chirped and twittered by the feeder outside, of camaraderie. I hadn't known how fragile and precious those mornings were or how content I had been. My heart seemed to clench like a fist. "I should probably get going," I muttered.

"There's a great show over at the International Center of Photography I'd encourage you to take a look at. See what other people do."

"Yeah, sure. I'll definitely go."

"You have the list I gave out on Saturday. All the information's there." When he smiled, his beard moved, revealing perfectly straight teeth. His blue eyes crinkled. He stood and we shook hands. His palm was warm and rough like Dad's, like Booner's. I almost leaned toward him for a kiss, overtaken by a sense of familiarity. But my heart beat out a warning panic, and I withdrew before I embarrassed myself.

"See you Saturday," he said.

" 'Bye!" I walked downstairs to the room where my negatives hung. They were dry and curling slightly at the ends. I laid them carefully in glassine envelopes, another item from the list of supplies I had bought. I got a job! I developed some negatives! I own a cool postcard! I was buoyed by a jubilance that usually took hold of me only when I was stoned or drunk. The thought of the pregnancy test flitted by, and I batted it away in my mind, like a moth.

I HEARD MUSIC blasting from somewhere as I climbed the stairs. It got louder as I approached our apartment and I opened the door to a solid wall of shrieking guitars and Van Halen screaming "And the Cradle Will Rock." Booner was sitting large and cross-legged in the middle of the living room, bent over, putting something together while he nodded to the beat, concentrating so deeply that he didn't sense me come in.

Fish, in separately sealed plastic bags, surrounded him like big bubbles on the sea of the orange shag rug, scattered with plastic plants and rocks and props. An empty fish tank sat on top of the stereo cabinet.

I picked up a piece of fake seaweed. AUTHENTIC AQUATIC PLANT REPLICA said the package. It landed soundlessly when I dropped it, but it must have caused a vibration because Booner looked up with his rare doofy grin, not his practiced handsome one. He held up a filter. "Check it out!"

Something shimmered near the sofa leg, a plastic castle. Glitter sprinkled off when I blew on it. I poked my pinkie through the window and wiggled my fingertip. The lovely princess was trapped by the evil witch in her castle. But she would find true love and set herself free.

"I knew you'd like the castle!" Booner shouted.

But he knew nothing. My job, my class, my "positive" belonged in a separate universe. "I got a job!" I screamed. His face didn't change. He rose awkwardly out of his seated position, obviously not used to sitting on the floor.

He picked up the tank and carried it into the kitchen. Had he completely not heard me? Had I not spoken out loud? Did I even exist anymore? I followed him. His sweatshirt was stained. His jeans were faded at the cheeks of his butt, wrinkling oddly. He was no longer mysterious.

I knew that beneath his jeans, he wasn't wearing underwear. I had seen him carefully brush the downy hairs above his upper lip with the same toothbrush he used to clean his teeth. I knew he didn't hold down the flusher on the toilet long enough and that his poop floated in circles.

He put the fish tank carefully in the sink and ran the water. "I got fish!" he shouted. It wasn't until the tank was half full and he turned the water off that he finally noticed me. "Why are you dressed like that? You look like a little old lady." And he laughed with his funny little squeak.

That did it. I turned and walked out, yanking off the hateful dress. "I'm not an old lady! I got a job! I've been trying to tell you!" I pushed through the beaded curtains and they swayed in my wake. My naked reflection in the mirror undulated exactly where I was pregnant. Booner didn't deserve to know. I put on sweatpants and a sweatshirt, slug clothes.

Carefully, I removed the necklace and laid it in the blue velvet case,

which I kept in my top drawer along with my few precious keep-
sakes, like the photograph of Barb holding up her I.D. and my
stuffed teddy bear from Dad. Mom's dress lay in a wrinkled heap on
the floor, and I despised it.

"Don't you wanna see the fish?" Booner's face appeared in the
mirror, peeking through the beaded curtains. I deliberately stamped
on the dress and kicked it out of the way as I left the bedroom.

"The filter's here." He touched it proudly. "And check it out." He
sprinkled food in and all the fish darted up in a diagonal stream of
color, their mouths sucking, eyes gaping.

"You got fish because Eugene has them, is that it? Monkey-see
monkey-do?" It came out even snottier than I had intended, and
Booner looked surprised, as if it didn't compute. Instantly sorry, I
tapped on the glass. "They're beautiful. That one looks like he's
smiling."

"Smiling. Yeah, you would say that." He put his arm around
me, stroked my back under my sweatshirt, and I leaned into
him, trying not to feel so angry inside, willing it away in order
to draw the comfort that his hard, thick fingers on my back were
offering. But his hand became more urgent, sliding down the waist
of my sweatpants, cupping my butt, pulling at the elastic on my
underwear.

His face came close and he kissed my cheek softly. I cringed when
his tongue circled my ear canal and he whispered into the wet, "You
looked so cute in your little old lady dress."

I twisted away, pretending to look at the fish, pretending that it
was just incidental that I had pulled away. It didn't work.

"What's with you?" He grabbed my arm.

I plopped onto the sofa. A coil poked out of the ripped cushion
and snagged my sweatpants. They were my only pair, and now they
were torn. Great.

But I could buy new ones. There had been good things in the day.
"I got a job," I said. "I'll take the subway every day. It's a brand-
new company. They'll train me to find the right person for the right
place. And vice versa."

He sat down next to me, weighting the cushion so our thighs
joined. "Did you say the subway? No. You don't want to do that.

How many times do I have to tell you? The subways are dangerous. Where's this job anyway?"

"It's in Manhattan, near Grand Central Station. Did you ever hear of the saying 'jump and the net will appear'?"

"Why do you want to work in Manhattan? There's bad influences there."

"There's no thirteenth floor in the building. It just goes from twelve to fourteen." I folded my arms over my chest. "Donna works in Manhattan."

He scratched the bridge of his nose. "You got this class, now you got this job. You're so damn independent. What about the job with Eugene? I've been trying to make that happen."

I thought of the garage, the smell of fuel, grease, and dirty rags, the roar of the trucks, and the makeshift toilet. It couldn't possibly compare with the newness, the freshly painted walls and vase of flowers at Corporate Liaisons Incorporated. "I can't wait around for that." I, who had so enjoyed waiting, couldn't wait around. It was strange. Where had this impatience come from?

"Yeah. All right. On one condition." He put his hand on my thigh. "When that GeneRo job comes through, you'll take it. So I can keep my eye on you and you won't be risking your life on the subways."

I leaned back into his strong shoulders, where my head fit perfectly. I was relieved, as though a great danger had just barely been avoided. If he thought he was giving me permission, that was fine. I was so grateful to be loved, to be real, to have someone who wanted to keep an eye on me. The filter on the fish tank bubbled away. The fire escape ladder clanged against the railing and the world became, for a moment, a benevolent place.

"You got me wrapped around your finger," Booner whispered. He shifted his position and rubbed my belly, moving his hand to my breasts under my sweatshirt. He pinched my nipples hard, first one, then the other, a miniature arc of pain he immediately soothed by softly stroking. My breath quickened, my nipples hardened. Sickness twisted my stomach. I pulled away.

"What's your problem?" He cupped his own crotch almost shyly, but his voice held a threat that made me squirm.

"I just don't feel like it."

"What's that supposed to mean? I'm not allowed to kiss my girl?" He stared me down, nailed me wriggling against the sofa with his steely green gaze. It was the same look he gave me when he paid for the meal in the diner at college, when he thought that I thought that he was a cheapskate.

"Why won't you let me love you?" Booner's arm lay around the back of the sofa. His thigh still touched mine. He took hold of my chin and twisted my face so I had to look at him as he pinned my arm back with his body and leaned in to kiss me, his eyes halfway closed.

I couldn't move unless I started kicking. "Booner, I don't know. It's about the fish." I tried to turn, to push him off. He wouldn't budge. "I mean, didn't Eugene get them for Rose because she was pregnant?"

"What are you talking about?"

"What would you do if I got pregnant?"

He released me and stared at the rug. "I would be the happiest man alive."

I had a forbidding sense of the world breaking open, the tenuous clarity of the picture changing, darkening until I couldn't see anything with certainty. It was a vaguely familiar feeling that one day things are one way and the next day everything has changed, and not for the better. Never for the better.

The summer I went to the county fair, the world had shifted like that. It had been my fault then, too. I heard the kids in school talking about winning stuffed animals and goldfish, eating cotton candy and caramelized popcorn, going on rides with magical names— Roundabout, Tilt-A-Whirl, Ferris wheel—and I had wanted those things with a physical want that kept me awake nights and lulled me to sleep just long enough for me to pee my bed.

Mom said, "No. We can't afford it. Who do you think you are?"

Dad said, "Come on, Gert. Every child should experience a fair." He held me on his big lap, bargaining. "Just help your mama, do your chores, and put on a happy face. Try to pee before you go to bed, okay? I'll do the rest."

I washed the dishes, but I broke one. I mopped the floor. Mom slipped and fell, bruising her hip. I threaded the needle on the sewing machine with the wrong color thread. I changed her sheets but messed up the hospital corners. I ironed her blouse and melted the polyester fabric. But the one thing I did correctly was polish her nails while she sat with her fingers spread and her voice friendly, not accusing at all. "Oh, that's the way. Yes, that nail always gives me problems. That one's the breakable one, be careful."

Dad would wink at me, announcing at every opportunity, "What a good girl Mandy's been. She sure deserves to go to the county fair!" Until at last one morning the three of us were off in the station wagon, even though Mom's esophagus bothered her and she sensed a lupus flare-up coming on.

I wore a dress that Mom had sewn, the same flowered fabric as hers. When she looked at me, she said, "My goodness, it's like I've given birth to myself."

"But I'm me!" I cried, and she wasn't offended. The Ferris wheel circled up ahead and music drifted on a breeze. Mom held one of my hands and Dad held the other. We were a family, like normal people! I wanted to melt with happiness.

Dad's presence next to me on the Ferris wheel calmed the breathless giddiness of being so high, swinging precariously, lurching, then swinging again. I could make out Mom on the ground, a tiny flower moving toward the bingo tent.

Dad bought me helium balloons and held on to them as he watched me whirl by myself on the Tilt-A-Whirl. He held the balloons again while I went on the bumper cars. I screamed, reversed, bumped, turned. I wanted to go once more, but Dad pulled his pockets inside out like a rabbit's ears to show me he had no money left.

Under the double Ferris wheel, which spun screaming people upside down as a tattooed man at the controls shouted, "You want more? You want more?" Dad pointed out a treasure trove of coins twinkling in the damp grass and mud. "Do it, Mandy girl, go for the gold." And he waited around the bend with my balloons so as not to attract attention while I scampered about, filling my skirt with change, making a little money sack out of my dress.

I was thrilled to hear the money clank as Dad dropped it all in his pockets, even the silver dollar, the first I had ever seen. He pried it from my fist, because it would be safe with him whereas I might lose it. "You're something special, Mandy!"

He tied the balloons around my wrist so they wouldn't fly away. And I was bursting with pride when, hand in hand, he led me to the beer tent, where men from the Griffin smacked him on the back, How goes it Frank? "Couldn't be better. I'll just have a quick one before I take my little girl on some more of those rides."

But a quick one turned into several and his friends kept buying. I seemed to be in everyone's way and I tugged at Dad's hand. "I want to go on the Roundabout." I knew what was happening. By the time Dad was done, all the money would be gone. I started to long for Mom.

I saw her march in before Dad did. Her face was flushed with rage. "What are you doing in this place?" She went to slap me, as if it were my fault. But I ducked. Her palm only grazed my cheek, so I didn't need to cry.

"We're going home. Right now. I have been looking all over for you two." Mom dug her fingernails into my arm.

The rest of the men were laughing. Dad lumbered along behind us, not upset in the least. "It's like this, Gert. You gamble, I drink."

"I don't gamble! How *dare* you!"

I felt the tug of the balloons on my wrist bobbing out behind me, remembrance of the fun part of the fair.

"Bingo's gambling."

"Bingo's raising money for the *church*!" Mom gripped my arm tighter, twisting so much that I knew there would be a bruise the next morning, which wasn't as bad as the prospect of a long ride home and them fighting the whole time. At least the bruise was something I could feel and look at before it went away.

When Dad turned the key in the ignition, the car gave a dry cough, then a sputter.

"What's happening?" Mom shouted.

He tried over and over while the same cough and sputter gradually weakened to an empty click. He sighed, got out, and went to the back, where he took out a hose and a gas can. "C'mon, Mandy girl, leave the balloons in the car. I'm going to need those sharp eyes of yours."

Mom kept a running monologue: ". . . can't even go the fair without nasty business. And you're making her just like you, the two of you thick as thieves, because that's what you are. Thieves."

Her voice wrapped around me as I followed Dad. I had stolen the money from under the double Ferris wheel, but how did Mom know? Dad gave me the hose to hold, and I wrapped it around my neck. Our shadows elongated before us and I stepped into mine. When I turned back toward the car, I saw my balloons in the window, like friends waiting.

Dad crouched behind a blue sedan, unscrewed the gas cap, and gestured for the hose. I watched as he dipped it in the tank and sucked on the end, though it was dirty. I turned to look for people, not knowing quite what Dad was doing but aware that it was wrong. He coughed and spit and golden liquid spilled like pee, clanging against the metal of the gas can, quieting as it filled. When the flow stopped, Dad pulled the hose out and screwed the cap back on and we made our way along the line of cars, crouching so no one would see us.

After three cars, with the can sloshing, the hose damp, and reeking of gasoline, we were back at the station wagon, where Mom sat like a crab in the front seat, red-faced, red-haired, her snapping claws folded over her chest. Dad poured the gas into the tank with a white funnel.

Someone shouted. "There's the guy!" I heard the clatter of the gas can, and then something pounded on the door. A rock. Dad was a dark blur coming around the driver's side. Mom ducked, screaming, "Don't kill my family!"

"That guy stole my fucking gas!" The can landed next to me in the backseat as another rock thudded across the car roof. A stain spread over my jumper from spilled gasoline. The car started right up. Dad wheezed like an old accordion, wheeling around the parking lot, tearing up the grass. His jaw pulsed all the way home. The rear windshield was cracked but not shattered. Mom started crying, gasping like crazy until she finally used her inhaler and her breath echoed mechanically and evenly through the car.

I wished I had never spoken of or wanted to go to the county fair. I stopped stating wants like that, or even feeling them. And the balloons, drained of their helium, puckered and deflated, were the only things I cried over when that day ended.

Booner's eyes bored into me. I turned to watch an iridescent orange fish with ruffled fins sway like a flower among the waving emerald strands of a fake plant. The power I held on to was in the secret growing inside me.

"If you were pregnant, I would marry you." Booner's fingers clenched around my face. He probed my lips with his tongue, pushed me back on the sofa, and yanked my sweatshirt up. "I love you."

I tried to turn my face away, but he held me fast.

"I love you," he repeated, pulling off my sweatpants. He put one hand between my legs and the other on my chest, pinning me down. "I can make you feel good. I know what you like." His voice was earnest, insistent, and heat spread through my body. It was easy to give in. I had a strange, transported sense of ceasing to exist and there was pleasure in it.

"I don't want to fight." He raised himself off to unzip his jeans. I was free enough to wiggle out and run away. But I didn't move. There was nowhere to go. When Booner's pants were off, I wrapped my legs around him and we maneuvered from the sofa to the rug. I welcomed the weight of his body and his hard, painful thrust. The rug chafed a burning soreness along my spine.

"Tell me you love me, Mandy, please tell me."

But a cold, hard, stubborn piece of me was locked away and I said nothing. It would soon be over.

"Talk to me." His hipbones jutted into mine.

He sounded desperate. I pitied him, with an overwhelming swell of sadness that I could float on. When he jammed his finger up my anus, the sharp pain only expanded my pity. Tears welled up, ran down my cheeks, and collected in the cups of my ears.

He came with a moan, loving me the only way he knew. Because despite everything, the one place where I felt surely loved was lying on my back as Booner burst inside me. This pity and this sadness, then, was love.

"Oh man, what you do to me." Booner took a deep breath and rolled off. He fished out a towel from under the sofa, wiped his penis and balls, and threw the towel over near the coffee table. Then he sat on the rug, leaning back against the sofa, and reached for his bag of pot. He sprinkled out some weed into an E-Z Wider bamboo paper and rolled up a joint. His penis dripped in the crook of his lap.

I rolled over on my side in order not to see him anymore. I couldn't stop crying. My muscles were cramped. I needed to blow my nose. Everything looked larger than me when I was lying on the floor, and I had never seen the place look uglier. I had to get out of here. But go where? Orange floated before me, a wash of color. I couldn't focus. Was there such a thing as true love? Booner tapped my back with his foot. "You want any of this?"

I sat up when he passed the joint and I took three deep, throat-burning hits before I passed it back. Then I wiped my nose on my sweatshirt. My tears ebbed. What was the point of crying? I shut my eyes and leaned my head against the armrest, picking out the good bits of the day: Priscilla Sherman's smile. Doug's postcard. My negatives. The ad on the subway: PREGNANT? WE CAN HELP.

Booner hoisted himself up so he was sitting on the sofa, not the floor. He tapped me with his foot again. "Mandy. Are you?"

"What?" I took another hit. Then another. I felt as though I were underwater. The orange shag rug waved its rough tentacles.

"If you are, it's mine, right?"

Moisture trickled out from between my legs. What if it wasn't even his? I hadn't thought of that. "First of all, I'm not sure if I am. Okay? As for your second question, fuck you, too."

"Well, how'm I supposed to know?"

The joint was finished, but I needed to keep smoking, so I lit a cigarette. I felt as though I had reached the end of the line and yet it was easy, a familiar place to be. "You could act a little nicer to me, you know."

"If you're pregnant, you shouldn't be smoking those cancer sticks." He patted the sofa cushion. "Come on up here by me."

Staying put on the floor, I blew a perfect smoke ring, a doughnut floating up in space.

He got up then and stood over me, gesturing with his big, clumsy hands at the fish tank. "I got them for you."

I knew he was gesturing because I saw the shadows on the rug. But I wouldn't look at him, towering naked above me. I molded the ash at the end of my cigarette into a perfect cone. I wondered what Dad had said when Mom told him she was pregnant. I wondered how Tracy's boyfriend had taken the news. I felt the tears coming on again. I didn't want to cry in front of Booner, but I didn't know how to stop.

"Don't cry." He squatted next to me on the rug and wiped my eyes with his fingers. I allowed it, wishing there were more of these tender gestures. Or none at all.

"I don't know if I am, Booner. I have to go to a clinic and make sure. I don't know if I'm ready . . ." I couldn't finish that line of thought. I wasn't ready for anything. I had never been ready. I squeezed my cigarette so tight, it flattened between my fingers. I barged ahead. "I never liked taking the pill to begin with, and now it seems that it didn't even work. And you act like birth control doesn't exist. It's all on me."

"But, Mandy, that's what being a girl's all about. It's like you're mad you were born a girl."

"But you're telling me I can't even smoke cigarettes!"

"I only nag because I care." His eyelashes cast pointy shadows on his cheeks, bestowing a shy, angelic aspect to his face.

"Stop caring then." I was tired.

"I can't, Mandy. Even if I wanted to. Look. Why don't I get you the name of Rose's doctor?"

"Oh no! If you tell anyone, I'll kill myself." I lit a cigarette off the one I had just finished.

He touched my cheek. "You look so beautiful. You got that, um, watchamacallit, that glow."

"Booner, everything you say is wrong." The rug was a vast expanse of swaying orange worms of yarn. Beyond Booner, the fish quivered in their tank, mouths opening and closing, milking moment by moment.

"I don't know what you want from me, Mandy. I mean, I never felt the way I'm feeling . . ." Again he circled the air with his big, ungainly hands.

But I knew what I wanted. Very clearly. I wanted him to be the pregnant one.

"Come on. Let's go eat." He stood. "I know you're hungry."

I stared at my toes, then my knees and my thighs, anything but Booner pulling on his jeans. I didn't want to see him carefully holding his penis while he zipped them. I looked when the zip was done.

He reached for me and I let him hoist me up off the floor. Then he put his arms around me and I rocked gently in his hug, warm and safe. Booner was two people, and one of them protected me. The other needed my protection. "Mandy Boyle, here's the thing. We have to get married."

The strength of his arms around me pushed out all the dangers and other possibilities.

"We'll move out of this place into a nice apartment until I have enough money and then we'll get a house." Booner talked in fast bursts, like I never heard him talk before. "I want to marry you. I gotta marry you. Will you marry me?"

There was no one else but him and nothing but his love. "Well," I said, feeling suddenly reckless and exuberant. Yes would settle everything. Yes would ease the gnawing fear and soothe the sadness. "Well, okay then. Sure."

He squeezed me. "Does that mean yes?"

"Yes." I laughed, loud, shrill, and unrecognizable. "Yes means yes."

MY DESK WAS large, L-shaped, with lots of drawers. It surrounded me like a wooden fortress. On the short side was the brand-new Wang machine on which I typed, stored, and personalized letters and résumés. I found the user's manual in one of the drawers.

On the wider section of my desk, along with the phone and a small radio, were a vase of fresh flowers delivered weekly, a box of tissues supplied by Priscilla, a large blotter with a calendar where I kept the schedule of appointments, and a plaque that was supposed to face out toward the door, like I did. The plaque said you have only failed when you have failed to try. I turned it to face myself. I believed it absolutely. Whatever happened, I would give it a try.

My chair had wheels and an adjustable back. The phone was sleek, tan. It didn't ring like a normal phone but emitted a humming chirp. My job was to answer it and take messages, always bearing in mind that my voice was the first indication of what kind of company Corporate Liaisons Incorporated was.

Neither Priscilla nor Leonard smoked, but they gave me a special smokeless ashtray with a domed cover and three small openings in which to lay a lit cigarette. Leonard said, "Try to keep the smoking down to a minimum, okay?" He spent the day in his office, on the phone.

But Priscilla lingered in the reception area, near me. "My boyfriend smokes so I have a little bit of tolerance, but Leonard hates it. He used to smoke, that's why." She perched her slim hip on the edge of my desk, talking as though she were letting me in on a secret.

"I remember what it was like to be your age. I wanted to be an actress," she said. "In college I majored in theater. And after I graduated, I moved to New York. I got my head shots, my résumé. I memorized monologues for auditions. But acting doesn't pay the rent, and I started doing office temp work."

"Wow, really." I had never thought of being an actress. I shifted toward her, hoping some of her glamour and elegance would land on me.

"Dreams like that just don't come true for everyone. I became a full-time secretary for six years before I moved on. But I don't regret it. In those six years I got my M.B.A., and the company paid for it. And you know what, the job I do now is like theater, so I haven't given anything up, really. Sales is theater. It's all theater, Miranda."

"So your boyfriend smokes, huh?" I wanted to get back to that, to learn all about him. Then I could tell her about Booner and how I said yes. "Did he want to be an actor, too?"

"I'm not willing to share that information." Priscilla slid off my desk. "Okay. Here's a word I want you to learn so well you live and breathe it. Repeat after me: *professionalism.*" She enunciated, pursing and widening her lips.

"Professionalism," I echoed. I wondered if Booner knew it.

The phone hummed. I picked it up. "Good morning, Corporate Liaisons," I enunciated exactly like Priscilla, since she was watching me.

"Priscilla?" said the man on the line.

"No. This is Miranda. Who's calling, please?"

"You sound just like Priscilla. It's Charles Hartnit."

"One moment please." I put him on hold. The other line rang and I picked it up. "Good morning, Corporate Liaisons."

"Leonard Glass, please."

"One moment." I was proud of my ease with juggling phone lines, proud of how far I had come in the two days I had worked here, and especially proud when I was mistaken for Priscilla. "Charles Hartnit on line one for you."

"Chuck!" Priscilla laughed and clapped her hands before she turned suddenly solemn and wagged her finger at me. "Miranda, you should always ask what it's in reference to. As it happens, I already know. But that was just luck. Anyway, I'll take it in my office. Thank you."

As soon as she left, I popped a piece of bubble gum into my mouth and lit a cigarette. It was perfect timing. On one wall of the reception area hung a round clock that ticked loudly, and I only allowed myself a cigarette every hour on the quarter past. If I missed that moment, I forced myself to wait until the next permitted time. I was in control.

On the other wall hung a framed print by Georgia O'Keeffe called *Two Calla Lilies on Pink*. Swirls of white and pale green filled the frame while a pink background, subtly shaded, peeked through. A stiff yellow stamen protruded from each flower, casting a muted yellow reflection on the white. The painting changed throughout the day, depending on how long I stared at it. In the morning, the calla lilies were cool, aloof, waiting, though not expectant. In the afternoon they shifted, slowly becoming richer, drawing me into a whirlpool of blending color, and I began to daydream about Booner and the stiff yellow stamens. I dreamed myself into the evening when I would arrive home and it wasn't night yet because the days were getting longer. Booner would kiss me until I felt as though I were melting like the heroines in the bodice-buster novels that Tracy and I used to read.

Then I couldn't remember if any of those heroines ever got pregnant. I opened the mail that arrived throughout the day, ripping, slicing, and slashing the envelopes with the letter opener that I stored in the top drawer of my desk. It distracted me from the one thought that blanked out all others as soon as it entered my mind. How could I sit here, behind this desk day after day, hour after hour, with a baby growing inside me? It seemed that my life was made up of many separate realities with no connection to each other except where they intruded.

Résumés arrived daily, and each new one deserved its own manila folder. I wrote the last names on the folder tabs and filed them according to specialty, like Fiduciary, Estates and Trusts, Insurance, and credential, like LL.B. and J.D.

In a little room off to the right of the reception area, there was a seemingly endless supply of manila folders on the shelves, plus yellow legal pads, copy paper, pens, pencils, Post-its, and more. The postage meter machine was in that room, too, along with the Xerox machine and coat rack. Also in the stock room stood a water cooler. The blue spigot poured out cold water and the red poured out hot for Priscilla's tea, very luxurious. It was my favorite room, the room of plenty.

I filed. I made Xerox copies. I purchased office supplies and took deposits to the bank. After I opened the mail, I went through the classified sections in *The Wall Street Journal* and *The New York Times,* circling ads relevant to the firm so Leonard and Priscilla could send résumés there. I liked the orderliness of the day, the knowing what I had to do and doing it, and the precise marching manner in which the day progressed.

The phone hummed. "Good afternoon, Corporate Liaisons."

"Yeah. Can I talk to Mandy Boyle?"

"May I ask what this is in reference to?" I waited for Booner to recognize my voice.

"Huh? What? Is Mandy there?"

"One moment please." With a strange lightness, I put him on hold. The flowers on my desk bowed to me. The clock ticked and the calla lilies swirled, hypnotizing. I could utterly fool Booner, and this gave me a larger sense of myself. Like when I first started smoking, it was something that only I could do. Though Tracy could sign my name in study hall and Mom could dress me up and read my diary, only I could actually smoke my own cigarette, which meant no one else could breathe my breath for me.

I put on my normal, comparatively sluggish voice. "Hello."

"Mandy? What kind of bitch do you work for? She wanted references."

"References?" I tried to imagine Booner walking through the door, waiting in one of the chairs for an interview. But I couldn't see him in a suit and tie. I touched the diamond on the chain around my neck and loved him. He needed my protection. I would teach him. "Hey, Booner, did you ever hear of the word *professionalism?*"

"I hate that phony stuck-up shit."

"Well, I have to learn to live and breathe it." I laughed as though it were all phony stuck-up shit. But I felt disloyal to Priscilla by laughing. She had been so nice to me, and I wanted to learn whatever I could.

"So what else do you do all day besides sit on your pretty butt living and breathing stupid shit?"

Mom, too, had wanted to know what I did all day.

"I answer the phone, send out résumés, type up letters. Lots of stuff." I didn't mention opening mail or circling want ads. Booner wouldn't think of those as work.

"I still don't know why you have to work there. It's fucking crazy. I worry about you. When I call, I expect your boss to say, 'Mandy? No, she's not here. She was murdered on the subway.' "

"Well, first of all, she would call me Miranda." I held the receiver to my ear and shut my eyes.

"I'm putting the screws on Eugene now. Any day, he'll fire the ditz so you can work here at the garage with me."

"Great." But I hoped that Eugene wouldn't fire anyone. The garage didn't have a water cooler, unlimited manila folders, flowers, or a plaque that said YOU HAVE ONLY FAILED WHEN YOU HAVE FAILED TO TRY. I liked being at my desk.

"So, girl, anyway, when are we gonna get married? We have to plan. You know, Lumpy told me that Donna's taking care of everything for their wedding. She's got magazines and shit. So maybe you ought to give her a call."

"You didn't tell anyone about . . ."

"No. What do you think I am? But Lumpy was going on about it. I'm just telling you. And I'm calling because I think I'm gonna get out early today. You should've been here at lunch, it was fucking funny!"

I could tuck the phone between my shoulder and my ear, correcting documents on the Wang machine while I listened to Booner's voice. He was like a little man living in my ear, talking away, my own Tom Thumb.

". . . just before lunch Hot Shot was in the shower. He got sprayed with some wicked black shit from this basin out in Brooklyn. Anyway, he thought the ditz was out to lunch, so he came out of the shower butt naked just as she was walking out of the office. Man, he almost bumped right into her!" Booner cracked up. I could tell he was stifling just a little, holding his mouth shut so chewing tobacco wouldn't fly out. I heard it in his voice. I knew him so well. "She ran screaming back to the office and wouldn't come out until Eugene escorted her."

"Lucky it wasn't you in the shower."

"Hey, if it was me in the shower, I'm the one who'd need an escort."

Priscilla buzzed me on her intercom. "Miranda, what time is my appointment?"

"Just a second," I told Booner, and pushed the hold button, leaving him in the limbo land of hold. I checked the calendar, buzzed Priscilla. "Bruce Davis. Three o'clock."

Then I picked up Booner again. "Sorry. I'm back."

"I hate that."

"I can't help it," I said. "It was my boss."

"You wouldn't find Eugene playing those games with me while I'm talking to you."

"It's a different kind of thing."

"Well, it'll be a whole different kind of thing when you're working here."

It was beautifully, luxuriously warm in the office, but I felt an inner iciness. The job at GeneRo was beginning to sound like a punishment. And what if the ditz quit? The last thing I wanted to see during my working day was Hot Shot in the flesh with his double chin, beer gut, and penis hanging out there in the open.

"I gotta go, little girl. Love me?"

"Sure do." He kissed the receiver first. Then I kissed it and hung up the phone.

Bruce Davis was large, almost fat, but with a handsome, tanned face and a chiseled chin. His straight, dark hair was trimmed short and parted on the side. His ears lay close to his skull. "I'm here to see Priscilla Sherman," he said in a deep voice. His eyes were brown, alert, and as friendly as an intelligent dog's. He was a tax attorney seeking a base salary of 85K+.

I learned on my first day at Corporate Liaisons Incorporated what K was in terms of dollar amounts. I took home just over two hundred dollars a week gross, which meant that I made 11K a year, which meant Bruce Davis and I lived on two separate planets. It amazed me to be in the same room with so rich and handsome a man.

My fairy godmother, who looks like Priscilla, helps dress me for the ball. Bruce Davis is the prince who finds my delicate glass slipper and searches the nation for the girl who ran from his arms at midnight. But Booner suddenly transforms into an even more powerful prince from a foreign land. He brandishes a flashing sword. "Stay away from my love, you beast, or I'll cut your head off!" I swoon in fear, crumpling gracefully to the ground while Bruce Davis scurries off, lowly and despicable. Booner takes me in his arms and awakens me with kisses.

"Have a seat. I'll tell Ms. Sherman you're here." I gave a little bow, aware of the ill-fitting cream-colored dress of Mom's I was wearing and how I was bowing like a lackey, as Booner never would. He was proud. He would rather die on his feet than live on his knees. I had to stop bowing.

I scurried around my desk so Bruce Davis wouldn't notice the sole flapping off one of my run-down loafers. I resolved to buy a new pair of shoes as soon as I received my first paycheck. I opened the door to Priscilla's office. "Bruce Davis is here."

She cupped her compact mirror, applying lipstick, smooshing her lips together. "Put him in the conference room please, Miranda."

He was still sitting in the reception area, reading the plaque on my desk. I imagined picking him up and dragging him through the office, setting him like a giant dummy in one of the conference room chairs.

"I have to put you in the conference room." I laughed at the absurdity of putting him anywhere. He didn't laugh back, probably just didn't get it. But I felt hurt by his not responding. If he had said something funny that I didn't get, I would have laughed, if only to be courteous.

You should see me in my photography class, I wanted to say. I don't need you. I'm going to my teacher's show in a gallery. "You can sit there." I pointed to the chair I had sat in for my interview.

He obeyed, seating himself opposite the print of the figure on the mountaintop.

"What the mind can conceive, the body can achieve," I said, pointing to it, craving at the very least a polite chuckle. But he gazed at me, his expression blank, friendly and unchanged.

Priscilla strode in, all business, power, and womanhood in her tailored suit and sheer stockings, her calves well defined in her sleek black pumps. Bruce Davis blushed, half stood, then sat. Who could blame him? Priscilla's lips were perfect, her smile large and welcoming. "Did our little assistant here offer you coffee?"

"I'm sorry," I said. "Do you want coffee?"

He shook his head and nervously adjusted his tie. But it had looked better before.

"Miranda. Tea. Lemon." Priscilla turned to Bruce Davis as she laid a manila folder on the table. "We're training her and she's learning very fast."

I cut Priscilla's lemon in two, holding it over the garbage can in the stock room as juice dripped over my fingers. "She's learning very fast" didn't feel like a compliment. Maybe Booner was right and Priscilla was a phony bitch who thought she was better than anyone else. And what would Booner have said about Bruce Davis? An egghead with money who never had to work a day in his life and he wouldn't last two seconds in Booner's job.

"Will that be all?" I set the tea down in front of Priscilla.

"Yes, thank you, Miranda."

Well, she had thanked me at least. I returned to my desk, having missed my moment for a cigarette. I washed off my phone receiver with lemon-scented spray cleaner. Then, spray cleaner in hand, I knocked on the door to Leonard's office. "Do you need your phone cleaned?"

"Sure, come on in."

•   •   •

THE DARKROOM WAS the best place to be. Warm, dark, and deep red. I could hide here. There were twelve enlargers, each one built into its own booth. They ran along opposite walls. The developing trays were set up on the counter down the middle.

"Yo, listen *up*! If you must leave for any reason, you announce it first. You never open the door. We don't want to screw up anyone's print." Doug paced the room. His shoelaces dragged. I heard them softly clicking along the floor in the silence between his words.

The first print I made was of Rose at the baby shower. I put the negative into the removable carrier and set the carrier tightly in place in the enlarger. Then I projected the image onto the easel. I focused, cropped, adjusted the contrast, and exposed the image onto a sheet of printing paper, which I carried to the developer tray and agitated with my tongs.

The blank sheet transformed into a laughing pregnant woman crowned with a hat made of ribbons. She was so huge that she spilled over the seat of her rocking chair. Her face was sharply focused, right down to the lines around her eyes. She stared at the camera with her mouth in a smile that looked more like a scream than a laugh. The image floated in liquid, revealing a terror in Rose I didn't remember seeing at the baby shower. I plucked it out, allowed it to drip off one corner, and laid it in the stop bath, then the fixer. It was my first print. I rinsed it and hung it on the line above the sink.

"Discoveries are made in the darkroom, and we want to be open to them . . ." Doug was talking to someone in the booth across from mine, but I felt as though he were talking to me.

"Damn. Shit. Can't fucking believe it." The guy at the enlarger next to mine banged things around, talked to himself. "Hey." He leaned into my booth. "Can I just borrow your tongs for a second, because I forgot . . ."

I handed him my photographic tongs and he dipped his blank paper into the developer. "Fucking A, man. I took some pictures, they are *out there*! I was totally fucking inspired!"

I wondered what it was like to feel inspired. An orgasm? An ear-ache? I couldn't ask. But I didn't have to put on a smile or an attentive expression, because it was dark. I watched as a figure slowly emerged on his paper and a gray shape became an old man with matted hair and layers of grimy clothes. He was spitting into a garbage can, his spit droplets suspended midair. I might have seen that man carrying a huge sack of soda cans the day I went with Booner to the Fresh Kills landfill, but it wasn't information I wanted to offer.

"Pretty powerful." I wished I knew his name. I liked him, even though he was loud, because he didn't seem to care what people thought.

"I'm gonna call this one *Die Yuppie Scum*!" he shouted.

"Enthusiasm is good. Loud mouth is not good," Doug called over. He was talking to a tall, dark-haired woman who wore a hat with a netted veil over her face. I had seen her in the hall before class and the hat was definitely cool. But how could she see anything in the darkroom with a veil over her eyes?

I turned back to my enlarger.

My next print was a picture of the living room window. I exposed it and then came my favorite part of the process, watching the blank page transform as it floated in the developer. A dark grid appeared, the burglar gates. Diamond shapes of soft light seemed to hover in the space behind the grid.

The others in the class were also quietly developing prints. The loud guy settled down, using my tongs, which I set on the counter. The only sounds were the dribble of liquid, the whisper of paper, and the click and hum of various enlargers.

Doug walked from one booth to the next. There were occasional questions and murmurs, but an underlying respect for the process prevailed. Prints lay in all stages of development in the trays and hung drying on the line above the sink.

The woman in the veiled hat was developing a print of a skinny naked guy, shoulder blades like sharp wings and a rib cage so pronounced that the shadows striped him like a zebra. He twisted in an odd position, facing a mirror, his back to the camera. Would Booner ever pose like that for me? I couldn't see it.

"He's my muse." The woman had addressed me through her veil as she moved her print from the stop tray to the fixer.

"Wow, really." I tried to place this woman into the other realities of my life. I couldn't imagine her at Rose's baby shower. I tried to picture her at Corporate Liaisons Incorporated. No way. I put her on Main Street in Ransomville, but I had to erase her out. She belonged nowhere but here, in the darkroom.

I chose another view of the living room window. I had taken this one lying on my back and the gate loomed up at an angle. Light was glowing behind it like a window in one of the cathedrals I had studied in Art History. I had known so little then. It seemed like a lifetime ago.

"So you're the gate person." A graveled voice, very close, pulled me out of myself.

"Gate person?"

"Yeah," said Doug. "I saw the gate photo hanging over the sink and I'm glad you're doing another. It's a great use of negative space, and you want to get it just right. It's got a certain purity."

"Negative space." What was negative space? I hadn't learned that in Art History. If only college hadn't gone bad. I remembered the Ox, the gray concrete towers, Barb and Tiff in the cafeteria, underwear in a sealed plastic bag.

"Miranda, right? When did I see you? Tuesday?"

"Yes." I felt special, acknowledged, until I remembered what had happened after I saw Doug on Tuesday. There was before Booner knew my secret and there was after. Behind that was a mess I didn't want to look at. I had to be very careful not to let it all fall apart the way it did in college.

"Yeah, what I mean by negative space is the use of the entire rect-angle, the entire print. I mean not seeing merely the object but how it fills the space. You know, not just the thing but what's behind the thing."

My eyes were level with his lips, which were soft and eerie, sur-rounded by his beard as they moved in the shadowed red. I watched them purse and the hair around them shift as he brought a can of beer to his mouth and took a deep swallow. I assumed it was beer since it was tall, wrapped in a paper bag. Tallboys. I once drank them with Barb.

"You may want to expose that lower-right-hand corner a little longer. It fades off a bit. And you can use a piece of blank paper to cover your gate. Diagonal. Like so."

My skin tingled when he brushed my arm. I felt more fully alive, and it wasn't just because of Doug. It was the darkroom, where everything seemed possible and nothing was known or certain.

The woman in the veiled hat interrupted. "Doug? Pardon me, but could you take a look at what I'm doing, because I'm trying to capture the fragmentary nature of . . ."

"Not now, Celeste. I'm talking to Miranda." Doug touched his bearded chin.

If we were in a normally lit room, the heat of my blush would have pulsed out, humiliated me, caused the sweat to spurt from under my arms and slide down my sides. But no one saw my blush in the darkroom, and I didn't have to be embarrassed.

"I'm on the verge of a breakthrough," Celeste insisted.

"Not now." Doug didn't even turn in her direction. "It's like a formalist plea." He pointed to the image projected on my easel. "Here's this massive structure blocking the light, like a prison gate. Are you with me?"

"So far."

"But the light, the light has life. It's like an imprisoned, um . . ." He paused to gulp more beer. "Soul. Yeah. That's it. An imprisoned soul. Or spirit."

I swallowed at the same time he did. My face grew hot and seemed to swell. My fingers throbbed. The air around me was heavy, pulsating, pushing me into a little hole where I couldn't marry Booner or have a baby and still be this person in the darkroom discussing negative space. Every part of my life contradicted every other.

Doug was still talking. ". . . and we want to avoid artificiality. Dishonesty." He gestured with the barest movement of his hand, as if he just couldn't be bothered. "Yet photography is lies and artifice. It's the ultimate conflict, really."

I tried to concentrate on what he was saying, but I was too nervous. My face was so close to his that if I leaned toward him slightly, shut my eyes, and moved my lips, the world would drop away in one long kiss of gratitude. But I shifted my position, careful not to touch him, offend him.

"The thing is, you've got something here, so, um, keep doing it." His sneakers, all different colors in the daylight, were mottled shades of red and black in the darkroom.

"And since you're into gates, check out some gates around the city. Get out of your apartment. Find the gates that mean the most to you. That's your assignment for next week."

But I hadn't said I was into gates. "What about people? Can't I take pictures of people?"

"Just for the week. Take at least one roll of film, only gates. And you know why I can say that?" He clasped my shoulder, a friendly gesture with no agenda, so different than Booner's. "Because I'm the teacher." He laughed and turned toward the center of the room. "Everybody listen! My show is opening Wednesday night. Charis Gallery on Prince Street. I don't have any more postcards, but there's a notice on the bulletin board. So I'll see you all there, I hope."

I had placed my postcard in Dad's hidden shoe, and I was looking forward to Doug's opening as if it were my own.

"We're clear, right, Miranda? Take pictures of all the people you want, but get an entire roll of gates." Doug moved on to the next enlarger, his shoelaces dragging and clicking behind him.

"Oh, Doug!" Celeste called from across the room. "I need you for a second!"

I tried the same window again, exposed the corner slightly longer, as Doug had suggested, and he was right. It was better when it didn't fade off. A structure imposed on light. Negative space. Boundless space. Buoyant as the air, fluid as the chemicals in their trays, I could do anything I wanted. Unless I had a baby.

Suddenly dizzy, I groped my way back to the enlarger and leaned against the wall of the divider, pressing my cheek against its smooth, solid coolness. I shut my eyes. The meaning of the gates expanded and circled back to me. I was pregnant.

"Are you okay?" The loud guy peered into my booth.

"Yeah. Thanks." I straightened up, grateful that he noticed. I decided to do a print of Booner emerging from the shower with steam rising off his warm, wet body and the towel wrapped perfectly around him, as though he were posing for the camera. It struck me that Booner was pretty much always posing, and I liked him better that way, because without his pose, he disintegrated and he wasn't what I needed.

It was a surprise when Doug clapped his hands. "People. Start winding down. Start cleaning up. Everyone has their own assignment, right? Good!"

Three hours had slipped by like a minute. By the end of the class, I had developed twelve prints. I took care. I paid attention. I patted the prints dry and put them in an envelope with a piece of cardboard so they wouldn't bend and curl.

THE CLINIC WAS located in a large, many-storied brownish brick building, as anonymous as any other building in the city except for a small plaque out front that said STUYVESANT WOMEN'S CENTER. Even so, a group of people stood vigil on the sidewalk, holding hands and praying.

Their chanting wasn't intrusive as I approached but soft, almost comforting, until a man broke from the huddle talking urgently. "We're trying to save lives in that building. There's a murder factory on the third floor. An abortuary." He thrust a leaflet at me that said RESCUE THOSE BEING DRAGGED TO DEATH, PROVERBS 24:11, with a crude drawing of a fetus.

I wanted to reassure the man that I was only there for a test, that Booner had asked me to marry him, but I was unable to interrupt. "Don't you feel it?" he cried. "We're standing in a place of horror, where innocent babies are being ripped to shreds one by one!"

I had heard of these people, had seen them on TV, but was unprepared for their effect on me. I marched past the man, fighting the urge to run away, go back to Queens, to Booner, to Rose Economopolous.

A woman directly in front of the entrance held up a plaster statue of a blue-robed Virgin Mary, big as a child, paint flaking off her arms and face. "Don't kill your baby!" the woman wailed. But she stepped aside as I pushed the door open. My heart was thudding, my body ached, and my backpack felt heavy, weighing down my shoulders.

The elevator was old, jolting and rattling. The doors opened directly into a very crowded, shabby waiting room. Some women sat in folding chairs with crying babies in their laps. Others sat alone. Every chair was taken. A poster showing the stages of fetal development hung crookedly on the paint-chipped wall. Another poster showed pictures of birth control methods. An oldies tune was playing on the radio, in the background, *". . . no, you just have to wait. Love don't come easy. It's a game of give-and-take . . ."*

The receptionist was about my age, bent over a textbook, Hi-Liter in hand, brown hair pulled back in a perky ponytail. She was probably in college. I felt a tug toward Barb, toward the library with its rows of books, the classrooms, blackboards, and chairs with foldout desktops. I missed the hope I had felt when I first glimpsed the university towers on the approach from the thruway. The clinic at college was much cleaner, newer, and kinder than this one, which seemed deliberately drab and run-down.

The receptionist took my name. "It might be a while. Not that long, but a while."

I didn't care how long it took. I had nowhere to go. I went to the pay phone, which was against the wall, next to the elevator, and dialed Booner, letting it ring fourteen times before I hung up. Where was he? His deep, familiar voice was supposed to strengthen me. Instead I felt helpless, as though I were being swooped into a panicked whirl. I needed a voice in my ear to ground me. Throwing countless quarters into the coin slot, I dialed Barb long-distance at college, expecting nothing.

"Start talking." The miracle of her immediate voice rendered me speechless, dizzy, almost ill.

"Hello? Hello?" she said.

"Uh, Barb? Hi, it's Mandy." Everyone in the waiting room could hear me.

"Mandy, how the hell are ya? You wouldn't believe! They gave me a new roommate and she put up posters of unicorns! It's not the black hole anymore! You *have* to come back, I can't take it!" But she was laughing about the unicorns. Life was funny for her, not the dead-serious issue it had become for me. I felt desperate, with the painful familiar prickling of tears coming on. Why had I called?

"What else is new with you?" I asked.

"Me? Shit. I'm studying like crazy because I missed so many classes and . . ."

I pictured her on the phone, pushing her frizzy hair off her face, leaning heavily against the wall, and fidgeting with her skirt. If I had been there, I too would have studied like crazy, looking forward to completing my freshman year. I might already have declared my major. What would it have been? Philosophy? Humanities? English? Political science?

"Barb," I whispered. "I think I'm pregnant. I don't know what to do."

There was silence.

"I'm at a clinic right now, to make sure."

More silence. She probably wished she hadn't answered the phone. "Barb?" My voice squeaked.

"Mandy, look," she said quickly. "This isn't something I tell everyone, but I had an abortion over Christmas break. The mother'rent dragged me there."

Although I was aware of the controversy, had seen debates on TV and pictures of crowds chaining themselves to clinics, abortion had always been an abstraction, something far away. Now it became a reality. My forehead was drenched. My sweater was damp, sticking to the small of my back. I couldn't fend off the unbearable sense of regret and exclusion. She hadn't told me. "Barb. I'm so sorry. I didn't know. Was it hard?"

"Please deposit five cents for the next two minutes."

I threw a nickel in. "Barb?" There was silence. Of course, there had been no room for her to tell me.

"It wasn't so bad," Barb finally said. "It only takes about five minutes. I mean, those barefoot-and-pregnant days are over, you know?"

"Did you think about, you know, having it?" I remembered Tracy holding Junior out toward me, Tracy, in her stretch wedding gown, throwing the bouquet. I pictured Junior playing with the steering wheel on Booner's car, and I wondered if Tracy had ever considered having an abortion. Then again, in Ransomville there was nowhere to get one. You had to drive fifty miles away, and if you made that trip, you kept it secret. Girls had babies, not abortions.

"Well. Yeah. Sure. But I'm still in college, and I want to go to graduate school. I didn't exactly know who the father was either. Tiff's been like my best friend through it all."

I felt a sharp pang of envy. I wanted to be her best friend.

"Miranda Boyle." The receptionist called my name.

"Barb, I have to go. Can I call you later?"

"Does the pope shit in the woods, silly?" I hung up with her laughter echoing in my ear.

A nurse in a white coat took my blood. "When was your last period?" she asked.

"I don't exactly remember," I said, ashamed.

She led me to an examining room, where I undressed. Then she helped me onto the table. I lay back with my feet in the stirrups. "The doctor will be in soon, okay?" She left the room, shutting the door behind her, and I was alone, waiting. Would I ever get used to this horrible, awkward position? I envied Booner and all the males in the world, who went through their days oblivious and free.

The doctor finally came in. She had a brisk, efficient manner. She didn't smile, but she wasn't unkind. The examination was over quickly.

"Well, you're pregnant. In fact, you're about ten weeks." She let the words sit there as she gazed solemnly at me, her hands folded in front of her. She looked at me until I felt the sobs come on, dry and almost forced. She was telling me what I already knew, which meant nothing had changed, nothing was any clearer.

Then she handed me a tissue, and the small kindness caused me to choke up. Burning tears gushed out. I was crying again. Always crying. I hated it. How had I traveled so far only to come to this?

"You have some options, and it's important that you consider them now," said the doctor. "Nod if you can hear me."

I nodded through my tears. I wished I could let my hair down to hide my face. I wished I had a hat with a veil.

"Understand that if you don't make a decision, that *is* a decision. If you want to terminate, for instance, it will have to be done as soon as possible, because if it isn't, you'll be talking about a much more complicated procedure. If you want to have this baby, you must begin prenatal care immediately."

"I don't know what to do!"

She patted my shoulder. "What about the father? Do you know who the father is? Can you talk to him?"

What more could I say to Booner? I tried to think, to measure the days out. Ten weeks. We were almost at the end of March, which meant ... I couldn't concentrate, and stared at the floor. Free-floating flecks of dull green, gray, and yellow shifted like fractured clouds. The floor was a moving whirlpool of molecules, drawing me in, sucking me down.

She handed me another tissue. "We offer counseling on Monday evenings. You should come to our next session. But you ought to make an appointment for a D-and-C before you leave here. We get very crowded, and you want to make sure you get yourself a spot if you need it. After the counseling session, you can always change your mind and cancel your appointment."

I blew my nose, finding comfort in the fact that I could always change my mind.

"It's tough," said the doctor. "It's really tough. You'll have some hard choices in the next few days. But you seem like a smart girl."

I picked up my backpack, wanting to hug this doctor, this woman I didn't know at all. I walked out of the examination room to the reception area and, dabbing my eyes with a tissue, did exactly as she had suggested.

BOONER WAS STANDING shirtless over the stove, his back to me, when I walked in. Grease spattered as he held a fork with a hot dog stuck on the end of it over the flame on a burner. "Where the fuck were you?" He didn't turn around.

"I went to a clinic." I was confused. I tried to recall if Booner had always talked with such a cruel tone. But I couldn't pause to puzzle it out. I had something to say quick, before I lost my nerve. "I've been thinking that I might not be ready to have a baby. Like maybe I could have an abortion. I mean, those barefoot-and-pregnant days are over, you know."

"What the hell are you talking about?"

"I just don't know if I'm ready to be a mother."

"Speaking of that. Your mom called, talking a lot of Jesus shit." Booner turned, holding his fork with the hot dog dripping oil on the floor. "She's a couple cans short of a six-pack, that's for damn sure."

His words stung. He had no right to say that. "She's sensitive." I repeated what Dad would have said. "She hasn't had an easy life. And her health's always been bad, but she makes the best of it."

"Yeah well, maybe you're as mental as her." He bit into his hot dog and spit it on the floor, puffing noisily. "Whoa. Hot."

"That's disgusting, Booner." I couldn't stand being in the same room as him, not one more second. I walked into the living room, where the fish tank glowed aqua against the wall, quietly bubbling. I lit a cigarette and it was a relief to breathe the smoke in.

The fish seemed faded, drooping, suspended in place. Their mouths opened and closed in slow motion. Did they know of the larger tank in which their small tank existed? When I poured in some food, not a single fish swam up. The crumbs descended slowly to settle invisibly among the brightly colored pebbles. I dabbled my finger in the water. It was ice-cold.

Booner came to the doorway, chewing. "I don't know if I'm ready to be a father, either. But guess what. Rose said she thought it was great news. She said it was the best thing that could happen to me. Said it would straighten me right out." His voice was too loud for the room. It sprang off the walls, hitting against the fish tank, the TV, and me. His chewing, too, was loud and moist. The whole space seemed to be chewing, filled with the suck of a tongue pulling bites off a fork and the muffled chomp of hot dog jammed into molars, sloshed with saliva, and swallowed.

"You said you wouldn't tell anyone, Booner." I got up and went to the window, putting as much distance between us as possible. I curled my fingers around the gate, blackened with dirt and dust. It needed washing desperately. And I was the one who would have to do it, just as the half-scraped bathroom, with its look of perpetual, permanent incompletion, needed desperately for me to finish it. The tasks only grew and expanded until they were larger than my ability.

I heard the heavy stomp of Booner walking before I felt the warmth of his big hands circling my waist. "What could I do, Mandy? I was freaking out. I needed to talk to someone. You're making me crazy. It seems like all I do, all day long, is worry about you while you're off doing our own fucking thing."

Outside, lights twinkled from golden rectangles, each one a window leading directly onto lives unrelated to me or to each other.

Booner moved his hands up to cup my breasts. I stiffened with the urge to spit, to scream, to kick. I needed air. I tore myself away from him, ran to the kitchen, and grabbed my camera off the table, ignoring Booner's "Where the fuck are you going?" I ran out to the hall and up the stairs to the roof, where I unbolted the thick metal door.

The air was soft and damp against my skin. The sun had gone down and a wash of lavender and pink spread across the sky, darkening like a bruise. How far I had come from the first evening I stood out here with Booner. I had known his loneliness then from the inside out and thought it was love. It wasn't.

I set the camera on the ledge with the f-stop wide open. I needed a flash for the close-ups, but it was downstairs on the dresser. I could capture the twilight without it, I hoped. Far away, lights pulsed and flickered like stars, each light an offering to its own private heaven.

Would I ever know a heaven to have faith in? No long-range universal vision existed, only randomness, the luck of the draw. There was only me, alone on the roof looking out over the lights, hoping that, maybe, at the top of one of those other buildings someone else was standing, gazing, who might catch a glimpse of me. And we would recognize each other.

I heard a metallic click. Thunk, and the roof door shut. A gray figure approached through the falling evening and gradually took on Booner's shape. He hunched inside himself, shoving his hands in his front pockets. I became aware of the chill then, aware I was cold. He stopped, too far away to touch. "Are you mad at me?" His voice vibrated oddly, as if the air affected it.

"I don't know." If I was mad, it was larger than Booner. It was because life had arranged itself like this.

He held a squarish object out toward me. Why was he offering me his beeper? I took a step to him, and he stretched his hand further, holding out my flashbulb. "Thought you could use this."

Maybe he understood a few things after all. Maybe I wasn't as alone as I thought. I clicked the flash into place and listened to the hum as it warmed up.

"You'll make a real good mother, you know. Rose says she was afraid at first, too. You're not the only one having a hard time."

I focused in on Booner, hunched and twisted in some kind of misguided repentance. Click. I got him, just like that, with the metal door behind him. Then I turned and walked toward the edge where the roof dropped off into the street five flights below.

I could keep walking until I dropped right off this life, because there was no reason not to. Because Booner handing me my flashbulb was not enough. All small kindnesses only brought out my longing for more. What was the use?

Booner grabbed my shoulder, jerking me backward, solid, strong, and sure of what he wanted. He enfolded me in his arms so I couldn't move, squeezing my camera painfully in my chest. "Let go of me, Booner. You said you wouldn't tell anyone. You promised."

"But Rose is different. And she was so happy for us. And I'll marry you."

"I want an abortion, Booner." My voice was clearer than my conviction. The streetlights all shot on at once along the sidewalk. Each round glow reflected the damp air, small artificial moons.

He was breathing hard, almost sobbing, but dry sobs, shedding no tears. He kneeled down, his arms still circled around me, pulling at my shirt, pulling at my pants, until he hugged my knees. "Please don't leave me."

"Booner, did you hear me? I can't take care of a baby."

He released me and I pulled my pants up, balanced on my own two feet, while Booner, crouching like an injured man, wiped his nose on his sweatshirt sleeve. "When I was a kid, my mother always had these guys stay with her and . . ." He was sobbing for real now. His tears reflected shiny trails down his cheeks. ". . . there was one who, I don't know, he came in and yanked me out of bed, started beating me up with his belt and then he got a piece of wood." Booner hunched up in a fetal position. He was drawing me in again. His hardships were greater than mine and his sadness more profound, the cruelty he had endured solid and unmistakable.

"Where was your mother?" I asked softly. "Why would he beat you?"

"What do you mean, why? I don't know why. I left my toys out or something. I don't know! He just came in and he was beating on me. My mother didn't do shit. She was drunk." He looked up, eyes liquid, staring at me like a sick, helpless dog. "She told me I should've been an abortion. And after that I lived with a foster family for three months. Then the guy left and my mother took me back."

I kneeled down and hugged him. I held his head, which felt large and heavy between my palms. I took the suffering he offered and for that moment it was enough, this chance to comfort and diminish all the wrongs inflicted on the innocent child who Booner once was. His wide, hard shoulders heaved with his weeping and the power was mine, the power to nurture, to give love, to undo.

AWARENESS

WHEN I OPENED the door to the office in the morning, the fresh scent of flowers, the tidy sight of my desk, and the inevitable presence of the computer greeted me with the promise of order. My trial period was over in a week and it seemed pretty certain I was here to stay, so I could forget about myself for a while.

"Let's try you at phone sales." Priscilla thumped the Yellow Pages down in front of me. Then she cloaked herself in her fake mink and sailed out the door to an appointment.

"Hello. My name is Miranda Boyle and I'm calling from Corporate Liaisons Incorporated. We're a placement firm specializing in tax professionals, how are you this morning? Oops. I mean, this afternoon."

"Not interested," said a woman on the other end, cutting me off with a soft click.

"How did you get this number?" demanded a man.

"I don't have time for this," said another.

After six phone calls, I needed a cigarette to recover from the feeling of rejection. I straightened out my desk, typed a few letters, and filed some résumés before I reluctantly went back to the Yellow Pages.

"Hello, I'm calling from Corporate Liaisons . . ."

"I don't take marketing calls." The woman on the other end hung up.

I shut the phone book. Wasn't there anything to photocopy?

"How's it going?" Leonard ambled out, cleaning his ear with the end of an uncurled paper clip.

"I don't know if I'm cut out for these cold calls."

"Let me see. I'll sit with you and you go ahead. Make a call."

I opened the Yellow Pages again, inadvertently landing on C: clinics, pregnancy, and abortion services, two columns of them.

"Don't use the Yellow Pages! Who gave you the Yellow Pages?"

"Priscilla."

"I can't believe Priscilla would do that." He got up and went to his office, emerging with an enormous hardcover Dun & Bradstreet directory. "Use this."

I dialed, conscious of my gestures and how I was slouching. My fingertips seemed too big as I clumsily pushed the buttons on the phone. Then I saw that Leonard was facing the Georgia O'Keeffe print, not looking at me. I relaxed a little.

"Hello, my name is Miranda Boyle and I'm calling from Corporate Liaisons Incorporated . . ."

"Forget it," said a woman.

Perspiration trailed a long drop from my armpit to my waist. I dialed the next number. "Hello, my name is Miranda Boyle and I'm calling from Corporate Liaisons Incorporated to find out if you have any openings in your firm."

"Well now," said the man on the other end. "I got openings, all right."

Leonard shifted in his seat, crossing his legs so his pants hiked up, revealing a small area of hairy skin above his sock and below his trouser cuff.

"You do? Well, how about for tax professionals? You see we're a . . ."

"How about you spread your legs and I eat your cunt out?"

"I must have the wrong number." I hung up, hands trembling. "I don't like doing this, Leonard. I'd rather just answer the phone."

"You sound too wooden." He jiggled his tassel-loafered foot. "You've got to engage."

I doodled on an index card. There was a stack of them for writing down who had been called and what was said. But there hadn't been a single phone call worthy of an index card.

"While we're at it, let me give you a little bit of advice."

I waited. I drew a swirl and then a swirl inside that swirl and another and another.

"That necklace and those earrings. Miranda. No. They don't go together, c'mon."

I shook my head to hear the earrings tinkle. My gift from Barb. I touched the cool, smooth teardrop on the chain. My gift from Booner. "What do you mean?"

"There's a word I want to give you the meaning of—*professionalism*. You heard of it?"

I nodded. "Priscilla clued me in."

"Did she mention the earrings?"

I was afraid of where this was going. I shook my head. She had not mentioned the earrings. She told me I did a good job, that my word-processing skills were invaluable, that my phone voice had improved, and that I took good, detailed messages. I drew another swirl, loving the flow of the pen on the paper. Razor Point pens drew beautiful textured lines, like velvet. They were a definite fringe benefit.

"Turquoise and silver, they're kid stuff. You're in the working world now. The necklace isn't bad, but you're better off wearing no earrings at all than wearing those."

I took off one earring, then the other, as he was talking. "Anything else?"

"The dress, Miranda. I don't want to hurt your feelings. You're very competent, but you're the first person a client sees when they walk in here, and quite frankly, you look like shit."

I was too surprised to get upset. "Are you telling me to take my dress off?"

"No, of course not. I'm telling you that how you look is inappropriate for this office."

But the dress was Mom's. Since she knew how to earn a living, I thought she at least knew what kind of dress to wear for it. I thought the two skills were somehow related.

The key clicked in the lock and Priscilla waltzed in like a blessing, trailing cold air and perfume. "Another highly successful meeting!" she declared in a singsong voice. Beneath her fur coat she wore a cream-colored two-piece suit and two-tone pumps. Her earrings were small pearls. She set a small blue shopping bag on my desk. "What's this? Are you two having a little powwow?"

"Priscilla, the opportunity came up and I was just sharing some thoughts with Miranda about professionalism."

"Ah, you're having that talk without me." Priscilla plucked one of my turquoise earrings off the desk. "I hope he was tactful. Did he hurt your feelings, Miranda?"

"I don't know." I hadn't really thought about my feelings, though it saddened me to see Barb's earrings shunted and rejected on my desk.

"Your appearance is extremely important," said Priscilla. "You're the first person a client sees, so what you wear and how you look, well, it matters. You're required to look professional." She held the earring up to the light. "It's not real silver, you know. It's an alloy."

I snatched it away and swept both earrings into my desk drawer.

Priscilla pretended to flinch. "Ooh, touchy. But, Miranda, you haven't looked in the bag."

On the blue shopping bag, in little white type, it said TIFFANY. It was too nice. I didn't want to touch it.

"Don't worry. Just the bag is from Tiffany's." Priscilla reached in and pulled out a mustard-colored blouse, as whispery smooth as the blouses she wore. She pulled out another deep green blouse made from identical material. "Silk." She let them float out of the bag.

The silk slid through my fingers as I laid the blouses on my desk. Folded beneath them in the bag were two straight wool skirts, one gray and the other tan, with lining. As I held the gray skirt up, I felt an excitement as if it were Christmas. The wool seemed to crackle with it. But I was, as Mom called me, chunky, not to mention pregnant. The skirts were slim and long. They would never fit.

"I was going through my closet this weekend and I found some things I haven't worn in over a year, so I put them in a bag to give to the Salvation Army. But after the meeting, it suddenly came to me that you could use them, so I stopped by my apartment and picked them up." Priscilla's eyes were shiny with self-satisfaction as she smoothed out a wrinkle in the blouse. "They're good as new. They were very expensive when I bought them."

I felt the want like a lump in my throat. But I recognized the thick sound of a charitable voice, and I remembered the church people, with their stinky old clothes and coffee cans full of sweat-stained dollar bills.

The blouses lay before me like a vivid temptation. "I don't think they'll fit," I said. "I'm not petite like you."

"Nonsense." Priscilla danced the green blouse in my face so its sleeves brushed my cheeks. "I've got an idea. Why don't you go into the Xerox room and try them on."

"I'm with Priscilla on this A-one hundred percent," said Leonard. "Some mix-and-match and you've got yourself almost a whole week's worth of clothes."

"Listen to the fashion consultant!" laughed Priscilla.

I wanted the clothes, wanted to look like Priscilla and talk like her, to become Priscilla, snap my fingers and say: Booner. Tea. Lemon. "Really?" I pulled the bag toward me.

"Go on, we'll take care of the phones."

"We always do anyway." Leonard guffawed.

The thrill of carrying a Tiffany shopping bag across the brand-new carpet into the brand-new Xerox room, where reams of paper were stacked on shelves and if we got below three, I was supposed to order more, was delicious. I had never felt this good when we received gifts from the church. All the stupid junk in those boxes had never added up to anything worthwhile.

I yanked off my dress and pulled at the buttons of the green silk blouse. They were covered by a delicate fold and difficult to button in a rush. The blouse fit, though it pulled a little at my chest. I could use a safety pin there, no problem.

The skirt was tight in the waist, so when I inhaled, my belly ballooned out beneath the waistband. It made me look pregnant. I couldn't get away from that fact. I punched myself in the gut. Maybe if I punched myself ten times a day, it would dislodge the thing and I would miscarry. Then I felt sorry, sorry for the poor innocent being growing inside me, filling me up. It wasn't the baby's fault. The skirt would have been tight on me anyway, and the solution was to move the button closer to the edge, make the waist wider. I had learned that from Mom, at least.

I opened the door and Priscilla, perched on my desk, burst out laughing. "Look at you."

"Don't laugh." I was already backing into the Xerox room. I shut the door quietly, though I wanted to slam it, then hurl the Xerox machine against it. Knock over the water cooler, rip apart the shelves, tear open the postage meter machine. Why was I the butt of jokes?

"Miranda, come back. We're not laughing at you, but the way you scowled just seemed funny."

I leaned my face against the warm glass of the Xerox machine. I felt like crying, but no tears came out.

"No, Leonard, I'll handle this. I started it." I heard Priscilla's voice as if from far away.

I pressed start and the machine expelled a sheet of paper with my muddy, fat, mashed profile in black and white. Why did everything I came into contact with turn ugly?

She tapped on the door with her rings. "Miranda, lighten up. You look very nice. I'm sorry I laughed. Please come out."

"I prefer not to, thank you." I looked down at myself in Priscilla's cast-off clothes, ashamed that I needed them. I poured myself a cup of water from the cooler. It wasn't her fault I didn't have nice things. I had to remember where I was and what I was supposed to be doing: living and breathing professionalism.

"I shouldn't have made you try them on. Please, come out." Priscilla pushed on the door but I pushed back.

"I prefer not to right now."

"You prefer not to?"

It was no use. She was too persistent, and I couldn't hide here forever. I stepped into my loafers and opened the door. Leonard applauded. "Can we all go back to work now?"

Priscilla was smiling eagerly, tilting her head to catch my eye. "You look great."

"Thank you." I pushed by her and around my fortress of a desk until I was safe behind it.

Priscilla laughed. "You know what I'm going to call you from now on?"

"Don't make fun of me." I picked up my pen and began to doodle on my desk blotter. Swirls within swirls gave me comfort. The bad feeling ebbed away. This was nothing compared to the rest of my life.

"Don't worry, Bartleby. Hey, Leonard, I think we have Bartleby the Scrivener working for us."

"If it's any consolation to you, Miranda," Leonard said, rapping on my desk, forcing me to look up, "I don't know who this Bartle-schmuck is and I'll continue to address you by your name."

I smiled, catching a glimpse of my green silk sleeve and wanting to laugh along with Priscilla and Leonard. "That's very professional of you. Thank you."

"You see! You see!" Priscilla clapped her hands. "A sense of humor is just as important as professionalism! You get a gold star!"

The buzzer at the entrance startled us. Priscilla quickly turned the plaque so it faced outward. Leonard opened the door to a small, freckled man, slightly hunched, holding an enormous bouquet of pink roses in a white vase. He shuffled in and placed the roses on my desk. They were covered in clear plastic that crackled when I touched it, barely able to control the tremble in my hands. Was Booner so romantic? If he was, I forgave everything.

Your daddy sent roses to my office when I was pregnant with you, I murmur to the rosy-cheeked, laughing infant in my lap. My baby rewards me with her touch, patting my face with her soft, chubby hands, stretching up to kiss me. Yes, she's a girl, and we are united in a perfect bond of love.

I let out a giggle as I tried to peel off the tape. I needed fingernails.

The freckled man was looking at his clipboard. "It's a delivery for Shoyman, Persall Shoyman."

"That's me," said Priscilla.

I backed away from the roses, embarrassed. I had already unwrapped them, but there was her name on a little white envelope, which she opened to read the card inside.

Leonard shut the door after the messenger. "You gotta tell us who they're from, Pris."

"Bruce Davis." Priscilla blushed.

"Whoa. You didn't even place him yet. He's smitten. Worse than that, he's out of his gourd."

"I think he would be better for Miranda," she said. "He's really too young for me." According to his file, Bruce Davis was thirty-two years old. According to how many years she admitted, Priscilla was thirty-five.

I put limits on the charity I accepted. I remembered Dad dropping the unwanted boxes off at the church. "I don't want Bruce Davis. I already have a boyfriend." I touched my diamond teardrop. "He asked me to marry him."

"Marry? Are you crazy? How old are you? What's this guy's name? What does he do for a living?" Leonard's pudgy face creased into a smile that just wouldn't quit.

"His name is Booner. He's in infrastructure."

"Infrastructure?" Priscilla looked up from her roses. They flattered her. Their pinkness lent an appealing flush to her cheeks, softened the tightness around her mouth.

"Yeah. He cleans catch basins. It's a necessary job."

They were looking at each other. "What are catch basins?"

"You know, those basins at the curb where water's supposed to drain. He makes good money." I couldn't believe it. I sounded just like him.

"You mean those sewers?" Priscilla wrinkled her nose.

"He loves me." I stared down at my loafers. She was exactly the kind of person who thought she was too good for the rest of the world. Then again I had once thought they were sewers, too.

"You can't marry for love, Miranda," said Leonard. "You've got to marry for money."

"How'd you get so smart, Leonard?" Priscilla laughed up and down the musical scales. "Come on, Miranda. I'll set you up with Bruce Davis. Like a corporate merger. What do you think, Leonard? Of course there'll be our fee, but Bruce can pay that."

When I had my baby, I could quit this job and never have to deal with these two again. "You can stop laughing at my life now." With a calmness and certainty that I couldn't remember ever feeling before, I picked up the vase full of flowers and carried it around my desk, past the two laughing hyenas who employed me. I walked into Priscilla's office and placed it carefully on her desk, where the one single rose she always had in a long, slender black container was now greatly outnumbered by a chorus of pink ones in a fat white vase.

I FELT LUCKY in my new skirt and blouse and a brand-new pair of patent leather pumps with low heels. They squeezed my toes into a point, so I carried them in my purse and wore my loafers, stopping at the corner to change, the way city women did.

A few people milled about outside the Charis Gallery. I strolled past them in my pinching pumps, wishing Booner or someone in my life were interested in photography. I walked straight through the double glass doors before I lost my nerve. The room was much too bright, with white walls, high ceilings lined with pipes and vents, and blazing fluorescent lights washing out the faces floating beneath.

The lights accentuated the contrast with the black outfits everyone else was wearing, as though it were a funeral. While I, with freckles like beacons, in my gray skirt, dark green blouse from Priscilla, and black pumps, looked as if I had stepped into this place from an unknown faraway universe. An office. I was relieved that Booner hadn't come after all.

I had asked him to go, knowing he would refuse. "I don't think so, Mandy. And you shouldn't go, either. It's a waste of time," he had said.

When it struck me that he might feel intimidated about attending the opening of a photography show in SoHo, I had even tried to convince him. "C'mon, Booner, it'll be a lot of fun," I said. "There'll be wine, and probably cheese and crackers." I was nervous about going, too, and I remembered how I had hovered by the food table at Rose's baby shower. A food table was a safe place, an oasis, at a party.

"You're a piece of work," he said. "I can pick up cheese and crackers at the Grand Union anytime, and eat in the comfort of my own home."

As if our home were so comfortable. "We have to try new things, Booner. Get out of this rut."

"I got news for you. I'm not in a rut."

But I was in a rut. And I was out of place. Priscilla's clothes were fine for the office, but I needed a new wardrobe for an event like this. Everyone looked sophisticated, confident.

Maybe Booner was right. It was so much easier when I gave up my own half-formed notions to his rightness. I could be at home getting comfortable, getting stoned, looking into his warm green-brown eyes. But I was here, anxious and stiff.

I spotted Doug standing in a crowd with a large can of Foster's in his hand. He wouldn't have to put it in a paper bag at his own show. He and everyone else in the group moved their mouths in an odd mouth-moving dance. The noise and buzz of people talking filled the room, the volume steadily amplifying. It was hard to distinguish what was coming from where.

I walked as naturally as I could toward a table where clear plastic cups of wine glittered like jewels in alternating rows of white and red. I grabbed a red, and armed with that, I was ready to look at Doug's photographs. They were very large, hung in clusters.

One cluster was a set of enlarged photographs of noses. Below the noses were pictures of hands, palms up and palms down, and below those were photographs of—the heat of a blush rose up my neck and into my face—erect penises. Below the penises were photographs of bare, long-toed human feet. The small sign that named the cluster said MYTH: TRUE OR PHALLUS." I knew my face was splotched with red, and my own awareness of it only made it worse. What could I say about compositional space when all I saw were penises?

I moved on to the next cluster: TUNNEL VISION. These pictures were smaller than the others and more abstract. I stared until I realized they were ear canals, open mouths, nostrils, anuses, vaginas, all shot in extreme close-up. There were a couple of them I simply couldn't make out.

I wiped my forehead with the back of my hand and dried my damp hand on my skirt. The light was too bright, the air too hot, and there was too much to learn. I shut my eyes, ostrichlike, and the darkness was a sanctuary. A breeze seemed to stroke my face like soft fingers and I remembered Dad brushing the hair from my eyes, saying, *It's okay. You know your mama loves you; she's just a little high-strung. She hasn't had an easy life.* Sadness swept over me as though it were new.

When I opened my eyes, the guy with the loud voice from my class was standing in front of me. The breeze was caused by a brown portfolio he waved in my face. "Feel better? You weren't looking so good."

"Yeah. Thanks. I'm just a little tired." I casually dabbed my eyes, pretending the brightness had caused them to tear.

"Talk about tired. I'm, like, in this band, you know? We're called Vortex Pig, right? We got five guitarists and . . . have you heard of us?"

I shook my head. His torn T-shirt said RITUAL TENSION. His jeans were faded, ripped at the knees. He had tied a flannel shirt around his waist. His hair was long, black, and shaggy, and I loved him because he had fanned me with his envelope and was standing there talking to me. But I didn't know his name.

"Well, I was up all fucking night rehearsing. I mean, we just entered the zone and it was four o'clock in the morning, we were jamming. But can you believe this? My stupid fucking *fascist* neighbors called the cops. If they don't like my art, they should get some fucking attenuators, man."

His eyes were greener than Booner's.

"Why are you looking at me like that? You probably don't know what attenuators are, do you?"

"You got that right," I said before I realized Booner always used those exact words. I didn't even have my own phrases anymore.

"They're earplugs!" shouted the guy.

If it were me talking, not Booner, what would I say? I had to find my own side of the conversation. "I'm glad I'm not your neighbor," I squeaked out.

"Hey! You're funny!" His eyes flashed a light of kindness, shining out like Barb's. I couldn't look at him without feeling sadness well up. I shifted my gaze to the wall, landing directly on a picture of the hairy lips of a vagina. No. Look somewhere else. When I glanced back at the guy, he was looking at the picture, too.

"You know, this *Nude as landscape* is tactile and everything, and Doug's definitely got his own point of view here, but haven't we seen enough flesh to last till the next millennium? It's cliché. It's static. I'm into the kind of scene where the art surrounds you. Multimedia, it's the latest thing. Like, I'm a visual kind of guy, but I'm also into music, so I need something where I can use my whole creative person. And the viewer comes in—he has to use his whole creative person, too. Like, he's got to really participate, you know?"

How people knew what they needed and what their whole creative person consisted of was a mystery. "What if the viewer's a she, not a he?" I asked.

"Same thing." He shrugged.

A flash of memory from my Women's Studies class struck me like a message from the great beyond. "Woman as object," I murmured. But it wasn't just women in the photographs. What about the penises? "He's dealing with stereotypes." My breath came hard and fast.

"Yeah. I guess if you judge it on its own terms, it's pretty outstanding."

If I thought of them as studies of stereotypes, as fragmented body pieces, as objects, looking at the photographs of the penises wasn't a problem. I tested it. I stared at an erect penis, looked away, took a step toward it. Okay, now look again. I stared. No big deal.

My head was swimming. I felt as though I had conquered a massive human problem. *Are you seeing the object in front of you, or is it just a concept of the object?* Dad had asked.

The guy tapped my arm. "When I go to museums, you know, I hate this stupid bullshit way of looking at each picture. I'm not a sheep. You're supposed to stop, then look, then move on to the next one. You stop, you look, you move on. I hate that shit, so when I go in, I stare at one picture for an hour until I really get it. Then I leave. Next time I'm gonna bring a cattle prod for the sheep."

Museums! There were so many possibilities, so much to know. "Baaaa." I imitated a sheep and then felt like an jerk.

"Baaaa." He did an imitation, too. Not as good as mine, but then he wasn't from Ransomville.

"What's art anyway?" When he smiled, a dimple appeared on his chin, lending him an eager look. "Art's a fucking commodity these days."

A skinny girl in a velvet miniskirt and fishnet stockings, her hair a mass of bleached, scraggly, teased-up split ends, slunk in behind the guy whose name I didn't know. "Hey, Romeo," she said in a throaty voice.

"Hey, honey, you just get here? What do you think?" He turned his back on me to talk to her. "The show could use some music, right? Some light and sound? Want some wine?"

Just as I was feeling forgotten, he turned around. "Nice talking to you. See you in class. Saturday, right?" He snapped his fingers, pointed at me, and off he bopped with his girlfriend, taking his smile and his eager dimple away with him. She hadn't even looked at me, no sign of curiosity.

I felt deflated again, the familiar state of wanting to exist in anyone else's skin but my own. The erect penises weren't embarrassing anymore, but it wasn't because I had just conquered a great human problem. It was because they were pointless and stupid.

"Miranda, what do you think?" Doug was right beside me and I hadn't even noticed him walking over. I had been too busy thinking negatively about his photographs. Would I never be free of myself? I ducked my head, looking at the floor, and I saw he had tucked the laces inside his sneakers but hadn't tied them.

"Speechless, eh?" he said.

"Oh no. I like your stuff, what you're doing with stereotypes here. And it's funny, too. And textural . . ."

He held a pack of foreign cigarettes out to me. "Cancer?"

"Sure. Love one." Steady she goes. I plucked one from the pack.

"I saw Malcolm bending your ear." Doug's friendly blue eyes squinted when he smiled.

"Who?"

"Malcolm." He nodded at the loud guy, who was talking and gesturing heatedly while his girlfriend gazed beyond him at a tall man in black leather pants.

"If only he worked as much as he talked." Doug chuckled as he blew out smoke, which a draft of air steered directly into my face. I stifled a cough.

He ineffectually fanned the smoke away. "I'm sorry. I'm nervous."

"You are?"

"Yeah. It's daunting to stand in a room full of my stuff." He had trimmed his beard into a goatee. "It's funny, but by the time the stuff is on display, I'm already on to something else. I'm following a new creative impulse and what you see here is the past, like an old skin of a snake."

He puffed on his cigarette. I puffed on mine. We were equals. He wasn't talking at me like Malcolm. He was telling me something like Dad used to do, including me in an understanding, a creative expansion that I was a part of. He was taking it for granted, too, and that was the best thing. He said, "One day you'll know how it feels, you keep working the way you do."

I was so twisted inside with pleasure that I couldn't look at him, or anything.

He squeezed my arm. "I gotta mingle. I spot a critic over there, and it's good to be nice to art critics." He winked. "Makes 'em feel like they're human."

" 'Bye." I pretended to look at a picture on the wall, but I was staring at the memory of Doug Harrison, his black T-shirt, wiry arms, and goatee. I smiled at his image in my mind. Then I realized I was grinning like an idiot at a photograph of a belly button, magnified so it looked almost like the mouth of a volcano.

One day I would know the feeling of standing at my own show. But I wouldn't wear these shoes, pinching my toes together. The French cigarette, the best cigarette I had ever smoked, was down to the filter. I ground it out, disappointed, finished my last sip of sour red wine, and took a stroll past a group of more abstract photographs, unidentifiable curves of flesh. The card said WHERE ARE WE NOW?

I looked at the door, thinking that it might be time to leave, when I saw Celeste, without her veil, step in and head for the wine table. The rims of her eyes had been darkened with eyeliner. In her slinky black dress, which accentuated her prominent hipbones, she glided rather than walked. Her face was pale, her hair long and dark, her lips purple with lipstick. She looked like a vampire.

Then—oh, dear Jesus, protect me from all evil—through the entrance stomped Booner, with a strange heavy trudge that revealed his drunkenness. The headache that had hinted from the sidelines of my skull began pounding for attention.

"Oh, I recognize you!" Celeste came over and touched my arm very softly and slowly, giving me the chance to look at the tattoos encircling her wrists like bracelets. "It was *such* a journey over here. So many obstacles, so many strange visions . . ." She was scanning the room as she talked.

"Yeah, I know what you mean," I murmured.

"Mandy." Booner stumbled around Celeste to get to me. "There she is, the girl that drives me crazy." He draped his arm around my shoulders, leaning heavily. "Baby, I missed you. I came to get you." He moved his hand up around the back of my neck, where he fingered the chain clasp. Then he bit my earlobe, a steady sharp pressure.

"It might just be the change of seasons," Celeste continued, oblivious to Booner gaping at her as though she were a freak. "I saw a fire truck parked at the curb near the supermarket. And there were flowers on the dashboard. Explain that to me."

"Maybe one of the firemen likes flowers." Was Celeste crazy? Or was she just honest in her way? It was impossible to judge.

"This your friend?" Booner asked, sickeningly good-humored. He shook Celeste's hand, squeezing her fingers. I noticed her wince.

"Celeste, this is Booner," I mumbled. "Booner, Celeste."

She trained her gaze on Booner, unintimidated. "I know you. I have seen you in the dark room." She said it like two words instead of one.

"You must come from Manhattan," said Booner. "They all dress like you in Manhattan."

"Ah, there's Doug," said Celeste. "I will see you on Saturday." She glided off to Doug, unaffected by Booner's insulting tone. What did she care that Doug stood in a closed circle, talking to the art critic and others? She approached that circle so fearlessly, it opened to allow her in. She made it look easy.

In his black leather jacket and big brown cowboy boots, Booner could have fit in. But his sneer and his hunched posture made his discomfort so obvious and extreme that he looked even more out of place than I did. And why was he normal while Celeste wasn't? Maybe she was the normal one. My head was going to explode.

"But what the fuck is it? That's what I want to know." Booner gave a grand sweep of his arm toward the nearest photograph, which might have been a wide expanse of hairy thigh. But it wasn't just that. It also looked like a landscape from another planet. Though his snicker turned my stomach, okay, I would try to help him understand.

"You can tell it's some part of the human body, but you know, it's taking the familiar and making it unfamiliar."

"Unfamiliar. That's for sure. *Doo-doo doo-doo.*" He sang the theme from *The Twilight Zone.* The room was crowded enough for his crudeness to blend with the babble of gallery talk, and I was relieved that no one was paying attention to us.

I watched Doug disengage himself from the circle. I pretended not to watch, pretended to be interested in the photograph on the wall, but I was looking as he scratched his head, momentarily baffled. He must have felt my eyes on him because he turned and waved before he took off in the opposite direction.

"Who's that?" Booner nudged me hard.

"Oh, that's my teacher."

"So he did all these masterpieces." He swept his arm at the cluster of photographs. "Shit, so this is art." It was time to go home. But Booner stomped along the wall with a threatening gait that influenced people to step out of his way. When he reached the corner, he turned with a salute and walked back to me.

I shut my eyes in a long dark blink in which I heard snatches of conversation. ". . . the pull of opposing elements . . ." ". . . vibrancy of lights and darks . . ." ". . . play of shadows on the skin surfaces . . ." I wanted to feel the give-and-take of intelligent conversation. I wanted to be included. I wanted to contain inside myself all the different angles and realities. I was hungry with want and I felt very tired. My feet hurt. I had to work tomorrow. "We should go," I said.

"No, baby. I just got here. And this is better than *Playboy* or *Penthouse,* believe me."

"Come on, Booner, please. I want to go home."

He sensed my humiliation. "What, I don't look good enough for you in front of these fucking fancy folks you want to impress?" He gripped my shoulder and gave me one sharp, brusque shake. My neck cramped. "We were having a little celebration over at the apartment and I came all the way here to get you. But you don't appreciate shit, do you?"

"I'm sorry." I swallowed around my words. There was a clear path to the door, and I grabbed Booner's arm. "I want to go to the celebration."

" 'Bye, everybody!" He waved as I practically pushed him out the door. "You fucking happy now?" he shouted. But at least we were outside. I gulped the air into my lungs, parched for it, desperate. We had made it.

Booner drove fast and dangerously, drunkenly, slamming his foot on the gas pedal, then the brake. Neither of us spoke, and I watched out the side window, too scared to look ahead as we wove and lurched through traffic. This is the father of my baby, I thought, and my insides felt like ice.

THE HALL WAS dark, the bulb burnt out. But under the apartment door the light was a narrow rectangle. Music was playing. When Booner tried to unlock the door, he dropped his keys and they landed with a rattling clank on the hallway linoleum. He groped for them in the glow along the floor and I bent down, too, pretending to search so he would believe I was being helpful. But the linoleum was cold and gritty. It was impossible to see and my actions were a total pretense.

"Goddamn motherfucker." Booner kicked the door. "*Goddamn motherfucker!*"

I felt the cool metal of my own keys in the side pocket of my purse, but I was afraid to interrupt. The door swung open from the inside. "Well, well, well, look who's here." Hot Shot, mustache dripping with beer, was puffing on a cigar, surrounded by a haze of acrid smoke.

Lynyrd Skynyrd was on the stereo. "Gimme Two Steps." Lumpy was sitting on the sofa, sucking on an aqua-colored bong. Hot Shot went and sat next to him, planting his work boots firmly on the floor and placing his can of Budweiser between them. The air was thick with the cloying stench of cigars and marijuana.

"We're back." Booner reached for a cigar from a small box on the coffee table. I understood that cigars meant babies, and I didn't want to know.

Lumpy passed me the bong in slow motion. "You're lookin' at the Tidy Bowl man, here." He laughed as if he were coughing, huh huh huh huh.

Fumes of stale water rose from the bong like swamp gas.

"Yeah, the Tidy Bowl man! You got that fuckin' right." Hot Shot handed me a pack of matches with a 900 number on them. Dial-a-sex fantasy. I lit the bong, inhaled deeply, and was off and running, no longer here. Or anywhere.

"Shit ahoy!" yelled Lumpy. He and Booner cracked up, and Booner slapped his knee, bent over in silent, helpless laughter.

I smiled halfway, testing the grounds. The photography show and all that had occurred there was quickly fading in the reality of these guys, this apartment. "Did you all work late or something?" I kneeled carefully so my skirt wouldn't hike up, and I took another deep hit off the bong.

"Yeah, we were out in Brooklyn." Lumpy squeezed his empty beer can.

"We had to clear an obstruction in this huge drainage basin. Eugene rented a rubber raft to go down and take a look. Lumpy did the honors." Booner waved his cigar crazily, snorting out small explosions of laughter. "Man, I thought he'd capsize!"

Lumpy shouted, "The Tidy Bowl man never capsizes! You seen the commercials. The Tidy Bowl man never capsizes!"

"Shit ahoy!" yelled Hot Shot. And they were off in their own private world, the three of them, their laughter merging into a closed circle of hilarity that I didn't want to be part of. Booner flicked a cigar ash into the fish tank. No one else seemed to notice.

"Fucking Lumpy's down there, goin' DOY!" Booner opened his mouth, forming a round O.

Lumpy laughed so hard he choked on his cigar smoke. He hacked and coughed and stamped his feet until I worried. He could die, with Booner and Hot Shot watching him choke to death, laughing at him all the while. Then Hot Shot smacked him good and hard on the back. Lumpy stopped coughing but kept on laughing. "Just thinking about it . . . aw, man." He wiped away a tear.

There was a roaring in my ears, rushing through my brain like the sound of the ocean in a large seashell. I crawled over to the fish tank and sat in the blur of the blue light. The fish were pale and still. A little one trailed through the water, so translucent its sharp comb of a skeleton glowed white through the clear sheath of its body. Its gills quivered. A ghost fish. It looked at me. I looked at it. I felt hopeless. "What's with the cigars?" I asked, resigning myself to the inevitable.

"Eugene gave them out this afternoon," said Lumpy. "Rose had the baby, so he was passing cigars to everyone. Booner took a whole box of 'em just for himself."

"It's a girl. They'll have to keep trying, won't they?" Hot Shot acted like he was cracking a joke. "I know Gene wanted a boy. Rose did, too."

But I remembered that Rose had known it would be a girl. Was that supposed to be secret? I put my hand on the rug to steady myself as I brought my legs out from under me. "So she had the baby, then. Wow."

The room began to tilt and keel. Smoke swirled above. So. Rose Economopolous had her baby girl, right on schedule. I flashed on the clinic: If you don't make a decision, that *is* a decision. My heart pumped so hard, my body expanded and contracted with it. I felt as though I were empty inside except for the pumping, which stretched and shrank my skin around it. I shouldn't have gotten stoned.

I sprinkled food into the tank and one fish rose slowly up to bite. The others only floated, submerged and accusing, staring out sideways like fish did, while crumbs fell through the water. The fish were so faded that their paraphernalia—the glittery castle, shrill pebbles, and fake, vividly green plants—were more real than the fish themselves. It was not supposed to be like this. Was I just stoned, or were they all slowly dying?

But I already knew they were dying. I had known it days ago. Inertia, like a sickness, said, They're not mine, they're Booner's, so it's not my fault.

Booner was saying, "Eugene was so fuckin' happy, man. I never saw that guy so happy."

At the top near the filter, jostled about by the water bubbles, floated a small dead fish. Not even a whole one, but three quarters of it, as if a chunk had been taken out. It just floated on its side on top of the water, surrounded by a brush of ashes from Booner's cigar.

"The fish tank isn't an ashtray, and the fish are dying." My voice was surprisingly calm.

Booner shoved his cigar between me and the fish tank. "Eugene was so happy, man. I never saw that guy so fuckin' happy. He was so happy it was like he was in *pain*." He blew smoke in my face, making my eyes tear.

"There." I pointed toward the filter. "See. A dead fish with a part missing."

"Yeah, so? It's been there awhile. It didn't appear just because you decided to notice it. The big guy's been eating them."

"The big guy?" Sure enough, a pale bloated fish lurked in the fake greenery below the dead one, a smug look to his fish mouth.

Lumpy and Hot Shot cracked jokes. "Fish for dinner! First a brain-fry then a fish-fry!" They were so loud, I wished I could turn down the volume. Lumpy's raspy voice somehow always carried in a room. He was like a small car beeping in a traffic jam, an irritating beep that made itself heard over all the other honking.

"Booner, didn't they tell you when you bought them, which fish could live with each other? Aren't they supposed to know about those things at Sealand?"

Booner puffed on his cigar, which was soggy at the mouth end. "Yeah, right. In your perfect world. Obviously, the guy didn't know what he was doing and he wanted to make a sale. That's how life is on this planet. I don't know what it's like out in space where you are. But we can get new ones, not that you care."

His voice triggered a stubborn strength inside me. On his planet, living things were replaceable and the hypocrisy of his pretending he wanted a baby when he couldn't even take care of fish made me tremble.

"What do you mean *new* ones? You mean you're going to let them die! Don't you see how they're dying?" I stared at all the guys with their thick cigars.

I could tell by the silence, the nervous energy, that they were verging on hysterical laughter. Lumpy and Hot Shot held their mouths shut, but the effort was obvious and laughter burst from their eyes. Lumpy let out a snort, then held his nose.

"We'll buy new ones, Mandy. That's all." Booner's tone was condescending, as if I were a crazy person. His voice quivered with suppressed laughter and he shrugged.

"That's not the point." I stood, though my knees had stiffened and my foot was asleep, prickling with pins and needles.

"Why don't you tell me what the *point* is if that's not the *point*." Booner's voice, not laughing anymore, rose like rust on an old car, corrosive and unstoppable. "Because I don't fucking know what the *point* could be when you cry over dead fish while you want to kill my baby. Does my baby know the *point?*"

I flinched. How could he talk to me like this in front of other people? Then regret washed over me. I had only wanted love, not to kill anything. And a girl who didn't want her baby was a despicable, horrible, unnatural subhuman. I didn't want to be that. My voice huddled in my throat. "It's just that you should have taken better care of them," I mumbled.

But Booner had moved beyond me. He had his audience with him. "Why do you care what lives or dies, Mandy? What the fuck do you care, that's what I want to know?"

"Come on, Booner, we're celebrating, remember?" Lumpy stood. "I'm gettin' a beer. Anyone else need one?"

"Yeah." Hot Shot and I spoke in unison.

"Lumpy, you fucking bastard. Don't think I don't know what's going on. I seen you making eyes at *my* girl!" Booner lunged. Lumpy leaped backward and stumbled toward the kitchen.

"Come on, Booner," said Hot Shot.

But Booner didn't even glance at Hot Shot. He stared intensely at me, his eyes hard with a chilly glow. His mouth curled, tight and ugly. "Do you know what Eugene says? Eugene says Rose wants *lots* of babies, that's what Eugene says." His spit sprayed my face, but I couldn't wipe it off. My hands were like weights, my arms too heavy to move.

"What's with that guy?" Lumpy passed a can of beer to Hot Shot. Was he asking me? Didn't he know? He couldn't hand me a beer without stretching past Booner, so he placed it on the rug, way out of my reach.

"Moody," said Hot Shot. "Booner's always been moody. It's like he's got the rag on."

What a relief. Booner shifted his fury to Hot Shot. "What the fuck do you know about me?" He stomped into the bedroom, which gave me an opportunity to snatch my beer.

He became entangled in the beaded curtains like an animal in a trap. He lashed out. "What the fuck? Why the fuck do we have these stupid goddamn pussy curtains!" He pulled ferociously at them and they snapped. Beads flew off, dropping and rolling in every direction, like hailstones in a windy, long-awaited storm.

I willed my own disappearance, afraid to breathe, backing up slowly, quietly through the doorway into the kitchen. Then I shot into the bathroom and shut the door behind me. I was alone, blood racing. When I placed my beer on the floor, the act made my head spin. I clutched the sink for balance and stared into the mirror at a face, small and pale behind the toothpaste spots. It was the face of someone in need, and if I saw it on the street, I would think, Poor girl, she looks scared and sad. But it wasn't someone else's. It was my face and I didn't know what to think, or do.

At my feet were three little stacks of bathroom tiles, small grayish octagons that once were white. A cockroach crept among them, a flick of brown disappearing into a crack in the wall. The bathtub had gone filthy gray again. The shower curtain was glommed together with sticky dirt and mildew.

I lived here, in this filth. This was my bathroom, my project. How far had I gotten? How far had I gone with anything in my life? How far would I ever really get? If only I knew what was true, what was real, what was right or wrong. But there was nothing solid inside or outside myself.

At least Booner knew what he wanted. He didn't pretend to be something he wasn't, unlike me, always pretending, stuck inside a shifting, changing skin.

He thought I was a certain kind of girl because I let him think it. I could have told him I wasn't a virgin. I could've said I didn't want to live in Ransomville or the city version of it, Astoria, for the rest of my life. But I didn't. I was dishonest, a liar. And a liar was the worst kind of person. "Once a liar, always a liar," Mom used to say.

I heard the guys' heavy footsteps in the kitchen, their voices loud, competing with each other. I couldn't make out particular words, just noise. But I was safe in the bathroom, alone with my lies. I heard banging on the kitchen shelf. I heard Hot Shot's doggy laughter, Lumpy's coughing, and I had to know what was going on. I tried to open the bathroom door, just a crack. But it stuck shut until I shoved it with my shoulder. Then it hurled open, startling the guys who stood near the front door, putting on their coats.

"Where are you going?" I asked

"Out," said Booner, stoned, drunk, and hateful, hell-bent on having the last word. "To celebrate. For *Eugene*. Not for *me*."

He wanted to have it out in front of his friends? Give them all a good laugh? Forget it. I wasn't playing his game. A smile was a weapon, too. "Have fun, boys." I laughed lightly, turned my back on them, and stepped, like a princess without a care in the world, into the living room.

I leaned against the living room wall. It was cool, bumpy, and rough against my hot cheek. I knew Booner was standing just on the other side, the thread between the two of us stretched tight as a scream.

"We goin' or what?" said Lumpy.

A thumping of boots, rattle of keys, Hot Shot muttered something. I waited for Booner to change his mind, to stay. I existed to wait. *I'm sorry, baby, I love you so much. He lets the guys go and comes toward me. Oh, Booner, even though I said I didn't want a baby, I wasn't sure and I really do want one, because I want you to love me. And you and I can make a human being, born of love, who will love me too, unconditionally, like I want to love you. Mandy, I've never known anyone like you and I can't bear to lose you. I'll change. I want to learn all about photography. And I want to be a husband and a father and love you as no one else has ever been able to. Oh thank you, Booner. We'll be so happy then.* But the door slammed shut and I was panting in the silence that held the echo of the slam. It reverberated inside me.

The world was out there and I was in here. Wherever I was not, there was the center and excitement of existence. The place I wanted to be was never where I ended up. I slumped against the wall, trapped alone in an apartment that wasn't mine. I didn't know who I was or had ever been. Or could be. There was only that wall, those gates, the ugly green sofa. A plastic bag glinted from beneath it.

Relief. It was a bag of pot, forgotten by the guys. I gratefully rolled a joint, switched on the TV, and the fog rolled in over the razor edge of my panic.

A car commercial came on, followed by a beer commercial, then a dog food ad, then tinfoil. Back to the news, and who cared about that? I lay on the sofa while the voices on the television jabbered on. The orange shag rug waved its tentacles back and forth. In the tank, the fish were dying.

THE ALARM JARRED me awake at 5:30 A.M. A cold terror set itself in my bones. I was alone in bed. The sofa was bare. Booner had stayed out all night. But I was so tired that after I reset the alarm for seven, I fell instantly asleep. I didn't even know I was sleeping until the alarm went off a second time, yanking me out of a dream. I glimpsed Dad through a large crowd. I was at some outdoor event, a county fair. There were so many people, I couldn't be sure the man walking with a familiar gait, one shoulder held slightly higher than the other, was Dad. I tried to follow him, pushing bodies out of my way.

The dreariness outside the window reminded me. I felt sick.

After I finished throwing up, I put the water on for instant coffee and lit a cigarette. My fingers were yellow from nicotine. My nails were tiny bitten slivers. I would have showered, but the water was frigid, even from the hot tap.

I dusted baby powder in my hair to disguise the greasiness. I buttoned up the mustard-colored silk blouse. It smelled of cigarette smoke and needed cleaning, but it would have to do. I stepped into the dark skirt Priscilla had given me. My panty hose ran from my toe to mid-calf as soon as I pulled them on, so the hell with it. I rolled on knee-highs. Priscilla's skirt was long enough that the knee-highs looked like panty hose if I didn't sit down too carelessly.

I had to get out of this place.

I packed a bag, threw in my camera, the photographs I had taken, the extra blouse and skirt from Priscilla, socks, underwear, and jeans. I had to be gone when Booner returned. I walked eleven blocks to the subway.

The train that pulled into the station was so crowded I didn't even try to get on. "It's not worth it." The weary voice next to me belonged to an enormously pregnant woman. I wanted to pull my camera out, take her picture, and confess that I was pregnant, too. But wordlessly, we hung back together as the crowd on the platform shoved and pushed their way in and the train seemed to swell to the breaking point with all those bodies crammed inside. The doors flattened people up against them when they closed, and as the train pulled away, a flap of someone's coat poked out between them. The next train was the same. The one after that, too.

By the time I reached Grand Central Station I was twenty minutes late. Leonard was on the phone. "Look, Ira, I don't want to beat a dead horse, but we gotta level the playing field here. You're not listening to me, Ira." I was relieved he was distracted. I peeked my head in and he waved me away as if I were a bothersome fly.

I resolved to lose myself in my work, opening mail, rip slash with my letter opener. I filed the résumés, writing the last names of the candidates on the folder tabs with my left hand. It was my personal goal to teach myself to write with my left hand. In between, I waited for the coffee bell to ring at 10:30. I didn't notice Leonard until a shadow darkened my stack of folders and I looked up quickly.

"So. Half hour late. Do you have an excuse?" His scalp was flushed.

"The subways were really bad. They were so crowded I couldn't even get on. I'm sorry."

"Sorry this, sorry that. I'm wondering, do you take this job seriously? Priscilla may be a pushover, but I'm not. We're a small office, and when you're not here, I can't do my job because I'm doing your job. I don't want to do your job, because that's what I pay you to do. Kapeesh?"

"Yes." I touched my necklace, but it was just a necklace and offered no love, only a reminder of Booner in a rage.

"Good. We need to renew the postage on the machine. You're supposed to keep your eye on that. I had something I wanted to send with the morning mail, but we had run out of postage." He laid a hundred-dollar bill on my stack of manila folders.

"I'm sorry," I mumbled, rising from my desk to head to the supply room, where the postage meter machine was stored.

"Sorry didn't do it. You did." Leonard walked back into his office and shut the door. I stuck my tongue out at it. The universe was against me.

It was a relief to get away. The air was cold and neutral. It didn't accuse. But I waited on an endless line at the post office, only to realize that the person in the window, framed like a badly thought out photograph, didn't do meter machines, just stamps. I moved to another line in order to wait endlessly, imagining how Leonard was going to scold me for taking so much time. But it was a long line, I would say. Yeah sure, I believe you. You're fired, he would say. I was waiting for that, too.

My whole life was waiting. And I had been waiting always for the one thing that seemed due to happen any minute, any day: for Mom to die. A longing to see her swept over me, surprising me.

While I waited, life was happening. If I were still at college, the semester would be gearing up for finals. I kicked the machine ahead as the line moved forward. I didn't care if it broke. I wanted to break it. But I kicked a little too hard and it hit the ankle of the man in front of me. He was round, with a fat face and greasy black hair slicked over a bald patch. "What's your problem, sister?"

"Sorry," I said, not sorry at all. My life was my problem. The three days I hated most were yesterday, today, and tomorrow. "Stupid bitch," he muttered.

Back at the office, Priscilla was the only one in. Her door was open. She sat at her desk with her chair swiveled toward the center of the room. In her lap, she held a pretty, framed picture of her two Siamese cats. "I was worried." Her eyes were red around the rims, her nose blotched and swollen pink.

"I had to renew the postage on this." I hoisted up the machine as proof. "Where's Leonard?"

"He had an appointment."

"Oh." Relieved, I turned, heading toward the supply room to put the meter machine down where it belonged. It was heavy. Priscilla followed.

"Someone called for you while you were gone."

"Someone?" I was careful to control my voice, smooth wrapping over the jagged fear and excitement in my body. I put the meter machine on its table and plugged it in.

"I believe it was your boyfriend." She leaned in the doorway, her eyebrows raised and her mouth in a sort of pout that I knew was pity.

I couldn't control the surge of happiness, though I didn't want to feel it. Love wouldn't just vanish, and this proved it. Booner would come around in his own time. He would become interested in photography and we would have discussions like the ones Doug and I had. And maybe I could actually have a baby and live happily ever after with Booner as he a become a better, different sort of man, little by little.

"I answered the phone," said Priscilla. "He thought I was you."

"Everyone thinks I'm you, too." I wanted to hug her.

"Miranda, he was *extremely* rude to me, believing I was you. I have *never* been spoken to like that in my life."

I went cold, leaned against the table, my hands shifting envelopes, sorting them, and sliding them across. "He's not really rude, he just sounds that way."

"He used a terrible tone of voice and foul language. He attacked and abused me verbally because he thought he was talking to you."

Okay. I got it. She was angry it had landed on her rather than me, the one it was meant for. The worst thing about it was the shame. If I told her why he was mad, if I said, "I'm pregnant and I don't want to have a baby, but he wants to marry me and thinks I'm killing his baby," she would agree with him, not me. I was sure of it. She would accuse me, like Mom did, of selfishness. And maybe she would be right.

"I'm sorry for what you had to go through, Priscilla. I'm sorry he thought you were me." I forced out a chirpy little laugh and, with shaking hands, started putting letters through the machine. They whipped across and zinged into the box at the other end. Priscilla was still standing there, waiting, it seemed, for an explanation.

"You have to listen between his words, Priscilla," I offered. "He hasn't had an easy life."

Her mask of sadness and outrage didn't change. The triumph lurking beneath the mask didn't change, either. I sensed it, glimpsed it with my peripheral vision as I pretended to ignore her. Of course she wouldn't understand, with her dozen roses from Bruce Davis and silk blouses to give away.

"I would never let any man talk to me that way. Never."

I said I was sorry, didn't I? Why did she persist? It was Leonard's

fault for sending me to the post office. Booner was probably on the
job, repentant, hung over, and he probably had to search for a pay
phone, ask someone for change, but when he finally got through, I
wasn't even there to receive the call. I felt as though I had failed a test
and on top of that Priscilla needed to add her own punishment. What
was she getting at? "Are you going to fire me?"

"What? No. Of course not." Priscilla took a step back, leaving just
enough space for me to slink by her and escape from the tight little
room with the fluorescent light flickering like a migraine. She kept
following me. "Is he abusive, Miranda? Is he mistreating you?"

She grabbed me by the arm so hard her rings dug into my skin
where I had rolled up the sleeves of my blouse. There was an opal
ring with a tiny diamond on either side, a ruby ring with sapphires,
and a gold band circled with diamonds, which cut the most. Our
faces were so close, energy crackled between us. Powder had collected in the furrows on her forehead and in the tiny lines around her
eyes.

"What do you mean, abusive?" I hung my head, dull heavy stone.
Was it abusive that Booner wanted what I couldn't give? Were his
temper tantrums abusive? He had never hit me, and his temper was
only half the truth. He had saved me, comforted me, cuddled and
loved me. He had never clutched my arm, digging rings in with sharp
points of pain like Priscilla was doing now.

"Abusive can mean many things. I mean physically harm you, but
I also mean psychologically undermine you." When she released
me, I took a quick sideways step and ducked behind my desk, my
fortress, where she couldn't grab me without an effort of reaching. I
knew nothing, and I wanted to scream, *What the hell are you talking
about?*

But if she thought I was going to drag out the conversation by
asking her what she meant by "psychologically undermining," she
had better think again. I sniffed the sweet aroma of the flowers on
my desk and in the waft of their scent I realized that I could ask Barb.
I felt an opening inside, an unlocking.

"Maybe it's I who abuse him." I lit a cigarette and poked the
match in through the slot of my smokeless ashtray. Priscilla backed
away, as I knew she would. YOU HAVE ONLY FAILED WHEN YOU HAVE

FAILED TO TRY said the plaque. But failed what? Tried what? It was too vague. It was stupid, and a lie.

"You think I don't understand you, but I do, Miranda. I once had an abusive boyfriend." She paused. I nodded, wanting to know more. "He had keys to my apartment, but that was just for emergencies. I told him never, never go to my apartment when I'm not there. But he didn't care. One afternoon he went into my home and hid in the closet. I came in from work, you know, turned on the TV, and I went to hang up my clothes. He jumped out and I swear I had a heart attack. I was so terrified. I still feel the terror at night sometimes. Later I was furious. I told my doorman, 'Don't ever let him up to my place again.' I had my locks changed and . . ."

I flicked an ash, took a drag, and waited for her story to become relevant. I felt no sympathy or connection, only curiosity that she turned on her TV as soon as she got home. She had her own apartment, with a doorman standing guard at the entrance. She had enough money on hand to change her locks. And she took it all for granted.

"That's when I realized he had to go." She crossed her beautiful legs, with their well-defined calves wrapped in sheer stockings, tossed back her thin brown flyaway hair, and stared level at me with her cool gray eyes. "But it didn't end there. He started following me. He ripped up pictures of me and mailed them to my address. I had to get a restraining order on him. It was years ago and I'm still frightened, do you understand?"

I didn't move. I didn't know how to respond.

"I'm telling you this because I feel as if I know you and you think you're all alone but you're not. Others have gone through it. Your boyfriend's tone of voice implied that I have less right to be on this earth than he does. You don't have to put up with that."

But I did. I had no money, no apartment, no doorman. "I'm not complaining, Priscilla."

"Miranda, you're obviously unhappy. You've been moping around, dragging your feet as if everything is a hardship. Leonard says you've come in late the past few days and I can see you're always yawning, always tired. Your face is breaking out. Then I hear how that man talks to you and I gather you're in a bad situation.

You don't look healthy. You're not taking care of yourself. Are you anemic?"

I wanted to believe she cared, but she was coming at me from all angles and I couldn't take it in. "We live together," I said. *I'm pregnant,* I didn't say. *He wants a baby and I don't. He's mad because I'm a murderer.* I wanted to keep Priscilla on my side and she might not stay there if I mentioned the word *abortion.* Pregnancies, miscarriages, fibroid tumors, they were all events that could be shared, but an abortion could only be a shameful secret.

"Oh, Miranda, you can do better. I have to ask. Are you pregnant?"

"Of course not!" I snapped. I wanted to light another cigarette instantly, but I knew she would notice. I tried to find some plateau in my mind, a stable ledge to make decisions from. Dad used to say, *What does it matter what others think? Only you can know yourself.*

Priscilla was trying to weaken me. How dare she tell me my face was breaking out! Did she think I wasn't completely, painfully aware of it? She was treating me like a loser. I didn't need anyone passing judgment on my life, not anymore. She wasn't Mom. She wasn't the Church of Assemblies. I wasn't a child. I didn't need help from the likes of her. I wanted to scratch her eyes out.

Instead, I reached under my desk into my bag and withdrew my camera, intact, full of film. I shifted the f-stop knob. "I can take care of myself, Priscilla. You don't know Booner. You don't understand him, and you don't know what kind of life I live."

She was looking at the camera, too. "You don't have to get hostile, Miranda. I never said you couldn't take care of yourself. Frankly, you do a good job here, which enables me to do a better job. I want to keep that going."

She tilted her face, trying to make me look at her, and said, almost plaintively, "I only want to help."

"Thanks." I stared at the camera. *I lied. I am pregnant,* I wanted to say. *Please help me.* But I couldn't say a word. I framed her in the viewfinder. Click. I got a picture of her looking sad and lonely, aching for a purpose.

"It's not easy being a girl, starting out in the world." She came over and laid her hand gently, hesitantly on my arm, as if she were afraid to touch my failure, afraid she'd catch my life.

"I'm not a girl. I'm a woman."

"Nineteen years old does not make a woman, Bartleby." She laughed.

I focused in on her smile, which opened her soul, genuine and kind, even loving. Maybe she wasn't just a meddling snob.

Keys rattled and Leonard stepped through the door, right into the frame of my camera. "Say cheese," I said.

His resentment showed in his scowl and the blush on his bald scalp. But I caught him—click—in a moment when his face was twisted in unmistakable fear. His disgust was only a disguise for his fear. I had never seen that before. What could Leonard, with his shiny tassel loafers, possibly be afraid of? I wanted to tell him it was okay, he had no reason to be frightened. But that would be way out of line. "What the hell is this? Don't you people have work to do?" He put on his joking grin. But I understood that Leonard was afraid sometimes, and knowing that made me a little less scared.

I DIDN'T TELL Mom I was coming. I trudged with the crowd to Port Authority after work and caught a six o'clock bus to Ransomville. In the front seat to the right of the driver, I relaxed with the jostling rhythm, watching the dark highway being sucked down beneath the bus.

The waxy sound of unwrapped fast food floated up the bus aisle, carrying the smell of grease and meat, which mingled with the cold, metallic odor of the seats and windows and the heavy stench of diesel fuel. When a nauseous, woozy feeling bubbled up inside me, I clamped my hand over my mouth and clenched my teeth to shut it out. That seemed to help. I closed my eyes and tried to sleep. It didn't work. Booner's voice shouted through my skull: "What's the point of crying over fish when you want to kill my baby?"

His. Not ours. Not mine. It weighed me down, this thing inside, a heavy fact of life, growing like a tumor. It became everything I didn't want to think about. I envied Mom her miscarriages. She was allowed to be sad and helpless, a victim of fate and worthy of sympathy.

It was overcast and night was falling. Traffic was heavy but moving. Swoosh by unchanging mini-malls, lit up to reveal their grayness, one sameness after another. Swoosh by the streetlights and the trees shadowed behind them. Swoosh by the cars below my bus window. Swoosh by intermittent concrete cliffs and guardrails. At least this movement felt a little like progress.

I remembered Priscilla's face when she asked, *Is he mistreating you?* Booner didn't treat me any worse than I treated myself. And I thought of the orange shag rug, the unfinished bathroom, the grease-spattered stove, and the pigeons on the windowsill. They pulled me back to the life I had made there, drawing me in like a vortex. At least I knew that life. What lay beyond could always be worse.

Would Booner throw my clothes out the window? What did it matter? I was wearing my necklace, still valuable without its power. I had my camera and my photographs, earrings from Barb, and Priscilla's clothes. I had packed my favorite jeans. Then alarm hit me like an icy-cold patch in a lake, washing over my body. I was numb. I had forgotten Dad's shoes.

I had hidden them away so well that I concealed them from myself. I could picture them high up in the closet, positioned slightly pigeon-toed with the obituary in one shoe and the postcard for Doug's show in the other. I had to go back. I couldn't go back. But how could I leave them? My skin shrank around my body. I was trapped.

By the time we pulled off the thruway onto the exit, passing the prison and the hospital and turning onto the two-lane highway, I was the only passenger left on the bus. I couldn't see the Pine Hills Rest Center where Dad was buried, but I knew it was out there.

I got off at the Ransomville bus station, where he used to meet the buses. The movie theater on Main Street was playing *Top Gun*. The Lincoln Motel across the street featured tickling fingers and X-rated movies on TV. Just because I came from here didn't make it home.

A skinny guy with a cap on his head advertising pig feed approached me. "Need a taxi?"

"No, thanks." I picked up my bag and tried to shift by him.

"Got any spare change then? I've been sick and they cut off my disability, but I can't work and . . ." He took off his hat and held it out while I dug in my pocket for change. I dropped in a couple dimes and a quarter and started the uphill walk toward Mom's house.

Did Dad ever ask for change when people declined a taxi? No. Impossible. He worked for his money. He did odd jobs, business deals at the Griffin, various projects. But he had pocketed my change off the bar the day he drove me to college. He must have asked for money. Of course he did.

I dragged myself up Piler Road. It was almost nine o'clock, and the houses I passed were hulking shadows in the dark. But I knew without seeing them that they had deteriorated slightly, duller and more run-down with each passing winter. I knew the old barn on the left was sinking deeper into itself. The three trailers in a row probably had new tenants, since no one ever lived there for more than six months. There was a light burning outside Loretta's house, so I could read her faded sign BEAUTY SHOPPE. Further on, I saw through a window someone watching a color TV. It was ordinary, predictable, even a little comforting.

The air was sweet and light, cold as a Popsicle. The seasons were in control here. The only sign of spring was the mud at the side of the road. The roots of the trees were so large they cracked up through the cement sidewalk, breaking out of their prison, unlike the tree in front of Booner's place. His. Not mine. At least I could take my time walking. In Ransomville there was nothing to do, so you might as well do it slow.

The station wagon sat in the driveway, but the house was dark, heavy with quiet, and closed against me. There was something strange about it that I couldn't put my finger on. Then I realized the junk in the front yard had been cleared. No more rusted bed frames and pieces of cars, no more "found objects." I walked around to the back door. It was never locked.

I stepped in and turned the light on. The first thing I saw was the sewing machine set up on the kitchen table, a bolt of floral material on the floor by the foot pedal. That sewing machine couldn't have gotten there without someone bringing it up from the basement.

"Mom?" No answer. She's supposed to be here, I thought. Where was she? I wanted her. Yet I knew if she had been there, I would have wished to be alone.

The kitchen was clean, the counters clear. The refrigerator was covered in a lively assortment of magnets with sayings and colorful illustrations: "What the world needs now is a breath of fresh prayer." "Jesus is coming. Look busy." "God-fearer." "I ♡ Jesus." "WWJD: What would Jesus do?" "Salvation is a state of mind." They hadn't been there in December, and they seemed loud in the silence.

The living room was a larger shock. Dad's BarcaLounger was gone and in its place bulked an immovable armchair covered with one of the bedspreads from my room. "Mom!" I called. There was no answer.

I walked down the basement steps. Someone had taken the mobiles and the birdhouses. But the cot was still in the corner on the carpet, where it had always been. Dad's ragged slippers with the hole in the sole and the flattened heels were still by the cot, and I remembered how they used to flap off his feet when he walked around in the morning. The sound of his shuffle-flap would wake me up. But I felt strangely distant from the memory. It didn't hit me in the chest or make my eyes burn. His things no longer emanated life. They were as cold and dead as the necklace I was wearing.

I lay in the sagging bow of the cot. Even in my coat, I was cold and my breath emerged in a white fog. I wrapped my coat tight around my body, trying to feel a claim on his space, a connection. His philosophy books were still on the shelves. But someone had been here. The heater he had set up on the carpet was gone. Where the dollhouse had stood for years there was only a dark rectangle. The floor was faded and dusty around it. The puppet theater was set up neatly by the foot of the stairs, probably waiting for a pickup.

Dad was being dismantled bit by bit—his things, even his memory.

I ran back upstairs to the bathroom and it was a relief to see the walls had only primer on them still, a sort of vindication for the fact that I hadn't finished Booner's bathroom and a reminder of Dad's unfinished plans. I would move back here and complete the job. I would have the baby and take care of both it and Mom. I should have stayed here from the beginning, as she had wanted. But I was stubborn and selfish. I couldn't remember why it had seemed so important to leave.

I didn't hear a car pull up, but suddenly voices approached, already close. A man said, "You left the lights on." One set of footsteps clomped and scraped and another, lighter set tapped up the flagstone path. I ran out of the bathroom in a panic, ran toward my bedroom, stopped, ran to the living room, and stopped in the kitchen just as Mom walked in the back door, clutched her heart, and screamed.

I recognized a panic attack and threw my arms around her.

The man shouted, "Trudi, where are your pills, Trudi?"

"Xanax!" I yelled. "Refrigerator!"

"Give her space, let her breathe! Let go of her!" he shouted at me.

Mom tried to shake me off, too, but she was weak and gasping while I was stronger than I had ever been. "Breathe, Mom. You'll be okay. It's a panic attack." I held her as I had countless times in the past. Then, as now, as always, the fear held me in a grip of hope and terror. What if this time it wasn't panic but her heart? What if she died? Only my fear prevented her death.

"You'll be all right," I murmured. But she moved and gasped in my arms like a flapping fish. The man shook a pill from a vial and pressed it into Mom's palm. She choked it back, reached for the water he offered, and took a loud gulp. Her breath quieted almost instantly. The man took the water, and Mom jabbed me hard with her elbows until I released her.

"How dare you give me such a fright, Miranda? What are you trying to do, scare me to death? You were hanging on to me so I couldn't breathe! You were trying to kill me!"

I had thought I was helping. I sat in the chair next to the sewing machine feeling useless. "I didn't mean to, Mom. I'm sorry." I understood that it was I who wanted help. I began to cry, quiet endless tears, as though they had been building and, now released, would go on forever. I had snatched at Mom like a drowning person. Had it always been so? I laid my head in my arms.

"Are you all right, Trudi? Are you all right?" I recognized the smooth, oily voice that Pastor Bob liked to use. Why was he calling her Trudi when everyone called her Gert? Where was my welcome?

I smelled the cigarette smoke, harsh and comforting. I felt Mom's fingers on my head and didn't move, afraid she would draw away when I wanted her touch. Whatever price I had to pay for her affection, I would pay it. I hugged her around the waist. "Mom!"

"Well really, Miranda." Her hand was cool on the back of my neck, smooth, dry, and comforting. "Well really," she said again. And again. Well really, Miranda, well really, like a lullaby. I heard the scrape of a match and the gust of the oven going on. Pastor Bob was lighting it as though he lived here and knew exactly how we did things. I pulled away from Mom to wipe my eyes.

"Don't do that. It's a sure way to get the conjunctivitis. Here, have a cigarette." Mom handed me one of her menthols, which I usually didn't like, but I lit it anyway. The confusion in her face mirrored my own.

"I think we should all take a silent moment for prayer." Pastor Bob was sitting, hands outstretched on the table. Mom put her cigarette in the ashtray before she reached for him, then me. Her skin was papery. Smoke rose off the glowing ends of our cigarettes in pale swirls of intertwining lace. Pastor Bob stretched his arm out over the sewing machine to clasp my other hand. He closed his eyes. Mom's were already shut, her lips softly moving. I pretended to shut mine but only lowered my eyelids until the figures of Mom and Pastor Bob were dim, indistinct.

I didn't know how to pray. It had been too long. I remembered packing boxes in the church basement with Mom and other women. I remembered not wanting to be there, but a family had been burned out of their home and it was a relief at least that the charity of the Church of Assemblies was aimed on someone other than us.

I had been placing cans of food into a cardboard box, careful not to stuff it too full or make it so heavy that no one could lift it. And I kept getting up, surreptitiously grabbing handfuls of sugar cubes from the coffee table to suck on while I packed. Mom sighed with pain and limped over to sit in a chair in the corner because her back hurt. Two other women were chatting as they worked and their words slowly defined themselves until I knew they were talking about Mom in her chair, bent over with pain.

"One illness after another, poor thing."

". . . used to be so lively."

". . . no help from that husband."

". . . always at the bar."

". . . she's not right in the head but . . ."

"Mmm-hmm. A shame." Tight-lipped nods between them sealed their reality. I stared at the round, dull metal tops of the cans, circles next to circles, contained inside a square. My cheeks burned. I sided with Dad, who told me Mom wasn't really sick but most likely malingering. It was a word I looked up in the large dictionary at the school library.

I pretended to prepare another box, but I had lost the sense of how to arrange things. I wanted to scream, *She's malingering!* I wanted to tell them how she waited behind the door for me when I got off the school bus, how she pulled me in and shook me—"What are you saying about me? What?"—until my head flopped on my neck while I tried desperately to recall the events of the school day, to figure out where I had slipped and said the wrong thing and how she could have known.

How was I supposed to know it was shameful to tell my teacher that our phone was turned off because we hadn't paid the bill or to reveal that I had always thought Dad drank water all day but in fact it was vodka. Vodka? My science teacher showed such intense curiosity, I clammed up.

The worst disclosure was at Sunday school, when I told Brother Joe that Mom and I took baths together and afterward she examined my body and let me love her breasties. I quickly learned it was to be secret that we played dress-up, that she put makeup on me and curled my hair so I could be the mommy and she could be the baby and she could cry, *I'm hungry, Mommy. I want milk!* She had sucked on my nipples until they were the only part of me that existed. I thought I was telling Brother Joe how much my mother loved me, how much I loved her. But she hit me when she found out, and when Brother Joe came to pray with her.

Mom and Pastor Bob pulled their hands free. The prayer was over. I was at the kitchen table, not in the church basement. "Miranda." Mom was staring at me. Her pale blue eyes bulged with bewilderment. She was wearing mascara and a light powdering of lavender eye shadow.

Pastor Bob was staring, too, regarding me suspiciously with his slate-gray eyes. I didn't know what to say and, apparently, neither did they. What mattered, and what I tried to hold on to, was that

Mom had laid her cool fingers on the back of my neck when I was crying. What mattered was the cigarette she had offered. What was most important was that I had come home.

Pastor Bob said, "No matter what pain or affliction your mother has to face, she pushes on. She's the wonder of the church store, and I don't know what we'd do without her. I'm not trying to embarrass you now, Trudi, but I'm a man who speaks his mind as Jesus spoke his." He patted her arm gently with his pudgy, thick-fingered hand. "Your mother's got a fan club in me."

Mom's thin lips sagged into a smile. Her mousy grayish hair was red at the ends, where the dye had not yet been cut off. She looked old and harmless. "Pastor Bob's been very good to me, as you know."

I felt inertia settle into my body. Forget about Booner, about Corporate Liaisons Incorporated, about Doug Harrison, photography, and all the rest. Let Dad's shoes go. I would stay here, sleep in my room, and take care of Mom. It was what I should have done anyway. I could bear the son Mom never had. She needed me, and the surrender to her need was a welcome feeling, like a release.

The sound of a car in the driveway and the slam of first one then another car door disrupted the sense of peace at the table. Pastor Bob looked at his watch. "Just in time."

"Are you expecting someone?"

"I wasn't expecting you," said Mom, "and you're here."

When Pastor Bob got up and walked through the living room to the front door, I seized the moment. "Mom. I left the city. I want to stay here for a while. The apartment where I was living has ugly gates on every window and now . . ."

She shook her head. "You want to live in the city. That's how they live in the city." She half stood in her seat as Pastor Bob returned to the kitchen, followed by two vaguely familiar people.

I didn't care about them. I grabbed Mom's hand and whispered urgently. "Mom? I'm sorry I ever left and . . ."

"You remember Scott and Melissa, don't you Trudi?" Pastor Bob interrupted.

"You find us as we are." Mom sank back into her seat with a sigh. "I'd stand if my soft-tissue arthritis would let me. It's the lupus, don't you know. Not that I haven't learned to live with it, mind you. The symptoms haven't brought me down yet."

I cringed at her nonsense. But I would learn to accept her. I would try harder.

The couple behind Pastor Bob stood arm in arm, fidgeting, looking everywhere but in my eyes as I studied them. The guy had a bland, inoffensive face, a thick neck, and a fat middle, probably used to be a jock in high school. But I recognized the girl because of her unchanged long, blond hair and sharp nose. She had been a few years above me in school and she traveled with a pack, the popular kids.

Once when I was sitting on the bleachers watching a basketball game, I felt a tap on my shoulder. "Excuse me, whatever your name is, could you move down because Melissa has to fit in here." I left my seat to move down two rows, where I saw an empty spot. But someone else got to it before me and I stood, baffled, exposed, and frightened. They laughed at me, Melissa and her friends, and I felt like I was nothing.

"What are you doing in my house?" I said.

"Excuse me?" It was her turn to look baffled. She didn't remember me at all.

"I'll just show them around again. Stay where you are, Trudi," said Pastor Bob.

We were alone again. Meanwhile heavy footsteps stomped through the house, examining and judging. "Why are those people here?"

"I need my tablet. Bring me my pills, please."

"Don't do this. Tell me at least, why is the sewing machine out?"

"Because I'm sewing again, Miranda. There are people who appreciate what I can sew. I'm coming out of my shell. I want to enjoy life without the weight of this house on my soul."

I brought her the box of pills while her words sank in. "You're selling the house?"

"I don't know."

"But that bathroom . . ."

"Good price. Good location," Pastor Bob was saying. "You've hit our rock bottom. We're not going any lower than that."

"We have to think it over." Scott lifted his firm chin, giving a manly look over Mom, me, and the kitchen. Melissa hung back, no longer a member of the beautiful people's pack from high school, just a woman looking at a house, silently assenting to the loudly stated opinion of her husband.

"Are you finished already?" said Mom. "Is there anything I can do?"

"I'll walk them out," said Pastor Bob. "You just stay put."

"I can't believe you're selling the house." I laid my hand on the scratched, nicked, and faded Formica table. It felt solid. But it wasn't solid at all. "I just can't believe it."

"Sure, blame Gert," said Mom. "You always do."

"It's *Trudi* now, isn't it?" I stared at the sewing machine, the pale green of its body, the sharp, glinting point of the threaded needle. How I despised the whirring noise it made when Mom used to sew! "If you sell the house, I have nowhere to go, Mom."

"I thought you were all settled down there in the city. You didn't need anyone. How was I to know you'd come back?" She sniffed. Guttural and gross, the mucus dragged down her throat. "You're like your father, Miranda. You will always find someone to take care of you. I'm not worried."

Pastor Bob let the door slam behind him. "Well, I have a hunch about these things. I believe, God willing and I'm putting it in my prayers tonight, that we are going to get an offer."

Mom clapped her hands like a child. Grinned like one, too. And she looked pretty and young as she might have looked in high school, when her nickname had actually been Trudi.

I picked up my suitcase. Pastor Bob sidestepped to let me by, and I felt the rake of their eyes down my back as I carried my bag to my bedroom. The twin beds were in the same position, but one was a bare mattress, without bedding. Cluttered on it, instead of my stuffed animals, were flowery cushions, the same pattern as the bolt of fabric near the sewing machine. One side of each pillow had been embroidered with a Christian fish design. Dad had told me it was a secret sign from the times when Christianity was a forbidden sect. He had said that being a Christian probably meant something real back then.

Boxes were stacked and arranged haphazardly in front of the vanity table. They were open, filled with merchandise from Evangelical Enterprises. There were loads of Bibles with leather covers, Bibles on tape, T-shirts, posters, postcards, medals, and coffee mugs with the face of a mournful loving Jesus. There was an entire box of bumper stickers with JESUS IS MY CO-PILOT and I BRAKE FOR JESUS.

My bedroom was a stockroom for the church store. Like Dad, I was being dismantled bit by bit, and I wasn't even dead yet.

At least my key to the honor society still hung off the closet doorknob. I felt more attached to that one solid moment of accomplishment than I did to the room, which had never truly been mine. It had been Mom's, and I, too, had been hers.

My hope for finding refuge here was gone. I couldn't stay. Where could I go? Headlights flashed across the window and slanted down the wall. Pastor Bob was leaving. Very shortly afterward came a light tap on my door. "Miranda. Do you want to play rummy five hundred?"

She hadn't barged in on me.

I took the camera with me to the living room, where she had dealt the cards out on the coffee table. I sat in the unfamiliar armchair, which was soft and held me like a hug. There was a cushion, springy and warm, positioned at my lower back. It was like the small pillows on my bed, embroidered with the Christian fish. "Did you make the pillows, Mom?"

Her face brightened. "Do you like them? I sew and Loretta embroiders. It's been so good that we can't keep up with the demand. People are amazed at my abilities. But I feel Jesus inside me when I'm at that sewing machine."

I shifted my position. "What happened to Dad's chair?"

"Don't you love that new one? Loretta sits there, and, oh, she says it's the most comfortable chair she ever sat in."

Mom never answered my questions. And what right did she have to be so happy? "Does that mean you threw it away? Where? In the dump?"

She fanned out her cards. "I donated several items to the church. They were having a fund-raising social."

"The church. I wonder what Dad would've said about that." I picked up my cards. A double in tens and not much else. I held them gently, very gently, to counteract the urge to hurl them in her face. *If I've found someone to take care of me, it was because I had to! Because you never did!* I wanted to spit in her face.

"That chair was a piece of junk," she said.

It was as though she were saying that Dad was a piece of junk. She thought she was so superior. "Did you donate the stuff in the basement, too? How about all that stuff out in the yard?"

"I took a mortgage out for the funeral, and now I have to sell the house to pay off his debts. When will you get it through your head that he was a bum?"

We glared at each other, gripping our cards. She lowered her gaze before I did. "You should pick a card," she said.

I picked up a three and threw it on the discard pile, feeling an explosive pressure building inside me, feeling the weight of the growing fetus and the realization of what I had known now for a while. Dad always had body odor, salty, pickled. He didn't wash often enough. His face was unshaven. He was fat, a bum. He collected junk in town, asked strangers for money. He was a drunk. I had known that even when he was alive. But how could I admit it? If I loved him, what did that make me?

Mom's lined face, with her eyelids sagging in her downturned gaze and her thin, disapproving lips, was no longer powerful enough to fight. She was weak, and her weakness made her the winner. Was there anything left to lose? "You used to come into my room at night and make me feel you." It slid out tearfully, like water trickling from a faucet that hasn't been turned off tightly enough.

"What?" She picked a card, inserted it among the cards in her hand, and discarded the queen of clubs, which I grabbed only because I already knew what it was, not that it would do me any good. I wanted to pack up my things and leave, never looking back. But I couldn't. I felt drugged.

Mom gave a dry cough. "I've lived here all my life in this house, Miranda. Just try to imagine how hard it is for me."

"I don't want to imagine how hard it is for you. I'm sick of knowing how hard everything is for you." The cards bent under my grip.

"You just love to hurt me, don't you."

"It's you who love to hurt me."

"I could die any day."

"Why don't you!" I screamed, and couldn't say any more.

The silence was long and hostile.

"When I came to in the hospital after I almost died giving birth to you . . ."

"Here we go again!" I crumpled the cards in my hand. "I don't want to hear it again!"

"Just like your father. You shut your ears and your eyes and tell yourself the world's flat."

"I'm not a drunk! I'm not a bum!"

She raised her eyebrows in an unbearable gesture of triumph that said, *Aha, so you finally admit what he was.*

"I'd rather be like him than you!" I yelled. But I didn't want to be like either of them.

"I came to, and all I could think was, Where's my baby? I was alone and in pain while your father was three sheets to the wind at the Griffin. I called for my baby, 'Where's my baby?' and the nurse carried you in and gave you to me. The nurses wore little name tags and hers said Miranda, so I named you after her because she was so nice. But even from the start, you didn't love me back. You screamed. You wanted to stay with her. You were vicious, with your sucking mouth like a demon spawned from hell. You never loved me. You only wanted me to be your cow."

I thought of Rose with her crown of ribbons, of Tracy and Junior hugging, of Barb's mother dragging her off for an abortion. "You're sick," I said.

"I'd see you with your father, all smiles and dancing. But as soon as I walked in the room, you'd clam up with that sneer on your face, giving me the worst of yourself. Do you think it was easy putting food on the table with him doing nothing? And the ladies in the church, the ones who came into Lack's to shop, I knew them in school when they envied me because I was prettier and all the rest of it. Wouldn't you know, they loved to watch misfortune raining down on me."

"You made me touch your tits." I sounded gross, a pig.

"You rejected everything I gave you, the clothing I sewed, the love

I offered. You rejected me, and now you're turning it around and trying to make it my fault. You peed your bed like an animal just to spite me. Your father put you up to it." She was starting to gasp. "Grow up, Miranda. It's time you just grow up."

"*No!*" I screamed, feeling faint. Blackness closed in around me as a staticky noise rushed through my ears. I hugged my camera, thinking to head for the basement, but I couldn't move. Just stared at the camera in my lap with its lens and its body, the f-stops and aperture opening. If I could show her the photographs I had developed in the darkroom, I could prove to her that I was somebody, doing things. I wasn't a demon or an animal.

"I was smart!" she said. "I could've gone to college."

"It wasn't me that stopped you. You got what you wanted in your life." My voice was a jagged whisper. My muscles were tense from bending toward her and the coffee table. What if my baby came out hating me? I didn't want one if it didn't come with love. Did that mean I was just like Mom?

"It was a long time ago," she said.

I couldn't answer. I was drained. My throat felt red and raw from screaming. After a pause Mom picked a card, discarding the queen of spades like an offering. "For you. Since you seem to like queens."

I was grateful for the gesture. Maybe it was her way of apologizing. But I didn't want her discards and I wouldn't take the queen. I pulled a jack of clubs and it fit in nicely between the queen and ten of clubs to make a flush, which I laid down.

Mom marked her pad, keeping score while I picked up my camera, looked through the viewfinder, cropped out the TV, which was on with the volume off. She glanced up with startled eyes and looked quickly back down. She was afraid of me. She knew exactly what she had done. I pitied her like I had pitied Booner, a pity so powerful I knew it as love. The camera was shaking in my hands.

"Here comes the headache. Oh dear God, I'm sorry." Mom gripped her temples.

I couldn't tell if she was apologizing to me or to God, but either way, it was enough. I helped her into bed, turned on the electric heater, tucked the blanket around her chin. She clutched my hand

and made a noise. I listened, only wanting some sense of love, true and simple, between us. I leaned close to hear what I longed to hear. *I've been wrong for all these years, Miranda. I mistreated you and your father. He loved you, too. We both did. And I'm so sorry for the unhappiness I've caused you. I will change. I promise you that.*

I leaned in so close that I felt her warm breath on my cheek.

"That's a lovely necklace," she whispered.

THE HOUSE WAS asleep, dark and quiet, all the televisions turned off. I felt safe in my bedroom with the lights on, awake. I opened my bag and took out the envelope that held my photographs. One by one, I withdrew them, lining them up against the stacks of boxes. There were three pictures of the gates on the living room windows. There was Donna shielding herself from the camera. Rose, in her rocking chair, laughed away a hidden terror. She was pregnant then, but she had a baby now.

There was a picture of Booner in front of his building, stepping over a shadow into the light, with a bulge in his cheek from chewing tobacco. There was Booner, fresh from the shower and wrapped in a towel. The steam rising off him softened his outlines and he looked insubstantial, like a phantom. There was a photograph of the mother and girl, mirrored profiles, one looking down and the other gazing up.

These were pictures of the truth, pieces of my life. They were windows that revealed what I saw, and their existence alone proved that what I saw mattered. Mom was never going to change. Dad had been a bum, though I loved him. I wanted to know and to recognize what I knew so it wouldn't always catch me by surprise. *Grow up,* Mom had said.

Grow up, said Rose in her rocking chair. *Grow up,* said Donna and Booner. *Grow up and get out,* said the gates. *It's time for you to just grow up.* They repeated in a long moment that echoed through the room, through the house, *grow up, grow up, grow up,* until I had to lie down.

Exhaustion closed me off like a heavy curtain. With the photographs around me, the lights in my room shining down, and the softness of a pillow with a Christian fish pressed against my cheek, I was able to sleep in fits and starts.

I snapped awake early, shivering and light-headed in the gray dawn. Mom was still sleeping. I crept to the kitchen, not wanting to wake her, and walked down the steps to the basement. There, I gathered Dad's philosophy books and carried them upstairs, piling what didn't fit in my suitcase on my bed.

Then I lugged up some of the other odds and ends: the guitar with the broken strings, the deflated kickballs, basketballs, tennis, golf and Spaldeen balls, a broken birdcage, a bit of hose, the piece of carpet, his slippers, and the skinny tie he used to wrap his robe shut. These, I carried to the car, which sported a new bumper sticker: JESUS IS MY CO-PILOT.

I drove to the cemetery with balls flapping and flopping around on the car floor. The temporary placard still stood. I laid the guitar on his grave. He only ever played one song, which went, *"when I die please bury me deep, lay a rock at my head and my feet so they know I've gone to sleep. Freight train freight train, going so fast."* We should have sung that at his funeral.

The tennis balls and golf balls, I placed around the body of the guitar. I put the kickball, the Spaldeens, and the basketball at the top, his slippers at the base of the guitar's neck. I draped the tie over the placard. Maybe if there was extra money after Mom sold the house we could buy Dad a real gravestone.

I stood and tried to remember his laugh, but I couldn't. I tried to see his face, but I could only see it in parts, not the whole. He loped away, one shoulder slightly higher than the other. His eyes twinkled. He knocked back a drink at the Griffin, laying his glass with a clunk on the bar. He shambled around the front yard. I glimpsed Dad in fragments. I stood until it grew too cold to stand and dampness soaked through the hole in my boot, drenching my sock. Then I got into the car and went home.

The cards were on the coffee table in the living room, exactly as we left them last night. They were waiting for us to pick up the game and go on. Mom was still sleeping. The phone gave off a dial tone. I called long-distance.

"Yeah, what, hello." The sound of Booner's voice brought on the familiar overwhelming pity and longing to submit.

"Hi, Booner, it's me."

"Aw shit. You gotta come back. Where are you? I was about to call the cops. I'm sick with worrying. I'm sorry for acting like a schmuck. I mean, the guys really set me straight with that. But I was upset, see, when you don't want my baby, it's like you don't want me. You understand?"

I understood. But it wasn't just his baby, and I had no answer.

"Why did you leave me? I thought you loved me. You're the only one who ever loved me for who I am. We could be such a great family. You don't want an abortion. You've been brainwashed by your college days. We can work it out. Come on."

"Brainwashed? I am not."

"Just come back. You'll be a great mother. We'll talk it over."

"Booner, there's nothing you can say that will convince me we should make such a huge mistake."

There was an uneasy moment of quiet.

"Then fuck you, Mandy."

It hurt like a cold plunge in the river. I quietly hung up and tried to stifle my terror. I dialed Barb. The phone rang and rang and rang. I felt desperate. Who else could I call? My fingers stiffened in the rotary. I was panicking. Then it came to me in a flood of warmth. I dialed information. "Can I have the number for Priscilla Sherman on East Sixty-eighth Street?"

She was actually listed, and she answered after the first ring with a simple "Hello."

"Priscilla? It's Mandy. Miranda."

"Miranda. Are you okay?"

"Um. Not really. I . . . remember how you said you could help me?"

Silence. I pounded through it. "Well, I'm uh . . ." The lump in my throat stopped me.

"Do you need money?" Her tone was wary.

"Just a loan and maybe a place to stay. I have to get an . . ." I stopped.

"Abortion?" she asked. Then she added, "Sure."

Did that mean yes? Was she really going to help? "I didn't know who else to call," I said. "And I need to find an apartment or something or go back to school or something. Or move up in your company or something . . ." I was whipping up a frenzy of somethings.

"One thing at a time, right?" said Priscilla.

"Yeah!" I was crying with relief. She would help me. She was going to help!

"Who are you talking to?" Mom shuffled out.

"Do you have a doctor? Is anything arranged?" asked Priscilla.

"I have an appointment. I'm, uh, going to have to take the day off work."

The rattle of Mom's pillbox was distracting.

"You can stay here for a couple of days. I can't give you more than that, unfortunately, because on Thursday I'm having a visitor."

"That's all I need. I'll figure something out." I hung up the phone, laughing and crying, while Mom swallowed her pills at the table. I had no reason for this exuberance. Yet there it was.

"You've gone stark, raving lunatics." Mom gulped her water. But she seemed pleased.

"I have to go back to the city, Mom. You were right. My life is there."

"I'd like to simply turn over a new page, Miranda. Can we do that? Can we stop being cruel and find some forgiveness in our hearts?"

"I don't know," I said. "Maybe."

"Let me drive you to the bus, at least."

"Thanks, Mom. I don't have a lot of time." I carried my suitcase to the car. Then I went back inside for the shopping bag with Dad's books. I had my camera slung over my shoulder with my purse.

The phone was ringing as I walked back into the kitchen. Mom picked it up. "Boyle residence."

I waited, drumming my fingers on the counter. If I missed the morning bus, I would have to wait another five hours. Too long.

"Just a second. She's right here." Mom handed me the phone and shuffled out of the room.

"Hello?"

"I want you back." Booner was crying. "Whatever you need to

do, I'll go along with it. You're right. We're not ready to have a kid. I'm on my knees here and there's beads all over the fucking floor. Just come back. It's empty without you."

"I don't know," I said. "I need time to think."

"Please! I'm begging you! What more can I do!"

I knew that this was all Booner could do. He didn't have any more in him. He wasn't going to change. "I'm sorry. I have to go." I hung up as Mom returned to the kitchen, a coat slung over her robe. She carried one of her fish pillows, and she held a small stack of photographs out to me. "You almost forgot these. And this is for you." She handed me the pillow.

"Thanks, Mom." We walked out to the car together, down the flagstone path. Mom slipped her arm through mine and I allowed it, pulling away only when we reached the car. I carefully slid the photographs into the side pocket of my suitcase. But as Mom started the car, Loretta pulled into the driveway in her little gray Toyota.

She rolled her window down. "I was just over at the church! Apparently, Frank's grave has been vandalized!"

"Good God." Mom was pounding on the gas pedal with her foot. The car sounded like it was sobbing.

I knew immediately that Loretta was referring to my little shrine. But I hadn't vandalized anything. I had honored Dad. The useless-ness of pointing it out spurred me on. "Mom, we really have to go."

"We're in a rush, Loretta!" Mom was shouting. "I have to drive my daughter to the bus." She drove real slow, so careful that she was a menace. She braked for nothing, swerved away from nothing. "I'm not getting out of the car," she said.

I didn't answer. I checked behind us. Loretta was following.

"Did you take those pictures I found?" asked Mom. "You know, with that old camera?

"Yeah."

"How come they're black and white? Why don't you take color pictures?"

"Some other time." I saw the bus in front of the station, and I itched to get on. She would never understand. But, oddly, I didn't feel angry about it. "Let me know about the house, Mom. I want to help."

"Will do."

I glanced at her in time to see her smile and I felt uncommonly pleased. She turned off the ignition and took both my hands. She wouldn't let them go. I pulled away, but she was strong when she wanted to be, staring into my eyes. She said, "Miranda Jane, I don't know if I will ever understand you."

LIFE

RISCILLA LIVED IN a white-brick luxury high-rise. At the entrance, in the center of a circular drive, was a fountain where water sprayed in arcs, surrounded by small trees, bushes, and blooming crocuses. A man in a blue uniform opened the front door. Her apartment, 15F, was immaculate, as though she didn't spend any time there. The living room window faced east over the river, a beautiful view, with Queens on the other side, miniaturized like a toy world over which I had power.

"Please shut the drapes," she said. "I don't want the light to fade my carpet or my furniture."

It was gloomy with the curtains closed. I had opened them to brighten up the place. I switched on one of her halogen lamps. Her two Siamese cats posed elegantly on the radiator, watching. Under the lamplight their pupils slit their blue eyes vertically. With their dusky fur and perfect faces, they were so gorgeous I wanted to hug them. But when I reached to pet one, it hissed and snapped at my fingers.

"My little dears simply don't like being touched," said Priscilla.

I had been here for one night. I slept on her pullout couch and, in the morning, put it back together carefully so it looked like it had never been slept in. I missed Booner and our five-floor walk-up, peeling linoleum, tattered sofa, and mattress. I missed being able to relax.

"I'm afraid I can't allow you to smoke in my home. If you absolutely *have* to, you can go outside," said Priscilla.

So I went outside and smoked a cigarette by her fountain, which spread a fine mist around. When I came back up, she coughed. "My God, you smell like an ashtray!"

I was afraid to eat or go to the toilet or take a shower or even sit on the couch, which was hard and had no bounce. I accidentally left some fingerprints on her glass end table when I reached for my iced tea. Everything I did, I seemed to make a mess.

She placed coasters beneath glasses, washed every dish directly after using it, and had someone come in twice a week to clean. If she saw a cat hair somewhere, she used a small hand vacuum to remove it. The hours I spent in her apartment with her widened and yawned. Time trickled slowly by.

"Can I use your phone?" I was scared to touch anything without asking.

"As long as you don't call that sewer cleaner. I can't believe you would ever want to talk to him again." She shuddered.

Her phone sat on a high small table in her front hall. I dialed Queens. "Yeah," Booner answered.

"Hi. It's me. I'm at Priscilla's. Do you still want me back?" I tried to talk calmly, professionally. "Will you pick me up from the clinic tomorrow?"

"Who's Priscilla?"

"My boss." I glanced around nervously. But Priscilla had put her slippered feet up on a hassock while she watched *60 Minutes* on a large-screen color TV. She seemed completely absorbed.

"Your boss," he snorted. "Man, I knew that Manhattan job was a shitty idea."

I didn't answer.

"Where are you? I'll come get you right now."

I paused, tempted. But Priscilla muted the television and walked past me to the kitchen. What would she say if Booner came and got me? I couldn't leave like that. I didn't even want her to know I was talking to him. She had already offered to take me to the clinic before she went to work. It had already been arranged. "No, thanks. I'll just stay here one more night and . . ."

"No thanks? Are you kidding me? Where the hell are you?"

I felt threatened and said nothing. He would try to destroy my job. After tomorrow, I would be free to make changes, and the first thing I had to do was find another place to live, a place to call my own. Priscilla passed by me again, this time carrying her frozen low-fat meal, which she had heated in her microwave. "I'm going to eat my dinner now," she announced.

"It's been hell for me," said Booner. "I can't sleep. I can't eat. But okay. You got your way. Where should I meet you?"

I gave him the address of the Stuyvesant Women's Center.

"Are you happy now?" he said.

"No, I'm sorry. I'll see you tomorrow." Unsure that he would actually show, I hung up Priscilla's phone. Then I wiped the receiver off with my shirt, erasing all evidence of myself, and sat on her sofa to watch *60 Minutes*.

She had set up a tray on her lap for her microwaved meal, which consisted of a small piece of fish, some vegetables, and a pudding, each in its own section. She dabbed her mouth with a cloth napkin. "Did you do your chore today, Miranda?"

"Oh, darn, I forgot." I wiped off the white sofa cushion and fluffed it carefully to get rid of any indentation.

My chore was to change the cat litter. Priscilla like it cleaned every day. "I absolutely despise the odor of cat poo," she had said when I arrived yesterday. "But I have an idea. Why don't we make that your chore while you stay here? It's the one and only thing you'll have to do, and you can start right now."

I poured the pissy graveled stuff into a garbage bag and poured clean stuff into the box. I wouldn't have minded if I had liked her cats.

"Help yourself to a frozen dinner," she said.

But my stomach was in such a knot that I didn't want to eat. I felt like I was in limbo. I couldn't sit still. On her bookshelves, the books were perfectly aligned and I was impressed that she owned the complete works of Shakespeare and Charles Dickens. She also had many true-crime books, thrillers, and mysteries. One of her bookshelves held only photographs. A framed picture of Priscilla and a handsome silver-haired man in formal dress caught my eye. "Is that your dad?" I asked.

She grabbed it. "No. It's my boyfriend." She stroked his face with her finger, her voice going dreamy. "My Chuck. One day he'll leave his wife."

"His wife?"

"You didn't hear that, Miranda." She placed the picture back exactly where it had been. "I'm going to take my bath now. But first I'll clean up."

It seemed that Priscilla found it necessary to announce whatever she was doing just before she did it. Or was it me? I felt cramped with gratitude. She cleared away her meal, washed her utensils. Then she spent an hour in her bath before she retired to her bedroom, her two cats dashing after her. I waited until she shut her bedroom door. Then I was temporarily free.

Starving, I tiptoed to her kitchen and quietly opened drawers. Her refrigerator had an ice maker. When I checked her cabinets, I found a box of Stella D'Oro biscuits, which I tore open and carried into the living room. I sat under the sheet of the pullout sofa bed, shoving one after another into my mouth, spilling crumbs. Abortion tomorrow, I thought, sick with fear. I remembered I wasn't supposed to be eating anything until afterward, but I finished the box anyway.

I lay awake a long time on Priscilla's sofa bed. Her drapes were so thick that the room was completely black. The darkness level was the same whether I opened my eyes or shut them. Would Booner do what he said? Would he pick me up? I missed the guy I had fallen in love with, the one who had saved me. He had been replaced by an angry, ugly man I didn't know at all, and I wanted Booner back.

THE SOUND OF running water and dishes clanking in the kitchen woke me up. The lamp was on. The cats stared balefully from the radiator. "We've got to get moving," said Priscilla. I wrapped the crumbs in the sheets and threw them in her hamper. The empty box of cookies I folded and shoved into my suitcase. I threw on jeans and a sweater. Then I washed my face, brushed my teeth, wiped all stray droplets off the sink, and I was ready to go.

Priscilla held the door as I carried my suitcase and the shopping bag full of Dad's books, along with my purse and my camera. "Why are you bringing all that?" she asked as we waited for the elevator.

"Well, a friend is going to pick me up at the clinic and I'll probably stay with . . . her, him." I sort of coughed over the last word. I didn't want her to know it was Booner. "I really appreciate your putting me up and giving me some days off and everything. I just don't want to be a bother."

"I said you could stay until Wednesday." She shook her head. "Of course, it's up to you." I thought I heard relief in her voice, which confirmed that I was doing the right thing. The elevator rode fast and smooth. The doorman ushered us out the front entrance.

In a plum-colored suit and long brown coat and pumps, Priscilla flicked her wrist at a cab. It pulled up in front of us with a shriek of brakes on the corner of Second Avenue and Sixty-eighth Street. He popped the trunk open for my stuff. I had never taken a taxi before, never stood on a curb and hailed one. Priscilla's ease amazed me. "Second Avenue and Twenty-first Street, please," she told the driver sternly.

It was not quite 7 A.M. on a Monday and the streets were quiet. Many stores were locked and gated. But diners and delis were open. People were walking dogs. A girl leaned in a doorway, smoking. She could've been me. I felt rigid with tension, as though my muscles were turning to bone. My stomach growled.

Priscilla rolled the taxi window halfway down and took huge gulps of air before she turned to me. "We're going to expand Corporate Liaisons Incorporated, hire a new placement person. It'll mean a heavier workload for you. To be honest, I had hoped you could take the position and we would train you, but Leonard and I just don't think you're ready."

"You won't tell Leonard about this, will you?" I hugged myself in protection from the wind blowing in through her open window. We were getting close, passing Thirty-fourth Street and hurtling through a series of green lights. I began digging through my pockets, intending to pay for the taxi.

When we passed Twenty-third Street, I was faint with panic. I almost cried when I saw the people marching in front of the building. SAVE THE UNBORN! said a sign that tilted above them.

"Uh-oh." Priscilla echoed my thoughts.

I fumbled with my money as the taxi pulled up to the curb opposite the crowd. "Oh, no. I have this one," said Priscilla.

"No. Please. Let me."

"Don't be ridiculous." Priscilla pushed a twenty at the driver.

"Please!" I screamed. "I want to pay for this!"

But the driver was already counting out change. Priscilla said, "Miranda, you're hysterical. Calm down."

I felt worthless as I got out of the cab. I reached into the trunk for my suitcase.

"Let me help." Priscilla tried to pull it, grunting with the effort.

"It's okay, Priscilla." She could throw her money around, but I was physically stronger. She clutched my arm as we crossed the street toward the small group of protestors, who were marching in a circle, praying out loud. Some of them held steaming cups of coffee in their gloved hands.

A hugely pregnant young girl with a laminated sign—LET ME LIVE—taped on her full belly, shouted, "Don't kill your baby! You *can* take care of your innocent child! They made me have an abortion last year! Don't let them do it to you!" I steeled myself, gritted my teeth, and barged ahead.

Someone thrust a flyer at Priscilla. She looked at it and gasped before she crumpled it up and threw it in the catch basin at the curb. Booner might be the one to clean that basin one day.

"Hail Mary full of grace, the Lord is with thee . . ." prayed the crowd. The chant was almost comforting, as though they were praying for me, not against me. Surrounding us, they jostled me and my suitcase banged into my shin. The handles of my shopping bag cut into my palm. But the protestors weren't forming a human chain or throwing themselves on the sidewalk in front of me like I had once seen on the news. Priscilla was practically crying, but I couldn't comfort her.

The glass doors loomed ahead and we pushed ourselves inside the quiet lobby, where the sounds of the crowd were muffled and distant. She muttered through clenched teeth as we stepped on the elevator. "I could've gotten you a private doctor. Why didn't you tell me?"

I had no answer. The clinic was all I knew. *Don't be ridiculous,* I wanted to say. *You're getting hysterical.*

The elevator lurched up to the third floor. The doors jerked open directly into the waiting room, where the same frayed posters hung on the wall, showing pictures of birth control methods and the stages of fetal development. All the faces turned toward us and then away, back to their own private daydreams. A baby cried. The air was heavy and smelled of damp, soggy diapers. A radio played quietly and the low murmur of women's voices could be heard over the music.

There weren't enough chairs. A few women leaned against the wall, arms folded, eyes shut. Two little girls sat at their mother's feet playing with dolls, while the mother leaned her head back, staring blankly. Other children slumped in women's laps. A weariness seemed to have fallen over everyone. It was the same as my last visit here. The only thing different this time was me.

I looked at the floor and followed the path where the carpet had faded and browned from so many people walking up to the reception desk. I leaned in close, my face hot and a pulse beating in my temples, reminding me why I was here. I felt ashamed. "I have a seven-thirty appointment for an . . ." I lowered my voice to a whisper, glancing quickly behind me, but no one was paying attention. I looked back at the receptionist, with her intelligent eyes and clear skin. She held her finger between the pages of her book, saving her spot to return to. ". . . abortion," I finished.

"We're kinda overbooked today because we lost some hours Saturday, so just take a seat. I'll call you."

"I have someone here who's going to pay for it. But she can't stay, so I wonder if we can do that now."

With a sigh she slowly tore a piece of paper in half, stuck the torn scrap into her book, shut it, and pushed it away. "All right."

I tried not to feel hurt. I gestured to Priscilla, who stood uncomfortably near the pay phone, wrinkling her nose in disgust as she